Johann Wolfgang von Goethe

Before he was thirty, Goethe had proven himself a master of the novel, the drama, and lyric poetry. But even more impressive than his versatility was his unwillingness ever to settle into a single style or approach; whenever he used a literary form, he made of it something new.

Born in 1749 to a well-to-do family in Frankfurt, he was sent to Strasbourg to earn a law degree. There he met the poet-philosopher Herder, discovered Shakespeare, and began to write poetry. His play *Götz von Berlichingen* (1773) made him famous throughout Germany. He was invited to the court of the duke of Sachsen-Weimar, where he quickly became a cabinet minister. In 1774 his novel of Romantic melancholy, *The Sorrows of Young Werther*, electrified all Europe. Soon he was at work on the first version of his *Faust*, which would finally appear as a fragment in 1790.

In the 1780s Goethe visited Italy and immersed himself in classical poetry. The next decade saw the appearance of *Wilhelm Meister's Apprenticeship*, his novel of a young artist's education, and a wealth of poetry and criticism. He returned to the *Faust* material around the turn of the century and completed Part 1 in 1808.

The later years of his life were devoted to a bewildering array of pursuits: research in botany and in a theory of colors, a novel (*Elective Affinities*), the evocative poems of the *West-Eastern Divan*, and his great autobiography, *Poetry and Truth*. In his eighties he prepared a forty-volume edition of his works; the forty-first volume, published after his death in 1832, was the second part of *Faust*.

Goethe's wide-ranging mind could never be confined to one form or one philosophy. When asked for the theme of his masterwork, *Faust*, he could only say, "From heaven through all the world to hell"; his subject was nothing smaller.

Bantam Classics
Ask your bookseller for classics by these international writers:

Aeschylus
Aristophanes
Anton Chekhov
Euripides
Dante
Fyodor Dostoevsky
Alexandre Dumas
Gustave Flaubert
Johann Wolfgang von Goethe
The Brothers Grimm
Homer
Victor Hugo
Henrik Ibsen
Franz Kafka
Pierre Choderlos de Laclos
Gaston Leroux
Niccolo Machiavelli
Thomas Mann
Plato
Edmond Rostand
Sophocles
Marie-Henri Beyle de Stendhal
Leo Tolstoy
Ivan Turgenev
Jules Verne
Virgil
Voltaire

Faust
Part I
by Johann Wolfgang von Goethe

Revised Edition
Translated with an Introduction
and Notes by Peter Salm

BANTAM BOOKS
NEW YORK · TORONTO · LONDON · SYDNEY · AUCKLAND

FAUST

A Bantam Book

PUBLISHING HISTORY

*Bantam Dual-Language edition published
November 1962
Bantam World Drama edition published February 1967
Bantam Classic revised edition / May 1985*

*Cover art, Faust and Mephistopheles, by Delacroix.
Reproduced by permission of the Trustees, the Wallace
Collection, London.*

ISBN 0-553-21348-2

*Published simultaneously in the United States
and Canada*

*Bantam Books are published by Bantam Books, a division of Bantam Doubleday Dell Publishing Group, Inc.
Its trademark, consisting of the words "Bantam Books"
and the portrayal of a rooster, is Registered in U.S. Patent
and Trademark Office and in other countries. Marca
Registrada. Bantam Books, 1540 Broadway, New York,
New York 10036.*

O   11

CONTENTS

INTRODUCTION

A man who called himself Faust, or Faustus, lived in the early part of the sixteenth century and left his traces in cities like Erfurt, Leipzig, and Wittenberg. We have the testimony of Martin Luther, for example, who in the context of one of his "Table Talks" (1536–7) incidentally referred to Faust, his contemporary, as a conjurer and necromancer who was wont to refer to the devil as his brother-in-law. In the mid-sixteenth century, about ten years after Faust's death, Philip Melanchthon, Luther's close friend and adjutant, spoke of Faust with a mixture of awe and fervent repugnance:

> Once upon a time [Faust] intended to put on a spectacle in Venice and he said that he would fly into the heavens. Soon the devil took him away and pummelled and mauled him so terribly that, upon coming back to earth, he lay as if dead. But this time he did not die. (*Faust, eine Anthologie*, Reklam, Leipzig, n.d., p. 16, translation mine)

There are other bits of documentary evidence, but while Faust's goings-about are not ascertainable in detail, the legends proliferated and in due time began to envelop the scanty verifiable facts. Whatever contributed to the object lesson in the necromancer's reprobate life was worthy of being singled out and enlarged upon for the benefit of pious souls who lived in hope of salvation.

Magic and alchemy were related endeavors, and their practitioners inspired both awe and suspicion; awe because they could produce near-miracles in their vials, alembics, and retorts. They were, after all, in pursuit of ancient and persistent dreams: transmutating base metals into gold, discovering the elixir of eternal youth, achieving human flight, finding panaceas for the plague, and, finally, the dream of possessing superhuman wisdom. There were reports that the alchemists Paracelsus and Agrippa had performed feats that came close to attaining those wondrous goals, reports that, along with other fanciful tales, often became transmuted into Faustian lore.

On the other hand, the alchemists and necromancers were regarded with suspicion because to bring about their marvels in

the laboratory they "obviously" had to resort to black magic and
hence had to be motivated by evil purposes, much like the power-
ful "evil scientist" of our day as he appears in animated cartoons
on Saturday morning television. In the sixteenth century, an age
of great religious turmoil and fervor, the alchemist-magicians
were seen as tampering with the divine order of things. They
furtively took minerals, crystals, and waters out of God's nature
and carried them off into their laboratories and, by compound-
ing, boiling, distilling, and filtrating, forced them to minister to
their dark purposes. They were "speculating the elements," illic-
itly prying into deeply hidden mysteries. In our own century,
rather more tolerant of scientific probings into nature's inmost
recesses, Thomas Mann put to good use a tenacious ambiguity
still embedded in the language. In his novel *Doctor Faustus*
(1947), he has the narrator play on the common root in the
German words *versuchen*, meaning to try or test, *Versuch*,
experiment, and *Versuchung*, temptation—all by way of evoking
the alchemists' suspect trade. Here is the passage in English:

> But the enterprise of experimenting on Nature, of teasing
> her into manifestations, "tempting" her, in the sense of
> laying bare her workings by experiment . . . that all this . . .
> was itself the work of the "Tempter," was the conviction of
> earlier epochs. (Thomas Mann, *Doctor Faustus*, New York,
> 1960, p. 17, trans. H. T. Lowe-Porter)

Surely where there is temptation, the devil, or Mephistopheles,
cannot be far behind. After all, Jesus himself, having been led
into the wilderness by the Evil Spirit, had to confront three temp-
tations, and three times he stood fast against their lure (Luke 4:
1–12).

The stories that were circulating about Faust were excellent
raw material for the newly established printing shops. It should
not be forgotten that during the sixteenth century printers were
on the lookout for new, preferably sensational stories that might
be offered to the public. After Johannes Gutenberg invented
movable type, the books printed during the remainder of the
fifteenth century were largely of a religious nature: editions of the
Bible, collections of religious songs, and prayer books. But print-

ing presses constituted a big investment and became econom-
ically interesting only if they were also used for nonreligious
ends. There were the medieval legends about Virgil, the Roman
poet and author of the *Aeneid*, whom the Middle Ages had endowed with superhuman wisdom and prophetic powers; and
much entertainment was found in the rude tricks perpetrated by
the arch-prankster Till Eulenspiegel. The printers produced
cheap, pamphletlike chapbooks and hawked them at street corners and country fairs. The hair-raising episodes in the life of the
mighty conjurer Johann Faust, who in the end paid in full for his
impious life, quickly captured the imagination of people looking
to be both entertained and edified. The first Faust book, marketed
by the printer Johannes Spiess in 1587, was a popular and finan-
cial success, which soon spread to the north of Europe by way of
an English translation. It appealed powerfully to Christopher
Marlowe, who was moved to compose *The Tragical History of
Doctor Faustus* sometime between 1588 and 1593. Marlowe's
drama, in turn, became the basis for puppet and marionette
shows that were given at various communal festivities, a ready
market for slapstick versions of the damnable life of Faust.

In his autobiography, Goethe noted that "the important puppet fable [of Faust] continued to echo and buzz many-toned
within me" (*Poetry and Truth* II, 10). While Goethe's and Marlowe's dramas arose from the same folklore, there is a spiritual
and emotional distance between them that reflects a seismic shift
in cultural history. To be sure, in one respect all the stories—the
puppet-theater versions and the crudely written *Faust*
chapbooks—were alike: in order to acquire limitless riches and
power, Faust had succumbed to the blandishments of the devil;
for twenty-four years Mephistopheles would do Faust's bidding,
after which he would collect his soul to be roasted in Hell. It was a
plot made to order to be a warning not to do as Faust did—not to
reach for powers that lay beyond one, not to "speculate the elements"—but to rest content with the approved answers that were
provided by the Scriptures and by the inspired and approved
ancient philosophers.

To the eighteenth century, however, the interpretation of the
Faust story in the dim light of old biases and medieval supersti-
tions must have seemed quaintly picturesque, superannuated,

and irrelevant to the sensibilities of modern man. Faust's chafing at his human limitations could no longer in itself be regarded as sinful. A new pride in the grandeur of the individual, fed by a rekindled confidence in the capacity of human reason to unravel nature's mysteries, made it possible to see in Faust not only the sinner but also a representative example of what is noble and divine in man: an unquenchable thirst for knowledge and an inborn need to explore—by spiritual as well as sensuous means—the limits of human potential. Indeed at the end of the second part of Goethe's drama Faust has earned the right to divine Grace.

In 1773, as a twenty-four-year-old law student at the University of Strasbourg, Goethe sketched out the first doggerel verses of the opening monologue of *Faust*—intentionally "bad" verse, a reminiscence of the puppet theater. From then on—though with many interruptions—the ever-growing poetic edifice of *Faust* remained Goethe's chief preoccupation, running like a red thread through an immensely productive life.

A momentous Goethean departure from the old legend occurred in Goethe's version of the transaction between Faust and Mephistopheles. The traditional twenty-four-year contract was done away with and transformed into a wager. Faust says to Mephisto:

> If ever I should tell the moment:
> Oh stay! You are so beautiful!
> Then you may cast me into chains,
> then I shall smile upon perdition!
> (1699–1702)

In his long life as a scholar, Faust has reached the melancholy conclusion that he will never know what is truly worth knowing, that he would be blinded by the light of truth, and must therefore be resigned to live with mere reflections and counterfeit images. Since he has little faith in even the devil's ability to satisfy his craving to the full, he is confident—though by no means cheerfully so—that he will win the bet. He fully expects that he will continue to live as he lived before, not truly advancing beyond the condition that made him say in the opening monologue:

> yet here I am, a wretched fool,
> no wiser than I was before.
> ·
> I don't pretend to know a thing worth knowing.
> I don't pretend that I can teach,
>
> (358–72)

Faust's prospects are grim. Despair and the idea of suicide are ever his close companions.

But suppose that Faust were to lose the wager and that through Mephisto's machinations he indeed were to experience the supreme Moment, the incomparable, all-encompassing pinprick of time. In that case, for a single instant of usurped divinity, Faust would look upon even hellfire as trivial punishment. The stakes of the wager—no doubt by design—are not what they seem to be at first sight. They require "speculation" in the alchemical sense, meaning intellectual probing and testing. As it turns out, an accounting of who won or who lost is not finally at issue in *Faust*. All is secondary to the quest for the transcendent Moment. It is Faust's irrepressible striving to extend the human potential and to break through the restrictions inherent in human nature that finally tips the balance in favor of Faust's salvation, even though, in legalistic terms, he may have lost his bet with Mephisto.

The first part of the drama, *Faust I*—offered in this volume in an English translation as well as in the original German—sparkles in its manifold poetic modes and impresses us with a substantial integrity. It stands on its own dramatic feet without *Faust II* and is frequently performed, even though it leaves the hero's destiny and the outcome of the wager in abeyance. At the end of our play, one sees Gretchen lying on her prison pallet uttering, Ophelia-like, deranged shreds of truth that pierce Faust's inmost being. She is guilty of murdering her illegitimate baby, whose father is her seducer-lover, Faust. We, as readers of the play, know that Gretchen was moved by love alone and was driven to despair by love. Having seen her despised and humiliated by her own people, we are relieved to see her find mercy in God's eyes and grateful for a hint that she will be given a luminous place in Heaven. Faust, on the other hand, must continue to live, bound to a minion of Hell and inextricably enmeshed in Evil.

The modes and moods of Goethe's dramatic discourse are never for long the same or reliably predictable. There is the solemn and metrically uniform celebration of divine majesty manifested in the rolling planetary spheres of the "Prologue in Heaven," immediately followed by the irregular, doggerel-like verses of the opening monologue. Shakespearean blank verse is never far removed from medieval hymnic chants. Strictly composed four-foot stanzaic lines may still echo in our minds when, near the drama's end, we reach the ragged and harsh shreds of prose in "Gloomy Day—Field." It is apparent that we must not look to verse forms as such to provide us with any unifying principle in *Faust*. The mood may shift from high seriousness to levity, from profound sentiment to callousness, from optimism to despair, oscillations that seem almost instantaneous, like an alternating current. They soon reveal themselves as important reflections of the theme or content of the drama; for are not the ambivalences and paradoxes inherent in human existence—and the absence of absolutes—important aspects of Faust's frustration and are they not near the source of what Goethe explicitly named a "tragedy"?

Even before the "Prologue in Heaven" ends, the vision of celestial magnificence is suddenly cut short by the ironic colloquialisms of Lucifer-Mephisto:

> From time to time it's good to see the Old Man;
> I must be careful not to break with him.
> How decent of so great a personage
> to be so human with the devil.
>
> (350-3)

And a bit later, when we witness Faust bemoaning his painfully futile encounter with the Earth Spirit, there is a knock on the door. It is Wagner, his disciple and assistant, who had listened to his master's outcries as they echoed through the corridors. As a devotee of traditional scholarship and loyal defender of the sanctity of venerable texts, he says upon entering the study:

> Excuse me, but I heard your declamation;
> was it a passage from Greek tragedy?

I should like to profit from such elocution,

(522–4)

Wagner radically misjudges his master. By his ludicrously inappropriate reference to the travails of Faust's soul, he reveals himself—through an ironic shaft directed at the audience—as a prototypal philistine.

Often there is no temporal sequence of contrary positions, but a simultaneous presence of mutually exclusive polarities. Consider the following: when Faust tells Mephisto that he is bent on a life of all-encompassing experience beyond the reach of ordinary men, Mephisto answers mockingly:

> Make your alliance with a poet,
> and let that gentleman think lofty thoughts,
> and let him heap the noblest qualities
> upon your worthy head:

(1789–92)

The lines are deceptively simple. Actually they contain multi-leveled ironies. The poet with whom Faust is to ally himself here stands for a person who conjures up empty illusions of the kind Faust continuously creates for himself. The reader realizes—perhaps in a double-take response—that the images of Faust's fantasy are indeed the stuff of poetry and are constitutive elements of the *Faust* poem itself. It is a case of involuted paradoxes: Mephisto, the no-nonsense materialist contemptuous of poetic imagination, scoffs at Faust and recommends that he make himself over into a dramatic character—only in this manner could he hope to find fulfillment. It is a provocation directed not only at Faust but at the reader-spectator as well. And it is the *Faust* drama—itself a poetic battleground between poetry and anti-poetry—that continuously generates provisional answers to Mephisto's challenge. After all, acting counter to Mephisto's corrosive stance is our realization that Faust need not bother himself to make an "alliance with a poet." Surely, in his case such a step would be redundant. For the public, on the other hand, Mephisto's suggestion may be only partially ironic, because it is aware of the "as if" condition of the stage. Mephisto's radical critique opens unsuspected avenues into our minds and nerve centers. We are compelled to measure the distance between fantasy and quotidian reality and "get inside" the process of poetic transformation. We might indeed take upon ourselves a share of Faust's own frustration:

> Two souls, alas, dwell in my breast,
> each seeks to rule without the other.
> (1112–13)

as we come upon the one explicit and unironic expression of Faustian ambivalence.

While a diversity of approaches to the *Faust* poem have, over the approximately century-and-a-half of its existence, produced indispensable insights, critics with an all too single-minded perspective tended to obscure values that are accessible only to a different optic. The poem's philosophical problems—for example, those having to do with the nature of truth and of cosmic governance—have been explored perhaps more intensively than any other aspect. Psychological analyses of the characters have been carried out, as well as researches dealing exclusively with the rich field of Faustian imagery. We are fortunate in having comparative studies dealing with the literary and spiritual influences that went into the composition of both parts of the poem. A considerable body of evidence also has been marshaled in support of the proposition that a far-reaching analogy exists between Goethe's vision of life-forms in the earth's flora—such as dicotyledonous plants—and the principles governing the structure of *Faust*.

When all is said and done, however, the simple question, What is *Faust* about? is still capable of eliciting fresh responses, if only for the reason that by looking for meaning we are implicitly searching for some underlying coherence or for a metaphor that might convincingly convey a sense of structure. To find textual confirmation for one's own intuited image of unity in *Faust* is the exhilarating reward of devoted study. Certainly, even after only a fleeting acquaintance, one must ask the question: What is it that keeps Faust dissatisfied, even though he has mastered all the academic disciplines of his day? Why could he not be proud of his accomplishments and have faith in human progress like his redoubtable assistant Wagner? At least part of the answer may be found in the most concentrated symbol of Faust's imperious need: the all-encompassing Moment, the *Augenblick*, that is the subject of the wager with Mephisto and the thematic undercurrent of the entire drama. To experience, in a single instant, the succession of events that mark our existence in time is equivalent to eliminating time altogether; it means an existence in a continuous present tense. As temporal creatures, nervously feeding a shortening future into a lengthening past, we attribute to the gods a timeless mode of being and an existence in total simultaneity. Therefore Faust's craving for the "highest moment" really amounts to the ultimate *hubris*; he is reaching for more than mere superiority among men—more than Macbeth, who would be king, and more than Oedipus, the incomparable solver of riddles who *was* the king and came to know it too late. Faust reaches for divinity and is "hell-bent" to burst out of his imprisonment in temporality.

Since Goethe's death, in 1832, the Faust story, through its various transmutations, has become one of the central myths of the Western world. The theme fascinated composers like Wagner, Schumann, Berlioz, Gounod, Boito, and Mahler, all of whom created important operatic or orchestral scores inspired by Goethe's drama. American writers have recently paid renewed attention to the earlier chapbook accounts. Stephen Vincent Benét's play *The Devil and Daniel Webster* and the musical comedy *Damn Yankees*, transposed from a novel by Douglass Wallop, were successful Broadway productions and continue to be popular on stage and on television. Intellectually more demanding and ambitious are Thomas Mann's last big novel, *Doctor Faustus* (1947), whose plot parallels the pre-Goethean story, but which also contains unmistakable imprints of Goethe's *Faust*, and the 1981 motion picture *Mephisto*, loosely based on a novel concerned with the career and questionable morality of a German actor-director who achieved fame in his role of Mephisto. The film is a remarkable directorial accomplishment by Istvan Szabo.

The headlong strides in the natural sciences and in technology, the imperious reach for nature's inmost secrets by twentieth-century "speculators of the elements" operating in computerized laboratories, the thrust toward man-made velocities that seemingly approach the impassable limits this side of omnipresence—can these not be seen as assaults on hitherto forbidden realms? In our day the search for the *Augenblick* is proceeding with increasing intensity. According to the Gospel of Luke, Satan showed to Jesus "all the kingdoms of the world in an instant of time" and then offered them to him; and it is not difficult to see in this second temptation a prefiguration of the Faustian wager, a "harking forward" to late-twentieth-century technological wizardry.

A NOTE ON THE TRANSLATION

To make great poetry accessible by translation is a joy as well as a harsh discipline. The joy is of the kind that follows the completion of any difficult piece of work. The discipline and harsh constraints flow from the peculiar forces at play. On the one hand, there is the obligation to remain as close as possible to the original text and to avoid "irresponsible" departures from it. From that point of view, each recasting or remolding of the poet's carefully chosen phrases can be judged to be a little betrayal.

The position at the other extreme has its source in the conviction that a good or faithful translation is only very rarely a literal transfer, that it is rather the transmigration of feeling, form, and thought from the imprecisions of one language to the quirks and coincidences of another.

It is important to give heed to both contrary impulses without entirely submitting to either, maintaining, wherever possible, a delicate balance between them. I have striven toward an ideal of a vital, rhythmic, American idiom so that the general impression might be similar to what a German reader might receive from the original. By relinquishing rhyme and strict meter, except in the interspersed songs and ballads, I gained the freedom to be more faithful to sense and spirit than I could otherwise have been. I believe that a consistent adherence to all the details of prosody cannot be sustained in a work of the scope of *Faust* without doing violence to natural diction. Moreover, it has for some time been clear to me that a German rhymed line is not necessarily rendered most felicitously—or most faithfully—by an equivalent English rhyme. Such a translation easily suffers from a jingling quality that may vitiate or even falsify the mood of the original.

The language of this translation is meant to be neither archaic nor wholly colloquial. Instead I tried to steer an intermediate course, in the hope of conveying a sense of the poetic immediacy and continual urgency of the German text.

This Bantam *Faust* was first published in 1962, reissued in 1967, and now—more than twenty years after its first appearance—is being granted a new life. It is not very often that translators are given a second chance, and it is strangely il-

luminating—when reviewing the earlier version—to be con-
veyed into one's own past and, as it were, to come face-to-face
with one's translating persona of an earlier day. There is a ner-
vous "hello" and also a firm "good-bye."

I feel inwardly connected to all those readers who came to
Faust by way of my English version, and I am now tentatively
confident that the changes in this new edition will further con-
tribute to the understanding and enjoyment of one of the world's
supreme poetic works.

1749   August 28. Johann Wolfgang Goethe born in Frankfurt, Germany.

1765   Enrolls as a law student at the University of Leipzig; takes private lessons in art.

1768   Falls seriously ill. Returns to Frankfurt. Reads Shakespeare for the first time; also books on alchemy. First anonymous collection of poems called *Neue Lieder*, set to music and published by Breitkopf.

1770   Travels to Strasbourg, in Alsace. Resumes his studies at the university. Falls in love with Friderike Brion, a parson's daughter living in nearby Sesenheim. Meets German critic and essayist Herder.

1771   Receives law degree. First plans for drama *Götz von Berlichingen*, profoundly influenced by Shakespeare. Also possible first sketches for a Faust drama.

1773   Much preoccupied with drawing and portraiture. Completes *Götz von Berlichingen*.

1774   Epistolary novel: *The Sorrows of Young Werther*.

1775   Accepts invitation of the reigning duke of Weimar, Carl August, to join his court.

1777   First version of *Wilhelm Meister*, a bildungsroman. Group of dithyrambic odes, "Prometheus," etc.

1780   Poems: "Der Fischer," "Erlkönig," and other ballads.

1782   Receives title of nobility from the emperor.

1784   Scientific writings: treatise concerning granite; discovery of the intermaxillary bone in humans.

1785   Common-law marriage with Christiane Vulpius (legalized 1806).

1786– First Italian journey. Dramas: *Iphigenie auf Tauris, Eg-*
1788   *mont*.

1789   Birth of son, August von Goethe. Poetry: *Roman Elegies*.
       Drama: *Torquato Tasso*.

1790   Second Italian journey. *Faust I* first published as a frag-
       ment.

1791   Becomes general manager of Weimar Court Theater.
       Completes treatise in biology: *The Metamorphosis of
       Plants*.

1794   Meets Schiller. Beginning of collaboration and friend-
       ship between the two poets.

1795   Completes first volume of *Wilhelm Meister*. Epic poem:
       Hermann und Dorothea. Second series of ballads, among
       them "The Sorcerer's Apprentice."

1804   Madame de Staël visits with Goethe in Weimar.

1805   Schiller dies.

1808   Conversation with Napoleon. *Faust I* appears in com-
       plete form.

1812   Meeting with Beethoven.

1816   His wife Christiane dies.

1822   *Theory of Color* (*Farbenlehre*), opposing the physics of
       Isaac Newton.

1823   First visit of Johann Peter Eckermann, subsequently
       Goethe's secretary and faithful recorder of conversations
       with him.

1831   Completes *Faust II*.

1832   Dies in Weimar on March 22.

FAUST

ZUEIGNUNG

Ihr naht euch wieder, schwankende Gestalten,
Die früh sich einst dem trüben Blick gezeigt.
Versuch' ich wohl, euch diesmal festzuhalten?
Fühl' ich mein Herz noch jenem Wahn geneigt?
Ihr drängt euch zu! nun gut, so mögt ihr walten,
Wie ihr aus Dunst und Nebel um mich steigt;
Mein Busen fühlt sich jugendlich erschüttert
Vom Zauberhauch, der euren Zug umwittert.

Ihr bringt mit euch die Bilder froher Tage,
Und manche liebe Schatten steigen auf;   10
Gleich einer alten, halbverklungnen Sage
Kommt erste Lieb' und Freundschaft mit herauf;
Der Schmerz wird neu, es wiederholt die Klage
Des Lebens labyrinthisch irren Lauf,
Und nennt die Guten, die, um schöne Stunden
Vom Glück getäuscht, vor mir hinweggeschwunden.

Sie hören nicht die folgenden Gesänge,
Die Seelen, denen ich die ersten sang;
Zerstoben ist das freundliche Gedränge,
Verklungen, ach! der erste Widerklang.   20
Mein Leid ertönt der unbekannten Menge,
Ihr Beifall selbst macht meinem Herzen bang,
Und was sich sonst an meinem Lied erfreuet,
Wenn es noch lebt, irrt in der Welt zerstreuet.

Und mich ergreift ein längst entwöhntes Sehnen
Nach jenem stillen, ernsten Geisterreich,
Es schwebet nun in unbestimmten Tönen
Mein lispelnd Lied, der Äolsharfe gleich,
Ein Schauer faßt mich, Träne folgt den Tränen,
Das strenge Herz, es fühlt sich mild und weich;   30
Was ich besitze, seh' ich wie im Weiten,
Und was verschwand, wird mir zu Wirklichkeiten.

DEDICATION[1]

Wavering forms, you come again;
once long ago you passed before my clouded sight.
Should I now attempt to hold you fast?
Does my heart still look for phantoms?
You surge at me! Well, then you may rule
as you rise about me out of mist and cloud.
The airy magic in your path
stirs youthful tremors in my breast.

You bear the images of happy days,
and friendly shadows rise to mind.   10
With them, as in an almost muted tale,
come youthful love and friendship.
The pain is felt anew, and the lament
sounds life's labyrinthine wayward course
and tells of friends who went before me
and whom fate deprived of joyous hours.

They cannot hear the songs which follow,
the souls to whom I sang my first,
scattered is the genial crowd,
the early echo, ah, has died away.   20
Now my voice sings for the unknown many
whose very praise intimidates my heart.
The living whom my song once charmed
are now dispersed throughout the world.

And I am seized by long forgotten yearnings
for the solemn, silent world of spirits;
as on an Aeolian harp my whispered song
lingers now in vagrant tones.
I shudder, and a tear draws other tears;
my austere heart grows soft and gentle.   30
What I possess appears far in the distance,
and what is past has turned into reality.

3

Direktor, Theaterdichter, Lustige Person.

DIREKTOR.

Ihr beiden, die ihr mir so oft,
In Not und Trübsal, beigestanden,
Sagt, was ihr wohl in deutschen Landen
Von unsrer Unternehmung hofft?
Ich wünschte sehr der Menge zu behagen,
Besonders weil sie lebt und leben läßt.
Die Pfosten sind, die Bretter aufgeschlagen,
Und jedermann erwartet sich ein Fest.   40
Sie sitzen schon, mit hohen Augenbraunen,
Gelassen da und möchten gern erstaunen.
Ich weiß, wie man den Geist des Volks versöhnt;
Doch so verlegen bin ich nie gewesen:
Zwar sind sie an das Beste nicht gewöhnt,
Allein sie haben schrecklich viel gelesen.
Wie machen wir's, daß alles frisch und neu
Und mit Bedeutung auch gefällig sei?
Denn freilich mag ich gern die Menge sehen,
Wenn sich der Strom nach unsrer Bude drängt   50
Und mit gewaltig wiederholten Wehen
Sich durch die enge Gnadenpforte zwängt,
Bei hellem Tage, schon vor vieren,
Mit Stößen sich bis an die Kasse ficht
Und, wie in Hungersnot um Brot an Bäckertüren,
Um ein Billett sich fast die Hälse bricht.
Dies Wunder wirkt auf so verschiedne Leute
Der Dichter nur; mein Freund, o tu es heute!

DICHTER.

O sprich mir nicht von jener bunten Menge,
Bei deren Anblick uns der Geist entflieht.   60
Verhülle mir das wogende Gedränge,
Das wider Willen uns zum Strudel zieht.
Nein, führe mich zur stillen Himmelsenge,
Wo nur dem Dichter reine Freude blüht,
Wo Lieb' und Freundschaft unsres Herzens Segen
Mit Götterhand erschaffen und erpflegen.

PRELUDE IN THE THEATER

Manager, Dramatic Poet, Comic Character.

MANAGER.

You two who often stood by me
in times of hardship and of gloom,
what do you think our enterprise
should bring to German lands and people?
I want the crowd to be well satisfied,
for, as you know, it lives and lets us live.
The boards are nailed, the stage is set,
and all the world looks for a lavish feast.   40
There they sit, with eyebrows raised,
and calmly wait to be astounded.
I have my ways to keep the people well disposed,
but never was I in a fix like this.
It's true, they're not accustomed to the best,
yet they have read an awful lot of things.
How shall we plot a new and fresh approach
and make things pleasant and significant?
I'll grant, it pleases me to watch the crowds,
as they stream and hustle to our tent   50
and with mighty and repeated labors
press onward through the narrow gate of grace;
while the sun still shines—it's scarcely four o'clock—
they fight and scramble for the ticket window,
and as if in famine begging at the baker's door,
they almost break their necks to gain admission.
The poet alone can work this miracle
on such a diverse group. My friend, the time is now!

OET.

Oh, speak no more of motley crowds to me,
their presence makes my spirit flee.   60
Veil from my sight those waves and surges
that suck us down into their raging pools.
Take me rather to a quiet little cell
where pure delight blooms only for the poet,
where our inmost joy is blessed and fostered
by love and friendship and the hand of God.

5

Ach! was in tiefer Brust uns da entsprungen,
Was sich die Lippe schüchtern vorgelallt,
Mißraten jetzt und jetzt vielleicht gelungen,
Verschlingt des wilden Augenblicks Gewalt.   70
Oft, wenn es erst durch Jahre durchgedrungen,
Erscheint es in vollendeter Gestalt.
Was glänzt, ist für den Augenblick geboren,
Das Echte bleibt der Nachwelt unverloren.

LUSTIGE PERSON.

Wenn ich nur nichts von Nachwelt hören sollte.
Gesetzt, daß i c h von Nachwelt reden wollte,
Wer machte denn der Mitwelt Spaß?
Den will sie doch und soll ihn haben.
Die Gegenwart von einem braven Knaben
Ist, dächt' ich, immer auch schon was.   80
Wer sich behaglich mitzuteilen weiß,
Den wird des Volkes Laune nicht erbittern;
Er wünscht sich einen großen Kreis,
Um ihn gewisser zu erschüttern.
Drum seid nur brav und zeigt euch musterhaft,
Laßt Phantasie mit allen ihren Chören,
Vernunft, Verstand, Empfindung, Leidenschaft,
Doch, merkt euch wohl! nicht ohne Narrheit hören!

DIREKTOR.

Besonders aber laßt genug geschehn!
Man kommt zu schaun, man will am liebsten sehn.   90
Wird vieles vor den Augen abgesponnen,
So daß die Menge staunend gaffen kann,
Da habt Ihr in der Breite gleich gewonnen,
Ihr seid ein vielgeliebter Mann.
Die Masse könnt Ihr nur durch Masse zwingen,
Ein jeder sucht sich endlich selbst was aus.
Wer vieles bringt, wird manchem etwas bringen;
Und jeder geht zufrieden aus dem Haus.
Gebt Ihr ein Stück, so gebt es gleich in Stücken!
Solch ein Ragout, es muß Euch glücken;   100
Leicht ist es vorgelegt, so leicht als ausgedacht.
Was hilft's, wenn Ihr ein Ganzes dargebracht,
Das Publikum wird es Euch doch zerpflücken.

Alas! What sprang from our deepest feelings,
what our lips tried timidly to form,
failing now and now perhaps succeeding,
is devoured by a single brutish moment.   70
Often it must filter through the years
before its final form appears perfected.
What gleams like tinsel is but for the moment.
What's true remains intact for future days.

COMEDIAN.

Oh, save me from such talk of future days!
Suppose I were concerned with progeny,
then who would cheer our present generation?
It lusts for fun and should be gratified.
A fine young fellow in the present tense
is worth a lot when all is said and done.   80
If he can charm and make the public feel at ease,
he will not mind its changing moods;
he seeks the widest circle for himself,
so that his act will thereby be more telling.
And now be smart and show your finest qualities,
let fantasy be heard with all its many voices,
as well as mind and sensibility and passion,
and then be sure to add a dose of folly.

MANAGER.

Above all, let there be sufficient action!
They come to gaze and wish to see a spectacle.   90
If many things reel off before their eyes,
so that the mob can gape and be astounded,
then you will sway the great majority
and be a very popular man.
The mass can only be subdued by massiveness,
so each can pick a morsel for himself.
A large amount contains enough for everyone,
and each will leave contented with his share.
Give us the piece you write in pieces!
Try your fortune with a potpourri   100
that's quickly made and easily dished out.
What good is it to sweat and to create a whole?
The audience will yet pick the thing to pieces.

DICHTER.

   Ihr fühlet nicht, wie schlecht ein solches Handwerk sei!
   Wie wenig das dem echten Künstler zieme!
   Der saubern Herren Pfuscherei
   Ist, merk' ich, schon bei Euch Maxime.

DIREKTOR.

   Ein solcher Vorwurf läßt mich ungekränkt:
   Ein Mann, der recht zu wirken denkt,
   Muß auf das beste Werkzeug halten.   110
   Bedenkt, Ihr habet weiches Holz zu spalten,
   Und seht nur hin, für wen Ihr schreibt!
   Wenn diesen Langeweile treibt,
   Kommt jener satt vom übertischten Mahle,
   Und, was das Allerschlimmste bleibt,
   Gar mancher kommt vom Lesen der Journale.
   Man eilt zerstreut zu uns, wie zu den Maskenfesten,
   Und Neugier nur beflügelt jeden Schritt;
   Die Damen geben sich und ihren Putz zum besten
   Und spielen ohne Gage mit.   120
   Was träumet Ihr auf Eurer Dichterhöhe?
   Was macht ein volles Haus Euch froh?
   Beseht die Gönner in der Nähe!
   Halb sind sie kalt, halb sind sie roh.
   Der, nach dem Schauspiel, hofft ein Kartenspiel,
   Der eine wilde Nacht an einer Dirne Busen.
   Was plagt ihr armen Toren viel,
   Zu solchem Zweck, die holden Musen?
   Ich sag' Euch, gebt nur mehr und immer, immer mehr,
   So könnt Ihr Euch vom Ziele nie verirren.   130
   Sucht nur die Menschen zu verwirren,
   Sie zu befriedigen, ist schwer——
   Was fällt Euch an? Entzückung oder Schmerzen?

DICHTER.

   Geh hin und such dir einen andern Knecht!
   Der Dichter sollte wohl das höchste Recht,
   Das Menschenrecht, das ihm Natur vergönnt,
   Um deinetwillen freventlich verscherzen!
   Wodurch bewegt er alle Herzen?
   Wodurch besiegt er jedes Element?

POET.

You do not feel the baseness of such handiwork.
How improper for an artist worth his salt!
I see, the botchery of your neat companions
has been the maxim of your enterprise.

MANAGER.

Such reproaches leave me unperturbed.
A man who wants to make his mark
must try to wield the best of tools.   110
You have coarse wood to split, remember that;
consider those for whom you write!
A customer may come because he's bored,
another may have had too much to eat;
and what I most of all abhor:
some have just put down their evening paper.
They hurry here distracted, as to a masquerade,
and seek us out from mere curiosity.
The ladies come to treat the audience to their charms
and play their parts without a salary.   120
Now are you still a dreamer on poetic heights?
And yet content when our house is filled?
Observe your benefactors at close range!
Some are crude, the others cold as ice.
And when it's finished, this one wants a deck of cards
and that one pleasure in a whore's embrace.
Why then invoke and plague the muses
for such a goal as this, poor fools?
I say to you, give more and more and always more,
and then you cannot miss by very much.   130
You must attempt to mystify the people,
they're much too hard to satisfy—
What's got into you—are you anguished or ecstatic?

POET.

Go find yourself another slave!
The poet, I suppose, should wantonly give back,
so you'd be pleased, the highest right
that Nature granted him, the right of Man!
How does the poet stir all hearts?
How does he conquer every element?

Ist es der Einklang nicht, der aus dem Busen dringt   140
Und in sein Herz die Welt zurücke schlingt?
Wenn die Natur des Fadens ew'ge Länge,
Gleichgültig drehend, auf die Spindel zwingt,
Wenn aller Wesen unharmon'sche Menge
Verdrießlich durcheinander klingt,
Wer teilt die fließend immer gleiche Reihe
Belebend ab, daß sie sich rhythmisch regt?
Wer ruft das Einzelne zur allgemeinen Weihe,
Wo es in herrlichen Akkorden schlägt?
Wer läßt den Sturm zu Leidenschaften wüten?   150
Das Abendrot im ernsten Sinne glühn?
Wer schüttet alle schönen Frühlingsblüten
Auf der Geliebten Pfade hin?
Wer flicht die unbedeutend grünen Blätter
Zum Ehrenkranz Verdiensten jeder Art?
Wer sichert den Olymp? vereinet Götter?
Des Menschen Kraft, im Dichter offenbart.

LUSTIGE PERSON.

So braucht sie denn, die schönen Kräfte,
Und treibt die dichtrischen Geschäfte,
Wie man ein Liebesabenteuer treibt.   160
Zufällig naht man sich, man fühlt, man bleibt,
Und nach und nach wird man verflochten;
Es wächst das Glück, dann wird es angefochten,
Man ist entzückt, nun kommt der Schmerz heran,
Und eh' man sich's versieht, ist's eben ein Roman.
Laßt uns auch so ein Schauspiel geben!
Greift nur hinein ins volle Menschenleben!
Ein jeder lebt's, nicht vielen ist's bekannt,
Und wo ihr's packt, da ist's interessant.
In bunten Bildern wenig Klarheit,   170
Viel Irrtum und ein Fünkchen Wahrheit,
So wird der beste Trank gebraut,
Der alle Welt erquickt und auferbaut.
Dann sammelt sich der Jugend schönste Blüte
Vor eurem Spiel und lauscht der Offenbarung,
Dann sauget jedes zärtliche Gemüte
Aus eurem Werk sich melanchol'sche Nahrung,

Is it not the music welling from his heart   140
that draws the world into his breast again?
When Nature spins with unconcern
the endless thread and winds it on the spindle,
when the discordant mass of living things
sounds its sullen dark cacophony,
who divides the flowing changeless line,
infusing life, and gives it pulse and rhythm?
Who summons each to common consecration
where each will sound in glorious harmony?
Who bids the storm accompany the passions,   150
the sunset cast its glow on solemn thought?
Who scatters every fairest April blossom
along the path of his beloved?
Who braids from undistinguished verdant leaves
a wreath to honor merit?
Who safeguards Mount Olympus, who unites the gods?
Man's power which in the poet stands revealed!

COMEDIAN.

Very well, then put to use those handsome powers
and carry on the poet's trade,
as one would carry on a love affair.   160
One meets by accident, emotes, and lingers,
and by and by one is entangled,
one's bliss increases, then one is in trouble;
one's rapture grows, then follows grief and pain,
before you know, your story is completed.
We must present a drama of this type!
Reach for the fullness of a human life!
We live it all, but few live knowingly;
if you but touch it, it will fascinate.
A complex picture without clarity,   170
much error with a little spark of truth—
that's the recipe to brew the potion
whence all the world is quenched and edified.
The fairest bloom of youth will congregate
to see the play and wait for revelation;
then every tender soul will eagerly absorb
some food for melancholy from your work.

Dann wird bald dies, bald jenes aufgeregt,
Ein jeder sieht, was er im Herzen trägt.
Noch sind sie gleich bereit, zu weinen und zu lachen,   180
Sie ehren noch den Schwung, erfreuen sich am Schein;
Wer fertig ist, dem ist nichts recht zu machen;
Ein Werdender wird immer dankbar sein.

DICHTER.

So gib mir auch die Zeiten wieder,
Da ich noch selbst im Werden war,
Da sich ein Quell gedrängter Lieder
Ununterbrochen neu gebar,
Da Nebel mir die Welt verhüllten,
Die Knospe Wunder noch versprach,
Da ich die tausend Blumen brach,   190
Die alle Täler reichlich füllten.
Ich hatte nichts und doch genug:
Den Drang nach Wahrheit und die Lust am Trug.
Gib ungebändigt jene Triebe,
Das tiefe, schmerzenvolle Glück,
Des Hasses Kraft, die Macht der Liebe,
Gib meine Jugend mir zurück!

LUSTIGE PERSON.

Der Jugend, guter Freund, bedarfst du allenfalls,
Wenn dich in Schlachten Feinde drängen,
Wenn mit Gewalt an deinen Hals   200
Sich allerliebste Mädchen hängen,
Wenn fern des schnellen Laufes Kranz
Vom schwer erreichten Ziele winket,
Wenn nach dem heft'gen Wirbeltanz
Die Nächte schmausend man vertrinket.
Doch ins bekannte Saitenspiel
Mit Mut und Anmut einzugreifen,
Nach einem selbstgesteckten Ziel
Mit holdem Irren hinzuschweifen,
Das, alte Herrn, ist eure Pflicht,   210
Und wir verehren euch darum nicht minder.
Das Alter macht nicht kindisch, wie man spricht,
Es findet uns nur noch als wahre Kinder.

First one and then another thing is stirred,
so each can find what's in his heart.
They weep and laugh quite easily;   180
they honor fancy and they like their make-believe.
The finished man, you know, is difficult to please;
a growing mind will ever show you gratitude.

POET.

Then let me live those years again
when I could still mature and grow,
when songs gushed up as from a spring
that ceaselessly renewed itself within,
when all the world was veiled in mist
and every bud concealed a miracle,
when I gathered up a thousand flowers   190
that richly decked the slopes and fields—
then I had nothing, yet I had enough:
a yen for phantoms, and an urge for truth.
Give me back my unconstrained desires,
my deep and painful time of bliss,
the strength of hate, the force of love,
give me back my youth again!

COMEDIAN.

You need your youth in any case, my friend,
when pressed in battle by a surging foe,
when lovely girls with all their strength   200
lock their arms about your neck,
when far away the victor's wreath
lures the runner to a hard-won goal,
when after frenzied whirling dances,
you feast and drink throughout the night.
But to pluck the lyre's familiar strings
with courage and with graceful mien,
to sweep through charming aberrations
to a self-appointed goal,
that, gentlemen, is where your duty lies,   210
and we honor you no less for it.
They say that age makes people childish;
I say it merely finds us still true children.

DIREKTOR.

Der Worte sind genug gewechselt,
Laßt mich auch endlich Taten sehn!
Indes ihr Komplimente drechselt,
Kann etwas Nützliches geschehn.
Was hilft es viel von Stimmung reden?
Dem Zaudernden erscheint sie nie.
Gebt ihr euch einmal für Poeten,   220
So kommandiert die Poesie.
Euch ist bekannt, was wir bedürfen:
Wir wollen stark Getränke schlürfen;
Nun braut mir unverzüglich dran!
Was heute nicht geschieht, ist morgen nicht getan,
Und keinen Tag soll man verpassen.
Das Mögliche soll der Entschluß
Beherzt sogleich beim Schopfe fassen,
Er will es dann nicht fahren lassen
Und wirket weiter, well er muß.   230

Ihr wißt, auf unsern deutschen Bühnen
Probiert ein jeder, was er mag;
Drum schonet mir an diesem Tag
Prospekte nicht und nicht Maschinen.
Gebraucht das groß' und kleine Himmelslicht,
Die Sterne dürfet ihr verschwenden;
An Wasser, Feuer, Felsenwänden,
An Tier und Vögeln fehlt es nicht.
So schreitet in dem engen Bretterhaus
Den ganzen Kreis der Schöpfung aus   240
Und wandelt mit bedächt'ger Schnelle
Vom Himmel durch die Welt zur Hölle.

MANAGER.

Sufficient words have been exchanged;
now at last I want to see some action.
While you are turning pretty compliments,
some useful thing should be afoot.
What good is it to speak of inspiration?
To him who hesitates it never comes.
Since you are poets by profession,   220
call out and commandeer some poetry.
You are acquainted with our needs:
We wish to swallow potent brew,
so do not dally any longer!
What you put off today will not be done tomorrow;
you should never let a day slip by
Let resolution grasp what's possible
and seize it boldly by the hair;
then you will never lose your grip,
but labor steadily, because you must.   230

On our German stage, you know,
we like to try out all we can;
so don't be stingy on this day
with panoramas and machinery.
Employ the great and small celestial light
and scatter stars without constraint;
nor are we short of water, fire, rocky crags,
and birds and beasts we have galore.
Within the narrow confines of our boards
you must traverse the circle of creation   240
and move along in measured haste
from Heaven through the world to Hell.

PROLOG IM HIMMEL

Der Herr. Die himmlischen Heerscharen.
Nachher Mephistopheles.
Die drei Erzengel treten vor.

RAPHAEL.

Die Sonne tönt nach alter Weise
In Brudersphären Wettgesang,
Und ihre vorgeschriebne Reise
Vollendet sie mit Donnergang.
Ihr Anblick gibt den Engeln Stärke,
Wenn keiner sie ergründen mag;
Die unbegreiflich hohen Werke
Sind herrlich wie am ersten Tag.   250

GABRIEL.

Und schnell und unbegreiflich schnelle
Dreht sich umher der Erde Pracht;
Es wechselt Paradieseshelle
Mit tiefer, schauervoller Nacht;
Es schäumt das Meer in breiten Flüssen
Am tiefen Grund der Felsen auf,
Und Fels und Meer wird fortgerissen
In ewig schnellem Sphärenlauf.

MICHAEL.

Und Stürme brausen um die Wette,
Vom Meer aufs Land, vom Land aufs Meer,   260
Und bilden wütend eine Kette
Der tiefsten Wirkung rings umher.
Da flammt ein blitzendes Verheeren
Dem Pfade vor des Donnerschlags;
Doch deine Boten, Herr, verehren
Das sanfte Wandeln deines Tags.

ZU DREI.

Der Anblick gibt den Engeln Stärke,
Da keiner dich ergründen mag,
Und alle deine hohen Werke
Sind herrlich wie am ersten Tag.   270

PROLOGUE IN HEAVEN[2]

The Lord. The Heavenly Hosts.
Later, Mephistopheles.
Enter the three Archangels.

RAPHAEL.

The sun intones his ancient song
in contest with fraternal spheres,
and with a roll of thunder
rounds out his predetermined journey.
His aspect strengthens angels,
but none can fathom him.
The inconceivable creations
are glorious as from the first.   250

GABRIEL.

And swift beyond conception
the earth's full splendor wheels about.
The light of paradise is followed
by deep and baleful night;
the ocean's rivers churn and foam
and lash the rocks' foundations,
and rocks and water hurtle onward
in swift, perennial circles.

MICHAEL.

The roaring storms race through the skies
from sea to land, from land to sea,   260
and furiously they forge a chain
of deep pervading energy.
Then lightning wrecks the trail,
then comes the crash of thunder;
and yet, O Lord, your messengers revere
the gentle movement of your day.

THE THREE.

The spectacle gives strength to angels,
but none can fathom you,
and all your high creations
are glorious as from the first.   270

17

MEPHISTOPHELES.

Da du, o Herr, dich einmal wieder nahst
Und fragst, wie alles sich bei uns befinde,
Und du mich sonst gewöhnlich gerne sahst,
So siehst du mich auch unter dem Gesinde.
Verzeih, ich kann nicht hohe Worte machen,
Und wenn mich auch der ganze Kreis verhöhnt;
Mein Pathos brächte dich gewiß zum Lachen,
Hättst du dir nicht das Lachen abgewöhnt.
Von Sonn' und Welten weiß ich nichts zu sagen,
Ich sehe nur, wie sich die Menschen plagen.   280
Der kleine Gott der Welt bleibt stets von gleichem Schlag,
Und ist so wunderlich als wie am ersten Tag.
Ein wenig besser würd' er leben,
Hättst du ihm nicht den Schein des Himmelslichts gegeben;
Er nennt's Vernunft und braucht's allein,
Nur tierischer als jedes Tier zu sein.
Er scheint mir, mit Verlaub von Euer Gnaden,
Wie eine der langbeinigen Zikaden,
Die immer fliegt und fliegend springt
Und gleich im Gras ihr altes Liedchen singt;   290
Und läg' er nur noch immer in dem Grase!
In jeden Quark begräbt er seine Nase.

DER HERR.

Hast du mir weiter nichts zu sagen?
Kommst du nur immer anzuklagen?
Ist auf der Erde ewig dir nichts recht?

MEPHISTOPHELES.

Nein, Herr! ich find' es dort, wie immer, herzlich schlecht.
Die Menschen dauern mich in ihren Jammertagen,
Ich mag sogar die armen selbst nicht plagen.

DER HERR.

Kennst du den Faust?

MEPHISTOPHELES.

                    Den Doktor?

DER HERR.

                              Meinen Knecht!

MEPHISTOPHELES.

Fürwahr! er dient Euch auf besondre Weise.   300

MEPHISTOPHELES.
   Because, O Lord, you show yourself and ask
   about conditions here with us,
   and you were glad in former days to have me near,
   you see me now as one among your servants.
   Forgive me, but I can't indulge in lofty words,
   although this crowd will hold me in contempt;
   my pathos certainly would make you laugh,
   had you not dispensed with laughter long ago.
   I waste no words on suns and planets,
   I only see how men torment themselves.   280
   Earth's little god remains the same
   and is as quaint as from the first.
   He would have an easier time of it
   had you not let him glimpse celestial light;
   he calls it reason and he only uses it
   to be more bestial than the beasts.
   To me he seems—I beg your gracious Lord's indulgence—
   a kind of grasshopper, a long-legged bug
   that's always in flight and flies as it leaps
   and in the grass scrapes out its ancient litany;   290
   I wish that he had never left the grass
   to rub his nose in imbecility!

THE LORD.
   Is this all you can report?
   Must you come forever to accuse?
   Is nothing ever right for you on earth?

MEPHISTOPHELES.
   No, my Lord. I find it there, as always, thoroughly revolting.
   I pity men in all their misery
   and actually hate to plague the wretches.

THE LORD.
   Do you know Faust?

MEPHISTOPHELES.
                        The doctor?

THE LORD.
                                    My servant!

MEPHISTOPHELES.
   Indeed! He serves you in peculiar ways.   300

Nicht irdisch ist des Toren Trank noch Speise.
Ihn treibt die Gärung in die Ferne,
Er ist sich seiner Tollheit halb bewußt;
Vom Himmel fordert er die schönsten Sterne
Und von der Erde jede höchste Lust,
Und alle Näh' und alle Ferne
Befriedigt nicht die tiefbewegte Brust.

DER HERR.

Wenn er mir jetzt auch nur verworren dient,
So werd' ich ihn bald in die Klarheit führen.
Weiß doch der Gärtner, wenn das Bäumchen grünt,   310
Daß Blüt' und Frucht die künft'gen Jahre zieren.

MEPHISTOPHELES.

Was wettet Ihr? den sollt Ihr noch verlieren,
Wenn Ihr mir die Erlaubnis gebt,
Ihn meine Straße sacht zu führen!

DER HERR.

Solang' er auf der Erde lebt,
Solange sei dir's nicht verboten.
Es irrt der Mensch, solang' er strebt.

MEPHISTOPHELES.

Da dank' ich Euch; denn mit den Toten
Hab' ich mich niemals gern befangen.
Am meisten lieb' ich mir die vollen, frischen Wangen.   320
Für einen Leichnam bin ich nicht zu Haus;
Mir geht es wie der Katze mit der Maus.

DER HERR.

Nun gut, es sei dir überlassen!
Zieh diesen Geist von seinem Urquell ab,
Und führ' ihn, kannst du ihn erfassen,
Auf deinem Wege mit herab,
Und steh beschämt, wenn du bekennen mußt:
Ein guter Mensch in seinem dunklen Drange
Ist sich des rechten Weges wohl bewußt.

MEPHISTOPHELES.

Schon gut! nur dauert es nicht lange.   330
Mir ist für meine Wette gar nicht bange.
Wenn ich zu meinem Zweck gelange,
Erlaubt Ihr mir Triumph aus voller Brust.

He eats and drinks no earthly nourishment, the fool.
The ferment in him drives him on and on,
and yet he half-knows that he's mad.
He demands the fairest stars from heaven
and every deepest lust from earth.
The nearest and the farthest
leave his churning heart dissatisfied.

THE LORD.

If now he serves me only gropingly,
I soon shall lead him into clarity.
The gardener knows that when his sapling greens   310
the coming years will see it bloom and bear.

MEPHISTOPHELES.

What will you bet? You'll lose him in the end,
if you'll just give me your permission
to lead him gently down my street.

THE LORD.

So long as he walks the earth,
so long may your wish be granted;
man will stray so long as he strives.

observation about sin
if you sit and do nothing
you won't have lived,
or sinned.

MEPHISTOPHELES.

I thank you kindly; for I have never
enjoyed involvement with the dead.
I prefer the full and rosy cheek,   320
and I'm simply not at home to corpses.
Cats like mice alive—and so do I.

THE LORD.

Very well. I leave this much to you.
Draw this spirit from his primal source
and—if you can hold him—
lead him downward on your road;
but stand ashamed when in the end you must confess:
a good man in his dark and secret longings
is well aware which path to go.

MEPHISTOPHELES.

True enough! Except, it won't be true for long.   330
I'm not concerned about the outcome of my wager,
and once I have attained my goal,
please let me have my heartfelt triumph!

Staub soll er fressen, und mit Lust,
Wie meine Muhme, die berühmte Schlange.

DER HERR.

Du darfst auch da nur frei erscheinen;
Ich habe deinesgleichen nie gehaßt.
Von allen Geistern, die verneinen,
Ist mir der Schalk am wenigsten zur Last.
Des Menschen Tätigkeit kann allzuleicht erschlaffen,   340
Er liebt sich bald die unbedingte Ruh;
Drum geb' ich gern ihm den Gesellen zu,
Der reizt und wirkt und muß als Teufel schaffen.—
Doch ihr, die echten Göttersöhne,
Erfreut euch der lebendig reichen Schöne!
Das Werdende, das ewig wirkt und lebt,
Umfass' euch mit der Liebe holden Schranken,
Und was in schwankender Erscheinung schwebt,
Befestiget mit dauernden Gedanken.

(*Der Himmel schließt, die Erzengel verteilen
sich.*)

MEPHISTOPHELES.

Von Zeit zu Zeit seh' ich den Alten gern,   350
Und hüte mich, mit ihm zu brechen.
Es ist gar hübsch von einem großen Herrn,
So menschlich mit dem Teufel selbst zu sprechen.

Dust shall he eat, and that with pleasure,
as did my relative, the celebrated snake.

THE LORD.

I am glad to let you have apparent freedom;
I hold no hatred for the like of you.
Of all the spirits that negate,
the rogue to me is the least burdensome.
Man's diligence is easily exhausted,   340
he grows too fond of unremitting peace.
I'm therefore pleased to give him a companion
who must goad and prod and be a devil.—
But you, my own true sons of Heaven,
rejoice in Beauty's vibrant wealth.
That which becomes will live and work forever;
let it enfold you with propitious bonds of Love.
And what appears as flickering image now,
fix it firmly with enduring thought.
    (*The heavens close; the Archangels sep-
    arate.*)

MEPHISTOPHELES.

From time to time it's good to see the Old Man;   350
I must be careful not to break with him.
How decent of so great a personage
to be so human with the devil.

NACHT

In einem hochgewölbten, engen gotischen Zimmer
Faust unruhig auf seinem Sessel am Pulte.

FAUST.

Habe nun, ach! Philosophie,
Juristerei und Medizin,
Und leider auch Theologie
Durchaus studiert, mit heißem Bemühn.
Da steh' ich nun, ich armer Tor,
Und bin so klug als wie zuvor!
Heiße Magister, heiße Doktor gar,   360
Und ziehe schon an die zehen Jahr'
Herauf, herab und quer und krumm
Meine Schüler an der Nase herum—
Und sehe, daß wir nichts wissen können!
Das will mir schier das Herz verbrennen.
Zwar bin ich gescheiter als alle die Laffen,
Doktoren, Magister, Schreiber und Pfaffen;
Mich plagen keine Skrupel noch Zweifel,
Fürchte mich weder vor Hölle noch Teufel—
Dafür ist mir auch alle Freud' entrissen,   370
Bilde mir nicht ein, was Rechts zu wissen,
Bilde mir nicht ein, ich könnte was lehren,
Die Menschen zu bessern und zu bekehren.
Auch hab' ich weder Gut noch Geld,
Noch Ehr' und Herrlichkeit der Welt;
Es möchte kein Hund so länger leben!
Drum hab' ich mich der Magie ergeben,
Ob mir durch Geistes Kraft und Mund
Nicht manch Geheimnis würde kund;
Daß ich nicht mehr mit sauerm Schweiß   380
Zu sagen brauche, was ich nicht weiß;
Daß ich erkenne, was die Welt
Im Innersten zusammenhält,

THE FIRST PART OF THE TRAGEDY

NIGHT

A high-vaulted, narrow, Gothic room.
Faust, restless, in an armchair at his desk.

FAUST.

Alas, I have studied philosophy,
the law as well as medicine,
and to my sorrow, theology;
studied them well with ardent zeal,
yet here I am, a wretched fool,
no wiser than I was before.
They call me Magister, even Doctor,   360
and for some ten years now
I've led my students by the nose,
up and down, across, and in circles—
all I see is that we cannot know!
This burns my heart.
Granted I am smarter than all those fops,
doctors, masters, scribes, and preachers;
I am not afflicted by scruples and doubts,
not afraid of Hell or the devil—
but in return all joy is torn from me,   370
I don't pretend to know a thing worth knowing,
I don't pretend that I can teach,
improve, or convert my fellow men.
Nor have I property or gold,
or honor and glories of this world;
no dog would choose to live this way!
Therefore I have turned to magic,
so that by the spirit's might and main
I might yet learn some secret lore;
that I need no longer sweat and toil   380
and dress my ignorance in empty words;
that I might behold the warp and the woof
of the world's inmost fabric,

Schau' alle Wirkenskraft und Samen,
Und tu' nicht mehr in Worten kramen.

O sähst du, voller Mondenschein,
Zum letztenmal auf meine Pein,
Den ich so manche Mitternacht
An diesem Pult herangewacht:
Dann über Büchern und Papier,   390
Trübsel'ger Freund, erschienst du mir!
Ach! könnt' ich doch auf Bergeshöhn
In deinem lieben Lichte gehn,
Um Bergeshöhle mit Geistern schweben,
Auf Wiesen in deinem Dämmer weben,
Von allem Wissensqualm entladen,
In deinem Tau gesund mich baden!

Weh! steck' ich in dem Kerker noch?
Verfluchtes dumpfes Mauerloch,
Wo selbst das liebe Himmelslicht   400
Trüb durch gemalte Scheiben bricht!
Beschränkt von diesem Bücherhauf,
Den Würme nagen, Staub bedeckt,
Den, bis ans hohe Gewölb' hinauf,
Ein angeraucht Papier umsteckt;
Mit Gläsern, Büchsen rings umstellt,
Mit Instrumenten vollgepfropft,
Urväter-Hausrat drein gestopft—
Das ist deine Welt! das heißt eine Welt!

Und fragst du noch, warum dein Herz   410
Sich bang in deinem Busen klemmt?
Warum ein unerklärter Schmerz
Dir alle Lebensregung hemmt?
Statt der lebendigen Natur,
Da Gott die Menschen schuf hinein,
Umgibt in Rauch und Moder nur
Dich Tiergeripp' und Totenbein.

Flieh! auf! hinaus ins weite Land!

of its essential strength and fount
and no longer dig about in words.

O gentle moonlight, how I wish that you
could see the end of all my misery!
How often at this desk I sat
into the depth of night and looked for you
until over these books and papers   390
you appeared to me, my melancholy friend.
If I could roam on mountain heights in
your dear light,
drift with hovering spirits over caverns,
weave over meadows in your twilight glow,
I would expel the smoke of learning
and be drenched to wholeness in your dew.

Alas! am I still wedged within this prison cell?
You cursed, dank hole in the wall,
where even the sweet light of heaven   400
breaks wanly through the painted glass!
I'm cooped in heaps of worm-eaten books
thickly laden with dust,
with sooty papers fastened all around,
extending to the vaulted arches—
retorts and boxes strewn about
with pyramids of instruments,
the stuffing of ancestral rubbish—
This is my world! I must call it a world!

And still you wonder why your heart   410
claws anxiously against your breast?
And why a misery yet unexplored
stands in the way of stirring life?
Instead of pulsing nature,
where God had once placed man,
you're thrust into this soot and mold
and ringed by sundry bones and parched cadavers.

Away! Escape! Go out into the open fields!

Und dies geheimnisvolle Buch,
Von Nostradamus' eigner Hand,
Ist dir es nicht Geleit genug?   420
Erkennest dann der Sterne Lauf,
Und wenn Natur dich unterweist,
Dann geht die Seelenkraft dir auf,
Wie spricht ein Geist zum andern Geist.
Umsonst, daß trocknes Sinnen hier
Die heil'gen Zeichen dir erklärt:
Ihr schwebt, ihr Geister, neben mir;
Antwortet mir, wenn ihr mich hört!
      (*Er schlägt das Buch auf und erblickt das
      Zeichen des Makrokosmus.*)
Ha! welche Wonne fließt in diesem Blick   430
Auf einmal mir durch alle meine Sinnen!
Ich fühle junges, heil'ges Lebensglück
Neuglühend mir durch Nerv' und Adern rinnen.
War es ein Gott, der diese Zeichen schrieb,
Die mir das innre Toben stillen,
Das arme Herz mit Freude füllen
Und mit geheimnisvollem Trieb
Die Kräfte der Natur rings um mich her enthüllen?
Bin ich ein Gott? Mir wird so licht!
Ich schau' in diesen reinen Zügen   440
Die wirkende Natur vor meiner Seele liegen.
Jezt erst erkenn' ich, was der Weise spricht:
„Die Geisterwelt ist nicht verschlossen;
Dein Sinn ist zu, dein Herz ist tot!
Auf, bade, Schüler, unverdrossen
Die ird'sche Brust im Morgenrot!"
      (*Er beschaut das Zeichen.*)
Wie alles sich zum Ganzen webt,
Eins in dem andern wirkt und lebt!
Wie Himmelskräfte auf und nieder steigen
Und sich die goldnen Eimer reichen!   450
Mit segenduftenden Schwingen
Vom Himmel durch die Erde dringen,
Harmonisch all das All durchklingen!

And this volume of mysterious lore
in Nostradamus's[3] hand and pen—   420
is it not sufficient company?
Once you know the stars' procession,
and Nature is your guide and master,
when spirits speak to spirit—
your soul will then unfold its strength.
My barren thoughts are wasted
within the sight of sacred signs:
Spirits, now you hover close to me;
if you hear me, answer me!
   (*He opens the book and sees the sign of the
   macrocosm.*)
Ha! A rush of bliss   430
flows suddenly through all my senses!
I feel a glow, a holy joy of life
which sets my veins and flesh afire.
Was it a god that drew these signs
which soothe my inward raging
and fill my wretched heart with joy,
and with mysterious strength
reveal about me Nature's pulse?
Am I a god? The light pervades me so!
In these pure ciphers I can see   440
living Nature spread out before my soul.
At last I understand the sage's words:
"The world of spirits is not closed;
your mind is shut, your heart is dead!
Pupil, stand up and unafraid
bathe your earthly breast in morning light!"
   (*He gazes at the sign.*)
How all things are weaving one in one;
each lives and works within the other.
Heaven's angels dip and soar
and hold their golden pails aloft;   450
with fragrant blessings on their wings,
they penetrate the earthly realm from Heaven
and all make all resound in harmony.

Welch Schauspiel! Aber ach! ein Schauspiel nur!
Wo fass' ich dich, unendliche Natur?
Euch Brüste, wo? Ihr Quellen alles Lebens,
An denen Himmel und Erde hängt,
Dahin die welke Brust sich drängt—
Ihr quellt, ihr tränkt, und schmacht' ich so vergebens?
  (*Er schlägt unwillig das Buch um und erblickt*
  das Zeichen des Erdgeistes.)
Wie anders wirkt dies Zeichen auf mich ein!   460
Du, Geist der Erde, bist mir näher;
Schon fühl' ich meine Kräfte höher,
Schon glüh' ich wie von neuem Wein,
Ich fühle Mut, mich in die Welt zu wagen,
Der Erde Weh, der Erde Glück zu tragen,
Mit Stürmen mich herumzuschlagen
Und in des Schiffbruchs Knirschen nicht zu zagen.
Es wölkt sich über mir—
Der Mond verbirgt sein Licht—
Die Lampe schwindet!   470
Es dampft—Es zucken rote Strahlen
Mir um das Haupt—Es weht
Ein Schauer vom Gewölb' herab
Und faßt mich an!
Ich fühl's, du schwebst um mich, erflehter Geist.
Enthülle dich!
Ha! wie's in meinem Herzen reißt!
Zu neuen Gefühlen
All' meine Sinnen sich erwühlen!
Ich fühle ganz mein Herz dir hingegeben!   480
Du mußt! du mußt! und kostet' es mein Leben!
  (*Er faßt das Buch und spricht das Zeichen*
  des Geistes geheimnisvoll aus. Es zuckt eine
  rötliche Flamme, der GEIST *erscheint in der*
  Flamme.)
GEIST.
  Wer ruft mir?
FAUST (*abgewendet*).
              Schreckliches Gesicht!

What pageantry! But alas, a pageant and no more!
Where shall I clasp you, infinity of Nature?
You breasts, where? You wellsprings of all life?
Heaven and earth depend on you—
toward you my parched soul is straining.
You flow, you nourish, yet I crave in vain.
>   (*He reluctantly turns the pages of the book
>   and perceives the sign of the Earth Spirit.*)

How differently this new sign works on me!   460
You are nearer to me, spirit of the earth;
even now I feel my powers rise
and glow as from new wine.
I feel new strength to face the world,
to endure its woe and happiness,
to brave the blasts of hurricanes,
to scoff at my splintering ship.
The airs above me thicken,
the moon conceals her light—
the lamp goes dark!   470
Smoke envelops me—scarlet flashes
dart about my head—a chilling breath
sifts downward from the vault
and seizes me!
I feel it, you surround me, spirit that I crave.
Reveal yourself!
My heart, ah, how it tears in me!
How all my senses swirl,
well up to novel feelings.
I know my heart is at your bidding!   480
You must! You must, and if I die for it!
>   (*He grips the book and solemnly murmurs the
>   spell of the Earth Spirit. There is a flash of
>   reddish flame in which the* SPIRIT *appears.*)

SPIRIT.
Who calls?

FAUST (*averts his face*). Terrifying vision![4]

GEIST.

  Du hast mich mächtig angezogen,
  An meiner Sphäre lang' gesogen,
  Und nun—

FAUST.

        Weh! ich ertrag' dich nicht!

GEIST.

  Du flehst eratmend, mich zu schauen,
  Meine Stimme zu hören, mein Antlitz zu sehn;
  Mich neigt dein mächtig Seelenflehn,
  Da bin ich!—Welch erbärmlich Grauen
  Faßt Übermenschen dich! Wo ist der Seele Ruf?   490
  Wo ist die Brust, die eine Welt in sich erschuf
  Und trug und hegte, die mit Freudebeben
  Erschwoll, sich uns, den Geistern, gleich zu heben?
  Wo bist du, Faust, des Stimme mir erklang,
  Der sich an mich mit allen Kräften drang?
  Bist du es, der, von meinem Hauch umwittert,
  In allen Lebenstiefen zittert,
  Ein furchtsam weggekrümmter Wurm?

FAUST.

  Soll ich dir, Flammenbildung, weichen?
  Ich bin's, bin Faust, bin deinesgleichen!   500

GEIST.

  In Lebensfluten, im Tatensturm
  Wall' ich auf und ab,
  Webe hin und her!
  Geburt und Grab,
  Ein ewiges Meer,
  Ein wechselnd Weben,
  Ein glühend Leben,
  So schaff' ich am sausenden Webstuhl der Zeit
  Und wirke der Gottheit lebendiges Kleid.

FAUST.

  Der du die weite Welt umschweifst,   510
  Geschäftiger Geist, wie nah fühl' ich mich dir!

GEIST.

  Du gleichst dem Geist, den du begreifst,

SPIRIT.

    I felt a mighty pull from you,
    you have long been sucking at my sphere,
    and now—

FAUST.

              No! I can't endure you!

SPIRIT.

    You have sought me breathlessly,
    longed for my voice and countenance;
    your strong pleadings have my sympathy.
    Now I am here!—What pitiable terror
    seizes you, you superman? Where is the
        outcry of your soul,   490
    where the breast that built its inward world
    and bore and fostered it and swelled with joyful tremor,
    intent on rising to the level of the spirits?
    Where are you, Faust, whose voice rang out,
    who forced himself on me with all his might?
    Are you he who at my very exhalation
    shivers to his depths,
    a frightened, cringing worm?

FAUST.

    Should I flinch before you, flaming apparition?
    I stand my ground as Faust, your equal!   500

SPIRIT.

    In the tides of life and action
    I rise and descend
    and fling the shuttle back and forth.
    The cradle and the grave,
    a perennial sea,
    a flickering fabric,
    a glowing life,
    I toil at the whirring loom of time
    and weave the godhead's living vesture.

FAUST.

    You roam the ample world, my bustling spirit;   510
    how close I feel to you!

SPIRIT.

    You're like the spirit that you grasp.

Nicht mir!
  (*Verschwindet.*)
FAUST (*zusammenstürzend*).
  Nicht dir?
  Wem denn?
  Ich Ebenbild der Gottheit!
  Und nicht einmal dir!
  (*Es klopft.*)
  O Tod! ich kenn's—das ist mein Famulus—
  Es wird mein schönstes Glück zunichte!
  Daß diese Fülle der Gesichte   520
  Der trockne Schleicher stören muß!
  (WAGNER *im Schlafrocke und der Nacht-*
  mütze, eine Lampe in der Hand. FAUST
  wendet sich unwillig.)
WAGNER.
  Verzeiht! ich hör' Euch deklamieren;
  Ihr last gewiß ein griechisch Trauerspiel?
  In dieser Kunst möcht' ich was profitieren,
  Denn heutzutage wirkt das viel.
  Ich hab' es öfters rühmen hören,
  Ein Komödiant könnt' einen Pfarrer lehren.
FAUST.
  Ja, wenn der Pfarrer ein Komödiant ist;
  Wie das denn wohl zu Zeiten kommen mag.
WAGNER.
  Ach! wenn man so in sein Museum gebannt ist,   530
  Und sieht die Welt kaum einen Feiertag,
  Kaum durch ein Fernglas, nur von weiten,
  Wie soll man sie durch Überredung leiten?
FAUST.
  Wenn ihr's nicht fühlt, ihr werdet's nicht erjagen,
  Wenn es nicht aus der Seele dringt
  Und mit urkräftigem Behagen
  Die Herzen aller Hörer zwingt.
  Sitzt ihr nur immer! Leimt zusammen,
  Braut ein Ragout von andrer Schmaus,
  Und blast die kümmerlichen Flammen
  Aus eurem Aschenhäufchen 'raus!   540

You're not like me.
   (*The* SPIRIT *vanishes.*)
FAUST (*overwhelmed*).
  Not your equal?
  Then whom do I resemble?
  I, the image of the godhead!
  And not your equal?
    (*A knock at the door.*)
  Oh, death, I know that knock—my famulus—
  So ends my fairest hour!
  Why must this shriveled crawler   520
  destroy the fullness of my vision?
    (*Enter* WAGNER, *in dressing gown and night-*
    cap, lamp in hand. FAUST, *annoyed, turns to*
    him.)
WAGNER.
  Excuse me, but I heard your declamation;
  was it a passage from Greek tragedy?
  I should like to profit from such elocution,
  for nowadays it's a great help.
  I've often heard it said that an actor
  could give lessons to a preacher.
FAUST.
  Yes, whenever the preacher is also an actor,
  which may happen now and then.
WAGNER.
  Ah! when we're cooped in our chambers   530
  and scarcely see the world on holidays—
  from far away as through a telescope—
  how can we guide it by persuasion?
FAUST.
  You will never conquer it unless you feel it,
  unless a surging from your soul,
  a primal, joyful energy
  compels the heart of all your listeners.
  Go sit down and paste your words together,
  concoct a stew from morsels left by others
  and try to get some feeble flames   540
  from your puny heap of ashes!

Bewundrung von Kindern und Affen,
Wenn euch darnach der Gaumen steht—
Doch werdet ihr nie Herz zu Herzen schaffen,
Wenn es euch nicht von Herzen geht.

WAGNER.

Allein der Vortrag macht des Redners Glück;
Ich fühl' es wohl, noch bin ich weit zurück.

FAUST.

Such' Er den redlichen Gewinn!
Sei Er kein schellenlauter Tor!
Es trägt Verstand und rechter Sinn   550
Mit wenig Kunst sich selber vor;
Und wenn's euch Ernst ist, was zu sagen,
Ist's nötig, Worten nachzujagen?
Ja, eure Reden, die so blinkend sind,
In denen ihr der Menschheit Schnitzel kräuselt,
Sind unerquicklich wie der Nebelwind,
Der herbstlich durch die dürren Blätter säuselt!

WAGNER.

Ach Gott! die Kunst ist lang,
Und kurz ist unser Leben.
Mir wird, bei meinem kritischen Bestreben,   560
Doch oft um Kopf und Busen bang.
Wie schwer sind nicht die Mittel zu erwerben,
Durch die man zu den Quellen steigt!
Und eh' man nur den halben Weg erreicht,
Muß wohl ein armer Teufel sterben.

FAUST.

Das Pergament, ist das der heil'ge Bronnen,
Woraus ein Trunk den Durst auf ewig stillt?
Erquickung hast du nicht gewonnen,
Wenn sie dir nicht aus eigner Seele quillt.

WAGNER.

Verzeiht! es ist ein groß Ergetzen,   570
Sich in den Geist der Zeiten zu versetzen;
Zu schauen, wie vor uns ein weiser Mann gedacht,
Und wie wir's dann zuletzt so herrlich weit gebracht.

FAUST.

O ja, bis an die Sterne weit!

And if your palate craves for this,
you may have apes and infants stand in awe,
but you'll never move another's heart
unless your own pours forth its energy.

WAGNER.

Yet elocution is the speaker's greatest tool;
it's clear to me, I'm far behind.[5]

FAUST.

Go seek advancement honorably.
Don't be a jingling fool!
Clear thinking and some honesty   550
need little art for their delivery.
And once you speak in earnest,
must you still hunt for words?
The tinseled glittering phrases
with which one crimps the shredded bits of thought
are lifeless like a misty exhalation
that blows through withered autumn leaves.

WAGNER.

Oh, my, but art is long
and our life is fleeting.[6]
My head begins to swim   560
with the strain of critical endeavor.
How difficult it is to gain the means
that will lead one to the sources.
We poor devils labor long and hard
and die before we travel half the distance.

FAUST.

Is parchment then the sacred fount
from which a draft will quench our thirst forever?
You must draw it from your inward soul
or else you'll not be satisfied.

WAGNER.

Excuse me, but it gives the greatest satisfaction   570
to view the spirit of another age,
to see how wise men thought before our days,
and to rejoice how far we've come at last.

FAUST.

Oh yes, a journey to the stars!

Mein Freund, die Zeiten der Vergangenheit
Sind uns ein Buch mit sieben Siegeln.
Was ihr den Geist der Zeiten heißt,
Das ist im Grund der Herren eigner Geist,
In dem die Zeiten sich bespiegeln.
Da ist's denn wahrlich oft ein Jammer! 580
Man läuft euch bei dem ersten Blick davon:
Ein Kehrichtfaß und eine Rumpelkammer
Und höchstens eine Haupt- und Staatsaktion
Mit trefflichen pragmatischen Maximen,
Wie sie den Puppen wohl im Munde ziemen!

WAGNER.

Allein die Welt! des Menschen Herz und Geist!
Möcht' jeglicher doch was davon erkennen.

FAUST.

Ja, was man so erkennen heißt!
Wer darf das Kind beim rechten Namen nennen?
Die wenigen, die was davon erkannt, 590
Die töricht gnug ihr volles Herz nicht wahrten,
Dem Pöbel ihr Gefühl, ihr Schauen offenbarten,
Hat man von je gekreuzigt und verbrannt.
Ich bitt' Euch, Freund, es ist tief in der Nacht,
Wir müssen's diesmal unterbrechen.

WAGNER.

Ich hätte gern nur immer fortgewacht,
Um so gelehrt mit Euch mich zu besprechen.
Doch morgen, als am ersten Ostertage,
Erlaubt mir ein' und andre Frage.
Mit Eifer hab' ich mich der Studien beflissen; 600
Zwar weiß ich viel, doch möcht' ich alles wissen.
(*Ab.*)

FAUST (*allein*).

Wie nur dem Kopf nicht alle Hoffnung schwindet,
Der immerfort an schalem Zeuge klebt,
Mit gier'ger Hand nach Schätzen gräbt,
Und froh ist, wenn er Regenwürmer findet!

Darf eine solche Menschenstimme hier,
Wo Geisterfülle mich umgab, ertönen?

My friend, the days of history
make up a book with seven seals.
What you call the spirit of an age
is in reality the spirit of those men
in which their time's reflected.
And what you see is mostly misery,   580
the sight of which will make you run away.
Pails of garbage and heaps of trash,
at best a staged enactment of high history
with excellent pragmatic maxims
suitable for puppets.

WAGNER.

But what of the world? The human heart and intellect?
One tries so hard to gain some knowledge!

FAUST.

Oh yes! They like to call it knowledge.
Who can give the child its rightful name?
Those few who gained a share of understanding,   590
who foolishly unlocked their hearts,
their pent-up feelings, and their visions to the rabble,
have always ended on the cross and pyre.
Forgive me, friend, the night is well advanced,
we must suspend our conversation.

WAGNER.

I should have liked to stay much longer
to exchange such learned words with you.
But I hope that on tomorrow's Easter holiday
I may ask some further questions.
I always strive for erudition;   600
I know a lot, it's true, but I must know it all.

                                           (*Exit.*)

FAUST (*alone*).

How can such hope still dwell with him,
whose mind tenaciously adheres to rubbish,
who digs with eager hands for treasure
and is delighted when he finds a worm!

Should such a human voice intrude
when spirits held me in their spell?

Doch ach! für diesmal dank' ich dir,
Dem ärmlichsten von allen Erdensöhnen.
Du rissest mich von der Verzweiflung los,   610
Die mir die Sinne schon zerstören wollte.
Ach! die Erscheinung war so riesengroß,
Daß ich mich recht als Zwerg empfinden sollte.

Ich, Ebenbild der Gottheit, das sich schon
Ganz nah gedünkt dem Spiegel ew'ger Wahrheit,
Sein selbst genoß in Himmelsglanz und Klarheit,
Und abgestreift den Erdensohn;
Ich, mehr als Cherub, dessen freie Kraft
Schon durch die Adern der Natur zu fließen
Und, schaffend, Götterleben zu genießen   620
Sich ahnungsvoll vermaß, wie muß ich's büßen!
Ein Donnerwort hat mich hinweggerafft.

Nicht darf ich dir zu gleichen mich vermessen!
Hab' ich die Kraft dich anzuziehn besessen,
So hatt' ich dich zu halten keine Kraft.
In jenem sel'gen Augenblicke
Ich fühlte mich so klein, so groß;
Du stießest grausam mich zurücke,
Ins ungewisse Menschenlos.
Wer lehret mich? was soll ich meiden?   630
Soll ich gehorchen jenem Drang?
Ach! unsre Taten selbst, so gut als unsre Leiden,
Sie hemmen unsres Lebens Gang.

Dem Herrlichsten, was auch der Geist empfangen,
Drängt immer fremd und fremder Stoff sich an;
Wenn wir zum Guten dieser Welt gelangen,
Dann heißt das Beßre Trug und Wahn.
Die uns das Leben gaben, herrliche Gefühle,
Erstarren in dem irdischen Gewühle.

Wenn Phantasie sich sonst mit kühnem Flug   640
Und hoffnungsvoll zum Ewigen erweitert,
So ist ein kleiner Raum ihr nun genug,

Alas, this once you have my gratitude,
you smallest of all sons of the earth.
You snatched me from despondency   610
which threatened ruin to my senses.
Ah! the titanic spirit's visitation
made me gaze upon my dwarfish self.

I, the godhead's image, who thought myself
close to the mirror of eternal truth,
and stripped of my mortality,
saw Heaven's light and clarity reflect on me.
I, more than Cherub, with unbounded power
presumed to course through Nature's arteries,
to create and live the life of a divinity—   620
now I must do penance without measure;
one thunder-word has swept me off to nothingness.

I can't withstand comparison with you!
If I possessed the strength to draw you near,
I wanted strength to hold you close to me.
In that blessed, fleeting moment
I felt myself so small, so great—
you thrust me from you cruelly
into man's uncertain destiny.
Who will teach me? What must I shun?   630
Shall I obey my inward yearning?
Alas, our deeds as much as our sorrows
cramp the course of our waking days.

However glorious the mind's conception,
alien matter will in time intrude.
Whenever we achieve some good on our earth,
the better things are labeled frauds and fantasies.
The ecstasies that launched us on this life
congeal in the muddled business of living.

Once Imagination on her daring flight   640
reached boldly for eternity, but now
she deems a narrow chamber quite sufficient,

Wenn Glück auf Glück im Zeitenstrudel scheitert.
Die Sorge nistet gleich im tiefen Herzen,
Dort wirket sie geheime Schmerzen,
Unruhig wiegt sie sich und störet Lust und Ruh;
Sie deckt sich stets mit neuen Masken zu,
Sie mag als Haus und Hof, als Weib und Kind erscheinen,
Als Feuer, Wasser, Dolch und Gift;
Du bebst vor allem, was nicht trifft,   650
Und was du nie verlierst, das mußt du stets beweinen.
Den Göttern gleich' ich nicht! Zu tief ist es gefühlt;
Dem Wurme gleich' ich, der den Staub durchwühlt,
Den, wie er sich im Staube nährend lebt,
Des Wandrers Tritt vernichtet und begräbt.

Ist es nicht Staub, was diese hohe Wand
Aus hundert Fächern mir verenget,
Der Trödel, der mit tausendfachem Tand
In dieser Mottenwelt mich dränget?
Hier soll ich finden, was mir fehlt?   660
Soll ich vielleicht in tausend Büchern lesen,
Daß überall die Menschen sich gequält,
Daß hie und da ein Glücklicher gewesen?—
Was grinsest du mir, hohler Schädel, her,
Als daß dein Hirn wie meines einst verwirret
Den leichten Tag gesucht und in der Dämmrung schwer,
Mit Lust nach Wahrheit, jämmerlich geirret?
Ihr Instrumente freilich spottet mein
Mit Rad und Kämmen, Walz' und Bügel:
Ich stand am Tor, ihr solltet Schlüssel sein;   670
Zwar euer Bart ist kraus, doch hebt ihr nicht die Riegel.
Geheimnisvoll am lichten Tag
Läßt sich Natur des Schleiers nicht berauben,
Und was sie deinem Geist nicht offenbaren mag,
Das zwingst du ihr nicht ab mit Hebeln und mit Schrauben.
Du alt Geräte, das ich nicht gebraucht,
Du stehst nur hier, weil dich mein Vater brauchte.
Du alte Rolle, du wirst angeraucht,
Solang' an diesem Pult die trübe Lampe schmauchte.
Weit besser hätt' ich doch mein weniges verpraßt,   680

as every joy is foundering in the whirls of time.
Care nesting deep within the heart
will quickly wreak her secret pangs.
She sways and claws and dims our peace and joy
and never fails to don new masks,
as a homestead or as wife and child,
or else she shows herself as water, fire, poison, knife.
You dread the blows that do not strike   650
and you lament the things you never lose.
I am not like the gods—I feel it deeply now.
I am the worm that burrows in the dust
and, seeking sustenance in the dust,
is crushed and buried by a wanderer's heel.

Is it not dust which from a hundred shelves
imprisons me behind this towering wall?
Is it not rubbish and a thousand trifles
which stuff and choke my mothy world?
What I lack, am I to find it here?   660
Am I to fathom from a thousand books
that mankind suffered everywhere,
that here and there a lucky one turned up?—
Why do you grin at me, you hollow skull,
except to show that once your brain, perplexed like mine,
sought the light of day and lusted for the truth,
and lost its way in heavy twilight gloom?
Those instruments—they jeer at me
with all their flanges, wheels, and tackle.
I stood at the gate, you were to be the keys;   670
though deftly wrought you raised no latch for me.
Mysterious even in the light of day
Nature keeps her veil intact;
whatever she refuses to reveal
you cannot wrench from her with screws and levers.
Ancient gear, you served my father;
I cannot use you, yet you stand about.
Faded scroll, you turned a sooty brown
since this lamp began to smoulder at my desk.
Far better, had I squandered all I own   680

Als mit dem wenigen belastet hier zu schwitzen!
Was du ererbt von deinen Vätern hast,
Erwirb es, um es zu besitzen.
Was man nicht nützt, ist eine schwere Last,
Nur was der Augenblick erschafft, das kann er nützen.

Doch warum heftet sich mein Blick auf jene Stelle?
Ist jenes Fläschchen dort den Augen ein Magnet?
Warum wird mir auf einmal lieblich helle,
Als wenn im nächt'gen Wald uns Mondenglanz umweht?

Ich grüße dich, du einzige Phiole,   690
Die ich mit Andacht nun herunterhole!
In dir verehr' ich Menschenwitz und Kunst.
Du Inbegriff der holden Schlummersäfte,
Du Auszug aller tödlich feinen Kräfte,
Erweise deinem Meister deine Gunst!
Ich sehe dich, es wird der Schmerz gelindert,
Ich fasse dich, das Streben wird gemindert,
Des Geistes Flutstrom ebbet nach und nach.
Ins hohe Meer werd' ich hinausgewiesen,
Die Spiegelflut erglänzt zu meinen Füßen,   700
Zu neuen Ufern lockt ein neuer Tag.

Ein Feuerwagen schwebt auf leichten Schwingen
An mich heran! Ich fühle mich bereit,
Auf neuer Bahn den Äther zu durchdringen,
Zu neuen Sphären reiner Tätigkeit.
Dies hohe Leben, diese Götterwonne,
Du, erst noch Wurm, und die verdienest du?
Ja, kehre nur der holden Erdensonne
Entschlossen deinen Rücken zu!
Vermesse dich, die Pforten aufzureißen,   710
Vor denen jeder gern vorüberschleicht.
Hier ist es Zeit, durch Taten zu beweisen,
Daß Manneswürde nicht der Götterhöhe weicht,
Vor jener dunkeln Höhle nicht zu beben,
In der sich Phantasie zu eigner Qual verdammt,
Nach jenem Durchgang hinzustreben,

than now to sweat beneath my property!
What you inherit from your father,
earn it anew before you call it yours.
What does not serve you is a heavy burden,
what issues from the moment is alone of use.

But why do my eyes cling strongly to that spot?
Is that small flask a magnet to my sight?
Why this sudden sweet illumination,
as when a mellow moon flows through the woods at night?

I greet you, rare and precious vial   690
as I now devoutly reach for you.
In you I honor human wit and skill.
You summary of gentle slumber-juices,
you distillate of all deadly powers,
now show your favors to your master!
I look at you; my pain is much assuaged,
I grasp you; my restlessness abates,
the flood-tide of my spirit slowly ebbs away.
The ocean draws me to its deeper regions,
the glassy seas are gleaming at my feet,   700
a new day beckons me to newer shores.

A fiery chariot borne on nimble wings
approaches me. I am prepared to change my course,
to penetrate the ether's high dominions
toward novel spheres of pure activity.
Do you, scarcely better than a worm, deserve
this lofty life and heavenly delight?
Now be resolute and turn your back
on our earth's endearing sun!
Be bold and brash and force the gates   710
from which men shrink and slink away!
The time has come to prove by deeds
that man will not give in to gods' superior might
and will not quake before the pit where fantasy
condemns itself to tortures of its own creation
when he advances to the narrow passageway

Um dessen engen Mund die ganze Hölle flammt;
Zu diesem Schritt sich heiter zu entschließen,
Und wär' es mit Gefahr, ins Nichts dahinzufließen.

Nun komm herab, kristallne reine Schale!   720
Hervor aus deinem alten Futterale,
An die ich viele Jahre nicht gedacht!
Du glänztest bei der Väter Freudenfeste,
Erheitertest die ernsten Gäste,
Wenn einer dich dem andern zugebracht.
Der vielen Bilder künstlich reiche Pracht,
Des Trinkers Pflicht, sie reimweis zu erklären,
Auf einen Zug die Höhlung auszuleeren,
Erinnert mich an manche Jugendnacht;
Ich werde jetzt dich keinem Nachbar reichen,   730
Ich werde meinen Witz an deiner Kunst nicht zeigen;
Hier ist ein Saft, der eilig trunken macht;
Mit brauner Flut erfüllt er deine Höhle.
Den ich bereitet, den ich wähle,
Der letzte Trunk sei nun, mit ganzer Seele,
Als festlich hoher Gruß, dem Morgen zugebracht!
   (*Er setzt die Schale an den Mund.*)
   (*Glockenklang und Chorgesang.*)

CHOR DER ENGEL.
      Christ ist erstanden!
      Freude dem Sterblichen,
      Den die verderblichen,
      Schleichenden, erblichen   740
      Mängel umwanden.

FAUST.
Welch tiefes Summen, welch ein heller Ton
Zieht mit Gewalt das Glas von meinem Munde?
Verkündiget ihr dumpfen Glocken schon
Des Osterfestes erste Feierstunde?
Ihr Chöre, singt ihr schon den tröstlichen Gesang,
Der einst, um Grabes Nacht, von Engelslippen klang,
Gewißheit einem neuen Bunde?

CHOR DER WEIBER.
    Mit Spezereien

about whose mouth infernal flames are blazing.
Approach the brink serenely and accept the risk
of melting into nothingness.

And now come down, my goblet of pure crystal;   720
let me pluck you from your dusty pouch.
I have neglected you for many years.
Once you glittered at ancestral banquets,
cheering, as you passed from hand to hand,
the sober guests about the table.
The wealth of artful images engraved on you,
the drinker's duty to elucidate in rhymes
and drain the chalice in a single draft,
bring back some youthful nights of long ago;
now I shall not pass you to a neighbor   730
nor test my rhyming skill on you;
here is a juice that quickly will intoxicate;
the murky sap which I prepared
is now contained within this hollow shell.
With all my soul and festive salutation
to this day's beginning I consecrate this final drink.
     (*He puts the goblet to his mouth.*)
     (*Church bells and choir.*)
CHOIR OF THE ANGELS.
               Christ is arisen!
               Joy to all men
               Mortal and frail,
               Enmeshed in silent   740
               Inherited failings.[7]
FAUST.
   What organ resonance, what sunlit tones
   draw mightily the goblet from my lips?
   These muted bells, do they announce so soon
   the Easter Day's first festive hour? You choir,
   do you now sing the hymn of consolation
   which once angelically rang out at the nocturnal tomb
   pledging a new covenant?
CHOIR OF THE WOMEN.
               With precious spices

Hatten wir ihn gepflegt,   750
Wir seine Treuen
Hatten ihn hingelegt;
Tücher und Binden
Reinlich umwanden wir,
Ach! und wir finden
Christ nicht mehr hier.

CHOR DER ENGEL.

Christ ist erstanden!
Selig der Liebende,
Der die betrübende,
Heilsam' und übende   760
Prüfung bestanden.

FAUST.

Was sucht ihr, mächtig und gelind,
Ihr Himmelstöne, mich am Staube?
Klingt dort umher, wo weiche Menschen sind.
Die Botschaft hör' ich wohl, allein mir fehlt der Glaube;
Das Wunder ist des Glaubens liebstes Kind.
Zu jenen Sphären wag' ich nicht zu streben,
Woher die holde Nachricht tönt;
Und doch, an diesen Klang von Jugend auf gewöhnt,
Ruft er auch jezt zurück mich in das Leben.   770
Sonst stürzte sich der Himmelsliebe Kuß
Auf mich herab, in ernster Sabbatstille;
Da klang so ahnungsvoll des Glockentones Fülle,
Und ein Gebet war brünstiger Genuß;
Ein unbegreiflich holdes Sehnen
Trieb mich, durch Wald und Wiesen hinzugehn,
Und unter tausend heißen Tränen
Fühlt' ich mir eine Welt entstehn.
Dies Lied verkündete der Jugend muntre Spiele,
Der Frühlingsfeier freies Glück;   780
Erinnrung hält mich nun mit kindlichem Gefühle
Vom letzten, ernsten Schritt zurück.
O tönet fort, ihr süßen Himmelslieder!
Die Träne quillt, die Erde hat mich wieder!

CHOR DER JÜNGER.

Hat der Begrabene

We had tended Him.   750
We faithful ones
Had laid Him down;
Swathing and linen
We neatly bound,
Ah, only to find
An empty tomb.

CHOIR OF THE ANGELS.

Christ is arisen!
Blessed He who loves
And who emerges whole
From the grueling   760
Grievous ordeal.

FAUST.

Why do you seek me in the dust,
Heaven's tones, so mighty and so gentle?
On softer souls you may reverberate.
I hear your message, but I have no faith;
the miracle is faith's most treasured child,
but I dare not reach for these high regions,
the source and music of glad tidings.
And yet, accustomed to these harmonies from childhood,
I now can hear their summons to return to life.   770
Once the embrace of Heaven's love
rushed down to me in solemn Sabbath stillness;
the churchbell's pulsing tones were auguries
and each prayer was a lustful pleasure.
Ineffable sweet yearning
prompted me to roam through woods and fields,
and through a thousand burning tears
I felt my world come into being.
This song proclaimed the happy games of children,
unbounded rapture of a festival of Spring;   780
I remember—and a childlike feeling
constrains me from the last and gravest step.
O sounds of Heaven, do not fade away—
the tears well up, the earth has me again!

CHOIR OF THE DISCIPLES.

He who was buried,

Schon sich nach oben,
Lebend Erhabene,
Herrlich erhoben,
Ist er in Werdelust
Schaffender Freude nah: 790
Ach! an der Erde Brust
Sind wir zum Leide da.
Ließ er die Seinen
Schmachtend uns hier zurück;
Ach! wir beweinen,
Meister, dein Glück!

CHOR DER ENGEL.

Christ ist erstanden,
Aus der Verwesung Schoß;
Reißet von Banden
Freudig euch los!   800
Tätig ihn Preisenden,
Liebe Beweisenden,
Brüderlich Speisenden,
Predigend Reisenden,
Wonne Verheißenden
Euch ist der Meister nah,
Euch ist er da!

VOR DEM TOR

Spaziergänger aller Art ziehen hinaus.

EINIGE HANDWERKSBURSCHEN.
Warum denn dort hinaus?
ANDRE.
Wir gehn hinaus aufs Jägerhaus.
DIE ERSTEN.
Wir aber wollen nach der Mühle wandern.   810
EIN HANDWERKSBURSCH.
Ich rat' euch, nach dem Wasserhof zu gehn.
ZWEITER.
Der Weg dahin ist gar nicht schön.

The Lord of life,
Has ascended in glory
To Heaven on high,
In eager Becoming
Near joyous creation.   790
Ah! we dwellers on earth
Are here to suffer.
We followers stayed
And languished for Him.
In anguish, O Master,
We crave your bliss.

CHOIR OF THE ANGELS.

Christ is arisen
From the womb of decay.
Burst from your bonds
In freedom and joy!   800
Wandering pilgrims,
Givers of Charity,
Sharers of sustenance,
Preachers of Sanctity,
Prophets of bliss:
The Master is near you;
Now He is here!

BEFORE THE GATE[8]

Various groups of people, strolling.

SEVERAL APPRENTICES.
   Why go in that direction?
OTHERS.
   We're walking to the hunter's lodge.
THE FIRST.
   But we are heading for the mill.   810
ONE APPRENTICE.
   Take my advice, go to the River Inn.
SECOND APPRENTICE.
   I don't like the road up there.

DIE ZWEITEN.

Was tust denn du?

EIN DRITTER.

           Ich gehe mit den andern.

VIERTER.

Nach Burgdorf kommt herauf, gewiß dort findet ihr
Die schönsten Mädchen und das beste Bier,
Und Händel von der ersten Sorte.

FÜNFTER.

Du überlustiger Gesell,
Juckt dich zum drittenmal das Fell?
Ich mag nicht hin, mir graut es vor dem Orte.

DIENSTMÄDCHEN.

Nein, nein! ich gehe nach der Stadt zurück.   820

ANDRE.

Wir finden ihn gewiß bei jenen Pappeln stehen.

ERSTE.

Das ist für mich kein großes Glück;
Er wird an deiner Seite gehen,
Mit dir nur tanzt er auf dem Plan.
Was gehn mich deine Freuden an!

ANDRE.

Heut ist er sicher nicht allein,
Der Krauskopf, sagt er, würde bei ihm sein.

SCHÜLER.

Blitz, wie die wackern Dirnen schreiten!
Herr Bruder, komm! wir müssen sie begleiten,
Ein starkes Bier, ein beizender Toback   830
Und eine Magd im Putz, das ist nun mein Geschmack.

BÜRGERMÄDCHEN.

Da sieh mir nur die schönen Knaben!
Es ist wahrhaftig eine Schmach:
Gesellschaft könnten sie die allerbeste haben,
Und laufen diesen Mägden nach!

ZWEITER SCHÜLER (*zum ersten*).

Nicht so geschwind! dort hinten kommen zwei,
Sie sind gar niedlich angezogen,
's ist meine Nachbarin dabei;

OTHERS.

   And what will you do?

THIRD APPRENTICE.

                    I will go with the others.

FOURTH APPRENTICE.

   Come with me to Burgdorf,[9] all of you, I'll bet you find
   the prettiest girls and the finest beer up there
   and first-rate rows and squabbles.

FIFTH APPRENTICE.

   You're too much for me, you've had it twice,
   does your hide itch for another beating?
   I am not going there; the place gives me the shivers.

SERVANT GIRL.

   No, no! I'm going back to town.   820

OTHER SERVANT GIRLS.

   I think we'll find him standing by the poplar trees.

FIRST SERVANT GIRL.

   This doesn't make me very happy;
   he'll walk along with you,
   and he'll dance with you alone.
   What do I care about your pleasures!

OTHER SERVANT GIRL.

   He won't be by himself today, I'm sure.
   He is expecting Curly's company.

STUDENT.

   Wow! Just watch these lassies move!
   Let's go, my boy, let's walk with them,
   a jug of beer, a pipe that stings and bites,   830
   and a girl in her Sunday best, that's just to my taste.

BURGHER'S DAUGHTER.

   Look at the handsome boys!
   What a shame, when they might move
   in the very best society
   and instead are chasing after servant girls!

SECOND STUDENT (*to the first*).

   Wait a moment! Two of them are coming over here;
   they are done up so prettily,
   and one of them's my neighbor;

Ich bin dem Mädchen sehr gewogen.
Sie gehen ihren stillen Schritt   840
Und nehmen uns doch auch am Ende mit.

ERSTER.

Herr Bruder, nein! Ich bin nicht gern geniert.
Geschwind! daß wir das Wildbret nicht verlieren.
Die Hand, die Samstags ihren Besen führt,
Wird Sonntags dich am besten karessieren.

BÜRGER.

Nein, er gefällt mir nicht, der neue Burgemeister!
Nun, da er's ist, wird er nur täglich dreister.
Und für die Stadt was tut denn er?
Wird es nicht alle Tage schlimmer?
Gehorchen soll man mehr als immer,   850
Und zahlen mehr als je vorher.

BETTLER (*singt*).

    Ihr guten Herrn, ihr schönen Frauen,
    So wohlgeputzt und backenrot,
    Belieb' es euch, mich anzuschauen,
    Und seht und mildert meine Not!
    Laßt hier mich nicht vergebens leiern!
    Nur der ist froh, der geben mag.
    Ein Tag, den alle Menschen feiern,
    Er sei für mich ein Erntetag.

ANDRER BÜRGER.

Nichts Bessers weiß ich mir an Sonn- und Feiertagen   860
Als ein Gespräch von Krieg und Kriegsgeschrei,
Wenn hinten, weit, in der Türkei,
Die Völker auf einander schlagen.
Man steht am Fenster, trinkt sein Gläschen aus
Und sieht den Fluß hinab die bunten Schiffe gleiten;
Dann kehrt man abends froh nach Haus,
Und segnet Fried' und Friedenszeiten.

DRITTER BÜRGER.

Herr Nachbar, ja! so laß ich's auch geschehn,
Sie mögen sich die Köpfe spalten,
Mag alles durch einander gehn;   870
Doch nur zu Hause bleib's beim alten.

she always did appeal to me.
Both walk so primly and so unconcerned—   840
perhaps they'll let us go along with them.

FIRST STUDENT.

Brother, no! It's too much trouble.
Hurry! Don't let our quarry get away.
The hand that wields the broom on Saturdays
is best for Sunday's sweet caresses.

BURGHER.

The burgomaster goes against my grain!
Since he is in, his pride grows every day.
And what's he done for our town?
Conditions go from bad to worse!
He wants obedience from us all,   850
while taxes climb to untold heights.

BEGGAR (*sings*).

Fine gentlemen and ladies,
Decked out so well and rosy-cheeked,
If it please you, look at me,
Please look and ease my poverty.
Don't let me grind my tune in vain.
Content is he who likes to give.
This is a holiday for all the world.
Let it be a harvest day for me.

OTHER BURGHER.

On Sunday or on holidays I know of nothing better   860
than to converse of war and battle clamor,
when far away, perhaps on Turkish fields,
the nations maul each other zealously.
We stand by the window and we sip a glass
and see the painted ships glide down the river.
Then in the evening we go home content
and bless both Peace and peaceful times.

THIRD BURGHER.

Neighbor, I agree with you, yes indeed I do.
Let them crack their skulls for all I care,
let everything go topsy-turvy   870
while nothing changes here at home.

ALTE (*zu den* BÜRGERMÄDCHEN).

    Ei! wie geputzt! das schöne junge Blut!
    Wer soll sich nicht in euch vergaffen?—
    Nur nicht so stolz! Es ist schon gut!
    Und was ihr wünscht, das wüßt' ich wohl zu schaffen.

BÜRGERMÄDCHEN.

    Agathe, fort! ich nehme mich in acht,
    Mit solchen Hexen öffentlich zu gehen;
    Sie ließ mich zwar in Sankt Andreas' Nacht
    Den künft'gen Liebsten leiblich sehen—

DIE ANDRE.

    Mir zeigte sie ihn im Kristall,   880
    Soldatenhaft, mit mehreren Verwegnen;
    Ich seh' mich um, ich such' ihn überall,
    Allein mir will er nicht begegnen.

SOLDATEN.

        Burgen mit hohen
        Mauern und Zinnen,
        Mädchen mit stolzen
        Höhnenden Sinnen
        Möcht' ich gewinnen!
        Kühn ist das Mühen,
        Herrlich der Lohn!   890

        Und die Trompete
        Lassen wir werben,
        Wie zu der Freude,
        So zum Verderben.
        Das ist ein Stürmen!
        Das ist ein Leben!
        Mädchen und Burgen
        Müssen sich geben.
        Kühn ist das Mühen,
        Herrlich der Lohn!   900
        Und die Soldaten
        Ziehen davon.

    (FAUST *und* WAGNER.)

FAUST.

    Vom Eise befreit sind Strom und Bäche

OLD WOMAN (*to the* BURGHER'S DAUGHTERS).
    Eh, how sweet they look! The gay young blood!
    Who would not fall for you at a first glance?—
    Don't be stuck-up! There's no harm in what I say!
    You always end up with the thing you want.

BURGHER'S DAUGHTER.
    Agatha, come along, I say we should avoid
    the company of such a witch in public,
    although it's true that on St. Andrew's Night 10
    she let me see my future sweetheart in the flesh—

OTHER BURGHER'S DAUGHTER.
    I saw my own within her crystal ball,   880
    soldierlike and in the company of daring men.
    I look about and seek him everywhere,
    and yet he won't turn up for me.

SOLDIERS.
                    The sturdy castle,
                    The moat, and the tower,
                    The haughty girls
                    Who sit and glower,
                    I wish to conquer.
                    Great is the strife
                    And glorious the prize.   890

                    And our bugle
                    Sounds the call
                    To joy and to pleasure
                    And to a great fall.
                    A charging and storming
                    Is our life!
                    Maidens and castles
                    They all must surrender.
                    Great is the strife
                    And glorious the prize!   900
                    And the soldiers
                    Go marching away.

        (FAUST *and* WAGNER.)

FAUST.
    Streams and brooks are freed of ice

Durch des Frühlings holden, belebenden Blick;
Im Tale grünet Hoffnungsglück;
Der alte Winter, in seiner Schwäche,
Zog sich in rauhe Berge zurück.
Von dorther sendet er, fliehend, nur
Ohnmächtige Schauer körnigen Eises
In Streifen über die grünende Flur;   910
Aber die Sonne duldet kein Weißes:
Überall regt sich Bildung und Streben,
Alles will sie mit Farben beleben;
Doch an Blumen fehlt's im Revier,
Sie nimmt geputzte Menschen dafür.
Kehre dich um, von diesen Höhen
Nach der Stadt zurückzusehen.
Aus dem hohlen finstern Tor
Dringt ein buntes Gewimmel hervor.
Jeder sonnt sich heute so gern.   920
Sie feiern die Auferstehung des Herrn,
Denn sie sind selber auferstanden,
Aus niedriger Häuser dumpfen Gemächern,
Aus Handwerks- und Gewerbesbanden,
Aus dem Druck von Giebeln und Dächern,
Aus der Straßen quetschender Enge,
Aus der Kirchen ehrwürdiger Nacht
Sind sie alle ans Licht gebracht.
Sieh nur, sieh! wie behend sich die Menge
Durch die Gärten und Felder zerschlägt,   930
Wie der Fluß, in Breit' und Länge,
So manchen lustigen Nachen bewegt,
Und bis zum Sinken überladen
Entfernt sich dieser letzte Kahn.
Selbst von des Berges fernen Pfaden
Blinken uns farbige Kleider an.
Ich höre schon des Dorfs Getümmel,
Hier ist des Volkes wahrer Himmel,
Zufrieden jauchzet groß und klein.
Hier bin ich Mensch, hier darf ich's sein!   940

WAGNER.
    Mit Euch, Herr Doktor, zu spazieren,

by the reviving gracious eye of Spring;
Hope's greenery grows in the valley.
Ancient Winter's feeble self
has fallen back into the rugged mountains.
From there he sends in fitful flight
impotent showers of ice
in streaks across the greening fields,   910
but the sun will suffer no white;
all stirs with shaping and striving,
he endows each thing with his hue.
But in this region flowers are scarce,
the land is speckled with gay-colored people instead.
Turn about and from these heights
cast your glance back to the town.
Out from the hollow, gloomy gate
a motley crowd is surging today,
eager for the rays of the sun. They celebrate   920
the resurrection of the Lord,
for they themselves have arisen
from their glum quarters and tight little houses,
from bondage to their trade and labor,
from their oppressive roofs and gables,
from the crush of narrow alleyways,
and from the solemn night of churches;
they have all been brought into the light.
Look! Look, how nimbly the crowd
sallies and scatters through gardens and fields,   930
how the river moves its many skiffs
happily down its winding way,
and how the last of all these drifting barges
is over-brimming with its merry load.
And even from the mountain's far-off trails
comes the glitter of bright garments.
Now I hear the hum and bustle of the village.
This is the people's proper paradise;
they shout and revel—great and small:
I'm human here, here I can be!   940

WAGNER.
To stroll about with you, O master,

Ist ehrenvolle und ist Gewinn;
Doch würd' ich nicht allein mich her verlieren,
Weil ich ein Feind von allem Rohen bin.
Das Fiedeln, Schreien, Kegelschieben
Ist mir ein gar verhaßter Klang;
Sie toben wie vom bösen Geist getrieben
Und nennen's Freude, nennen's Gesang.

    (BAUERN *unter der Linde.*)

Tanz und Gesang.

Der Schäfer putzte sich zum Tanz,
Mit bunter Jacke, Band und Kranz,   950
Schmuck war er angezogen.
Schon um die Linde war es voll;
Und alles tanzte schon wie toll.
Juchhe! Juchhe!
Juchheisa! Heisa! He!
So ging der Fiedelbogen.

Er drückte hastig sich heran,
Da stieß er an ein Mädchen an
Mit seinem Ellenbogen;
Die frische Dirne kehrt' sich um   960
Und sagte: Nun, das find' ich dumm!
Juchhe! Juchhe!
Juchheisa! Heisa! He!
Seid nicht so ungezogen.

Doch hurtig in dem Kreise ging's,
Sie tanzten rechts, sie tanzten links,
Und alle Röcke flogen.
Sie wurden rot, sie wurden warm
Und ruhten atmend Arm in Arm,
Juchhe! Juchhe!   970
Juchheisa! Heisa! He!
Und Hüft' an Ellenbogen.

Und tu mir doch nicht so vertraut!
Wie mancher hat nicht seine Braut
Belogen und betrogen!

brings me much honor and much gain;
yet I should never come up here alone,
because I hate all forms of vulgar entertainment.
The fiddling, the shrieking, the rolling bowling balls,
all this is hateful noise to me.
The people rage as if the fiend possessed them
and then they call it happiness and song.

    (PEASANTS *under the Linden Tree.*)

           A Song and a Dance

In jacket, ribbon, fancy vest,
The shepherd boy was at his best   950
And joined the crowd to dance.
Beneath the linden tree they whirled;
Round and round they jumped and twirled;
Hurray, hurrah,
Tralala, hop-ho!
So went the fiddle bow.

He thrust himself into the crush
And with his elbow he did touch
The maiden with his knee.
The jolly girl was not so coy   960
And said to him, "You silly boy!"
Hurray, hurrah,
Tralala, hop-ho,
"Don't be so fresh with me."

And in a circle went the race,
To right and left at quickened pace,
The petticoats a-flying.
Their faces flushed, their cheeks were warm,
They rested panting, arm in arm.
Hurray, hurrah,   970
Tralala, hop-ho,
Their bodies were aglow.

"You're much too intimate with me!
In you and all the rest I see
How men deceive their women."

Er schmeichelte sie doch bei Seit',
Und von der Linde scholl es weit:
Juchhe! Juchhe!
Juchheisa! Heisa! He!
Geschrei und Fiedelbogen.   980

ALTER BAUER.

Herr Doktor, das ist schön von Euch,
Daß Ihr uns heute nicht verschmäht
Und unter dieses Volksgedräng',
Als ein so Hochgelahrter, geht.
So nehmet auch den schönsten Krug,
Den wir mit frischem Trunk gefüllt,
Ich bring' ihn zu und wünsche laut,
Daß er nicht nur den Durst Euch stillt:
Die Zahl der Tropfen, die er hegt,
Sei Euren Tagen zugelegt.   990

FAUST.

Ich nehme den Erquickungstrank,
Erwidr' euch allen Heil und Dank.
     (*Das Volk sammelt sich im Kreis umher.*)

ALTER BAUER.

Fürwahr, es ist sehr wohl getan,
Daß Ihr am frohen Tag erscheint;
Habt Ihr es vormals doch mit uns
An bösen Tagen gut gemeint!
Gar mancher steht lebendig hier,
Den Euer Vater noch zuletzt
Der heißen Fieberwut entriß,
Als er der Seuche Ziel gesetzt.   1000
Auch damals Ihr, ein junger Mann,
Ihr gingt in jedes Krankenhaus;
Gar manche Leiche trug man fort,
Ihr aber kamt gesund heraus;
Bestandet manche harte Proben;
Dem Helfer half der Helfer droben.

ALLE.

Gesundheit dem bewärten Mann,
Daß er noch lange helfen kann!

But off he whirled her to the side
Amidst the shouting far and wide.
Hurray, hurrah,
Tralala, hop-ho,
So went the fiddle bow.   980

OLD PEASANT.

Doctor, it is good of you
not to disdain us on this day
and as a deeply learned man
walk with us in this jostling crowd.
Please accept this handsome pitcher
filled this day for you to quaff.
I say, for everyone to hear,
"May it more than quench your thirst.
May the sum of drops contained therein
be added to your days.   990

FAUST.

I accept this wholesome drink
and thank you kindly for your wishes.
    (*The people form a circle around him.*)

OLD PEASANT.

We think it very fine of you
to be with us this festive day;
I remember how in times of trouble
you always proved a friend to us.
Many of us live today
because your father snatched us in the nick of time
from the fever's burning rage
when he stayed the plague at last.   1000
And you, then still a youngish man,
entered every stricken home,
and though they buried many bodies,
you always came out whole and well.
You overcame the harshest trials;
our helper's help came from the Lord in Heaven.

ALL THE PEASANTS.

Good health to our worthy friend;
long may he live and stand by us!

FAUST.

Vor jenem droben steht gebückt.
Der helfen lehrt und Hilfe schickt.   1010
  (*Er geht mit* WAGNERN *weiter.*)

WAGNER.

Welch ein Gefühl mußt du, o großer Mann,
Bei der Verehrung dieser Menge haben!
O glücklich, wer von seinen Gaben
Solch einen Vorteil ziehen kann!
Der Vater zeigt dich seinem Knaben,
Ein jeder fragt und drängt und eilt,
Die Fiedel stockt, der Tänzer weilt.
Du gehst, in Reihen stehen sie,
Die Mützen fliegen in die Höh':
Und wenig fehlt, so beugten sich die Knie,   1020
Als käm' das Venerabile.

FAUST.

Nur wenig Schritte noch hinauf zu jenem Stein,
Hier wollen wir von unsrer Wandrung rasten.
Hier saß ich oft gedankenvoll allein
Und quälte mich mit Beten und mit Fasten.
An Hoffnung reich, im Glauben fest,
Mit Tränen, Seufzen, Händeringen
Dacht' ich das Ende jener Pest
Vom Herrn des Himmels zu erzwingen.
Der Menge Beifall tönt mir nun wie Hohn.   1030
O könntest du in meinem Innern lesen,
Wie wenig Vater und Sohn
Solch eines Ruhmes wert gewesen!
Mein Vater war ein dunkler Ehrenmann,
Der über die Natur und ihre heil'gen Kreise
In Redlichkeit, jedoch auf seine Weise,
Mit grillenhafter Mühe sann;
Der, in Gesellschaft von Adepten,
Sich in die schwarze Küche schloß
Und, nach unendlichen Rezepten,   1040
Das Widrige zusammengoß.
Da ward ein roter Leu, ein kühner Freier,
Im lauen Bad der Lilie vermählt,

FAUST.

    We bow in reverence to Him above.

    The Lord instructs and helps the helper. 1010

      (*He walks on with* WAGNER.)

WAGNER.

    What feelings you must feel, great man,

    at the veneration of this crowd!

    Happy you who may derive

    such great advantage from your learning!

    The fathers show you to their sons,

    they all ask questions, push and hurry,

    the music stops, the dancer pauses.

    They stand in rows as you progress;

    they wave and fling their caps up in the air

    and almost fall upon their knees 1020

    as if the Host were passing by.

FAUST.

    A few more steps up to that rock,

    then let us rest from our wanderings.

    Here, deep in thought, I often sat alone

    and racked myself with fast and prayer.

    Rich in hope, and firm in faith,

    with tears and sighs and wringing hands

    I sought to wrest from the Lord in Heaven

    the means to end the pestilence.

    The crowd's acclaim now sounds like mockery. 1030

    Oh, could you read my inmost soul,

    you'd find how little son and father

    were worthy of the folk's acclaim.

    My father, man of darkling honor,

    brooded about Nature's sacred spheres

    in deep sincerity, yet in peculiar fashion,

    and with a crank's obsessive zeal,

    within a circle of adepts

    ensconced himself in his black kitchen

    and sought to fuse two hostile elements, or more, 1040

    according to his endless recipes.

    A daring wooer called Red Lion

    was wedded to the Lily in a tepid bath;

Und beide dann mit offnem Flammenfeuer
Aus einem Brautgemach ins andere gequält.
Erschien darauf mit bunten Farben
Di junge Königin im Glas,
Hier war die Arzenei, die Patienten starben,
Und niemand fragte: wer genas?
So haben wir mit höllischen Latwergen   1050
In diesen Tälern, diesen Bergen
Weit schlimmer als die Pest getobt.
Ich habe selbst den Gift an Tausende gegeben,
Sie welkten hin, ich muß erleben,
Daß man die frechen Mörder lobt.

WAGNER.

Wie könnt Ihr Euch darum betrüben!
Tut nicht ein braver Mann genug,
Die Kunst, die man ihm übertrug,
Gewissenhaft und pünktlich auszuüben?
Wenn du, als Jüngling, deinen Vater ehrst,   1060
So wirst du gern von ihm empfangen;
Wenn du, als Mann, die Wissenschaft vermehrst,
So kann dein Sohn zu höhrem Ziel gelangen.

FAUST.

O glücklich, wer noch hoffen kann
Aus diesem Meer des Irrtums aufzutauchen!
Was man nicht weiß, das eben brauchte man,
Und was man weiß, kann man nicht brauchen.
Doch laß uns dieser Stunde schönes Gut
Durch solchen Trübsinn nicht verkümmern!
Betrachte, wie in Abendsonneglut   1070
Die grünumgebnen Hütten schimmern.
Sie rückt und weicht, der Tag ist überlebt,
Dort eilt sie hin und fördert neues Leben.
O daß kein Flügel mich vom Boden hebt,
Ihr nach und immer nach zu streben!
Ich säh' im ewigen Abendstrahl
Die stille Welt zu meinen Füßen,
Entzündet alle Höhn, beruhigt jedes Tal,
Den Silberbach in goldne Ströme fließen.
Nicht hemmte dann den göttergleichen Lauf   1080

both were exposed to open, searing flames
and driven hapless to another Bridal Chamber.[11]
When thereupon in cheerful colors
the youthful Queen shone in her flask:
that was the medication; the patients died,
and no one asked: Did anyone get better?
And so with our hellish potions   1050
we raged about these plains and mountains
and were more deadly than the plague.
I myself administered the poison;
I saw thousands wilt, and now must live to see
how praise is heaped upon the shameless killers.

WAGNER.

How can you yield to such depression!
A worthy man can do no more
than execute with care and strict conformity
the art which was bequeathed to him.
If one reveres his father as a youth,   1060
one will accept his teachings eagerly,
and if you gain advances for your science,
your son may yet attain to higher goals.

FAUST.

Oh, happy he who still can hope in our day
to breathe the truth while plunged in seas of error!
What we don't know is really what we need,
and what we know is of no use to us whatever!
But the radiance of this hour
must not be marred by gloomy thoughts.
Mark the shimmering huts in green surroundings,   1070
basking in the evening sunlight's glow.
It fades and sinks away; the day is spent,
the sun moves on to nourish other life.
Oh, if I had wings to lift me from this earth,
to seek the sun and follow him!
Then I should see within the constant evening ray
the silent world beneath my feet,
the peaks illumined, and in every valley peace,
the silver brook flow into golden streams.
No savage peaks nor all the roaring gorges   1080

Der wilde Berg mit allen seinen Schluchten;
Schon tut das Meer sich mit erwärmten Buchten
Vor den erstaunten Augen auf.
Doch scheint die Göttin endlich wegzusinken;
Allein der neue Trieb erwacht,
Ich eile fort, ihr ew'ges Licht zu trinken,
Vor mir den Tag und hinter mir die Nacht,
Den Himmel über mir und unter mir die Wellen.
Ein schöner Traum, indessen sie entweicht.
Ach! zu des Geistes Flügeln wird so leicht   1090
Kein körperlicher Flügel sich gesellen.
Doch ist es jedem eingeboren,
Daß sein Gefühl hinauf und vorwärts dringt,
Wenn über uns, im blauen Raum verloren,
Ihr schmetternd Lied die Lerche singt;
Wenn über schroffen Fichtenhöhen
Der Adler ausgebreitet schwebt,
Und über Flächen, über Seen
Der Kranich nach der Heimat strebt.

WAGNER.

Ich hatte selbst oft grillenhafte Stunden,   1100
Doch solchen Trieb hab' ich noch nie empfunden.
Man sieht sich leicht an Wald und Feldern satt;
Des Vogels Fittich werd' ich nie beneiden.
Wie anders tragen uns die Geistesfreuden
Von Buch zu Buch, von Blatt zu Blatt!
Da werden Winternächte hold und schön,
Ein selig Leben wärmet alle Glieder,
Und ach! entrollst du gar ein würdig Pergamen,
So steigt der ganze Himmel zu dir nieder.

FAUST.

Du bist dir nur des einen Triebs bewußt;   1110
O lerne nie den andern kennen!
Zwei Seelen wohnen, ach! in meiner Brust,
Die eine will sich von der andern trennen;
Die eine hält, in derber Liebeslust,
Sich an die Welt mit klammernden Organen;
Die andre hebt gewaltsam sich vom Dust
Zu den Gefilden hoher Ahnen.

could then impede my godlike course.
Even now the ocean and its sun-warmed bays
appear to my astonished eyes.
When it would seem the sun has faded,
a newborn urge awakes in me.
I hurry off to drink eternal light;
before me lies the day, behind the night,
the sky above me, and the seas below.
A lovely dream; meanwhile the sun has slipped away.
Alas, the spirit's wings will not be joined   1090
so easily to heavier wings of flesh and blood.
Yet every man has inward longings
and sweeping, skyward aspirations
when up above, forlorn in azure space,
the lark sends out a lusty melody;
when over jagged mountains, soaring over pines,
the outstretched eagle draws his circles,
and high above the plains and oceans
the cranes press onward, homeward bound.

WAGNER.

I've had myself at times peculiar notions,   1100
but never have I felt an urge like that.
One quickly has one's fill of woods and meadows,
and I shall never envy birds their wings.
How differently the spirit's higher pleasures
buoy us up through many books and pages!
Those wintry nights hold charm and beauty,
a blessed life warms every limb,
and ah! when we unroll a precious parchment,
the very skies come down to us.

FAUST.

You're conscious only of a single drive;   1110
Oh, do not seek to know the other passion!
Two souls, alas, dwell in my breast,
each seeks to rule without the other.
The one with robust love's desires
clings to the world with all its might,
the other fiercely rises from the dust
to reach sublime ancestral regions.

O gibt es Geister in der Luft,
Die zwischen Erd' und Himmel herrschend weben,
So steiget nieder aus dem goldnen Duft   1120
Und führt mich weg, zu neuem, buntem Leben!
Ja, wäre nur ein Zaubermantel mein
Und trüg' er mich in fremde Länder!
Mir sollt' er um die köstlichsten Gewänder,
Nicht feil um einen Königsmantel sein.

WAGNER.

Berufe nicht die wohlbekannte Schar,
Die strömend sich im Dunstkreis überbreitet,
Dem Menschen tausendfältige Gefahr,
Von allen Enden her, bereitet.
Von Norden dringt der scharfe Geisterzahn   1130
Auf dich herbei, mit pfeilgespitzten Zungen;
Von Morgen ziehn, vetrocknend, sie heran
Und nähren sich von deinen Lungen;
Wenn sie der Mittag aus der Wüste schickt,
Die Glut auf Glut um deinen Scheitel häufen,
So bringt der West den Schwarm, der erst erquickt,
Um dich und Feld und Aue zu ersäufen.
Sie hören gern, zum Schaden froh gewandt,
Gehorchen gern, weil sie uns gern betrügen;
Sie stellen wie vom Himmel sich gesandt,   1140
Und lispeln englisch, wenn sie lügen.
Doch gehen wir! Ergraut ist schon die Welt,
Die Luft gekühlt, der Nebel fällt!
Am Abend schätzt man erst das Haus.—
Was stehst du so und blickst erstaunt hinaus?
Was kann dich in der Dämmrung so ergreifen?

FAUST.

Siehst du den schwarzen Hund durch Saat und Stoppel
    streifen?

WAGNER.

Ich sah ihn lange schon, nicht wichtig schien er mir.

FAUST.

Betracht' ihn recht! für was hälst du das Tier?

WAGNER.

Für einen Pudel, der auf seine Weise   1150

Oh, should there be spirits roaming through the air
which rule between the earth and heaven,
let them leave their golden haze and come to me,   1120
let them escort me to a new and bright-hued life!
Ah yes, if I could have a magic cloak
to whisk me off to foreign lands
I should not trade it for the richest robes,
nor for the mantle of a king.

WAGNER.

Do not invoke the well-known troop
that floats and streams in murky spheres,
a source of myriad dangers for all men,
issuing from every corner of the globe.
The sharp-toothed ghosts come from the north   1130
and chill you with their arrow-pointed tongues;
they move up, dry as bone, from eastern skies
and suck in moisture from your lungs.
Those churning up from southern desert sands
heap fire upon fire on your skull,
while western gusts will quench your thirst,
then drown you and your fertile fields.
They listen gladly and are glad to do you harm
and readily obey because they like to cheat;
they pretend to come to you from Heaven   1140
and lisp like angels when they lie to you.
But let us leave. The world is turning gray,
the air grows chill and mists are seeping down!
We come to prize our home at night—
Why do you stop short and look so startled?
What arrests you in this fading light?

FAUST.

Do you see the jet-black dog traversing field and stubble?

WAGNER.

I saw him long ago; it did not seem important.

FAUST.

Observe him well! What do you take him for?

WAGNER.

Why, for a poodle who, according to his kind,   1150

Sich auf der Spur des Herren plagt.

FAUST.

Bemerkst du, wie in weitem Schneckenkreise
Er um uns her und immer näher jagt?
Und irr' ich nicht, so zieht ein Feuerstrudel
Auf seinen Pfaden hinterdrein.

WAGNER.

Ich sehe nichts als einen schwarzen Pudel;
Es mag bei Euch wohl Augentäuschung sein.

FAUST.

Mir scheint es, daß er magisch leise Schlingen
Zu künft'gem Band um unsre Füße zieht.

WAGNER.

Ich seh' ihn ungewiß und furchtsam uns umspringen,   1160
Weil er, statt seines Herrn, zwei Unbekannte sieht.

FAUST.

Der Kreis wird eng, schon ist er nah!

WAGNER.

Du siehst! ein Hund, und kein Gespenst ist da.
Er knurrt und zweifelt, legt sich auf den Bauch.
Er wedelt. Alles Hundebrauch.

FAUST.

Geselle dich zu uns! Komm hier!

WAGNER.

Es ist ein pudelnärrisch Tier.
Du stehest still, er wartet auf;
Du sprichst ihn an, er strebt an dir hinauf;
Verliere was, er wird es bringen,   1170
Nach deinem Stock ins Wasser springen.

FAUST.

Du hast wohl recht, ich finde nicht die Spur
Von einem Geist, und alles ist Dressur.

WAGNER.

Dem Hunde, wenn er gut gezogen,
Wird selbst ein weiser Mann gewogen.
Ja, deine Gunst verdient er ganz und gar,
Er, der Studenten trefflicher Skolar.

   (*Sie gehen in das Stadttor.*)

sniffs out the footsteps of his absent master.

FAUST.

Observe the ample spiral turns
enclosing and racing ever closer!
Unless I'm wrong I see a trail of fire
follow swirling in his wake.

WAGNER.

I see a plain black poodle, and that's all,
it must be just an optical illusion.

FAUST.

I think he's softly weaving coils of magic
for future bondage round our feet.

WAGNER.

He is confused and leaps about us filled with fear   1160
at finding not his master but two strangers.

FAUST.

The circle tightens; now he's near!

WAGNER.

You see? He's no phantom but a dog.
He snarls and watches, crouching on his belly.
He wags his tail—all canine habits.

FAUST.

Come join with us. Come here! Come here!

WAGNER.

He is a poodly-foolish creature;
you stand still and he will wait for you;
you speak to him, he'll nuzzle you.
What you forget, he will retrieve for you;   1170
he'll jump into the water for your cane.

FAUST.

You may be right. I cannot find a trace
of any ghostly thing. It's all his training.

WAGNER.

A simple dog well-trained to heed commands
may even earn a learned man's affection.
Yes indeed, he quite deserves your favor
as a student and a fellow-scholar.
        (*They pass through the city gate.*)

FAUST (*mit dem Pudel hereintretend*).
Verlassen hab' ich Feld und Auen,
Die eine tiefe Nacht bedeckt,
Mit ahnungsvollem, heil'gem Grauen   1180
In uns die beßre Seele weckt.
Entschlafen sind nun wilde Triebe
Mit jedem ungestümen Tun;
Es reget sich die Menschenliebe,
Die Liebe Gottes regt sich nun.

Sei ruhig, Pudel! renne nicht hin und wider!
An der Schwelle was schnoperst du hier?
Lege dich hinter den Ofen nieder,
Mein bestes Kissen geb' ich dir.
Wie du draußen auf dem bergigen Wege   1190
Durch Rennen und Springen ergetzt uns hast,
So nimm nun auch von mir die Pflege,
Als ein willkommner stiller Gast.

Ach, wenn in unsrer engen Zelle
Die Lampe freundlich wieder brennt,
Dann wird's in unserm Busen helle,
Im Herzen, das sich selber kennt.
Vernunft fängt wieder an zu sprechen,
Und Hoffnung wieder an zu blühn,
Man sehnt sich nach des Lebens Bächen,   1200
Ach! nach des Lebens Quelle hin.

Knurre nicht, Pudel! Zu den heiligen Tönen,
Die jetzt meine ganze Seel' umfassen,
Will der tierische Laut nicht passen.
Wir sind gewohnt, daß die Menschen verhöhnen,
Was sie nicht verstehn,
Daß sie vor dem Guten und Schönen,
Das ihnen oft beschwerlich ist, murren;
Will es der Hund, wie sie, beknurren?

74

FAUST (*entering with the poodle*).
Behind me, all the fields and meadows
lie wrapped in shade and deepest night;
a holy and foreboding shudder   1180
wakes the better soul in us.
The rush of turbulent desire sleeps,
and every hint of stressful action.
The love of mankind is astir,
the love of God is all about us.

Poodle, be quiet! Stop racing back and forth!
Why must you sniff at the threshold?
Come now, lie down behind the stove,
I'll give you my softest pillow.
On the road out in the rolling meadows   1190
your leaps and capers entertained us well;
you did enough to earn my hospitality;
lie still then and be my welcome guest.

Ah, when the friendly lamp is burning
and glows within our narrow cell,
the darkened self grows clear again,
the heart that knows itself will brighten.
The voice of reason can be heard,
and hope begins to bloom again;
we crave to hold within our grasp   1200
the streams of life and ah, its sources!

Poodle, stop growling! that brutish snarl
is not in tune with the sacred sound
that now enthralls my soul.
I am used to men who mock and scorn
the things beyond their comprehension,
who mutter at the Good and Beautiful
because it is often too much trouble.
Will the dog snarl his displeasure like men?

Aber ach! schon fühl' ich, bei dem besten Willen,   1210
Befriedigung nicht mehr aus dem Busen quillen.
Aber warum muß der Strom so bald versiegen,
Und wir wieder im Durste liegen?
Davon hab' ich so viel Erfahrung.
Doch dieser Mangel läßt sich ersetzen:
Wir lernen das Überirdische schätzen,
Wir sehnen uns nach Offenbarung,
Die nirgends würd'ger und schöner brennt
Als in dem Neuen Testament.
Mich drängt's, den Grundtext aufzuschlagen,   1220
Mit redlichem Gefühl einmal
Das heilige Original
In mein geliebtes Deutsch zu übertragen.
     (*Er schlägt ein Volum auf und schickt sich an.*)
Geschrieben steht: „Im Anfang war das W o r t!"
Hier stock' ich schon! Wer hilft mir weiter fort?
Ich kann das W o r t so hoch unmöglich schätzen,
Ich muß es anders übersetzen,
Wenn ich vom Geiste recht erleuchtet bin.
Geschrieben steht: Im Anfang war der S i n n .
Bedenke wohl die erste Zeile,   1230
Daß deine Feder sich nicht übereile!
Ist es der S i n n , der alles wirkt und schafft?
Es sollte stehn: Im Anfang was die K r a f t !
Doch, auch indem ich dieses niederschreibe,
Schon warnt mich was, daß ich dabei nicht bleibe.
Mir hilft der Geist! Auf einmal seh' ich Rat
Und schreibe getrost: Im Anfang war die T a t !

Soll ich mit dir das Zimmer teilen,
Pudel, so laß das Heulen,
So laß das Bellen!   1240
Solch einen störenden Gesellen
Mag ich nicht in der Nähe leiden.
Einer von uns beiden
Muß die Zelle meiden.
Ungern heb' ich das Gastrecht auf,
Die Tür ist offen, hast freien Lauf.

But ah! though I am full of good intention,   1210
contentment flows no longer from my breast.
Why must this stream run dry so soon
and I be parched and thirsty once again?
I've had more than my share of it,
but I am able to relieve this want:
one learns to prize the supernatural,
one yearns for highest Revelation,
which nowhere burns more nobly and more bright
than here in my New Testament.
I feel impelled to read this basic text   1220
and to transpose the hallowed words,
with feeling and integrity,
into my own beloved German.
    (*He opens a volume and begins.*)
It is written: "In the beginning was the Word!"[12]   *opening of John*
Even now I balk. Can no one help?
I truly cannot rate the word so high.
I must translate it otherwise.
I believe the Spirit has inspired me
and I must write: "In the beginning there was Mind."   *his own Translation*
Think thoroughly on this first line,   1230
hold back your pen from undue haste!
Is it mind that stirs and makes all things?
The text should state: "In the beginning there was Power!"
Yet while I am about to write this down,
something warns me I will not adhere to this.
The Spirit's on my side! The answer is at hand:
I write, assured, "In the beginning was the Deed."

If you wish to share this cell with me,
poodle, stop your yowling;
bark no more.   1240
A nuisance such as you
I cannot suffer in my presence.
One of us must leave this room;
I now reluctantly suspend
the law of hospitality.
The door is open, you are free to go.

Aber was muß ich sehen!
Kann das natürlich geschehen?
Ist es Schatten? ist's Wirklichkeit?
Wie wird mein Pudel lang und breit! 1250
Er hebt sich mit Gewalt,
Das ist nicht eines Hundes Gestalt!
Welch ein Gespenst bracht' ich ins Haus!
Schon sieht er wie ein Nilpferd aus,
Mit feurigen Augen, schrecklichem Gebiß.
O! du bist mir gewiß!
Für solche halbe Höllenbrut
Ist Salomonis Schlüssel gut.

GEISTER (*auf dem Gange*).

 Drinnen gefangen ist einer!
 Bleibet haußen, folg' ihm keiner! 1260
 Wie im Eisen der Fuchs,
 Zagt ein alter Höllenluchs.
 Aber gebt acht!
 Schwebet hin, schwebet wider,
 Auf und nieder,
 Und er hat sich losgemacht.
 Könnt ihr ihm nützen,
 Laßt ihn nicht sitzen!
 Denn er tat uns allen
 Schon viel zu Gefallen. 1270

FAUST.

Erst zu begegnen dem Tiere,
Brauch' ich den Spruch der viere:
 Salamander soll glühen,
 Undene sich winden,
 Sylphe verschwinden,
 Kobold sich mühen.
Wer sie nicht kennte,
Die Elemente,
Ihre Kraft
Und Eigenschaft, 1280
Wäre kein Meister
Über die Geister.
 Verschwind in Flammen,

But what is this?
Is this a natural occurrence?
Is it shadow or reality?
How broad and long my poodle waxes!   1250
He rises up with mighty strength;
this is no dog's anatomy!
What a specter did I bring into my house!
Now he's very like a river horse
with glowing eyes and vicious teeth.
Oh! I am sure of you!
For such a half-satanic brood
the key of Solomon will do.

SPIRITS (*in the corridor*).[13]

    Someone is caught within!
    Stay out, and no one follow!   1260
    Like the fox in a snare
    The hell-lynx quakes.
    But take good care!
    Hover here, hover there,
    Flit up and down,
    And once he's loose,
    You may be of use,
    Don't leave him in the lurch.
    Remember that to all of us
    He granted many favors.   1270

FAUST.
First, to confront the brute
I must use the Spell of the Four.
    Glow, Salamander
    Undine, coil
    Sylph, meander
    Kobold, toil.[14]
Whoever is ignorant
of the four elements,
of the strength they wield
and of their quality,   1280
cannot master
the band of the spirits.
    Vanish in flames,

Salamander!
Rauschend fließe zusammen,
Undene!
Leucht in Meteoren-Schöne,
Sylphe!
Bring häusliche Hilfe,
Incubus! Incubus!   1290
Tritt hervor und mache den Schluß.
Keines der viere
Steckt in dem Tiere.
Es liegt ganz ruhig und grinst mich an;
Ich hab' ihm noch nicht weh getan.
Du sollst mich hören
Stärker beschwören.
Bist du Geselle
Ein Flüchtling der Hölle?
So sieh dies Zeichen,   1300
Dem sie sich beugen,
Die schwarzen Scharen!
Schon schwillt es auf mit borstigen Haaren.
Verworfnes Wesen!
Kannst du ihn lesen?
Den nie Entsproßnen,
Unausgesprochnen,
Durch alle Himmel Gegoßnen,
Freventlich Durchstochnen?

Hinter den Ofen gebannt,   1310
Schwillt es wie ein Elefant,
Den ganzen Raum füllt es an,
Es will zum Nebel zerfließen.
Steige nicht zur Decke hinan!
Lege dich zu des Meisters Füßen!
Du siehst, daß ich nicht vergebens drohe.
Ich versenge dich mit heiliger Lohe!
Erwarte nicht
Das dreimal glühende Licht!
Erwarte nicht   1320
Die stärkste von meinen Künsten!

Salamander!
In foam merge and flow,
Undine!
Light your stellar dome,
Sylph!
Bring comfort to the home,
Incubus, Incubus!   1290
Emerge and end it all.
None of the four
is lodged in the beast.
He lies quite still and grins at me.
I have not stung him yet.
I shall strike his core
with stronger conjurations.

Have you come to my cell
A refugee from Hell?
Then mark you this sign[15]   1300
To which all must incline,
All the black legions.
His fur is bristling now, and he swells and puffs!
Contemptible creature!
Face the Teacher!
The unconfined,
Never defined,
Heavenly presence
Pierced on the Cross.

My spell holds him fast behind the stove;   1310
now he swells to elephantine size
and fills the chamber with his bulk.
Now he wants to turn to vapor.
Do not rise up to the ceiling!
Lie at your master's feet!
You see, my threats are not in vain,
I scorch you with the sacred fire!
Do not await
the threefold glowing light![16]
Do not await   1320
the mightiest of my powers!

(MEPHISTOPHELES *tritt, indem der Nebel*
fällt, gekleidet wie ein fahrender Scholastikus,
hinter dem Ofen hervor.)

MEPHISTOPHELES.

Wozu der Lärm? was steht dem Herrn zu Diensten?

FAUST.

Das also war des Pudels Kern!
Ein fahrender Skolast? Der Casus macht mich lachen.

MEPHISTOPHELES.

Ich salutiere den gelehrten Herrn!
Ihr habt mich weidlich schwitzen machen.

FAUST.

Wie nennst du dich?

MEPHISTOPHELES.

                    Die Frage scheint mir klein
Für einen, der das Wort so sehr verachtet,
Der, weit entfernt von allem Schein,
Nur in der Wesen Tiefe trachtet.   1330

FAUST.

Bei euch, ihr Herrn, kann man das Wesen
Gewöhnlich aus dem Namen lesen,
Wo es sich allzudeutlich weist,
Wenn man euch Fliegengott, Verderber, Lügner heißt.
Nun gut, wer bist du denn?

MEPHISTOPHELES.

                    Ein Teil von jener Kraft,
Die stets das Böse will und stets das Gute schafft.

FAUST.

Was ist mit diesem Rätselwort gemeint?

MEPHISTOPHELES.

Ich bin der Geist, der stets verneint!
Und das mit Recht; denn alles, was entsteht,
Ist wert, daß es zugrunde geht;   1340
Drum besser wär's, daß nichts entstünde.
So ist denn alles, was ihr Sünde,
Zerstörung, kurz das Böse nennt,
Mein eigentliches Element.

FAUST.

Du nennst dich einen Teil, und stehst doch ganz vor mir?

(While the mist falls away, MEPHISTOPHELES
steps from behind the stove. He is dressed as a
traveling scholar.)

MEPHISTOPHELES.
   Why all this noise? What is the gentleman's pleasure?

FAUST.
   So this was the poodle's core!
   One of the traveling scholars. This *casus* makes me chuckle.

MEPHISTOPHELES.
   I salute the learned gentleman;
   I've sweated mightily for you.

FAUST.
   What is your name?

MEPHISTOPHELES.
                     This seems a trifling question
   for one so scornful of the word,
   for one removed from every outward show
   who always reaches for the inmost core.   1330

FAUST.
   The essence of the like of you
   is usually inherent in the name.
   It appears in all-too-great transparency
   in names like Lord of Flies, Destroyer, Liar.
   All right, who are you then?

MEPHISTOPHELES.
                           A portion of that power
   which always works for Evil and effects the Good.

FAUST.
   What is the meaning of this riddle?

MEPHISTOPHELES.
   I am the spirit that denies forever!
   And rightly so! What has arisen from the void
   deserves to be annihilated.   1340
   It would be best if nothing ever would arise.
   And thus what you call havoc,
   deadly sin, or briefly stated: Evil,
   that is my proper element.

FAUST.
   You call yourself a part and yet you stand before me whole?

MEPHISTOPHELES.

Bescheidne Wahrheit sprech' ich dir.
Wenn sich der Mensch, die kleine Narrenwelt,
Gewöhnlich für ein Ganzes hält—
Ich bin ein Teil des Teils, der anfangs alles war,
Ein Teil der Finsternis, die sich das Licht gebar,　　　　1350
Das stolze Licht, das nun der Mutter Nacht
Den alten Rang, den Raum ihr streitig macht,
Und doch gelingt's ihm nicht, da es, so viel es strebt,
Verhaftet an den Körpern klebt.
Von Körpern strömt's, die Körper macht es schön,
Ein Körper hemmt's auf seinem Gange,
So hoff' ich, dauert es nicht lange,
Und mit den Körpern wird's zugrunde gehn.

FAUST.

Nun kenn' ich deine würd'gen Pflichten!
Du kannst im Großen nichts vernichten　　　　1360
Und fängst es nun im Kleinen an.

MEPHISTOPHELES.

Und freilich ist nicht viel damit getan.
Was sich dem Nichts entgegenstellt,
Das Etwas, diese plumpe Welt,
So viel als ich schon unternommen,
Ich wußte nicht ihr beizukommen,
Mit Wellen, Stürmen, Schütteln, Brand—
Geruhig bleibt am Ende Meer und Land!
Und dem verdammten Zeug, der Tier- und Menschenbrut,
Dem ist nun gar nichts anzuhaben:　　　　1370
Wie viele hab' ich schon begraben!
Und immer zirkuliert ein neues, frisches Blut.
So geht es fort, man möchte rasend werden!
Der Luft, dem Wasser, wie der Erden
Entwinden tausend Keime sich,
Im Trocknen, Feuchten, Warmen, Kalten!
Hätt' ich mir nicht die Flamme vorbehalten,
Ich hätte nichts Aparts für mich.

FAUST.

So setzest du der ewig regen,
Der heilsam schaffenden Gewalt　　　　1380

MEPHISTOPHELES.

    I state the modest truth to you.

    While every member of your race—that little world of
        fools—

    likes best of all to think himself complete—

    I am a portion of that part which once was everything,

    a part of darkness which gave birth to Light,   1350

    that haughty Light which now disputes the rank

    and ancient sway of Mother Night;

    and though it tries its best, it won't succeed

    because it cleaves and sticks to bodies.

    The bodies mill about, Light beautifies the bodies,

    yet bodies have forever blocked its way—

    and so I hope it won't be long

    before all bodies are annihilated.

FAUST.

    Now I know your noble duties.

    You cannot wreck the larger entities,   1360

    and so you nibble away at the smaller things.

MEPHISTOPHELES.

    It isn't much when all is said and done.

    What stands opposed to Nothingness—

    the bungling earth, that something more or less—

    in spite of all I undertook

    I could not get my hands on it.

    After waves and quakes and fires,

    the lands and seas are still intact,

    and all that cursèd stuff, the brood of beasts and men,

    is too tenacious to be shaken.   1370

    Think of the multitudes I buried!

    Yet there is always fresh new blood in circulation.

    And so it goes; it drives me to distraction.

    In air and earth and water,

    through dryness, dampness, warmth, and cold,

    a thousand seeds will push their way to life.

    Had I neglected to reserve the flame for me,

    I should now be quite without a specialty.

FAUST.

    Against the ever working forces,

    the healing and creative powers,   1380

Die kalte Teufelsfaust entgegen,
Die sich vergebens tückisch ballt!
Was anders suche zu beginnen,
Des Chaos wunderlicher Sohn!

MEPHISTOPHELES.

Wir wollen wirklich uns besinnen,
Die nächsten Male mehr davon!
Dürft' ich wohl diesmal mich entfernen?

FAUST.

Ich sehe nicht, warum du fragst.
Ich habe jetzt dich kennen lernen,
Besuche nun mich, wie du magst.   1390
Hier ist das Fenster, hier die Türe,
Ein Rauchfang ist dir auch gewiß.

MEPHISTOPHELES.

Gesteh' ich's nur! daß ich hinausspaziere,
Verbietet mir ein kleines Hindernis,
Der Drudenfuß auf Eurer Schwelle—

FAUST.

Das Pentagramma macht dir Pein?
Ei sage mir, du Sohn der Hölle,
Wenn das dich bannt, wie kamst du denn herein?
Wie ward ein solcher Geist betrogen?

MEPHISTOPHELES.

Beschaut es recht! Es ist nicht gut gezogen;   1400
Der eine Winkel, der nach außen zu,
Ist, wie du siehst, ein wenig offen.

FAUST.

Das hat der Zufall gut getroffen!
Und mein Gefangner wärst denn du?
Das ist von ungefähr gelungen!

MEPHISTOPHELES.

Der Pudel merkte nichts, als er hereingesprungen,
Die Sache sieht jetzt anders aus:
Der Teufel kann nicht aus dem Haus.

FAUST.

Doch warum gehst du nicht durchs Fenster?

MEPHISTOPHELES.

's ist ein Gesetz der Teufel und Gespenster: 1410

you thrust your cold, infernal fist
in truculence; it's clenched in vain.
So you'd better seek some other work,
you fantastic son of Chaos.

MEPHISTOPHELES.

Well, let us give this matter further thought,
and discuss it when we meet again.
May I withdraw this time? With your permission . . .

FAUST.

I see no reason for your question.
Since we have now become acquainted,
you have leave to visit me at will.   1390
Here's the window; the door is over there;
feel free to use the chimney, too.

MEPHISTOPHELES.

I must confess, there is a little obstacle
that prevents my exit from this room,
the wizard's symbol on the sill—

FAUST.

The pentagram17 should cause you pain?
Why, tell me, son of Hades,
if it holds you now, how did you enter here?
How did you swindle such a spirit?

MEPHISTOPHELES.

Look closely now; the figure is not drawn too well,   1400
One of the corners facing outward,
as you can see, is slightly open at the tip.

FAUST.

A lucky accident has come my way!
You my prisoner? well I'll be damned!
It seems I've turned a handsome profit!

MEPHISTOPHELES.

The dog knew nothing when he first jumped in;
but now the tables have been turned;
the devil's caught and cannot leave the house.

FAUST.

Why can't you slip out through the window?

MEPHISTOPHELES.

A hellish law stands in the way: 1410

Wo sie hereingeschlüpft, da müssen sie hinaus.
Das erste steht uns frei, beim zweiten sind wir Knechte.

FAUST.

Die Hölle selbst hat ihre Rechte?
Das find' ich gut, da ließe sich ein Pakt,
Und sicher wohl, mit euch, ihr Herren, schließen?

MEPHISTOPHELES.

Was man verspricht, das sollst du rein genießen,
Dir wird davon nichts abgezwackt.
Doch das ist nicht so kurz zu fassen,
Und wir besprechen das zunächst;
Doch jetzo bitt' ich hoch und höchst,   1420
Für dieses Mal mich zu entlassen.

FAUST.

So bleibe doch noch einen Augenblick,
Um mir erst gute Mär zu sagen.

MEPHISTOPHELES.

Jetzt laß mich los! Ich komme bald zurück,
Dann magst du nach Belieben fragen.

FAUST.

Ich habe dir nicht nachgestellt,
Bist du doch selbst ins Garn gegangen.
Den Teufel halte, wer ihn hält!
Er wird ihn nicht so bald zum zweiten Male fangen.

MEPHISTOPHELES.

Wenn dir's beliebt, so bin ich auch bereit,   1430
Dir zur Gesellschaft hier zu bleiben;
Doch mit Bedingnis, dir die Zeit
Durch meine Künste würdig zu vertreiben.

FAUST.

Ich seh' es gern, das steht dir frei;
Nur daß die Kunst gefällig sei!

MEPHISTOPHELES.

Du wirst, mein Freund, für deine Sinnen
In dieser Stunde mehr gewinnen
Als in des Jahres Einerlei.
Was dir die zarten Geister singen,
Die schönen Bilder, die sie bringen,   1440

wherever we steal in we must steal out.
We're free to choose the first, but the second finds us
    slaves.

FAUST.

So Hell itself has its legalities?
This suits me fine, and I suppose a pact
might be concluded with you gentlemen?

MEPHISTOPHELES.

The promises we make you shall enjoy in full;
we will not skimp or haggle.
But this business should not be done so hastily;
we shall have another meeting soon;
but now I must ask you most politely   1420
to let me out immediately.

FAUST.

Ah, please stay on a little while
and entertain me with some more details.

MEPHISTOPHELES.

Let me go, my friend! I'll soon return;
then you can ask me at your pleasure.

FAUST.

I did not stalk you in the fields.
It's you who came and fell into the snare.
Let him who snares the devil hold him fast!
A second chance will not occur so soon.

MEPHISTOPHELES.

If it pleases you, I am prepared   1430
to keep you company for now,
provided I may help you pass the time
with handsome tricks and conjurations.

FAUST.

Proceed, I'd like some entertainment,
but let your tricks be to my liking.

MEPHISTOPHELES.

My friend, in this one hour you will gain
far more for all your senses
than in a year's indifferent course.
What the tender spirits sing for you,
the lovely images they bring,   1440

Sind nicht ein leeres Zauberspiel.
Auch dein Geruch wird sich ergetzen,
Dann wirst du deinen Gaumen letzen,
Und dann entzückt sich dein Gefühl.
Bereitung braucht es nicht voran,
Beisammen sind wir, fanget an!

GEISTER.

Schwindet, ihr dunkeln
Wölbungen droben!
Reizender schaue
Freundlich der blaue   1450
Äther herein!
Wären die dunkeln
Wolken zerronnen!
Sternelein funkeln,
Mildere Sonnen
Scheinen darein.
Himmlischer Söhne
Geistige Schöne,
Schwankende Beugung
Schwebet vorüber.   1460
Sehnende Neigung
Folget hinüber;
Und der Gewänder
Flatternde Bänder
Decken die Länder,
Decken die Laube,
Wo sich fürs Leben,
Tief in Gedanken,
Liebende geben.
Laube bei Laube!   1470
Sprossende Ranken!
Lastende Traube
Stürzt ins Behälter
Drängender Kelter,
Stürzen in Bächen
Schäumende Weine,
Rieseln durch reine,
Edle Gesteine,

will not be empty magic play.
Blissful scents will come your way,
then your palate will be stimulated,
you will be bathed in ecstasy.
For this you need no preparation;
we are assembled, now begin.

SPIRITS.

                    Vanish, you gloomy
                    High-vaulting arches!
                    Let the blue ether
                    More gracefully shine   1450
                    Into this cell!
                    Let darkling clouds
                    Thin out and vanish!
                    The firmament sparkles;
                    Mellower suns
                    Now offer their light.
                    Spirit of Beauty's
                    Heavenly suns
                    Sway and incline,
                    And hover by.   1460
                    Follow beyond
                    The yearning bent!
                    And their garments'
                    Fluttering ribbons
                    Cover the fields,
                    Cover the arbor
                    Where, steeped in their thoughts,
                    Lovers entwine,
                    Yielding for life.
                    Arbor on arbor!   1470
                    Tendrils budding!
                    The weight of the grape
                    Received in the holds
                    Of ready presses;
                    Falling in torrents,
                    The foaming wines
                    Then seep through precious,
                    Crystalline stones,

Lassen die Höhen
Hinter sich liegen,   1480
Breiten zu Seen
Sich ums Genügen
Grünender Hügel.
Und das Geflügel
Schlürfet sich Wonne,
Flieget der Sonne,
Flieget den hellen
Inseln entgegen,
Die sich auf Wellen
Gauklend bewegen;   1490
Wo wir in Chören
Jauchzende hören,
Über den Auen
Tanzende schauen,
Die sich im Freien
Alle zerstreuen.
Einige klimmen
Über die Höhen,
Andere schwimmen
Über die Seen,   1500
Andere schweben;
Alle zum Leben,
Alle zur Ferne
Liebender Sterne,
Seliger Huld.

MEPHISTOPHELES.

Er schläft! So recht, ihr luft'gen zarten Jungen!
Ihr habt ihn treulich eingesungen!
Für dies Konzert bin ich in eurer Schuld.
Du bist noch nicht der Mann, den Teufel festzuhalten!
Umgaukelt ihn mit süßen Traumgestalten,   1510
Versenkt ihn in ein Meer des Wahns;
Doch dieser Schwelle Zauber zu zerspalten,
Bedarf ich eines Rattenzahns.
Nicht lange brauch' ich zu beschwören,
Schon raschelt eine hier und wird sogleich mich hören.

Leaving behind
The steeper heights; 1480
They spread to the lakes
To slake the thirst
Of greening hills.
And fluttering birds
Drink up the bliss,
Fly in blue space,
Fly to discover
Radiant isles
That bob on the waters
In friendly sway, 1490
Where many sing
And frolic together,
Over the meadows
Bounding and dancing.
Out in the open,
All scatter and run.
Some are scaling
Over the heights;
Others swimming
Over the lakes, 1500
And some soar free—
All toward life,
Toward the sphere
Of loving stars,
Of blissful favor.

MEPHISTOPHELES.

He sleeps! Well done, my airy, tender children!
Your lullaby has put him sound asleep!
This concert leaves me in your debt.
You are not the man yet who can hold the devil.
Weave about him shapes of honeyed dreams 1510
and plunge him into seas of sweet delusions.
But to break this threshold's magic spell
the devil needs the sharp tooth of a rat.
For this I need no lengthy conjuration;
there, it's rustling now, it'll quickly do my bidding.

Der Herr der Ratten und der Mäuse,
Der Fliegen, Frösche, Wanzen, Läuse
Befiehlt dir, dich hervorzuwagen
Und diese Schwelle zu benagen,
Sowie er sie mit Öl betupft—   1520
Da kommst du schon hervorgehupft!
Nur frisch ans Werk! Die Spitze, die mich bannte,
Sie sitzt ganz vornen an der Kante.
Noch einen Biß, so ist's geschehn.—
Nun, Fauste, träume fort, bis wir uns wiedersehn.

FAUST (*erwachend*).
Bin ich denn abermals betrogen?
Verschwindet so der geisterreiche Drang,
Daß mir ein Traum den Teufel vorgelogen,
Und daß ein Pudel mir entsprang?

STUDIERZIMMER

Faust, Mephistopheles.

FAUST.
Es klopft? Herein! Wer will mich wieder plagen?   1530
MEPHISTOPHELES.
Ich bin's.
FAUST.
      Herein!
MEPHISTOPHELES.
      Du mußt es dreimal sagen.
FAUST.
Herein denn!
MEPHISTOPHELES.
      So gefällst du mir.
Wir werden, hoff' ich, uns vertragen!
Denn dir die Grillen zu verjagen,
Bin ich als edler Junker hier,
In rotem, goldverbrämtem Kleide,
Das Mäntelchen von starrer Seide,
Die Hahnenfeder auf dem Hut,
Mit einem langen spitzen Degen,

The lord of rats, the lord of mice,
of flies and bedbugs, frogs and lice
commands you now to come into the open,
to gnaw away this bit of threshold timber
while he daubs it with a drop of oil—   1520
There—I see you scuttling out already!
Quick, to your task! The point that held me captive
is near the edge upon the outer angle.
Another bite—see, now it's done.
Now, Faust, dream on till next we meet again.

FAUST (*waking*).

Have I been cheated once again?
Do the vanished spirits prove no more
than that the devil was a dreamed-up counterfeit
and that a poodle ran away from me?

STUDY

Faust, Mephistopheles.

FAUST.

A knock? Come in! Who's plaguing me again?   1530

MEPHISTOPHELES.

It's I.

FAUST.

   Come in!

MEPHISTOPHELES.

      It must be said three times.

FAUST.

Come in then!

MEPHISTOPHELES.

      Now you please me better.
You and I shall get along, I hope.
For I have come a noble gentleman
that I may drive your doldrums out.
Observe my scarlet dress with golden trim,
the cloak of stiffened silk,
the rooster's feather in my hat,
the rapier hanging at my side.

Und rate nun dir, kurz und gut,   1540
Dergleichen gleichfalls anzulegen;
Damit du, losgebunden, frei,
Erfahrest, was das Leben sei.

FAUST.

In jedem Kleide werd' ich wohl die Pein
Des engen Erdelebens fühlen.
Ich bin zu alt, um nur zu spielen,
Zu jung, um ohne Wunsch zu sein.
Was kann die Welt mir wohl gewähren?
Entbehren sollst du! sollst entbehren!
Das ist der ewige Gesang,   1550
Der jedem an die Ohren klingt,
Den, unser ganzes Leben lang,
Uns heiser jede Stunde singt.
Nur mit Entsetzen wach' ich morgens auf,
Ich möchte bittre Tränen weinen,
Den Tag zu sehn, der mir in seinem Lauf
Nicht Einen Wunsch erfüllen wird, nicht E i n e n,
Der selbst die Ahnung jeder Lust
Mit eigensinnigem Krittel mindert,
Die Schöpfung meiner regen Brust   1560
Mit tausend Lebensfratzen hindert.
Auch muß ich, wenn die Nacht sich niedersenkt,
Mich ängstlich auf das Lager strecken;
Auch da wird keine Rast geschenkt,
Mich werden wilde Träume schrecken.
Der Gott, der mir im Busen wohnt,
Kann tief mein Innerstes erregen;
Der über allen meinen Kräften thront,
Er kann nach außen nichts bewegen;
Und so ist mir das Dasein eine Last,   1570
Der Tod erwünscht, das Leben mir verhaßt.

MEPHISTOPHELES.

Und doch ist nie der Tod ein ganz willkommner Gast.

FAUST.

O selig der, dem er im Siegesglanze
Die blut'gen Lorbeern um die Schläfe windet,
Den er, nach rasch durchrastem Tanze,

I now suggest, to make it brief,   1540
that you move in similar attire,
that you, without restraints and ties,
may learn what life is all about.

FAUST.

In every garment, I suppose, I'm bound to feel
the misery of earth's constricted life.
I am too old for mere amusement
and still too young to be without desire.
What has the world to offer me?
You must renounce! Renounce your wishes!
That is the never-ending litany   1550
which every man hears ringing in his ears,
which every hour hoarsely tolls
throughout the livelong day.
I awake with horror in the morning,
and bitter tears well up in me
when I must face each day that in its course
cannot fulfill a single wish, not *one*!
The very intimations of delight
are shattered by the carpings of the day
which foil the inventions of my eager soul   1560
with a thousand leering grimaces of life.
And when night begins to fall
I timidly recline upon my cot,
and even then I seek in vain for rest;
savage dreams come on to terrorize.
The god that lives within my bosom
can deeply stir my inmost core;
enthroned above my human powers,
He cannot move a single outward thing.
And so, to be is nothing but a burden;   1570
my life is odious and I long to die.

MEPHISTOPHELES.

But somehow death is never quite a welcome guest.

FAUST.

Oh, fortunate he for whom in victory's blaze
death binds bloody laurels on the brow
and whom he places in a maiden's arms

In eines Mädchens Armen findet!
O wär' ich vor des hohen Geistes Kraft
Entzückt, entseelt dahingesunken!

MEPHISTOPHELES.

Und doch hat jemand einen braunen Saft,
In jener Nacht, nicht ausgetrunken.　　　　　　1580

FAUST.

Das Spionieren, scheint's, ist deine Lust.

MEPHISTOPHELES.

Allwissend bin ich nicht; doch viel ist mir bewußt.

FAUST.

Wenn aus dem schrecklichen Gewühle
Ein süß bekannter Ton mich zog,
Den Rest von kindlichem Gefühle
Mit Anklang froher Zeit betrog,
So fluch' ich allem, was die Seele
Mit lock- und Gaukelwerk umspannt,
Und sie in diese Trauerhöhle
Mit Blend- und Schmeichelkräften bannt!　　　　1590
Verflucht voraus die hohe Meinung,
Womit der Geist sich selbst umfangt!
Verflucht das Blenden der Erscheinung,
Die sich an unsre Sinne drängt!
Verflucht, was uns in Träumen heuchelt,
Des Ruhms, der Namensdauer Trug!
Verflucht, was als Besitz uns schmeichelt,
Als Weib und Kind, als Knecht and Pflug!
Verflucht sei Mammon, wenn mit Schätzen
Er uns zu kühnen Taten regt,　　　　　　　　1600
Wenn er zu müßigem Ergetzen
Die Polster uns zurechtelegt!
Fluch sei dem Balsamsaft der Trauben!
Fluch jener höchsten Liebeshuld!
Fluch sei der Hoffnung! Fluch dem Glauben,
Und Fluch vor allen der Geduld!

GEISTERCHOR (*unsichtbar*).

　　　　　Weh! weh!
　　　　　Du hast sie zerstört,
　　　　　Die schöne Welt,

when the frenzied dance is over.
Oh, to have breathed my last and faded
exulting in the spirit's sway!

MEPHISTOPHELES.

Yet I know someone who in that night
did not quite drink a dark brown potion.   1580

FAUST.

It seems that spying is your specialty.

MEPHISTOPHELES.

I don't know everything, but I'm aware of much.

FAUST.

Ever since a sweet familiar note
drew me from my fearful bog
and deceived the remnants of my childlike faith
with allusions to a gladder day,
I curse all things that now entice my soul
with glittering toys and fantasies
and ensnare it in this cave of pain
with flattering hocus-pocus and with tinsel bait.   1590
I curse the high opinion, first of all,
with which the mind deludes itself!
I curse the glare of mere appearance
that presses hard upon our senses.
I curse the lies of our fondest dreams,
their promises of glory and of lasting fame!
I curse what flatters us as fine possessions,
wife and child, and serf and plow!
I curse Mammon and his golden treasures,
inciting us to daring enterprise,   1600
and all his silken cushions
on which to loll in pillowed ease.
My curse upon the blessings of the grape!
My curse on lovers' highest consummation!
My curse on Hope! My curse on Faith,
and my curse on Patience most of all!

CHORUS OF SPIRITS (*invisible*).

    Woe! Woe!
    You have destroyed
    The lovely world

Mit mächtiger Faust;   1610
Sie stürzt, sie zerfällt!
Ein Halbgott hat sie zerschlagen!
Wir tragen
Die Trümmern ins Nichts hinüber,
Und klagen
Über die verlorne Schöne.
Mächtiger
Der Erdensöhne,
Prächtiger
Baue sie wieder,   1620
In deinem Busen baue sie auf!
Neuen Lebenslauf
Beginne,
Mit hellem Sinne,
Und neue Lieder
Tönen darauf!

MEPHISTOPHELES.

Dies sind die Kleinen
Von den Meinen.
Höre, wie zu Lust und Taten
Altklug sie raten!   1630
In die Welt weit,
Aus der Einsamkeit,
Wo Sinnen und Säfte stocken,
Wollen sie dich locken.

Hör auf, mit deinem Gram zu spielen,
Der, wie ein Geier, dir am Leben frißt;
Die schlechteste Gesellschaft läßt dich fühlen,
Daß du ein Mensch mit Menschen bist.
Doch so ist's nicht gemeint,
Dich unter das Pack zu stoßen.   1640
Ich bin keiner von den Großen;
Doch willst du mit mir vereint
Deine Schritte durchs Leben nehmen,
So will ich mich gern bequemen,
Dein zu sein, auf der Stelle.
Ich bin dein Geselle,

With a heavy blow.   1610
It falls, it is shattered!
Smashed by a demigod's fist.
We carry the fragments
Into the Void,
And we bemoan
Beauty forlorn.
O mighty one
Of earthly sons,
Build it anew,
Build in your breast   1620
A brighter world!
Begin,
Begin once more
With senses purged!
Newer songs
Will sound for you.

MEPHISTOPHELES.

These are my little ones;
they belong to my tribe.
Mark their precocious counsel
to pleasure and action!   1630
They lure you away
into the open,
away from bitter solitude
where sense and juices clog.

Stop playing games with your affliction,
which like a vulture feeds upon your life.
The lowest company will yet allow
for you to be a full-fledged man among the rest.
But never fear, I do not wish
to throw you to the common pack.   1640
I am not really so great myself,
but if you travel at my side
and make your way through life with me,
then I shall do the best I can
to be your friend in need
and your traveling companion;

Und mach' ich dir's recht,
Bin ich dein Diener, bin dein Knecht!

FAUST.

Und was soll ich dagegen dir erfüllen?

MEPHISTOPHELES.

Dazu hast du noch eine lange Frist.   1650

FAUST.

Nein, nein! der Teufel ist ein Egoist
Und tut nicht leicht um Gottes willen,
Was einem andern nützlich ist.
Sprich die Bedingung deutlich aus;
Ein solcher Diener bringt Gefahr in Haus.

MEPHISTOPHELES.

Ich will mich h i e r zu deinem Dienst verbinden,
Auf deinen Wink nicht rasten und nicht ruhn;
Wenn wir uns d r ü b e n wiederfinden,
So sollst du mir das gleiche tun.

FAUST.

Das Drüben kann mich wenig kümmern;   1660
Schlägst du erst diese Welt zu Trümmern,
Die andre mag darnach entstehn.
Aus dieser Erde quillen meine Freuden,
Und diese Sonne scheinet meinen Leiden;
Kann ich mich erst von ihnen scheiden,
Dann mag, was will und kann, geschehn.
Davon will ich nichts weiter hören,
Ob man auch künftig haßt und liebt,
Und ob es auch in jenen Sphären
Ein Oben oder Unten gibt.   1670

MEPHISTOPHELES.

In diesem Sinne kannst du's wagen.
Verbinde dich; du sollst, in diesen Tagen,
Mit Freuden meine Künste sehn,
Ich gebe dir, was noch kein Mensch gesehn.

FAUST.

Was willst du armer Teufel geben?
Ward eines Menschen Geist, in seinem hohen Streben,
Von deinesgleichen je gefaßt?
Doch hast du Speise, die nicht sättigt, hast

And if I do things as you like,
you'll have me as your servant and your slave.

FAUST.

And in return, what do you ask of me?

MEPHISTOPHELES.

For that you still have ample time.   1650

FAUST.

No, no! The devil is an egoist
and does not easily, for heaven's sake,
do what is useful for another.
State clearly your conditions.
A servant of your kind is full of present danger.

MEPHISTOPHELES.

I pledge myself to serve you *here and now*;
the slightest hint will put me at your beck and call,
and if *beyond* we meet again,
you shall do the same for me.

FAUST.

With that *beyond* I scarcely bother.   1660
Once we smash this world to bits,
the other world may rise for all I care.
From this earth spring all my joys;
it's this sun which shines on all my sorrows.
Once I must take my leave of them,
then come what may, it is of no concern.
I wish to hear no more discussion
on whether love and hate persist forever,
or whether in those other spheres
the up and down be much like ours.   1670

MEPHISTOPHELES.

That's the spirit; take the risk.
Commit yourself to me and soon
you will enjoy some samples of my art.
I'll give you what no man has ever seen before.

FAUST.

What, poor devil, can you offer?
Was ever human spirit in its highest striving
comprehended by the like of you?
You offer food which does not satisfy,

Du rotes Gold, das ohne Rast,
Quecksilber gleich, dir in der Hand zerrinnt,   1680
Ein Spiel, bei dem man nie gewinnt,
Ein Mädchen, das an meiner Brust
Mit Äugeln schon dem Nachbar sich verbindet,
Der Ehre schöne Götterlust,
Die, wie ein Meteor, verschwindet?
Zeig mir die Frucht, die fault, eh' man sie bricht,
Und Bäume, die sich täglich neu begrünen!

MEPHISTOPHELES.
Ein solcher Auftrag schreckt mich nicht,
Mit solchen Schätzen kann ich dienen.
Doch, guter Freund, die Zeit kommt auch heran,   1690
Wo wir was Guts in Ruhe schmausen mögen.

FAUST.
Werd' ich beruhigt je mich auf ein Faulbett legen,
So sei es gleich um mich getan!
Kannst du mich schmeichelnd je belügen,
Daß ich mir selbst gefallen mag,
Kannst du mich mit Genuß betrügen,
Das sei für mich der letzte Tag!
Die Wette biet' ich!

MEPHISTOPHELES.
                    Topp!

FAUST.
                    Und Schlag auf Schlag!
Werd' ich zum Augenblicke sagen:
Verweile doch! du bist so schön!   1700
Dann magst du mich in Fesseln schlagen,
Dann will ich gern zugrunde gehn!
Dann mag die Totenglocke schallen,
Dann bist du deines Dienstes frei,
Die Uhr mag stehn, der Zeiger fallen,
Es sei die Zeit für mich vorbei!

MEPHISTOPHELES.
Bedenk es wohl, wir werden's nicht vergessen.

FAUST.
Dazu hast du ein volles Recht;
Ich habe mich nicht freventlich vermessen.

red gold which moves unsteadily,
quicksilver-like between one's fingers.   1680
You offer sports where no one gains the prize,
a girl perhaps who in my very arms
hangs on another with conspiring eyes.
Honors that the world bestows on man
which vanish like a shooting star.
Show me the fruit that rots before it's plucked
and trees that grow their greenery anew each day!

MEPHISTOPHELES.

A project of this nature does not trouble me.
I know I can produce such treasures.
But there will come a time, my friend,   1690
when we shall want to feast at our leisure.

FAUST.

If you should ever find me lolling on a bed of ease,
let me be done for on the spot!
If you ever lure me with your lying flatteries,
and I find satisfaction in myself,
if you bamboozle me with pleasure,
then let this be my final day!
This bet I offer you![18]

MEPHISTOPHELES.

                    Agreed!

FAUST.

                    Let's shake on it!

If ever I should tell the moment:
Oh, stay! You are so beautiful!   1700
Then you may cast me into chains,
then I shall smile upon perdition!
Then may the hour toll for me,
then you are free to leave my service.
The clock may halt, the clock hand fall,
and time come to an end for me!

MEPHISTOPHELES.

Weigh it thoroughly; we shall not forget.

FAUST.

You have a perfect right to this;
this is no rash or headlong action.

[handwritten marginal notes:] "if I'm ever content or complascent then 'let me die." life = experience + growth STRIVE!!

Wie ich beharre, bin ich Knecht,   1710
Ob dein, was frag' ich, oder wessen.

MEPHISTOPHELES.

Ich werde heute gleich, beim Doktorschmaus,
Als Diener, meine Pflicht erfüllen.
Nur eins!—Um Lebens oder Sterbens willen
Bitt' ich mir ein paar Zeilen aus.

FAUST.

Auch was Geschriebnes forderst du Pedant?
Hast du noch keinen Mann, nicht Manneswort gekannt?
Ist's nicht genug, daß mein gesprochnes Wort
Auf ewig soll mit meinen Tagen schalten?
Rast nicht die Welt in allen Strömen fort,   1720
Und mich soll ein Versprechen halten?
Doch dieser Wahn ist uns ins Herz gelegt,
Wer mag sich gern davon befreien?
Beglückt, wer Treue rein im Busen trägt,
Kein Opfer wird ihn je gereuen!
Allein ein Pergament, beschrieben und beprägt,
Ist ein Gespenst, vor dem sich alle scheuen.
Das Wort erstirbt schon in der Feder,
Die Herrschaft führen Wachs und Leder.
Was willst du böser Geist von mir?   1730
Erz, Marmor, Pergament, Papier?
Soll ich mit Griffel, Meißel, Feder schreiben?
Ich gebe jede Wahl dir frei.

MEPHISTOPHELES.

Wie magst du deine Rednerei
Nur gleich so hitzig übertreiben?
Ist doch ein jedes Blättchen gut.
Du unterzeichnest dich mit einem Tröpfchen Blut.

FAUST.

Wenn dies dir völlig G'nüge tut,
So mag es bei der Fratze bleiben.

MEPHISTOPHELES.

Blut ist ein ganz besondrer Saft.   1740

FAUST.

Nur keine Furcht, daß ich dies Bündnis breche!
Das Streben meiner ganzen Kraft

Such as I am, I am a slave—   1710
of yours or whosesoever is of no concern.

MEPHISTOPHELES.

This evening, promptly, at the scholar's table
I shall perform my duty as your servant.
But one thing more . . . for all contingencies
I must ask you for a line or two.

FAUST.

The pedant wants a legal document!
Have you never known a man who keeps his word?
Is it not enough that what I speak
shall govern all my living days?
Does not the world race by in tides and streams?   1720
And why should I be shackled by a promise?
It's a deep-engrained delusion,
we do not easily part with it.
Blessed is he who keeps his own integrity;
he will not rue the greatest sacrifice!
A skin inscribed and stamped officially
is like a specter to be feared and best avoided.
The word is dead before it leaves the pen,
and wax and leather rule the day.
What do you, evil spirit, want of me?   1730
Metal, marble, parchment, paper?
Shall I write with stylus, chisel, pen?
Feel free to exercise your option.

MEPHISTOPHELES.

Why is your talk so full of heat,
your eloquence so overwrought?
Any scrap will serve me well enough.
You simply sign it with a droplet of your blood.

FAUST.

If you are fully satisfied with that,
by all means, let us play the farce.

MEPHISTOPHELES.

Blood is a very special juice.   1740

FAUST.

Be not afraid that I might break this pact!
The sum and essence of my striving

Ist grade das, was ich verspreche.
Ich habe mich zu hoch gebläht,
In deinen Rang gehör' ich nur.
Der große Geist hat mich verschmäht,
Vor mir verschließt sich die Natur.
Des Denkens Faden ist zerrissen,
Mir ekelt lange vor allem Wissen.
Laß in den Tiefen der Sinnlichkeit   1750
Uns glühende Leidenschaften stillen!
In undurchdrungnen Zauberhüllen
Sei jedes Wunder gleich bereit!
Stürzen wir uns in das Rauschen der Zeit,
Ins Rollen der Begebenheit!
Da mag denn Schmerz und Genuß,
Gelingen und Verdruß
Mit einander wechseln, wie es kann;
Nur rastlos betätigt sich der Mann.

MEPHISTOPHELES.

Euch ist kein Maß und Ziel gesetzt.   1760
Beliebt's Euch, überall zu naschen,
Im Fliehen etwas zu erhaschen,
Bekomm' Euch wohl, was Euch ergetzt.
Nur greift mir zu und seid nicht blöde!

FAUST.

Du hörest ja, von Freud' ist nicht die Rede.
Dem Taumel weih' ich mich, dem schmerzlichsten Genuß,
Verliebtem Haß, erquickendem Verdruß.
Mein Busen, der vom Wissensdrang geheilt ist,
Soll keinen Schmerzen künftig sich verschließen,
Und was der ganzen Menschheit zugeteilt ist,   1770
Will ich in meinem innern Selbst genießen,
Mit meinem Geist das Höchst' und Tiefste greifen,
Ihr Wohl und Weh auf meinen Busen häufen,
Und so mein eigen Selbst zu ihrem Selbst erweitern,
Und, wie sie selbst, am End' auch ich zerscheitern.

MEPHISTOPHELES.

O glaube mir, der manche tausend Jahre
And dieser harten Speise kaut,
Daß von der Wiege bis zur Bahre

is the very thing I promise you.
I had become too overblown,
while actually I only rank with you.
Ever since the mighty spirit turned from me,
Nature kept her doorway closed.
The threads of thought are torn to pieces,
and learning has become repugnant.
Let in the throes of raging senses   1750
seething passions quench my thirst!
In never lifted magic veils
let every miracle take form!
Let me plunge into the rush of passing time,
into the rolling tide of circumstance!
Then let sorrow and delight,
frustration or success,
occur in turn as happenstance;
restless action is the state of man.

MEPHISTOPHELES.

For you there is no boundary nor measure.   1760
As you are pleased to grasp at what you can
and, flitting by, to see what you can get,
I hope your pleasures may agree with you.
But start at once and don't be shy!

FAUST.

I told you, I am not concerned with pleasure.
I crave corrosive joy and dissipation,
enamored hate and quickening despair.
My breast no longer thirsts for knowledge
and will welcome grief and pain.
Whatever is the lot of humankind   1770
I want to taste within my deepest self.
I want to seize the highest and the lowest,
to load its woe and bliss upon my breast,
and thus expand my single self titanically
and in the end, go down with all the rest.

MEPHISTOPHELES.

Believe you him who now for some millennia
has chewed this tough and wretched fare,
that from the cradle to the bier

Kein Mensch den alten Sauerteig verdaut!
Glaub unsereinem: dieses Ganze   1780
Ist nur für einen Gott gemacht!
Er findet sich in einem ew'gen Glanze,
Uns hat er in die Finsternis gebracht,
Und euch taugt einzig Tag und Nacht.

FAUST.

Allein ich will!

MEPHISTOPHELES.

Das läßt sich hören!
Doch nur vor einem ist mir bang:
Die Zeit ist kurz, die Kunst ist lang.
Ich dächt', Ihr ließet Euch belehren.
Assoziiert Euch mit einem Poeten,
Laßt den Herrn in Gedanken schweifen,   1790
Und alle edlen Qualitäten
Auf Euren Ehrenscheitel häufen,
Des Löwen Mut,
Des Hirsches Schnelligkeit,
Des Italieners feurig Blut,
Des Nordens Dau'rbarkeit.
Laßt ihn Euch das Geheimnis finden,
Großmut und Arglist zu verbinden,
Und Euch, mit warmen Jugendtrieben,
Nach einem Plane zu verlieben.   1800
Möchte selbst solch einen Herren kennen,
Würd' ihn Herrn Mikrokosmus nennen.

FAUST.

Was bin ich denn, wenn es nicht möglich ist,
Der Menschheit Krone zu erringen,
Nach der sich alle Sinne dringen?

MEPHISTOPHELES.

Du bist am Ende—was du bist.
Setz dir Perücken auf von Millionen Locken,
Setz deinen Fuß auf ellenhohe Socken,
Du bleibst doch immer, was du bist.

FAUST.

Ich fühl's, vergebens hab' ich alle Schätze   1810
Des Menschengeists auf mich herbeigerafft,

no man digests the ancient dough!
Believe the likes of me: the single whole   1780
was fashioned for a god alone,
who dwells in everlasting, radiant glow
and relegated us to darkness;
and you must content yourselves with day and night.

FAUST.
I am determined though.

MEPHISTOPHELES.
                          Splendid words, for sure!
However, one thing worries me:
Art is long and time is fleeting.
It occurs to me that you might yet be taught.
Make your alliance with a poet,
and let that gentleman think lofty thoughts,   1790
and let him heap the noblest qualities
upon your worthy head:
a lion's nerve,
a stag's rapidity,
the fiery blood of Italy,
the constancy of northern man.
Then let him find the secret mortar
to combine nobility of soul with guile
and show you how to love with youthful fervor,
according to a balanced plan.   1800
I'd like myself to meet with such a person,
whom I would greet as Mr. Microcosm.

FAUST.
What am I, if I can never hope
to hold the crown of my humanity
which is the aim of all my senses?

MEPHISTOPHELES.
You are—all things considered—what you are.
Put on a wig with myriad curls,
stalk about on foot-high stilts,
still what you are, you always must remain.

FAUST.
I feel it, I have hoarded all the treasures,   1810
the wealth of human intellect, in vain;

Und wenn ich mich am Ende niedersetze,
Quillt innerlich doch keine neue Kraft;
Ich bin nicht um ein Haar breit höher,
Bin dem Unendlichen nicht näher.

MEPHISTOPHELES.
   Mein guter Herr, Ihr seht die Sachen,
Wie man die Sachen eben sieht;
Wir müssen das gescheiter machen,
Eh' uns des Lebens Freude flieht.
Was Henker! freilich Händ' und Füße   1820
Und Kopf und H ——, die sind dein;
Doch alles, was ich frisch genieße,
Ist das drum weniger mein?
Wenn ich sechs Hengste zahlen kann,
Sind ihre Kräfte nicht die meine?
Ich renne zu und bin ein rechter Mann,
Als hätt' ich vierundzwanzig Beine.
Drum frisch! Laß alles Sinnen sein,
Und grad' mit in die Welt hinein!
Ich sag' es dir: ein Kerl, der spekuliert,   1830
Ist wie ein Tier, auf dürrer Heide
Von einem bösen Geist im Kreis herumgeführt,
Und rings umher liegt schöne grüne Weide.

FAUST.
   Wie fangen wir das an?

MEPHISTOPHELES.
                   Wir gehen eben fort.
Was ist das für ein Marterort?
Was heißt das für ein Leben führen,
Sich und die Jungens ennuyieren?
Laß du das dem Herrn Nachbar Wanst!
Was willst du dich das Stroh zu dreschen plagen?
Das Beste, was du wissen kannst,   1840
Darfst du den Buben doch nicht sagen.
Gleich hör' ich einen auf dem Gange!

FAUST.
   Mir ist's nicht möglich, ihn zu sehn.

MEPHISTOPHELES.
   Der arme Knabe wartet lange,

when at last I sit and ponder in my chair,
no fresh strength wells up within.
I am no hairbreadth taller than I was
nor any closer to infinity.

MEPHISTOPHELES.
Good sir, you clearly look upon these things
the way such things are usually looked upon;
we'll have to find a shrewder method
and not wait until the joys of living flee.
Who gives a damn! One's hands and feet and toes,   1820
one's head and bottom are one's own,
but if I seize and feel an alien thrill,
does it belong the less to me?
If I can buy six stallions for my stable,
is not then their strength my own?
I race along, I am a splendid specimen
as if two dozen legs were mine.
Go to it then! Leave off your ruminations,
and go with me into the teeming world!
To waste your time in idle speculation   1830
is acting like a beast that's driven in a circle
by evil spirits on an arid moor
while all about lie fair and verdant fields.

FAUST.
How shall we begin?

MEPHISTOPHELES.
                     We simply go away.
What kind of torture chamber is this place?
What kind of life is this you lead—
a bore for you, a nuisance for your pupils.
Go, leave that to the boob next door.
Why should you plague yourself with threshing straw?
The best of what you hope to know   1840
is something that you cannot tell the youngsters.
There—I hear one coming up the corridor.

FAUST.
I cannot bring myself to see him now.

MEPHISTOPHELES.
The boy has waited long and patiently;

Der darf nicht ungetröstet gehn.
Komm, gib mir deinen Rock und Mütze;
Die Maske muß mir köstlich stehn.
    (*Er kleidet sich um.*)
Nun überlaß es meinem Witze!
Ich brauche nur ein Viertelstündchen Zeit;
Indessen mache dich zur schönen Fahrt bereit!   1850
                              (FAUST *ab.*)
MEPHISTOPHELES (*in* FAUST *langem Kleide*).
Verachte nur Vernunft und Wissenschaft,
Des Menschen allerhöchste Kraft,
Laß nur in Blend- und Zauberwerken
Dich von dem Lügengeist bestärken,
So hab' ich dich schon unbedingt—
Ihm hat das Schicksal einen Geist gegeben,
Der ungebändigt immer vorwärts dringt,
Und dessen übereiltes Streben
Der Erde Freuden überspringt.
Den schlepp' ich durch das wilde Leben,   1860
Durch flache Unbedeutenheit,
Er soll mir zappeln, starren, kleben,
Und seiner Unersättlichkeit
Soll Speis' und Trank vor gier'gen Lippen schweben;
Er wird Erquickung sich umsonst erflehn,
Und hätt' er sich auch nicht dem Teufel übergeben,
Er müßte doch zugrunde gehn!
    (*Ein* SCHÜLER *tritt auf.*)
SCHÜLER.
Ich bin allhier erst kurze Zeit,
Und komme voll Ergebenheit,
Einen Mann zu sprechen und zu kennen,   1870
Den alle mir mit Ehrfurcht nennen.
MEPHISTOPHELES.
Eure Höflichkeit erfreut mich sehr!
Ihr seht einen Mann wie andre mehr.
Habt Ihr Euch sonst schon umgetan?
SCHÜLER.
Ich bitt' Euch, nehmt Euch meiner an!
Ich komme mit allem guten Mut,

he must not leave unsatisfied.
Quickly, let me take your cap and gown.
It should suit my person handsomely.
   (*He changes his clothes.*)
Now trust my wit to handle matters"
in no more than fifteen minutes' time.
Meanwhile, prepare for our trip together.   1850
                              (*Exit* FAUST.)

MEPHISTOPHELES (*in* FAUST's *gown*).
   If once you scorn all science and all reason,
   the highest strength that dwells in man,
   and through trickery and magic arts
   abet the spirit of dishonesty,
   then I've got you unconditionally—
   then destiny endowed him with a spirit
   that hastens forward, unrestrained,
   whose fierce and over-hasty drive
   leapfrogs headlong over earthly pleasures.
   I'll drag him through the savage life,   1860
   through the wasteland of mediocrity.
   Let him wriggle, stiffen, wade through slime,
   let food and drink be dangled by his lips
   to bait his hot, insatiate appetite.
   He will vainly cry for satisfaction,
   and had he not by then become the devil's,
   he still would perish miserably.
      (*A* STUDENT *enters.*)

STUDENT.
   I am only newly here.
   I am full of humble expectation
   to greet and stand before the man   1870
   whose name all speak with veneration.

MEPHISTOPHELES.
   You please me by your courtesy!
   You see a man like many another.
   Have you not cast about elsewhere?

STUDENT.
   I beg you, sir, to take me on!
   I have come here so full of fervor,

Leidlichem Geld und frischem Blut;
Meine Mutter wollte mich kaum entfernen;
Möchte gern was Rechts hieraußen lernen.

MEPHISTOPHELES.

Da seid Ihr eben recht am Ort.   1880

SCHÜLER.

Aufrichtig, möchte schon wieder fort:
In diesen Mauern, diesen Hallen
Will es mir keineswegs gefallen.
Es ist ein gar beschränkter Raum,
Man sieht nichts Grünes, keinen Baum,
Und in den Sälen auf den Bänken
Vergeht mir Hören, Sehn und Denken.

MEPHISTOPHELES.

Das kommt nur auf Gewohnheit an.
So nimmt ein Kind der Mutter Brust
Nicht gleich im Anfang willig an,   1890
Doch bald ernährt es sich mit Lust.
So wird's Euch an der Weisheit Brüsten
Mit jedem Tage mehr gelüsten.

SCHÜLER.

An ihrem Hals will ich mit Freuden hangen;
Doch sagt mir nur, wie kann ich hingelangen?

MEPHISTOPHELES.

Erklärt Euch, eh' Ihr weiter geht,
Was wählt Ihr für eine Fakultät?

SCHÜLER.

Ich wünschte recht gelehrt zu werden,
Und möchte gern, was auf der Erden
Und in dem Himmel ist, erfassen,   1900
Die Wissenschaft und die Natur.

MEPHISTOPHELES.

Da seid Ihr auf der rechten Spur;
Doch müßt Ihr Euch nicht zerstreuen lassen.

SCHÜLER.

Ich bin dabei mit Seel' und Leib;
Doch freilich würde mir behagen
Ein wenig Freiheit und Zeitvertreib
An schönen Sommerfeiertagen.

with pulsing blood and a supply of money.
My mother found it hard to let me go,
but I am out to gain some useful knowledge.

MEPHISTOPHELES.

Well yes, this is the very place for you to be.   1880

STUDENT.

To tell the truth, I want to run away already:
within these walls and corridors
I feel no cheer or happiness at all.
The air is close and heavy;
there is no glimpse of shrubbery or trees,
and in the lecture hall and on the benches
I'm frightened out of all my senses.

MEPHISTOPHELES.

You are not yet acclimated.
Just as a child does not at first
accept its mother's breast quite willingly,   1890
but soon imbibes its nourishment with zest,
you will feel a growing lust
when clinging to high wisdom's bosom.

STUDENT.

I will clasp her neck with great delight.
But tell me, please, how I may reach that goal?

MEPHISTOPHELES.

You must declare before proceeding
what special faculty you choose.

STUDENT.

I want to be a really learned man,
would like to comprehend
what is on earth and up in heaven,   1900
the things of nature and of science.

MEPHISTOPHELES.

I'm glad to say you're on the proper trail,
but be careful not to be distracted.

STUDENT.

I'm with it with my heart and soul;
but I should also like, if possible,
some time for play and entertainment
on lovely summer holidays.

MEPHISTOPHELES.

Gebraucht der Zeit, sie geht so schnell von hinnen,
Doch Ordnung lehrt Euch Zeit gewinnen.
Mein teurer Freund, ich rat' Euch drum   1910
Zuerst Collegium Logicum.
Da wird der Geist Euch wohl dressiert,
In spanische Stiefeln eingeschnürt,
Daß er bedächtiger so fortan
Hinschleiche die Gedankenbahn,
Und nicht etwa, die Kreuz und Quer,
Irrlichteliere hin und her.
Dann lehret man Euch manchen Tag,
Daß, was Ihr sonst auf einen Schlag
Getrieben, wie Essen und Trinken frei,   1920
Eins! Zwei! Drei! dazu nötig sei.
Zwar ist's mit der Gedankenfabrik
Wie mit einem Weber-Meisterstück,
Wo e i n Tritt tausend Fäden regt,
Die Schifflein herüber hinüber schießen,
Die Fäden ungesehen fließen,
E i n Schlag tausend Verbindungen schlägt:
Der Philosoph, der tritt herein
Und beweist Euch, es müßt' so sein:
Das Erst' wär so, das Zweite so,   1930
Und drum das Dritt' und Vierte so,
Und wenn das Erst' und Zweit' nicht wär',
Das Dritt' und Viert' wär' nimmermehr.
Das preisen die Schüler aller Orten,
Sind aber keine Weber geworden.
Wer will was Lebendigs erkennen und beschreiben,
Sucht erst den Geist heraus zu treiben,
Dann hat er die Teile in seiner Hand,
Fehlt leider! nur das geistige Band.
Encheiresin naturae nennt's die Chemie,   1940
Spottet ihrer selbst und weiß nicht wie.

SCHÜLER.

Kann Euch nicht eben ganz verstehen.

MEPHISTOPHELES.

Das wird nächstens schon besser gehen,

MEPHISTOPHELES.

Make use of time, it flits away so fast;
though you can save it by economy;
wherefore, my worthy friend, I counsel you   1910
to register in Logic first of all,
so your spirit will be neatly drilled
and tightly laced in Spanish boots;[19]
and thus, along its winding path,
the thought will creep henceforth more circumspect,
instead of skipping to and fro,
and back and forth like a will-o'-the-wisp;
and you will labor many days
on what you once performed summarily—
just as you ate and drank without constraint   1920
you'll do it now by "one!" and "two!" and "three!"
by sheer necessity. The living factory of thought
is like a master weaver's masterpiece,
where one treadle plies a thousand strands,
the shuttles shoot this way and that,
the quivering threads flow unobserved,
one stroke effects a thousand ties.
But now philosophy comes in
and proves it never could be otherwise.
If One is thus and Two is so,   1930
then Three and Four must needs be so,
and if the first and second had not been,
the third and fourth could not occur.
All this is praised by students everywhere;
though none has yet become a weaver.
Who wants to see and circumscribe a living thing
must first expel the living spirit,
for then he has the separate parts in hand.
Too bad! the spirit's bond is missing.
The chemists call it *Encheiresis Naturae*[20]   1940
and know not how they mock themselves.

STUDENT.

Forgive me, sir, I don't quite understand.

MEPHISTOPHELES.

It will come easier by and by

Wenn Ihr lernt alles reduzieren
Und gehörig klassifizieren.

SCHÜLER.

Mir wird von alle dem so dumm,
Als ging' mir ein Mühlrad im Kopf herum.

MEPHISTOPHELES.

Nachher, vor allen andern Sachen,
Müßt Ihr Euch an die Metaphysik machen!
Da seht, daß Ihr tiefsinnig faßt,   1950
Was in des Menschen Hirn nicht paßt;
Für was drein geht und nicht drein geht,
Ein prächtig Wort zu Diensten steht.
Doch vorerst dieses halbe Jahr
Nehmt ja der besten Ordnung wahr.
Fünf Stunden habt Ihr jeden Tag;
Seid drinnen mit dem Glockenschlag!
Habt Euch vorher wohl präpariert,
Paragraphos wohl einstudiert,
Damit Ihr nachher besser seht,   1960
Daß er nichts sagt, als was im Buche steht;
Doch Euch des Schreibens ja befleißt,
Als diktiert' Euch der Heilig' Geist!

SCHÜLER.

Das sollt Ihr mir nicht zweimal sagen!
Ich denke mir, wie viel es nützt;
Denn, was man schwarz auf weiß besitzt,
Kann man getrost nach Hause tragen.

MEPHISTOPHELES.

Doch wählt mir eine Fakultät!

SCHÜLER.

Zur Rechtsgelehrsamkeit kann ich mich nicht bequemen.

MEPHISTOPHELES.

Ich kann es Euch so sehr nicht übel nehmen,   1970
Ich weiß, wie es um diese Lehre steht.
Es erben sich Gesetz' und Rechte
Wie eine ew'ge Krankheit fort,
Sie schleppen von Geschlecht sich zum Geschlechte
Und rücken sacht von Ort zu Ort.

when you learn how to reduce
and duly classify all things.

STUDENT.

I feel so dizzy in my head,
as if a millstone ground within.

MEPHISTOPHELES.

And then, before you move to other disciplines,
you must first tackle metaphysics
and see with due profundity the things   1950
beyond the compass of the mind.
And for whatever will or will not fit,
a splendid word will serve for all contingencies.
But while you're here this first semester,
conform to strict punctuality.
Every day you have to take five hours,
and when each hour strikes, be present!
Come in prepared well in advance,
all paragraphs well memorized,
so you can see that only what stands written   1960
is spoken from the lectern's height.
Be sure to write each thing that's said
as though the Holy Ghost dictated.

STUDENT.

No need for more reminders, sir;
I can tell how helpful this will be;
what one has down in black and white
one can carry home contentedly.

MEPHISTOPHELES.

But you must choose an academic discipline!

STUDENT.

I feel no call to jurisprudence.

MEPHISTOPHELES.

In this I cannot find much blame;   1970
I'm well acquainted with that discipline,
whose laws and statutes are transmitted
like a never ending pestilence.
Laws drag on from old to newer generations
and creep about from place to place.

Vernunft wird Unsinn, Wohltat Plage;

Weh dir, daß du ein Enkel bist!
Vom Rechte, das mit uns geboren ist,
Von dem ist leider! nie die Frage.

SCHÜLER.

Mein Abscheu wird durch Euch vermehrt,　　　　1980
O glücklich der, den Ihr belehrt!
Fast möcht' ich nun Theologie studieren.

MEPHISTOPHELES.

Ich wünschte nicht, Euch irre zu führen.
Was diese Wissenschaft betrifft,
Es ist so schwer, den falschen Weg zu meiden,
Es liegt in ihr so viel verborgnes Gift,
Und von der Arzenei ist's kaum zu unterscheiden.
Am besten ist's auch hier, wenn Ihr nur E i n e n hört,
Und auf des Meisters Worte schwört.
Im ganzen—haltet Euch an Worte!　　　　1990
Dann geht Ihr durch die sichre Pforte
Zum Tempel der Gewißheit ein.

SCHÜLER.

Doch ein Begriff muß bei dem Worte sein.

MEPHISTOPHELES.

Schon gut! Nur muß man sich nicht allzu ängstlich quälen;
Denn eben wo Begriffe fehlen,
Da stellt ein Wort zur rechten Zeit sich ein.
Mit Worten läßt sich trefflich streiten,
Mit Worten ein System bereiten,
An Worte läßt sich trefflich glauben,
Von einem Wort läßt sich kein Jota rauben.　　　　2000

SCHÜLER.

Verzeiht, ich halt' Euch auf mit vielen Fragen,
Allein ich muß Euch noch bemühn.
Wollt Ihr mir von der Medizin
Nicht auch ein kräftig Wörtchen sagen?
Drei Jahr' ist eine kurze Zeit,
Und, Gott! das Feld ist gar zu weit.
Wenn man einen Fingerzeig nur hat,
Läßt sich's schon eher weiter fühlen.

Good sense is foolishness, and
    human decency plague.
Alas, my boy, you will inherit this!
Too bad that of our natural inborn gifts
there's never any question.

STUDENT.

You have increased my own distaste.   1980
Oh, lucky he who's taught by you!
I now feel strongly tempted by theology.

MEPHISTOPHELES.

I do not wish to see you go astray.
For as concerns this science,
it's very hard to shun a false direction.
There lurk in it great quantities of hidden poison,
so hard to tell from proper medicine.
You'll find it best to listen to a single Master,
and swear by each and every word he says.
In general—put all your faith in words,   1990
for then you will securely pass the gate
into the temple-halls of certainty.

STUDENT.

But each word, I think, should harbor some idea.

MEPHISTOPHELES.

Yes, yes indeed. But don't torment yourself too much,
because precisely where no thought is present
a word appears in proper time.
Words are priceless in an argument.
Words are building stones of systems.
It's splendid to believe in words;
from words you cannot rob a single letter.   2000

STUDENT.

Forgive me if I ask so many questions,
but I must trouble you still more.
Would you be kind enough to say to me
a pithy word concerning medicine?
Three years is not too long a time to study,
and, my God! the field appears so broad to me.
If one could only get some pointers,
it would be easier to grope one's way ahead.

MEPHISTOPHELES (*für sich*).

Ich bin des trocknen Tons nun satt,
Muß wieder recht den Teufel spielen.   2010
   (*Laut.*)
Der Geist der Medizin ist leicht zu fassen;
Ihr durchstudiert die groß' und kleine Welt,
Um es am Ende gehn zu lassen,
Wie's Gott gefällt.
Vergebens, daß Ihr ringsum wissenschaftlich schweift,
Ein jeder lernt nur, was er lernen kann;
Doch der den Augenblick ergreift,
Das ist der rechte Mann.
Ihr seid noch ziemlich wohl gebaut,
An Kühnheit wird's Euch auch nicht fehlen,   2020
Und wenn Ihr Euch nur selbst vertraut,
Vertrauen Euch die andern Seelen.
Besonders lernt die Weiber führen;
Es ist ihr ewig Weh und Ach
So tausendfach
Aus e i n e m Punkte zu kurieren,
Und wenn Ihr halbweg ehrbar tut,
Dann habt Ihr sie all' unterm Hut.
Ein Titel muß sie erst vertraulich machen,
Daß Eure Kunst viel Künste übersteigt;   2030
Zum Willkomm tappt Ihr dann nach allen Siebensachen,
Um die ein andrer viele Jahre streicht,
Versteht das Pülslein wohl zu drücken,
Und fasset sie, mit feurig schlauen Blicken,
Wohl um die schlanke Hüfte frei,
Zu sehn, wie fest geschnürt sie sei.

SCHÜLER.

Das sieht schon besser aus! Man sieht doch, wo und wie.

MEPHISTOPHELES.

Grau, teurer Freund, ist alle Theorie,
Und grün des Lebens goldner Baum.

SCHÜLER.

Ich schwör' Euch zu, mir ist's als wie ein Traum.   2040
Dürft' ich Euch wohl ein andermal beschweren,
Von Eurer Weisheit auf den Grund zu hören?

MEPHISTOPHELES (*aside*).

    Now I'm tired of this arid style;

    I must play the devil once again.   2010

      (*Aloud.*)

    To grasp the gist of medicine is easy;

    you study through the great and little world,

    in order in the end to let things be

    exactly as the Lord desires.

    In vain, that scientific rambling everywhere,

    each one of us will learn what he can learn, no more.

    But he who takes the moment by the tail,

    he proves himself the man of the hour.

    You have a laudable physique

    and virile daring in your blood.   2020

    If you will simply trust yourself,

    the other souls will trust in you.

    And learn to lead the ladies specially;

    their eternal "woes!" and "oh's!"

    are cured a thousandfold

    by working from a single spot.

    And if you have a halfway honorable air,

    they'll soon be safely in your pocket.

    Your title first must gain their confidence

    and make your name superior and bright.   2030

    You begin by touching all her tender points,

    around the which another may have roved for years,

    and learn to press her pulse with gentle care

    and then with fiery, understanding glances

    place your arm about her slender hip

    to see how tightly she is laced.

STUDENT.

    I like that better. One can see the wheres and hows.

MEPHISTOPHELES.

    Gray, my friend, is every theory,

    and green alone life's golden tree.

STUDENT.

    I swear to you I feel as if I'm dreaming.   2040

    Could I perhaps impose on you again

    and drink more deeply from your wisdom?

MEPHISTOPHELES.

Was ich vermag, soll gern geschehn.

SCHÜLER.

Ich kann unmöglich wieder gehn,
Ich muß Euch noch mein Stammbuch überreichen.
Gönn' Eure Gunst mir dieses Zeichen!

MEPHISTOPHELES.

Sehr wohl.

(*Er schreibt und gibt's.*)

SCHÜLER (*liest*).

Eritis sicut Deus, scientes bonum et malum.

(*Macht's ehrerbietig zu und empfiehlt sich.*)

MEPHISTOPHELES.

Folg' nur dem alten Spruch und meiner Muhme, der
    Schlange,
Dir wird gewiß einmal bei deiner Gottähnlichkeit
    bange!   2050

(*FAUST tritt auf.*)

FAUST.

Wohin soll es nun gehn?

MEPHISTOPHELES.

                        Wohin es dir gefällt.
Wir sehn die kleine, dann die große Welt.
Mit welcher Freude, welchem Nutzen
Wirst du den Cursum durchschmarutzen!

FAUST.

Allein bei meinem langen Bart
Fehlt mir die leichte Lebensart.
Es wird mir der Versuch nicht glücken;
Ich wußte nie mich in die Welt zu schicken.
Vor andern fühl' ich mich so klein;
Ich werde stets verlegen sein.   2060

MEPHISTOPHELES.

Mein guter Freund, das wird sich alles geben;
Sobald du dir vertraust, sobald weißt du zu leben.

FAUST.

Wie kommen wir denn aus dem Haus?
Wo hast du Pferde, Knecht und Wagen?

MEPHISTOPHELES.

 I shall be pleased to help you where I can.

STUDENT.

 It is impossible for me to leave
 before you see my book of autographs.
 Grant me the favor of a line from you.

MEPHISTOPHELES.

 Very well.
   (*He writes in the book and returns it.*)

STUDENT (*reads*).

 Eritis sicut Deus, scientes bonum et malum.[21]
   (*Closes the book reverently and withdraws.*)

MEPHISTOPHELES.

 Follow the ancient words and also my cousin the snake.
 That godlike spark in you will have you quaking soon
       enough.   2050
   (FAUST *enters.*)

FAUST.

 Where do we go from here?

MEPHISTOPHELES.

                                    Anywhere you please.
 We'll see the small world, then the great.
 With what profit and what pleasure
 you will sponge through this curriculum!

FAUST.

 With this flowing beard of mine
 I lack that easy, graceful manner.
 My experiment will be a failure.
 I never was at ease with other people,
 they make me feel so small
 and continually embarrassed.   2060

MEPHISTOPHELES.

 My friend, all that will finally subside.
 Trust yourself and life will go your way.

FAUST.

 In what manner do we leave this house?
 Where are the horses, coach, and stable boys?

MEPHISTOPHELES.

Wir breiten nur den Mantel aus,
Der soll uns durch die Lüfte tragen.
Du nimmst bei diesem kühnen Schritt
Nur keinen großen Bündel mit.
Ein bißchen Feuerluft, die ich bereiten werde,
Hebt uns behend von dieser Erde.   2070
Und sind wir leicht, so geht es schnell hinauf;
Ich gratuliere dir zum neuen Lebenslauf!

AUERBACHS KELLER IN LEIPZIG

Zeche lustiger Gesellen.

FROSCH.

Will keiner trinken? keiner lachen?
Ich will euch lehren Gesichter machen!
Ihr seid ja heut wie nasses Stroh,
Und brennt sonst immer lichterloh.

BRANDER.

Das liegt an dir; du bringst ja nichts herbei,
Nicht eine Dummheit, keine Sauerei.

FROSCH (*gießt ihm ein Glas Wein über den Kopf*).

Da hast du beides!

BRANDER.

Doppelt Schwein!

FROSCH.

Ihr wollt es ja, man soll es sein!   2080

SIEBEL.

Zur Tür hinaus, wer sich entzweit!
Mit offner Brust singt Runda, sauft und schreit!
Auf! Holla! Ho!

ALTMAYER.

Weh mir, ich bin verloren!
Baumwolle her! der Kerl sprengt mir die Ohren.

SIEBEL.

Wenn das Gewölbe widerschallt,
Fühlt man erst recht des Basses Grundgewalt.

MEPHISTOPHELES.
  We merely need to spread this mantle,
  which shall bear us through the atmosphere.
  Be sure that for this daring journey
  you only take the lightest bundle.
  A little fiery air that I will make
  will promptly lift us from this earth.   2070
  And if we're light, we'll quickly gain some altitude.
  Congratulations on your new career!

AUERBACH'S CELLAR IN LEIPZIG

A *lively and lusty drinking party*.

FROSCH.
  Is nobody drinking? And no laughs?
  I'll teach you to make sour faces!
  Damned if you're not like wet grass today;
  you always used to blaze like straw!
BRANDER.
  It's your fault; we get nothing from you,
  no horseplay, no dirty joke.
FROSCH (*pours a glass of wine over* BRANDER's *head*).
  There you've got both.
BRANDER.
                    You double swine!
FROSCH.
  You asked for it. We aim to please.   2080
SIEBEL.
  Out the door, if you must fight!
  Sing with your gullets wide open; guzzle and shout!
  Forward! Holla! Ho!
ALTMAYER.
                    Ah, I'm ruined!
  Get some cotton-wool; that man is bursting my ear!
SIEBEL.
  Only when the vaults rebound
  can you really enjoy the mighty growl of the basses.

FROSCH.

So recht, hinaus mit dem, der etwas übel nimmt!
Al tara lara da!

ALTMAYER.

Al tara lara da!

FROSCH.

Die Kehlen sind gestimmt.
    (*Singt.*)
                Das liebe heil'ge Röm'sche Reich,   2090
                Wie hält's nur noch zusammen?

BRANDER.

Ein garstig Lied! Pfui! ein politisch Lied
Ein leidig Lied! Dankt Gott mit jedem Morgen,
Daß ihr nicht braucht fürs Röm'sche Reich zu sorgen!
Ich halt' es wenigstens für reichlichen Gewinn,
Daß ich nicht Kaiser oder Kanzler bin.
Doch muß auch uns ein Oberhaupt nicht fehlen;
Wir wollen einen Papst erwählen.
Ihr wißt, welch eine Qualität
Den Ausschlag gibt, den Mann erhöht.   2100

FROSCH (*singt*).

                Schwing dich auf, Frau Nachtigall,
                Grüß' mir mein Liebchen zehentausendmal.

SIEBEL.

Dem Liebchen keinen Gruß! ich will davon nichts hören!

FROSCH.

Dem Liebchen Gruß und Kuß! du wirst mir's nicht ver-
    wehren!
    (*Singt.*)
                Riegel auf! in stiller Nacht.
                Riegel auf! der Liebste wacht.
                Riegel zu! des Morgens früh.

SIEBEL.

Ja, singe, singe nur und lob' und rühme sie!
Ich will zu meiner Zeit schon lachen.
Sie hat mich angeführt, dir wird sie's auch so machen.   2110
Zum Liebsten sei ein Kobold ihr beschert!
Der mag mit ihr auf einem Kreuzweg schäkern;

FROSCH.

That's right. Throw him out, whoever takes offense!
Ah! Tara lara dum!

ALTMAYER.

Ah! Tara lara dum!

FROSCH.

Our gullets are attuned.

(*Sings.*)

Oh, dear old Holy Roman Empire,   2090
How does it still cohere?

BRANDER.

A nasty song! A stinking political song.
A rotten song. Each morning you should thank the Lord
that you're not running the Roman Empire.
I for one consider it a great advantage
that I am neither emperor nor chancellor.
And yet we cannot be without a leader.
Let us proceed therefore to choose a pope.
You know the qualities that matter
and elevate a man.   2100

FROSCH (*sings*).

In soaring flight, O Lady Nightingale, ascend.
A thousand greetings to my sweetheart send.

SIEBEL.

Forget the greeting to your sweetheart. Don't annoy
me with that tripe.

FROSCH.

A thousand greetings and a kiss! You can't begrudge me
that.

(*Sings.*)

Lift the latch! Still is the night.
Lift the latch! My love waits below.
Bolt the latch! The sun rises bright.

SIEBEL.

Go to it, sing her praises and her glory!
I will chuckle in my own good time.
She's played a dirty trick on me, she'll do the same
for you.   2110
I hope she gets a hobgoblin for a lover!
Let him toy with her at a crossroads.

Ein alter Bock, wenn er vom Blocksberg kehrt,
Mag im Galopp noch gute Nacht ihr meckern!
Ein braver Kerl von echtem Fleisch und Blut
Ist für die Dirne viel zu gut.
Ich will von keinem Gruße wissen,
Als ihr die Fenster eingeschmissen!

BRANDER (*auf den Tisch schlagend*).

Paßt auf! paßt auf! Gehorchet mir!
Ihr Herrn, gesteht, ich weiß zu leben;   2120
Verliebte Leute sitzen hier,
Und diesen muß, nach Standsgebühr,
Zur guten Nacht ich was zum besten geben.
Gebt acht! Ein Lied vom neusten Schnitt!
Und singt den Rundreim kräftig mit!
    (*Er singt.*)
            Es war eine Ratt' im Kellernest,
            Lebte nur von Fett und Butter,
            Hatte sich ein Ränzlein angemäst't,
            Als wie der Doktor Luther.
            Die Köchin hatt' ihr Gift gestellt;   2130
            Da ward's so eng ihr in der Welt,
            Als hätte sie Lieb' im Leibe.

CHORUS (*jauchzend*).
            Als hätte sie Lieb' im Leibe.

BRANDER.
            Sie fuhr herum, sie fuhr heraus,
            Und soff aus allen Pfützen,
            Zernagt', zerkratzt' das ganze Haus,
            Wollte nichts ihr Wüten nützen;
            Sie tät gar manchen Ängstesprung,
            Bald hatte das arme Tier genung,
            Als hätt' es Lieb' im Leibe.   2140

CHORUS.
            Als hätt' es Lieb' im Leibe.

BRANDER.
            Sie kam für Angst am hellen Tag
            Der Küche zugelaufen,
            Fiel an den Herd und zuckt' und lag,
            Und tät erbärmlich schnaufen.

Some old goat returning from Block Mountain[22]
should gallop by and bleat good-night!
A red-blooded clean-cut fellow
is much too good for that slut.
Don't talk to me about greetings—
unless it's the kind that will smash her windows.

BRANDER (*pounding on the table*).

Attention! Now listen to me!
Gentlemen, admit it, I know how to live. 2120
Some lovesick boys are with us this evening,
and it is proper that I present them
with something for the night.
Watch me! I give you the latest in songs!
Be sure to come in strong at the chorus!
    (*Sings.*)

        A rat lived in a cellar nest,
        Her paunch could not be smoother.
        She liked her lard and butter best,
        And looked like Martin Luther.
        The cook she set some poison bait; 2130
        The rat got in an awful state,
        As if she had love in her belly.

CHORUS (*jubilant*).

        As if she had love in her belly.

BRANDER.

        She scurried here and scurried there;
        She guzzled puddle juice.
        She scraped and flitted everywhere,
        Her frenzy was no use.
        She leapt great leaps in mortal fear,
        Without a doubt, the end was near—
        As if she had love in her belly. 2140

CHORUS.

        As if she had love in her belly.

BRANDER.

        And in the glaring light of day
        She ran into the kitchen,
        Dropped at the hearth and jerked and lay
        Panting hard and pitching.

Da lachte die Vergifterin noch:
Ha! sie pfeift auf dem letzten Loch,
Als hätte sie Lieb' im Leibe.

CHORUS.

Als hätte sie Lieb' im Leibe.

SIEBEL.

Wie sich die platten Bursche freuen!   2150
Es ist mir eine rechte Kunst,
Den armen Ratten Gift zu streuen!

BRANDER.

Sie stehn wohl sehr in deiner Gunst?

ALTMAYER.

Der Schmerbauch mit der kahlen Platte!
Das Unglück macht ihn zahm und mild;
Er sieht in der geschwollnen Ratte
Sein ganz natürlich Ebenbild.

(FAUST und MEPHISTOPHELES treten auf.)

MEPHISTOPHELES.

Ich muß dich nun vor allen Dingen
In lustige Gesellschaft bringen,
Damit du siehst, wie leicht sich's leben läßt.   2160
Dem Volke hier wird jeder Tag ein Fest.
Mit wenig Witz und viel Behagen
Dreht jeder sich im engen Zirkeltanz,
Wie junge Katzen mit dem Schwanz.
Wenn sie nicht über Kopfweh klagen,
So lang' der Wirt nur weiter borgt,
Sind sie vergnügt und unbesorgt.

BRANDER.

Die kommen eben von der Reise,
Man sieht's an ihrer wunderlichen Weise;
Sie sind nicht eine Stunde hier.   2170

FROSCH.

Wahrhaftig, du hast recht! Mein Leipzig lob' ich mir!
Es ist ein klein Paris, und bildet seine Leute.

SIEBEL.

Für was siehst du die Fremden an?

FROSCH.

Laßt mich nur gehn! Bei einem vollen Glase

> And now the cook did laugh to boot,
> "Ha! This is her final toot,
> As if she had love in her belly."

CHORUS.

> As if she had love in her belly. 23

SIEBEL.

How the numbskulls enjoy themselves!   2150
That's what I call a skill to be admired,
sprinkling poison for poor and helpless rats!

BRANDER.

They enjoy, I see, your personal protection.

ALTMAYER.

The old potbelly with his bald pate!
Tough luck has made him tame and mellow;
he sees in the bloated rat
the living image of himself.

> (FAUST *and* MEPHISTOPHELES *enter.*)

MEPHISTOPHELES.

Above all, I must now introduce you
to some jolly company,
so that you can see how smooth your life can be.   2160
To these people every day becomes a holiday.
With little mind and lots of zest
they twirl and dance in a tight little circle,
like a kitten chasing its tail.
So long as they keep their hangovers down
and the host keeps their credit up,
they are cheerful and carefree.

BRANDER.

Look, they're just back from a journey;
you can see it by their strange getup.
They've been here barely an hour.   2170

FROSCH.

I'll be damned, you're right. A toast for my Leipzig!
It's a little Paris and gives a man polish. 24

SIEBEL.

What do you take these strangers for?

FROSCH.

Leave it to me. Once the glasses are filled,

Zieh' ich, wie einen Kinderzahn,
Den Burschen leicht die Würmer aus der Nase.
Sie scheinen mir aus einem edlen Haus,
Sie sehen stolz und unzufrieden aus.

BRANDER.

Marktschreier sind's gewiß, ich wette!

ALTMAYER.

Vielleicht.

FROSCH.

          Gib acht, ich schraube sie! 2180

MEPHISTOPHELES (*zu* FAUST).

Den Teufel spürt das Völkchen nie,
Und wenn er sie beim Kragen hätte.

FAUST.

Seid uns gegrüßt, ihr Herrn!

SIEBEL.

             Viel Dank zum Gegengruß.
    (*Leise,* MEPHISTOPHELES *von der Seite ansehend.*)
Was hinkt der Kerl auf einem Fuß?

MEPHISTOPHELES.

Ist es erlaubt, uns auch zu euch zu setzen?
Statt eines guten Trunks, den man nicht haben kann,
Soll die Gesellschaft uns ergetzen.

ALTMAYER.

Ihr scheint ein sehr verwöhnter Mann.

FROSCH.

Ihr seid wohl spät von Rippach aufgebrochen?
Habt ihr mit Herren Hans noch erst zu Nacht
    gespeist? 2190

MEPHISTOPHELES.

Heut sind wir ihn vorbeigereist!
Wir haben ihn das letzte Mal gesprochen.
Von seinen Vettern wußt' er viel zu sagen,
Viel Grüße hat er uns an jeden aufgetragen.
    (*Er neigt sich gegen* FROSCH.)

ALTMAYER (*leise.*)

Da hast du's! der versteht's!

I'll pull some worms of truth from their noses,
easy as pulling babies' teeth.
They seem to be of noble family
because they look proud and dissatisfied.

BRANDER.

I'll bet they're a couple of hucksters.

ALTMAYER.

Perhaps.

FROSCH.

        Watch me. I'll squeeze it out of them.   2180

MEPHISTOPHELES (*to* FAUST).

The dears would never suspect the devil,
even if he had them by the collar.

FAUST.

We salute you, gentlemen.

SIEBEL.

                We thank you and return your
   greeting.
   (*Softly, observing* MEPHISTOPHELES *from the
   corner of his eye.*)
Why does the rascal drag one foot?

MEPHISTOPHELES.

Allow us to join you at the table.
Since we can't have wine of any quality,
let the company make up for it.

ALTMAYER.

You are a fastidious one, I see.

FROSCH.

You left Rippach late, I guess.
Did you have supper with Master Hans?[25]   2190

MEPHISTOPHELES.

We passed him on the road today.
But we spoke to him on our previous trip.
He had a lot to say about his cousins
and had greetings for each one of you.
   (*He bows to* FROSCH.)

ALTMAYER (*softly*).

There you are. The fellow is no fool.

SIEBEL.
Ein pfiffiger Patron!

FROSCH.
Nun, warte nur, ich krieg' ihn schon!

MEPHISTOPHELES.
Wenn ich nicht irrte, hörten wir
Geübte Stimmen Chorus singen?
Gewiß, Gesang muß trefflich hier
Von dieser Wölbung widerklingen!   2200

FROSCH.
Seid Ihr wohl gar ein Virtuos?

MEPHISTOPHELES.
O nein! die Kraft ist schwach, allein die Lust ist groß.

ALTMAYER.
Gebt uns ein Lied!

MEPHISTOPHELES.
Wenn ihr begehrt, die Menge.

SIEBEL.
Nur auch ein nagelneues Stück!

MEPHISTOPHELES.
Wir kommen erst aus Spanien zurück,
Dem schönen Land des Weins und der Gesänge.
  (*Singt.*)
Es war einmal ein König,
Der hatt' einen großen Floh—

FROSCH.
Horcht! Einen Floh! Habt ihr das wohl gefaßt?
Ein Floh ist mir ein saubrer Gast.   2210

MEPHISTOPHELES (*singt*).
Es war einmal ein König,
Der hatt' einen großen Floh,
Den liebt' er nicht wenig,
Als wie seinen eignen Sohn.
Da rief er seinen Schneider,
Der Schneider kam heran:
Da, miß dem Junker Kleider
Und miß ihm Hosen an!

SIEBEL.

A slippery customer!

FROSCH.

All right, just wait. I'll trip him soon enough.

MEPHISTOPHELES.

Unless I am mistaken, we just heard
the sounds of well-trained voices.
These vaulted ceilings surely should provide
a splendid echo to such music!   2200

FROSCH.

You are a virtuoso, I suppose?

MEPHISTOPHELES.

Far from it! My strength is feeble, though
    my desire's great.

ALTMAYER.

Give us a song!

MEPHISTOPHELES.

As many as you like.

SIEBEL.

Let it be a brand-new one.

MEPHISTOPHELES.

We've just returned from Spain,
that lovely land of wine and song.
    (*Sings.*)
            In ages past there lived a king
            Who owned a large-size flea—

FROSCH.

Listen to that! A flea! Did you get that?
There's a neat fellow, a flea!   2210

MEPHISTOPHELES (*sings*).

            In ages past there lived a king
            Who owned a large-size flea.
            On him he lavished everything
            As if a son were he.
            He called the tailor of the court,
            Who quickly came a-running,
            To fit him doublets long and short
            And breeches that were stunning.

BRANDER.

    Vergeßt nur nicht, dem Schneider einzuschärfen,
    Daß er mir aufs genauste mißt,   2220
    Und daß, so lieb sein Kopf ihm ist,
    Die Hosen keine Falten werfen!

MEPHISTOPHELES.

           In Sammet und in Seide
           War er nun angetan,
           Hatte Bänder auf dem Kleide,
           Hatt' auch ein Kreuz daran,
           Und war sogleich Minister,
           Und hatt' einen großen Stern.
           Da wurden seine Geschwister
           Bei Hof' auch große Herrn.   2230
           Und Herrn und Fraun am Hofe,
           Die waren sehr geplagt,
           Die Königin und die Zofe
           Gestochen und genagt,
           Und durften sie nicht knicken,
           Und weg sie jucken nicht.
           Wir knicken und ersticken
           Doch gleich, wenn einer sticht.

CHORUS (*jauchzend*).

           Wir knicken und ersticken
           Doch gleich, wenn einer sticht.   2240

FROSCH.

    Bravo! Bravo! Das war schön!

SIEBEL.

    So soll es jedem Floh ergehn!

BRANDER.

    Spitzt die Finger und packt sie fein!

ALTMAYER.

    Es lebe die Freiheit! Es lebe der Wein!

MEPHISTOPHELES.

    Ich tränke gern ein Glas, die Freiheit hoch zu ehren,
    Wenn eure Weine nur ein bißchen besser wären.

SIEBEL.

    Wir mögen das nicht wieder hören!

BRANDER.

And don't forget to warn that tailor
to measure for a very tight fit; 2220
if he wants to save his neck,
there'd better be no wrinkles in those breeches.

MEPHISTOPHELES.

In velvet and in silkiness
The courtly flea was dressed
To the hilt with ribbons on his dress
And a shiny cross on his breast.
And he nobly brought to court
His brothers and his sisters,
For he was now a mighty lord,
One of the State's ministers. 2230
The lords and ladies of the State
Were very sorely tried.
The queen said to the chambermaid
"We cannot shield our hide."
The fleas did make them shiver
And squeal as they were nicked.
We slither and we quiver
As soon as we are pricked.

CHORUS (*jubilant*).

We slither and we quiver
As soon as we are pricked. 2240

FROSCH.

Bravo, bravo! That was beautiful!

SIEBEL.

It should happen to all fleas.

BRANDER.

Cock your fingers, squish them prettily.

ALTMAYER.

Long live wine, and long live liberty!

MEPHISTOPHELES.

I'd like to fill my glass and drink to freedom's honor,
if only you had wine of better quality.

SIEBEL.

Don't let us hear such talk again!

MEPHISTOPHELES.

    Ich fürchte nur, der Wirt beschweret sich;

    Sonst gäb' ich diesen werten Gästen

    Aus unserm Keller was zum besten.   2250

SIEBEL.

    Nur immer her! ich nehm's auf mich.

FROSCH.

    Schafft Ihr ein gutes Glas, so wollen wir Euch loben.

    Nur gebt nicht gar zu kleine Proben;

    Denn wenn ich judizieren soll,

    Verlang' ich auch das Maul recht voll.

ALTMAYER (*leise*).

    Sie sind vom Rheine, wie ich spüre.

MEPHISTOPHELES.

    Schafft einen Bohrer an!

BRANDER.

                    Was soll mit dem geschehn?

    Ihr habt doch nicht die Fässer vor der Türe?

ALTMAYER.

    Dahinten hat der Wirt ein Körbchen Werkzeug stehn.

MEPHISTOPHELES (*nimmt den Bohrer*). (*Zu* FROSCH).

    Nun sagt, was wünschet Ihr zu schmecken?   2260

FROSCH.

    Wie meint Ihr das? Habt Ihr so mancherlei?

MEPHISTOPHELES.

    Ich stell' es einem jeden frei.

ALTMAYER (*zu* FROSCH).

    Aha! du fängst schon an, die Lippen abzulecken.

FROSCH.

    Gut! wenn ich wählen soll, so will ich Rheinwein haben.

    Das Vaterland verleiht die allerbesten Gaben.

MEPHISTOPHELES (*indem er an dem Platz, wo* FROSCH *sitzt, ein Loch in den Tischrand bohrt*).

    Verschafft ein wenig Wachs, die Pfropfen gleich zu

          machen!

ALTMAYER.

    Ach, das sind Taschenspielersachen.

MEPHISTOPHELES (*zu* BRANDER).

    Und Ihr?

MEPHISTOPHELES.

    I fear the landlord might not like it,

    else I should treat our worthy guests

    to something rare from our cellar.   2250

SIEBEL.

    Let's have it, man. I'll take the blame for it.

FROSCH.

    If you'll produce the liquid, we'll sing your praises to the sky.

    But let me have a generous sample,

    for if I am asked to referee,

    I must guzzle deep and long.

ALTMAYER (*aside*).

    I can tell they come from the Rhine.

MEPHISTOPHELES.

    Bring me an auger now!

BRANDER.

                  What would you want with that?

    You have no casks outside the door, or else?

ALTMAYER.

    Back there the landlord keeps his box of tools.

MEPHISTOPHELES (*takes the auger*). (*To* FROSCH.)

    Now tell me, what's your favorite label?   2260

FROSCH.

    How do you mean? Do you have several kinds?

MEPHISTOPHELES.

    The choice is free. It's up to you.

ALTMAYER (*to* FROSCH).

    Aha! Even now he licks his lips.

FROSCH.

    All right, if I can choose, I want some Rhenish wine.

    The fatherland bestows the finest gifts of all.

MEPHISTOPHELES (*drills a hole into the edge of the table in
       front of* FROSCH).

    Get me some wax, so we may stanch the flow.

ALTMAYER.

    Ah, that's just a juggler's trick.

MEPHISTOPHELES (*to* BRANDER).

    And for you?

BRANDER.

   Ich will Champagner Wein,
 Und recht moussierend soll er sein!

MEPHISTOPHELES (*bohrt; einer hat indessen die Wachspfropfen gemacht und verstopft*).

BRANDER.

 Man kann nicht stets das Fremde meiden,   2270
 Das Gute liegt uns oft so fern.
 Ein echter deutscher Mann mag keinen Franzen leiden,
 Doch ihre Weine trinkt er gern.

SIEBEL (*indem sich* MEPHISTOPHELES *seinem Platze nähert*).

 Ich muß gestehn, den sauren mag ich nicht,
 Gebt mir ein Glas vom echten süßen!

MEPHISTOPHELES (*bohrt*).

 Euch soll sogleich Tokayer fließen.

ALTMAYER.

 Nein, Herren, seht mir ins Gesicht!
 Ich seh' es ein, ihr habt uns nur zum besten.

MEPHISTOPHELES.

 Ei! Ei! Mit solchen edlen Gästen
 Wär' es ein bißchen viel gewagt.   2280
 Geschwind! Nur grad' heraus gesagt!
 Mit welchem Weine kann ich dienen?

ALTMAYER.

 Mit jedem! Nur nicht lang gefragt.
  (*Nachdem die Löcher alle gebohrt und
  verstopft sind.*)

MEPHISTOPHELES (*mit seltsamen Gebärden*).

   Trauben trägt der Weinstock!
   Hörner der Ziegenbock;
   Der Wein ist saftig, Holz die Reben,
   Der hölzerne Tisch kann Wein auch geben.
   Ein tiefer Blick in die Natur!
   Hier ist ein Wunder, glaubet nur!
 Nun zieht die Pfropfen und genießt!   2290

ALLE (*indem sie die Pfropfen ziehen und jedem der verlangte
  Wein ins Glas läuft*).

 O schöner Brunnen, der uns fließt!

BRANDER.
                    Champagne for me,
        and make it sparkle and tingle.
MEPHISTOPHELES (*bores holes; one of the others has meanwhile
        made the wax stoppers and begun to plug the holes*).

BRANDER.
        Sometimes one can't abstain from foreign stuff;   2270
        what is good lies often far away.
        A German of fine blood dislikes the French,
        but he enjoys their wines the better.
SIEBEL (*as* MEPHISTOPHELES *approaches his seat*).
        I must confess, I never liked it sour.
        Pour me a glass of sweet and mellow wine.
MEPHISTOPHELES (*continues to bore holes*).
        Tokay for you; watch it flow in just a minute.
ALTMAYER.
        Now, gentlemen, look straight into my eyes!
        Ah yes, your joke's on us, I must confess.
MEPHISTOPHELES.
        Come, come! With guests of your distinction
        such sport would be a risky venture.   2280
        Be quick and speak out honestly:
        Which wine would be your pleasure?
ALTMAYER.
        Anything for me! Don't ask a lot of questions.
            (*The holes have been bored and plugged.*)

MEPHISTOPHELES (*gesturing mysteriously*).
                    The grape from living vines is fed;
                    The goat, it has a horned head.
                    Wine is juice, plants yield more,
                    From this plank the wine shall pour.
                    Profoundly into Nature peer!
                    Have faith, a miracle is here!
        Now draw the stoppers, drink your fill!   2290
TOGETHER (*as they pull the stoppers, and the desired wine
        pours into their glasses*).
        Flow on, O fairest spring!

MEPHISTOPHELES.
    Nur hütet euch, daß ihr mir nichts vergießt!
      (*Sie trinken wiederholt.*)
ALLE (*singen*).
    Uns ist ganz kannibalisch wohl,
    Als wie fünfhundert Säuen!
MEPHISTOPHELES.
    Das Volk ist frei, seht an, wie wohl's ihm geht!
FAUST.
    Ich hätte Lust, nun abzufahren.
MEPHISTOPHELES.
    Gib nur erst acht, die Bestialität
    Wird sich gar herrlich offenbaren.
SIEBEL (*trinkt unvorsichtig, der Wein fließt auf die Erde und
    wird zur Flamme*).
    Helft! Feuer! helft! Die Hölle brennt!
MEPHISTOPHELES (*die Flamme besprechend*).
    Sei ruhig, freundlich Element!   2300
      (*Zu dem Gesellen.*)
    Für diesmal war es nur ein Tropfen Fegefeuer.
SIEBEL.
    Was soll das sein? Wart! Ihr bezahlt es teuer!
    Es scheinet, daß Ihr uns nicht kennt.
FROSCH.
    Laß Er uns das zum zweiten Male bleiben!
ALTMAYER.
    Ich dächt', wir hießen ihn ganz sachte seitwärts gehn.
SIEBEL.
    Was, Herr? Er will sich unterstehn,
    Und hier sein Hokuspokus treiben?
MEPHISTOPHELES.
    Still, altes Weinfaß!
SIEBEL.
                Besenstiel!
    Du willst uns gar noch grob begegnen?
BRANDER.
    Wart' nur, es sollen Schläge regnen!   2310

MEPHISTOPHELES.
> Be very careful not to spill a single drop.
>> (*They drink repeatedly.*)

TOGETHER (*singing*).
>> We feel so good, so cannibalic jolly,
>> much like five hundred grunting sows.

MEPHISTOPHELES.
> The people are free. How they enjoy themselves!

FAUST.
> I am inclined to leave immediately.

MEPHISTOPHELES.
> Take notice first how their bestiality
> will stand revealed in glowing color.

SIEBEL (*drinks carelessly; the wine spills to the ground and
>> turns into flame*).
> Help! Fire! Hell's aflame!

MEPHISTOPHELES (*addressing the flame*).
> Be still, my friendly element!   2300
>> (*To the students.*)
> This time it was the merest drop of purgatory.

SIEBEL.
> What do you mean? Wait, man, you will pay for this!
> Do you know with whom you're dealing?

FROSCH.
> Don't try this trick a second time, you hear!

ALTMAYER.
> Let's ease him sideways out the door.

SIEBEL.
> What, sir? You have the audacity
> to play your hocus-pocus here on us?

MEPHISTOPHELES.
> Shut your mouth, you tub of wine!

SIEBEL.
>> You skinny broomstick, you!
> I think you want to play it rough.

BRANDER.
> Just wait. We'll knock you black and blue.   2310

ALTMAYER (*zieht einen Pfropf aus dem Tisch, es springt ihm Feuer
    entgegen*).
    Ich brenne! ich brenne!
SIEBEL.
Zauberei!

    Stoßt zu! der Kerl ist vogelfrei!
        (*Sie ziehen die Messer und gehn auf* MEPHI-
        STOPHELES *los*.)
MEPHISTOPHELES (*mit ernsthafter Gebärde*).
            Falsch Gebild und Wort
            Verändern Sinn und Ort!
            Seid hier und dort!
        (*Sie stehn erstaunt und sehn einander an.*)
ALTMAYER.
    Wo bin ich? Welches schöne Land!
FROSCH.
    Weinberge! Seh' ich recht?
SIEBEL.
                        Und Trauben gleich zur Hand!
BRANDER.
    Hier unter diesem grünen Laube,
    Seht, welch ein Stock! Seht, welche Traube!
        (*Er faßt* SIEBELN *bei der Nase. Die andern
        tun es wechselseitig und heben die Messer.*)

MEPHISTOPHELES (*wie oben*).
    Irrtum, laß los der Augen Band!   2320
    Und merkt euch, wie der Teufel spaße.
        (*Er verschwindet mit* FAUST, *die Gesellen
        fahren auseinander.*)
SIEBEL.
    Was gibt's?
ALTMAYER.
            Wie?
FROSCH.
                War das deine Nase?
BRANDER (*zu* SIEBEL).
    Und deine hab' ich in der Hand!

ALTMAYER (*pulls a plug from the table; fire leaps in his face*).
  I burn! I burn!

SIEBEL.
                That's sorcery!
  Cut him down! He is a public enemy.
    (*They draw their knives and move against*
    MEPHISTOPHELES.)
MEPHISTOPHELES (*with solemn gestures*).
                False when and false where,
                The foul and the fair
                Be here, be there!
    (*They stand amazed and stare at each other.*)
ALTMAYER.
  Where am I? What a lovely land!
FROSCH.
  Vineyards! Can I trust my eyes?
SIEBEL.
                            And grapes so near at hand!
BRANDER.
  And look! beneath the dark green arbor,
  what vines! and oh, what luscious grapes!
    (*He seizes* SIEBEL's *nose. The others do the
    same, one to the other, and raise their knives.*)

MEPHISTOPHELES (*more gestures*).
  Illusion, release these eyes from error!   2320
  And you take notice how the devil plays his game.
    (*He disappears with* FAUST. *The students
    scatter.*)
SIEBEL.
  What's up?
ALTMAYER.
        Eh?
FROSCH.
            Was that your nose?
BRANDER (*to* SIEBEL).
  And yours I hold here in my hand!

ALTMAYER.

Es war ein Schlag, der ging durch alle Glieder!
Schafft einen Stuhl, ich sinke nieder!

FROSCH.

Nein, sagt mir nur, was ist geschehn?

SIEBEL.

Wo ist der Kerl? Wenn ich ihn spüre,
Er soll mir nicht lebendig gehn!

ALTMAYER.

Ich hab' ihn selbst hinaus zur Kellertüre—
Auf einem Fasse reiten sehn——
Es liegt mir bleischwer in den Füßen.
    (*Sich nach dem Tische wendend.*)
Mein! Sollte wohl der Wein noch fließen?

2330

SIEBEL.

Betrug war alles, Lug und Schein.

FROSCH.

Mir deuchte doch, als tränk' ich Wein.

BRANDER.

Aber wie war es mit den Trauben?

ALTMAYER.

Nun sag' mir eins, man soll kein Wunder glauben!

HEXENKÜCHE

*Auf einem niedrigen Herde steht ein großer
Kessel über dem Feuer. In dem Dampfe, der
davon in die Höhe steigt, zeigen sich
verschiedene Gestalten. Eine Meerkatze sitzt
bei dem Kessel und schäumt ihn, und sorgt,
daß er nicht überläuft. Der Meerkater
mit den Jungen sitzt daneben und
wärmt sich. Wände und Decke sind mit dem
seltsamsten Hexenhausrat ausgeschmückt.*

Faust, Mephistopheles.

FAUST.

Mir widersteht das tolle Zauberwesen!
Versprichst du mir, ich soll genesen

ALTMAYER.

It was a shock that went through bone and marrow!
Bring me a chair, I think I'm fainting.

FROSCH.

Will someone tell me what has happened?

SIEBEL.

Where is he? If I can get my hands on him,
he won't come off alive this time.

ALTMAYER.

I'm sure I saw him on a cask—
riding out the open cellar door— 2330
My legs feel heavier than lead.
     (*Turning to the table.*)
Do you suppose the wine might still be running?

SIEBEL.

It was a fraud, a lie, and trickery.

FROSCH.

I was so sure that I was drinking wine.

BRANDER.

And how about those luscious grapes?

ALTMAYER.

Who says there are no miracles!

WITCH'S KITCHEN

*A great cauldron stands on the fire over a low
hearth. Various grotesque figures can be seen
through the rising smoke. A she-ape sits
by the cauldron, stirring and skimming it. A he-ape
with his young ones sits near her, warming
himself. Walls and ceilings are decorated with
bizarre household implements.*

Faust, Mephistopheles.

FAUST.

I am repelled by all this magic stew and fuss!
Can you promise me that I'll be cured

In diesem Wust von Raserei?
Verlang' ich Rat von einem alten Weibe?   2340
Und schafft die Sudelköcherei
Wohl dreißig Jahre mir vom Leibe?
Weh mir, wenn du nichts Bessers weißt!
Schon ist die Hoffnung mir verschwunden.
Hat die Natur und hat ein edler Geist
Nicht irgendeinen Balsam ausgefunden?

MEPHISTOPHELES.

Mein Freund, nun sprichst du wieder klug!
Dich zu verjüngen, gibt's auch ein natürlich Mittel;
Allein es steht in einem andern Buch,
Und ist ein wunderlich Kapitel.   2350

FAUST.

Ich will es wissen.

MEPHISTOPHELES.

                    Gut! Ein Mittel, ohne Geld
Und Arzt und Zauberei zu haben:
Begib dich gleich hinaus aufs Feld,
Fang an zu hacken und zu graben,
Erhalte dich und deinen Sinn
In einem ganz beschränkten Kreise,
Ernähre dich mit ungemischter Speise,
Leb mit dem Vieh als Vieh, und acht es nicht für Raub,
Den Acker, den du erntest, selbst zu düngen;
Das ist das beste Mittel, glaub,   2360
Auf achtzig Jahr dich zu verjüngen!

FAUST.

Das bin ich nicht gewöhnt, ich kann mich nicht bequemen,
Den Spaten in die Hand zu nehmen.
Das enge Leben steht mir gar nicht an.

MEPHISTOPHELES.

So muß denn doch die Hexe dran.

FAUST.

Warum denn just das alte Weib!
Kannst du den Trank nicht selber brauen?

MEPHISTOPHELES.

Das wär' ein schöner Zeitvertreib!
Ich wollt' indes wohl tausend Brücken bauen.

by wallowing in that whirling frenzy?
Should I seek counsel from an ancient hag?   2340
And can that filthy, frothing cookery
relieve my carcass of some thirty years?
I am lost if you can think of nothing better!
My dearest hope has vanished even now.
Why has not nature or a noble spirit
found some remedial balm for me?

MEPHISTOPHELES.

Now you speak more sensibly again, my friend!
You may yet naturally regain your youth,
but that is written in a different book
and constitutes a special chapter.   2350

FAUST.

I wish to know it.

MEPHISTOPHELES.

                    Good! A method can be used
without physicians, gold, or magic.
Go out into the open field
and start to dig and cultivate;
keep your body and your spirit
in a humble and restricted sphere,
sustain yourself by simple fare,
live with your herd and spread your own manure
on land from which you reap your nourishment.
Believe me, that's the best procedure   2360
to keep your youth for eighty years or more.

FAUST.

I am not used to that. I cannot bring myself
to take a spade and till the ground.
The narrow life has no appeal for me.

MEPHISTOPHELES.

Then, I suppose the witch is worth a try.

FAUST.

Why must it be that ancient hag?
Why can't you brew the drink yourself?

MEPHISTOPHELES.

A pretty pastime during which
I'd rather build a thousand bridges!

Nicht Kunst und Wissenschaft allein,   2370
Geduld will bei dem Werke sein.
Ein stiller Geist ist Jahre lang geschäftig,
Die Zeit nur macht die feine Gärung kräftig.
Und alles, was dazu gehört,
Es sind gar wunderbare Sachen!
Der Teufel hat sie's zwar gelehrt;
Allein der Teufel kann's nicht machen.
    (*Die* TIERE *erblickend.*)
Sieh, welch ein zierliches Geschlecht!
Das ist die Magd! das ist der Knecht!
    (*Zu den* TIEREN.)
Es scheint, die Frau ist nicht zu Hause?   2380

DIE TIERE.
        Beim Schmause,
        Aus dem Haus
        Zum Schornstein hinaus!

MEPHISTOPHELES.
Wie lange pflegt sie wohl zu schwärmen?

DIE TIERE.
So lange wir uns die Pfoten wärmen.

MEPHISTOPHELES (*zu* FAUST).
Wie findest du die zarten Tiere?

FAUST.
So abgeschmackt, als ich nur jemand sah!

MEPHISTOPHELES.
Nein, ein Diskurs wie dieser da
Ist grade der, den ich am liebsten führe!
    (*Zu den* TIEREN.)
So sagt mir doch, verfluchte Puppen,   2390
Was quirlt ihr in dem Brei herum?

DIE TIERE.
Wir kochen breite Bettelsuppen.

MEPHISTOPHELES.
Da habt ihr ein groß Publikum.

DER KATER (*macht sich herbei und schmeichelt dem* MEPHI-
    STOPHELES).
        O würfle nur gleich
        Und mache mich reich,

Art and science is not all we need,   2370
this business requires patience too.
A tranquil mind must labor many years,
the fermentation is supplied by time.
The recipe requires care
and strange, exotic condiments.
The devil showed the witch the way,
but the devil cannot stoop to brew the potion.
    (*Notices* THE ANIMALS.)
Observe the dainty couple here!
This is the houseboy, that's the maid.
    (*To* THE ANIMALS.)
It seems your mistress isn't home?   2380

THE ANIMALS.

          Slipped away to carouse,
          Flew from the house,
          Out through the chimney!

MEPHISTOPHELES.

When do her revels usually end?

THE ANIMALS.

When our paws feel warm and cozy.

MEPHISTOPHELES (*to* FAUST).

How do you like the tender pets?

FAUST.

As hideous a bunch as I have seen.

MEPHISTOPHELES.

But look, a discourse such as this
is of the type I like above all others.
    (*Addressing* THE ANIMALS.)
Do tell me, cursed puppets,   2390
What are you stirring in that slop?

THE ANIMALS.

We're boiling watery beggar soup.

MEPHISTOPHELES.

You're sure to find a large demand for it.

HE-APE (*slinks up and fawns on* MEPHISTOPHELES).

          Roll the dice, you honey,
          And get me some money.

> Und laß mich gewinnen!
> Gar schlecht ist's bestellt,
> Und wär' ich bei Geld,
> So wär' ich bei Sinnen.

MEPHISTOPHELES.

Wie glücklich würde sich der Affe schätzen,　　　　2400
Könnt' er nur auch ins Lotto setzen!
>　　*(Indessen haben die jungen Meerkätzchen
>　　mit einer großen Kugel gespielt und rollen sie
>　　hervor.)*

DER KATER.

>　　Das ist die Welt;
>　　Sie steigt und fällt
>　　Und rollt beständig;
>　　Sie klingt wie Glas—
>　　Wie bald bricht das!
>　　Ist hohl inwendig.
>　　Hier glänzt sie sehr,
>　　Und hier noch mehr:
>　　Ich bin lebendig!　　　　2410
>　　Mein lieber Sohn,
>　　Halt dich davon!
>　　Du mußt sterben!
>　　Sie ist von Ton,
>　　Es gibt Scherben.

MEPHISTOPHELES.

Was soll das Sieb?

DER KATER *(holt es herunter)*.

>　　Wärst du ein Dieb,
>　　Wollt' ich dich gleich erkennen.
>　　*(Er läuft zur* KÄTZIN *und läßt sie durch-
>　　sehen.)*
>　　Sieh durch das Sieb!
>　　Erkennst du den Dieb,　　　　2420
>　　Und darfst ihn nicht nennen?

MEPHISTOPHELES *(sich dem Feuer nähernd)*.

Und dieser Topf?

KATER UND KÄTZIN.

>　　Der alberne Tropf!

Be crooked and stealthy,
Impatient and rash;
Then I'll be healthy,
With plenty of cash.

MEPHISTOPHELES.

The monkey here would be so glad   2400
if he could also join a game of chance.
(*Meanwhile the young apes have been playing with a large sphere which they now roll
forward.*)

HE-APE.

The world is a ball,
A rise and a fall;
Its sparkling mass
Is hollow matter,
Can quickly shatter
Like shiny glass.
Here it's night,
There it's bright.
I am wild!   2410
My darling child,
Go away, go away!
You have to die.
It's only clay
And goes to pieces.

MEPHISTOPHELES.

What about that sieve?

HE-APE (*takes it down*).

If you came to thieve,
By this I can tell.
(*Runs to* SHE-APE *and lets her peer through it.*)

Peer through the sieve!
You know the thief well,   2420
And yet dare not name him?

MEPHISTOPHELES (*goes near the fire*).

And what of this pot?

HE-APE AND SHE-APE.

The simple sot

Er kennt nicht den Topf,
Er kennt nicht den Kessel!

MEPHISTOPHELES.

Unhöfliches Tier!

DER KATER.

Den Wedel nimm hier
Und setz' dich in Sessel!

(*Er nötigt den* MEPHISTOPHELES *zu sitzen.*)

FAUST (*welcher diese Zeit über vor einem Spiegel gestanden,
sich ihm bald genähert, sich von ihm entfernt hat*).

Was seh' ich? Welch ein himmlisch Bild
Zeigt sich in diesem Zauberspiegel!   2430
O Liebe, leihe mir den schnellsten deiner Flügel,
Und führe mich in ihr Gefild!
Ach! wenn ich nicht auf dieser Stelle bleibe,
Wenn ich es wage, nah zu gehn,
Kann ich sie nur als wie im Nebel sehn!—
Das schönste Bild von einem Weibe!
Ist's möglich, ist das Weib so schön?
Muß ich an diesem hingestreckten Leibe
Den Inbegriff von allen Himmeln sehn?
So etwas findet sich auf Erden?   2440

MEPHISTOPHELES.

Natürlich, wenn ein Gott sich erst sechs Tage plagt,
Und selbst am Ende Bravo sagt,
Da muß es was Gescheites werden.
Für diesmal sieh dich immer satt;
Ich weiß dir so ein Schätzchen auszuspüren,
Und selig, wer das gute Schicksal hat,
Als Bräutigam sie heimzuführen!

(FAUST *sieht immerfort in den Spiegel.*
MEPHISTOPHELES, *sich in dem Sessel dehnend
und mit dem Wedel spielend, fährt fort zu
sprechen.*)

Hier sitz' ich wie der König auf dem Throne,
Den Zepter halt' ich hier, es fehlt nur noch die Krone.

DIE TIERE (*welche bisher allerlei wunderliche Bewegungen
durcheinander gemacht haben, bringen dem* MEPHI-
STOPHELES *eine Krone mit großem Geschrei*).

Knows not the pot,
Knows not the kettle.

MEPHISTOPHELES.

Impertinent beast!

HE-APE.

Take that feather duster there
And sit back in your chair.

(*Motions* MEPHISTOPHELES *to sit down.*)

FAUST (*who all this time has been standing before a mirror,
   now drawing nearer, now moving away from it*).

I see a form of boundless beauty
give radiance to this magic glass.[26]   2430
O Love, lend me the swiftest of your wings,
and lead me to her bright regions.
Ah, if I try to move from here—
if I dare approach the mirror—
she quickly fades into a cloud of mist.
Oh, highest vision of a woman!
Can it be? Can this woman be so fair?
Do I see in her recumbent shape
the form and essence of the heavens?
Can this epitome be found on earth?   2440

MEPHISTOPHELES.

If a god will do six days of heavy labor
and in the end say "bravo" to himself,
then something decent should result from it.
Feast your eyes for now and sate yourself.
I can arrange for such a doll for you.
Good fortune will have blessed the lucky man
who takes her to his home and bed.

   (FAUST *continues to peer into the mirror.*
   MEPHISTOPHELES, *stretching in his armchair
   and fanning himself with the feather duster,
   continues.*)

I sit here like a king enthroned,
with scepter in hand; I only need a crown.

THE ANIMALS (*who until now had moved about in all kinds of
   curious ways, bring* MEPHISTOPHELES *a crown, chattering
   and shrieking*).

O sei doch so gut,   2450
Mit Schweiß und mit Blut
Die Krone zu leimen!

(Sie gehn ungeschickt mit der Krone um und
zerbrechen sie in zwei Stücke, mit welchen
sie herumspringen.)

Nun ist es geschehn!
Wir reden und sehn,
Wir hören und reimen—

FAUST *(gegen den Spiegel).*

Weh mir! ich werde schier verrückt.

MEPHISTOPHELES *(auf die* TIERE *deutend).*

Nun fängt mir an fast selbst der Kopf zu schwanken.

DIE TIERE.

Und wenn es uns glückt,
Und wenn es sich schickt,
So sind es Gedanken!   2460

FAUST *(wie oben).*

Mein Busen fängt mir an zu brennen!
Entfernen wir uns nur geschwind!

MEPHISTOPHELES *(in obiger Stellung).*

Nun, wenigstens muß man bekennen,
Daß es aufrichtige Poeten sind.

(Der Kessel, welchen die KÄTZIN *bisher außer*
acht gelassen, fängt an, überzulaufen; es ent-
steht eine große Flamme, welche zum
Schornstein hinausschlägt. Die HEXE *kommt*
durch die Flamme mit entsetzlichem Ge-
schrei heruntergefahren.)

DIE HEXE.

Au! Au! Au! Au!
Verdammtes Tier! verfluchte Sau!
Versäumst den Kessel, versengst die Frau!
Verfluchtes Tier!

(FAUST und MEPHISTOPHELES erblickend.)

Was ist das hier?
Wer seid ihr hier?   2470
Was wollt ihr da?
Wer schlich sich ein?

> Oh, be a clown   2450
> And paste the crown
> With blood and perspiration.

(*They handle the crown awkwardly and break
it; then gambol about with the two pieces.*)

> Now it is done!
> We crawl and we run;
> We speak, we hear, and we rhyme—

FAUST (*before the mirror*).

Ah, I shall lose my mind.

MEPHISTOPHELES (*pointing to* THE ANIMALS).

The devil's head itself is reeling.

THE ANIMALS.

> And if it goes well—
> A lucky spell—
> There will be thought in it.   2460

FAUST (*as above*).

A fire rises in my breast!
Let us quickly get away!

MEPHISTOPHELES (*still in the same attitude*).

Well, at least one should acknowledge:
these poets have sincerity.

(*The* SHE-APE *has for some time neglected the
cauldron. It begins to overflow; there is a
large flame which blazes up the chimney. The*
WITCH *comes down through the flame, emit-
ting horrible shrieks.*)

WITCH.

Ow! Ow! Ow! Ow!
The filthy beast! The dirty swine!
Neglects the pot, sears my behind!
You filthy beast!

(*She notices* FAUST *and* MEPHISTOPHELES.)

> What's this now?
> Who's that now?   2470
> What do you want here?
> Who crept in here?

>   Die Feuerpein
>   Euch ins Gebein!

(Sie fährt mit dem Schaumlöffel in den Kes-
sel und spritzt Flammen nach FAUST, MEPH-
ISTOPHELES *und den* TIEREN. *Die* TIERE
winseln.)

MEPHISTOPHELES *(welcher den Wedel, den er in der Hand*
hält, umkehrt und unter die Gläser und Töpfe schlägt).

>   Entzwei! entzwei!
>   Da liegt der Brei!
>   Da liegt das Glas!
>   Es ist nur Spaß,
>   Der Takt, du Aas,
>   Zu deiner Melodei.   2480

(Indem die HEXE *voll Grimm und Entsetzen*
zurücktritt.)

Erkennst du mich? Gerippe! Scheusal du!
Erkennst du deinen Herrn und Meister?
Was hält mich ab, so schlag' ich zu,
Zerschmettre dich und deine Katzengeister!
Hast du vorm roten Wams nicht mehr Respekt?
Kannst du die Hahnenfeder nicht erkennen?
Hab' ich dies Angesicht versteckt?
Soll ich mich etwa selber nennen?

DIE HEXE.

O Herr, verzeiht den rohen Gruß!
Seh' ich doch keinen Pferdefuß.   2490
Wo sind denn Eure beiden Raben?

MEPHISTOPHELES.

Für diesmal kommst du so davon;
Denn freilich ist es eine Weile schon,
Daß wir uns nicht gesehen haben.
Auch die Kultur, die alle Welt beleckt,
Hat auf den Teufel sich erstreckt;
Das nordische Phantom ist nun nicht mehr zu schauen;
Wo siehst du Hörner, Schweif und Klauen?
Und was den Fuß betrifft, den ich nicht missen kann,
Der würde mir bei Leuten schaden;   2500
Darum bedien' ich mich, wie mancher junge Mann,

Fire and flame
Consume your frame!
(*She dips the ladle into the cauldron and
squirts flames on* FAUST, MEPHISTOPHELES,
and THE ANIMALS. THE ANIMALS *whine.*)

MEPHISTOPHELES (*reverses the feather duster which he holds
in his hand and flails the pots and glasses with it*).
Bang! Crash!
There lies the trash!
The crystal is shattered,
Not that it mattered.
Here's a rhythm, you bitch,
For your sweet ditty.   2480
(*While the* WITCH *recoils, chagrined and terror-stricken.*)
You know me now, you hag! Abomination!
You recognize your lord and master?
I have a mind to strike you down,
to smash you and your horde of monkeys.
Is this your homage to my scarlet coat?
Can you not recognize my cap and feather?
I did not keep my visage out of sight.
Must I announce my name to you?

WITCH.
Forgive my uncouth greeting, master!
I failed to see the equine hoof,   •   2490
and your two ravens—where are they?
MEPHISTOPHELES.
This time I'll let you off unpunished,
for certainly it has been rather long
since last we saw each other face to face.
The world is now a cultured place,
where the devil has evolved accordingly.
The Nordic phantom is entirely passé, you see,
he's shed his horns and tail and crooked fingers.
As for the hoof, I cannot really do without it,
but it would harm me in society,   2500
and hence, like many youthful gentlemen,

Seit vielen Jahren falscher Waden.

DIE HEXE (*tanzend*).

Sinn und Verstand verlier' ich schier,
Seh' ich den Junker Satan wieder hier!

MEPHISTOPHELES.

Den Namen, Weib, verbitt' ich mir!

DIE HEXE.

Warum? Was hat er Euch getan?

MEPHISTOPHELES.

Er ist schon lang' ins Fabelbuch geschrieben;
Allein die Menschen sind nichts besser dran,
Den Bösen sind sie los, die Bösen sind geblieben.
Du nennst mich Herr Baron, so ist die Sache gut;   2510
Ich bin ein Kavalier, wie andre Kavaliere.
Du zweifelst nicht an meinem edlen Blut;
Sieh her, das ist das Wappen, das ich führe!
    (*Er macht eine unanständige Gebärde.*)

DIE HEXE (*lacht unmäßig*).

Ha! Ha! Das ist in Eurer Art!
Ihr seid ein Schelm, wie Ihr nur immer wart!

MEPHISTOPHELES (*zu* FAUST).

Mein Freund, das lerne wohl verstehn!
Dies ist die Art, mit Hexen umzugehn.

DIE HEXE.

Nun sagt, ihr Herren, was ihr schafft.

MEPHISTOPHELES.

Ein gutes Glas von dem bekannten Saft!
Doch muß ich Euch ums älteste bitten;   2520
Die Jahre doppeln seine Kraft.

DIE HEXE.

Gar gern! Hier hab' ich eine Flasche,
Aus der ich selbst zuweilen nasche,
Die auch nicht mehr im mindsten stinkt;
Ich will euch gern ein Gläschen geben.
    (*Leise.*)
Doch wenn es dieser Mann unvorbereitet trinkt,
So kann er, wißt Ihr wohl, nicht eine Stunde leben.

MEPHISTOPHELES.

Es ist ein guter Freund, dem es gedeihen soll;

I've worn false calves these many years.

WITCH (*dancing*).

I'll shriek with glee, I'll lose my brain,
my Squire Satan has come back again!

MEPHISTOPHELES.

Such appellation, hag, is out of place.

WITCH.

What's wrong, what harm is there in it?

MEPHISTOPHELES.

It's now a name for fairy tales and fables;
the people are as miserable as ever—
the Evil One is gone, the evil ones remain.
You call me Baron, that will do for now.   2510
I am a cavalier, like other cavaliers.
You cannot doubt the noble blood in me.
Just take a look at my escutcheon.
    (*Makes an obscene gesture.*)

WITCH (*bursts out laughing*).

Ha! Ha! Ha! There's my little devil!
As shameless now as ever!

MEPHISTOPHELES (*to* FAUST).

My friend, I hope you understand it well.
This is the way we deal with witches.

WITCH.

Now tell me, sirs, what's on your mind.

MEPHISTOPHELES.

Get me a glassful of your famous juice!
But please, the oldest you can find—   2520
where years of age have multiplied its strength.

WITCH.

With pleasure! I keep a handy bottle on my person,
from which I snitch a little now and then.
The stink has gone from it completely.
Yes, indeed, I'll gladly let you have a swig.
    (*Softly.*)
But if this man should drink it when he's not prepared,
he would die within the hour, as you know.

MEPHISTOPHELES.

He is my friend; he should be the better for the potion.

Ich gönn' ihm gern das Beste deiner Küche.
Zieh deinen Kreis, sprich deine Sprüche,   2530
Und gib ihm eine Tasse voll!

> (*Die* HEXE, *mit seltsamen Gebärden, zieht
> einen Kreis und stellt wunderbare Sachen
> hinein; indessen fangen die Gläser an zu
> klingen, die Kessel zu tönen, und machen
> Musik. Zuletzt bringt sie ein großes Buch,
> stellt die Meerkatzen in den Kreis, die ihr
> zum Pult dienen und die Fackel halten müs-
> sen. Sie winkt* FAUSTEN, *zu ihr zu treten.*)

FAUST (*zu* MEPHISTOPHELES).

Nein, sage mir, was soll das werden?
Das tolle Zeug, die rasenden Gebärden,
Der abgeschmackteste Betrug,
Sind mir bekannt, verhaßt genug.

MEPHISTOPHELES.

Ei Possen! Das ist nur zum Lachen;
Sei nur nicht ein so strenger Mann!
Sie muß als Arzt ein Hokuspokus machen,
Damit der Saft dir wohl gedeihen kann.

> (*Er nötigt* FAUSTEN, *in den Kreis zu treten.*)

DIE HEXE (*mit großer Emphase fängt an, aus dem Buche
zu deklamieren*).

Du mußt verstehn!   2540
Aus Eins mach Zehn,
Und Zwei laß gehn,
Und Drei mach gleich,
So bist du reich.
Verlier die Vier!
Aus Fünf und Sechs,
So sagt die Hex',
Mach Sieben und Acht,
So ist's vollbracht:
Und Neun ist Eins,   2550
Und Zehn ist keins.
Das ist das Hexen-Einmaleins.

FAUST.

Mich dünkt, die Alte spricht im Fieber.

He deserves the finest sample of your cookery.
Go draw your circle, speak your spells,   2530
pour him a gobletful.
    (*While making fantastic gestures, the* WITCH
    draws a circle and places strange objects into
    it; the glasses begin to ring, the kettles hum—
    a kind of music ensues. Finally the WITCH
    picks up a large tome and motions the apes to
    jump into the circle. Some hold torches, and
    the backs of others serve her as a reading lec-
    tern. She beckons FAUST *to approach.*)

FAUST (*to* MEPHISTOPHELES).
What is the drift of this performance?
What's all this nonsense, this frenzied mumbo-jumbo?
With such repugnant business
I am only too familiar by now.

MEPHISTOPHELES.
Don't be foolish! This is only for a laugh or two.
For once don't be the stern professor!
She adopts a healer's hocus-pocus
to make the juice agree with you.
    (*He makes* FAUST *step into the circle.*)

WITCH (*begins to declaim with great pathos from the book*).

                See how it's done!   2540
                Make ten from one,
                The two must go,
                And three is so,
                When four is lost,
                You earn the most.
                From five to six,
                By the witch's tricks,
                Come seven and eight
                In excellent state!
                And nine is lame   2550
                And ten is tame—
                All in the witch's numbers-game.[27]

FAUST.
I think the witch is running a high fever.

MEPHISTOPHELES.

    Das ist noch lange nicht vorüber,
    Ich kenn' es wohl, so klingt das ganze Buch;
    Ich habe manche Zeit damit verloren,
    Denn ein vollkommner Widerspruch
    Bleibt gleich geheimnisvoll für Kluge wie für Toren.
    Mein Freund, die Kunst ist alt und neu.
    Es war die Art zu allen Zeiten,   2560
    Durch Drei und Eins, und Eins und Drei
    Irrtum statt Wahrheit zu verbreiten.
    So schwätzt und lehrt man ungestört;
    Wer will sich mit den Narrn befassen?
    Gewöhnlich glaubt der Mensch, wenn er nur Worte hört,
    Es müsse sich dabei doch auch was denken lassen.

DIE HEXE (*fährt fort*).

          Die hohe Kraft
          Der Wissenschaft,
          Der ganzen Welt verborgen!
          Und wer nicht denkt,   2570
          Dem wird sie geschenkt,
          Er hat sie ohne Sorgen.

FAUST.

    Was sagt sie uns für Unsinn vor?
    Es wird mir gleich der Kopf zerbrechen.
    Mich dünkt, ich hör' ein ganzes Chor
    Von hunderttausend Narren sprechen.

MEPHISTOPHELES.

    Genug, genug, o treffliche Sibylle!
    Gib deinen Trank herbei, und fülle
    Die Schale rasch bis an den Rand hinan;
    Denn meinem Freund wird dieser Trunk nicht
        schaden: 2580
    Er ist ein Mann von vielen Graden,
    Der manchen guten Schluck getan.

DIE HEXE (*mit vielen Zeremonien, schenkt den Trank in eine
    Schale; wie sie* FAUST *an den Mund bringt, entsteht eine
    leichte Flamme*).

MEPHISTOPHELES.

    Nur frisch hinunter! Immer zu!

MEPHISTOPHELES.

You've barely heard the half of it.
I know it well—it is the tenor of her book;
I used it once and wasted time with it.
A bald and thorough contradiction
holds mystery for fools and clever men alike.
My friend, it is an old as well as novel art.
It was the custom then and now—   2560
by three and one and one and three—
to broadcast error instead of verity.
They teach and blabber undisturbed
and no one really doubts these fools.
So long as words will flow, there'll be the notion
that thought must be their part and parcel.

WITCH (*continues*).

When science lies buried,
The "why is" or "what is"
Need never be sought.
No one is worried;   2570
All science is gratis,
Need never be thought.

FAUST.

What kind of nonsense is she drooling?
Another dose of it will split my head in two.
It seems I hear a choir
of a hundred thousand fools.

MEPHISTOPHELES.

Enough, enough, O worthy Sibyl!
Bring on the drink, uncork the bottle,
and fill his goblet quickly to the brink.
No harm will come to our friend from this: 2580
He is a man of manifold degrees
who's quaffed a wholesome drink or two before.

WITCH (*while gesturing ceremoniously, she pours the potion into a
bowl; as* FAUST *puts it to his lips, a delicate flame leaps up*).

MEPHISTOPHELES.

Go to it, friend, don't hesitate.

Es wird dir gleich das Herz erfreuen.
Bist mit dem Teufel du und du,
Und willst dich vor der Flamme scheuen?
   (*Die* HEXE *löst den Kreis.* FAUST *tritt heraus.*)

MEPHISTOPHELES.
   Nun frisch hinaus! Du darfst nicht ruhn.
DIE HEXE.
   Mög' Euch das Schlückchen wohl behagen!
MEPHISTOPHELES (*zur* HEXE).
   Und kann ich dir was zu Gefallen tun,
   So darfst du mir's nur auf Walpurgis sagen.   2590
DIE HEXE.
   Hier ist ein Lied! wenn Ihr's zuweilen singt,
   So werdet Ihr besondre Wirkung spüren.
MEPHISTOPHELES (*zu* FAUST).
   Komm nur geschwind und laß dich führen;
   Du mußt notwendig transpirieren,
   Damit die Kraft durch Inn- und Äußres dringt.
   Den edlen Müßiggang lehr' ich hernach dich schätzen,
   Und bald empfindest du mit innigem Ergetzen,
   Wie sich Cupido regt und hin und wider springt.
FAUST.
   Laß mich nur schnell noch in den Spiegel schauen!
   Das Frauenbild war gar zu schön!   2600
MEPHISTOPHELES.
   Nein! Nein! Du sollst das Muster aller Frauen
   Nun bald leibhaftig vor dir sehn.
    (*Leise.*)
   Du siehst, mit diesem Trank im Leibe,
   Bald Helenen in jedem Weibe.

STRASSE

Faust, Margaret vorübergehend.

FAUST.
   Mein schönes Fräulein, darf ich wagen,
   Meinen Arm und Geleit Ihr anzutragen?

Before you know, your heart will soar with joy.
You are the devil's intimate—
and would retreat before a little fire?
    (*The* WITCH *breaks the circle.* FAUST *steps out.*)

MEPHISTOPHELES.
    Now out with you. Let's go, you must not rest.
WITCH.
    I hope the drink sits well with you.
MEPHISTOPHELES (*to the* WITCH).
    If you should ever need me for a favor,
    don't hesitate to call on me Walpurgis Night.[28]   2590
WITCH.
    Here is a song for you! If you would sing it now and then,
    you will experience its special powers.
MEPHISTOPHELES (*to* FAUST).
    Come quickly now, and let yourself be guided;
    you must perspire thoroughly
    so that the strength will penetrate within and out.
    Later on you'll learn to value leisure,
    and soon you'll sense with thorough satisfaction
    how Cupid stirs and prances to and fro.
FAUST.
    Just let me quickly look into the mirror!
    The woman's form was, oh, so fair!   2600
MEPHISTOPHELES.
    No! No! The paragon of womankind
    shall come before you in the flesh.
      (*Aside.*)
    With that potion in your belly
    you'll soon see Helena in every wench.

A STREET

Faust; Margaret passing by.

FAUST.
    My fairest lady, may I dare
    to offer you my arm and company?

MARGARET.

> Bin weder Fräulein, weder schön,
> Kann ungeleitet nach Hause gehn.
> (*Sie macht sich los und ab.*)

FAUST.

> Beim Himmel, dieses Kind ist schön!
> So etwas hab' ich nie gesehn.   2610
> Sie ist so sitt- und tugendreich,
> Und etwas schnippisch doch zugleich.
> Der Lippe Rot, der Wange Licht,
> Die Tage der Welt vergess' ich's nicht!
> Wie sie die Augen niederschlägt,
> Hat tief sich in mein Herz geprägt;
> Wie sie kurz angebunden war,
> Das ist nun zum Entzücken gar!
>   (*MEPHISTOPHELES tritt auf.*)

FAUST.

> Hör, du mußt mir die Dirne schaffen!

MEPHISTOPHELES.

> Nun, welche?

FAUST.

>   Sie ging just vorbei.   2620

MEPHISTOPHELES.

> Da die? Sie kam von ihrem Pfaffen,
> Der sprach sie aller Sünden frei;
> Ich schlich mich hart am Stuhl vorbei.
> Es ist ein gar unschuldig Ding,
> Das eben für nichts zur Beichte ging;
> Über die hab' ich keine Gewalt!

FAUST.

> Ist über vierzehn Jahr doch alt.

MEPHISTOPHELES.

> Du sprichst ja wie Hans Liederlich,
> Der begehrt jede liebe Blum' für sich,
> Und dünkelt ihm, es wär' kein' Ehr'   2630
> Und Gunst, die nicht zu pflücken wär';
> Geht aber doch nicht immer an.

FAUST.

> Mein Herr Magister Lobesan,

MARGARET.

Am neither lady, neither fair,
and need no escort to go home.
    (*She frees herself and exits.*)

FAUST.

My God, this child is beautiful!
I've never seen the like of it.   2610
She is so proper and so virtuous,
and yet a little snippy too.
The red of her lips, the light of her face,
will be forever in my mind!
The way she shyly drops her eyes
is stamped profoundly in my heart.
How pert and curt she was with me—
a sheer delight, an ecstasy!
    (MEPHISTOPHELES *enters.*)

FAUST.

Listen! Get that girl for me!

MEPHISTOPHELES.

Which girl?

FAUST.

                The one who just went by.   2620

MEPHISTOPHELES.

Oh, that one? She only left her priest just now
who absolved her soul from every sin;
I sneaked in right behind her bench.
She is a very innocent young thing
who went for nothing to confession.
I have no power over her.

FAUST.

But she's past fourteen already.

MEPHISTOPHELES.

You talk like Jack the Libertine,
who craves each lovely blossom for himself.
He fancies that all gifts and favors   2630
are free and ready for the plucking;
but there are times without successes.

FAUST.

My dear Professor Know-It-All,

Lass' Er mich mit dem Gesetz in Frieden!
Und das sag' ich Ihm kurz und gut:
Wenn nicht das süße junge Blut
Heut nacht in meinen Armen ruht,
So sind wir um Mitternacht geschieden.

MEPHISTOPHELES.

Bedenkt, was gehn und stehen mag!
Ich brauche wenigstens vierzehn Tag',   2640
Nur die Gelegenheit auszuspüren.

FAUST.

Hätt' ich nur sieben Stunden Ruh',
Brauchte den Teufel nicht dazu,
So ein Geschöpfchen zu verführen.

MEPHISTOPHELES.

Ihr sprecht schon fast wie ein Franzos;
Doch bitt' ich, laßt's Euch nicht verdrießen:
Was hilft's, nur grade zu genießen?
Die Freud' ist lange nicht so groß,
Als wenn Ihr erst herauf, herum,
Durch allerlei Brimborium,   2650
Das Püppchen geknetet und zugericht't,
Wie's lehret manche welsche Geschicht'.

FAUST.

Hab' Appetit auch ohne das.

MEPHISTOPHELES.

Jetzt ohne Schimpf und ohne Spaß.
Ich sag' Euch: mit dem schönen Kind
Geht's ein- für allemal nicht geschwind.
Mit Sturm ist da nichts einzunehmen;
Wir müssen uns zur List bequemen.

FAUST.

Schaff mir etwas vom Engelsschatz!
Führ mich an ihren Ruheplatz!   2660
Schaff mir ein Halstuch von ihrer Brust,
Ein Strumpfband meiner Liebeslust!

MEPHISTOPHELES.

Damit Ihr seht, daß ich Eurer Pein
Will förderlich und dienstlich sein,
Wollen wir keinen Augenblick verlieren,

don't lecture me on legal matters!
I'll be brief and to the point:
Unless that sweet and youthful blood
lies in my arms this very evening,
by midnight you and I part company.

MEPHISTOPHELES.

Don't ask for the impossible!
I need at least two weeks, and more,   2640
to ferret out an opportunity.

FAUST.

Had I but seven hours' peace,
I should not need the devil's help
to seduce that darling creature.

MEPHISTOPHELES.

You're talking almost like a Frenchman now;
there is no need to be discouraged.
What good is easy consummation?
The pleasure is not half so keen
as when you first must clear your way
through sundry growth and thickets.   2650
Mold your moppet, knead her into shape,
as you have read in those Italian stories.

FAUST.

Thank you, my appetite is good enough
          without such titillations.

MEPHISTOPHELES.

No nonsense now, I'm serious.
Once for all, the matter is not easy.
You need some time to get this child.
You cannot take the citadel by storm;
we must employ some skill and strategy.

FAUST.

Get me a token from my angel's dress!
Lead me to her bed and chamber!   2660
Get me a kerchief from her breast,
a garter for my passionate desire.

MEPHISTOPHELES.

Your pangs of love, as you shall see,
are not without my sympathy;
we must not lose a moment's time;

Will Euch noch heut in ihr Zimmer führen.

FAUST.

Und soll sie sehn? sie haben?

MEPHISTOPHELES.

                                    Nein!

Sie wird bei einer Nachbarin sein.
Indessen könnt Ihr ganz allein
An aller Hoffnung künft'ger Freuden   2670
In ihrem Dunstkreis satt Euch weiden.

FAUST.

Können wir hin?

MEPHISTOPHELES.

                        Es ist noch zu früh.

FAUST.

Sorg du mir für ein Geschenk für sie!

                                        (*Ab.*)

MEPHISTOPHELES.

Gleich schenken? Das ist brav! Da wird er reüssieren!
Ich kenne manchen schönen Platz
Und manchen altvergrabnen Schatz;
Ich muß ein bißchen revidieren.

                                        (*Ab.*)

ABEND

Ein kleines reinliches Zimmer.

MARGARET (*ihre Zöpfe flechtend und aufbindend*).

Ich gäb' was drum, wenn ich nur wüßt',
Wer heut der Herr gewesen ist!
Er sah gewiß recht wacker aus,   2680
Und ist aus einem edlen Haus;
Das konnt' ich ihm an der Stirne lesen
Er wär' auch sonst nicht so keck gewesen.

                                        (*Ab.*)

(MEPHISTOPHELES, FAUST.)

MEPHISTOPHELES.

Herein, ganz leise, nur herein!

I'll guide you to her room this very day.

FAUST.
   And shall I see her, have her?

MEPHISTOPHELES.

                              No!
   She will be in her neighbor's house.
   Meanwhile you may indulge yourself alone
   in your hopes of future ecstasies   2670
   and stay to breathe the fragrance of her chamber.

FAUST.
   May we go now?

MEPHISTOPHELES.
                       It's still too soon.

FAUST.
   Get me a gift for her this afternoon.

                                      (*Exits.*)

MEPHISTOPHELES.
   A gift so soon? That's nice! It bodes success for you.
   I know of several likely places
   and several treasures buried long ago;
   I'd better scout about a bit.

                                      (*Exits.*)

EVENING

A *small, neatly kept room.*

MARGARET (*braiding and tying up her hair*).
   I'd give anything if only I could know
   who was that gentleman today!
   I think he cut a gallant figure   2680
   and is of noble family.
   I could plainly see it in his face—
   else he'd not have been so bold with me.

                                      (*Exits.*)

   (MEPHISTOPHELES, FAUST.)

MEPHISTOPHELES.
   Step in—softly now—but enter!

FAUST (*nach einigem Stillschweigen*).
   Ich bitte dich, laß mich allein!
MEPHISTOPHELES (*herumspürend*).
   Nicht jedes Mädchen hält so rein.

                               (*Ab.*)

FAUST.
   Willkommen, süßer Dämmerschein,
   Der du dies Heiligtum durchwebst!
   Ergreif mein Herz, du süße Liebespein,
   Die du vom Tau der Hoffnung schmachtend lebst!   2690
   Wie atmet rings Gefühl der Stille,
   Der Ordnung, der Zufriedenheit!
   In dieser Armut welche Fülle!
   In diesem Kerker welche Seligkeit!
     (*Er wirft sich auf den ledernen Sessel am
     Bette.*)
   O nimm mich auf, der du die Vorwelt schon
   Bei Freud' und Schmerz im offnen Arm empfangen!
   Wie oft, ach! hat an diesem Väterthron
   Schon eine Schar von Kindern rings gehangen!
   Vielleicht hat, dankbar für den heil'gen Christ,
   Mein Liebchen hier, mit vollen Kinderwangen,   2700
   Dem Ahnherrn fromm die welke Hand geküßt.
   Ich fühl', o Mädchen, deinen Geist
   Der Füll' und Ordnung um mich säuseln,
   Der mütterlich dich täglich unterweist,
   Den Teppich auf den Tisch dich reinlich breiten heißt,
   Sogar den Sand zu deinen Füßen kräuseln.
   O liebe Hand! so göttergleich!
   Die Hütte wird durch dich ein Himmelreich.
   Und hier!
     (*Er hebt einen Bettvorhang auf.*)
          Was faßt mich für ein Wonnegraus!
   Hier möcht' ich volle Stunden säumen.   2710
   Natur! hier bildetest in leichten Träumen
   Den eingebornen Engel aus!
   Hier lag das Kind, mit warmem Leben
   Den zarten Busen angefüllt,
   Und hier mit heilig reinem Weben

FAUST (*after keeping silent for some time*).
   I beg of you—leave me alone!
MEPHISTOPHELES (*looking around*).
   Not every girl's this neat and tidy.

                        (*Exits.*)

FAUST.
   Welcome, lovely twilight glow,
   how you pervade this sacred shrine!
   Grip my heart, O keen-edged lover's pain,
   that languishes on mere dewdrops of a hope.   2690
   A sense of peace breathes in this room,
   of order and contentment!
   What fullness in this poverty,
   what blessedness within this cell.
     (*He throws himself into a leather armchair
     next to the bed.*)
   You who once with open arms received the joys
   and sorrows of a world gone by, oh, take me in!
   How often round about this soft ancestral throne
   have swarms of children clung!
   Perhaps on Christmas Eve, in gratitude,
   my round-cheeked sweetheart kissed her grandsire's wilted
       hand.   2700
   I feel, O girl, the whisper of your spirit,
   of order and abundance everywhere,
   which, motherly, instructs you daily how
   to spread the cloth upon the table,
   and even how to smooth the sand beneath your feet.
   Beloved hand, so godlike and so sweet!
   Through you this cottage is a paradise.
   And here!
     (*He lifts a bed-curtain.*)
           What raptures come over me!
   Here I could while away the fullest hours.   2710
   O Nature, here you shaped in airy dreams
   your very own angelic child!
   Here lay the girl, her tender bosom filled
   with warm and vibrant breath of life,
   and here, on Nature's purest looms,

Entwirkte sich das Götterbild!

Und du! Was hat dich hergeführt?
Wie innig fühl' ich mich gerührt!
Was willst du hier? Was wird das Herz dir schwer?
Armsel'ger Faust! ich kenne dich nicht mehr.   2720

Umgibt mich hier ein Zauberduft?
Mich drang's, so grade zu genießen,
Und fühle mich in Liebestraum zerfließen!
Sind wir ein Spiel von jedem Druck der Luft?

Und träte sie den Augenblick herein,
Wie würdest du für deinen Frevel büßen!
Der große Hans, ach wie so klein!
Läg', hingeschmolzen, ihr zu Füßen.

MEPHISTOPHELES (*kommt*).
    Geschwind! ich seh' sie unten kommen.
FAUST.
    Fort! Fort! Ich kehre nimmermehr!   2730
MEPHISTOPHELES.
    Hier ist ein Kästchen leidlich schwer,
    Ich hab's wo anders hergenommen.
    Stellt's hier nur immer in den Schrein,
    Ich schwör' Euch, ihr vergehn die Sinnen;
    Ich tat Euch Sächelchen hinein,
    Um eine andre zu gewinnen.
    Zwar Kind ist Kind und Spiel ist Spiel.
FAUST.
    Ich weiß nicht, soll ich?
MEPHISTOPHELES.
                    Fragt Ihr viel?
    Meint Ihr vielleicht den Schatz zu wahren?
    Dann rat' ich Eurer Lüsternheit,   2740
    Die liebe schöne Tageszeit
    Und mir die weitere Müh' zu sparen.
    Ich hoff' nicht, daß Ihr geizig seid!
    Ich kratz' den Kopf, reib' an den Händen—

was wrought the semblance of divinity.

And you, what led you to this chamber?
How deeply you are stirred!
Your heart is heavy, and you feel so out of place.
Wretched Faust! Who are you anyway?   2720

Am I moving in a magic haze?
I came to seize the crassest pleasure,
and now I dissolve in dreams of love!
Are we the sports of every whim of the weather?

And should she enter at this very moment,
how you would rue your crude transgression!
Then Faust would suddenly be very small
and languish helpless at her feet.

MEPHISTOPHELES (*entering*).
  Quick, my friend! I see her coming down below.

FAUST.
  Away from here, and never to return!   2730

MEPHISTOPHELES.
  I have a little jewel box, not very heavy,
  which I acquired at another place.
  Relax, and put it in the wardrobe there;
  I swear she'll be beside herself with pleasure.
  I enclosed some little trinkets
  which were meant for someone other.
  But a child's a child and a game is a game.

FAUST.
  I don't know—shall I?

MEPHISTOPHELES.
                    Don't ask questions!
  You mean to keep the trinkets for yourself?
  May I advise Your Lustfulness   2740
  to use the happy daylight hours
  and spare me further toil and trouble!
  I hope you're not a stingy man!
  I scratch my head and rub my palms—

(Er stellt das Kästchen in den Schrein und
drückt das Schloß wieder zu.)
Nur fort! geschwind!—,
Um Euch das süße junge Kind
Nach Herzens Wunsch und Will' zu wenden;
Und Ihr seht drein,
Als solltet Ihr in den Hörsaal hinein,
Als stünden grau leibhaftig vor Euch da   2750
Physik und Metaphysika!
Nur fort!

                      (Ab.)

MARGARET *(mit einer Lampe)*.
Es ist so schwül, so dumpfig hie,
    (Sie macht das Fenster auf.)
Und ist doch eben so warm nicht drauß.
Es wird mir so, ich weiß nicht wie—
Ich wollt', die Mutter käm' nach Haus.
Mir läuft ein Schauer übern ganzen Leib—
Bin doch ein töricht furchtsam Weib!
    (Sie fängt an zu singen, indem sie sich
    auszieht.)

               Es war ein König in Thule
               Gar treu bis an das Grab,   2760
               Dem sterbend seine Buhle
               Einen goldnen Becher gab.

               Es ging ihm nichts darüber,
               Er leert' ihn jeden Schmaus;
               Die Augen gingen ihm über,
               So oft er trank daraus.

               Und als er kam zu sterben,
               Zählt' er seine Städt' im Reich,
               Gönnt' alles seinem Erben,
               Den Becher nicht zugleich.   2770

               Er saß beim Königsmahle,
               Die Ritter um ihn her,
               Auf hohem Vätersaale,

(*He places the box in the wardrobe and clicks the lock shut.*)

Away from here! Let's hurry—
so we may bend the sweet young thing
to your wish and heart's desire.
You stand there with a sad expression
like a student entering the lecture hall,
as if before you in gray majesty   2750
stood Physics and Metaphysics in person!
Away from here!

(*Exits.*)

MARGARET (*carrying a lamp*).
   It is so close, so sultry here,
      (*She opens the window.*)
   and yet it's not too warm outside.
   It makes me feel so—I don't know.
   If only Mother would come home.
   I feel a chill go down my spine—
   I'm such a silly, fearful girl.
      (*She begins to sing, while undressing.*)

            There was a king in Thule,
            Was true unto the grave.
            To him his dying lady   2760
            A golden goblet gave.

            And he prized nothing dearer;
            At feasts he drained it dry.
            And when he held the goblet,
            The tears would fill his eye.

            And when he came to dying,
            He counted land and town.
            He gave all to his children,
            But kept the cup his own.   2770

            With him in his great chamber
            Sat knights of high degree.
            They held the royal dinner

Dort auf dem Schloß am Meer.

Dort stand der alte Zecher,
Trank letzte Lebensglut,
Und warf den heiligen Becher
Hinunter in die Flut.

Er sah ihn stürzen, trinken
Und sinken tief ins Meer,   2780
Die Augen täten ihm sinken,
Trank nie einen Tropfen mehr.

(Sie eröffnet den Schrein, ihre Kleider ein-
zuräumen, und erblickt das Schmuck-
kästchen.)

Wie kommt das schöne Kästchen hier herein?
Ich schloß doch ganz gewiß den Schrein.
Es ist doch wunderbar! Was mag wohl drinne sein?
Vielleicht bracht's jemand als ein Pfand,
Und meine Mutter lieh darauf.
Da hängt ein Schlüsselchen am Band,
Ich denke wohl, ich mach' es auf!
Was ist das? Gott im Himmel! Schau,   2790
So was hab' ich mein' Tage nicht gesehn!
Ein Schmuck! Mit dem könnt' eine Edelfrau
Am höchsten Feiertage gehn.
Wie sollte mir die Kette stehn?
Wem mag die Herrlichkeit gehören?

(Sie putzt sich damit auf und tritt vor den
Spiegel.)

Wenn nur die Ohrring' meine wären!
Man sieht doch gleich ganz anders drein.
Was hilft euch Schönheit, junges Blut?
Das ist wohl alles schön und gut,
Allein man läßt's auch alles sein;   2800
Man lobt euch halb mit Erbarmen.
Nach Golde drängt,
Am Golde hängt
Doch alles. Ach wir Armen!

In the castle by the sea.

There stood the old carouser
And drank his last red wine,
Then flung the holy vessel
Into the foamy brine.

He saw it sway and falter
And slip into the sea;   2780
His eyes did sink forever,
And nevermore drank he.[29]
(*She opens the wardrobe to arrange
her dresses and notices the jewel box.*)

How did that handsome jewel case get here?
I am quite sure I locked the wardrobe door.
It's very strange! I wonder what's inside?
Perhaps some neighbor brought it as a pawn,
for which my mother lent some money.
There is a key tied neatly to a ribbon;
I have a mind to open it and see.
What's that? My God in Heaven! Look!   2790
I never saw the like of this before.
It's jewelry! The greatest lady
could wear this piece on highest holidays.
How would these jewels look on me?
Whose could they ever be?
(*She adorns herself with the jewels and steps
before the mirror.*)
I wish these earrings were my own.
One looks so different right away.
What good is youth and beauty for the like of us!
They say, "All that is very good,"
and then they leave us as we are.   2800
Their praise is half in pity.
They race after gold
and cling to gold,
and we stay poor forever.

SPAZIERGANG

Faust in Gedanken auf und ab gehend.

Zu ihm Mephistopheles.

MEPHISTOPHELES.

Bei aller verschmähten Liebe! Beim höllischen Elemente!
Ich wollt', ich wüßte was Ärgers, daß ich's fluchen könnte!

FAUST.

Was hast? was kneipt dich denn so sehr?
So kein Gesicht sah ich in meinem Leben!

MEPHISTOPHELES.

Ich möcht' mich gleich dem Teufel übergeben,
Wenn ich nur selbst kein Teufel wär'!   2810

FAUST.

Hat sich dir was im Kopf verschoben?
Dich kleidet's, wie ein Rasender zu toben!

MEPHISTOPHELES.

Denkt nur, den Schmuck, für Gretchen angeschafft,
Den hat ein Pfaff hinweggerafft!—
Die Mutter kriegt das Ding zu schauen,
Gleich fängt's ihr heimlich an zu grauen:
Die Frau hat gar einen feinen Geruch,
Schnuffelt immer im Gebetbuch,
Und riecht's einem jeden Möbel an,
Ob das Ding heilig ist oder profan;   2820
Und an dem Schmuck da spürt' sie's klar,
Daß dabei nicht viel Segen war.
Mein Kind, rief sie, ungerechtes Gut
Befängt die Seele, zehrt auf das Blut.
Wollen's der Mutter Gottes weihen,
Wird uns mit Himmels-Manna erfreuen!
Margretlein zog ein schiefes Maul,
Ist halt, dacht' sie, ein geschenkter Gaul,
Und wahrlich! gottlos ist nicht der,
Der ihn so fein gebracht hierher.   2830
Die Mutter ließ einen Pfaffen kommen;
Der hatte kaum den Spaß vernommen,

PROMENADE

*Faust, lost in thought, walking
up and down.*

Mephistopheles enters.

MEPHISTOPHELES.

By all rejected lovers! By every hellish element!
I wish I had a better malediction.

FAUST.

What ails you now? What's pinching you?
In all my life I've never seen a face like that.

MEPHISTOPHELES.

I'd give myself over to the devil,
if I were not he himself.   2810

FAUST.

Is there a screw loose in your head?
Your ravings are a telling symptom.

MEPHISTOPHELES.

Just think! The jewelry you gave to Gretchen—
slipped in the pocket of a priest!
When her mother took a look at it,
she got the secret shudders!
That woman has an excellent sense of smell
always sniffing in her prayer book.
Her nose can tell from far away
which is sacred, which profane.   2820
And those jewels left no doubt in her
that their presence was not wholly blessed.
"My child," she cried, "ill-gotten gain
ensnares the soul and saps the blood.
We'll offer it to our blessed Virgin,
who will make God's manna rain on us!"
Little Margaret made a face and pouted.
"It's a gift horse after all," she thought,
"whoever brought it here so cleverly
could never be a godless person."   2830
The mother asked the priest to have a look,
and he had scarcely heard what was afoot

Ließ sich den Anblick wohl behagen.
Er sprach: So ist man recht gesinnt!
Wer überwindet, der gewinnt.
Die Kirche hat einen guten Magen,
Hat ganze Länder aufgefressen,
Und doch noch nie sich übergessen;
Die Kirch' allein, meine lieben Frauen,
Kann ungerechtes Gut verdauen.   2840

FAUST.

Das ist ein allgemeiner Brauch.
Ein Jud' und König kann es auch.

MEPHISTOPHELES.

Strich drauf ein Spange, Kett' und Ring',
Als wären's eben Pfifferling',
Dankt' nicht weniger und nicht mehr,
Als ob's ein Korb voll Nüsse wär',
Versprach ihnen allen himmlischen Lohn—
Und sie waren sehr erbaut davon.

FAUST.

Und Gretchen?

MEPHISTOPHELES.

                    Sitzt nun unruhvoll,
Weiß weder, was sie will noch soll,   2850
Denkt ans Geschmeide Tag und Nacht,
Noch mehr an den, der's ihr gebracht.

FAUST.

Des Liebchens Kummer tut mir leid.
Schaff du ihr gleich ein neu Geschmeid'!
Am ersten war ja so nicht viel.

MEPHISTOPHELES.

O ja, dem Herrn ist alles Kinderspiel!

FAUST.

Und mach, und richt's nach meinem Sinn!
Häng dich an ihre Nachbarin!
Sei, Teufel, doch nur nicht wie Brei,
Und schaff ein neuen Schmuck herbei!   2860

MEPHISTOPHELES.

Ja, gnäd'ger Herr, von Herzen gerne.

                              (FAUST *ab*.)

when he eyed the gems with muted glee
and said: "You've done the proper thing!
Who conquers self will be rewarded in the end.
The church has always had an iron belly,
has swallowed states and countries now and then,
and yet it never overate.
The church alone, dear women, can digest
ill-gotten gains without a stomachache."   2840

FAUST.

That is a universal custom;
a Jew or king might do the same.

MEPHISTOPHELES.

He then took brooch and chain and ring
as if they had been chicken feed
and made no greater show of gratitude
than for a basketful of nuts.
He promised them rewards of every kind,
and they were highly edified.

FAUST.

And Gretchen?

MEPHISTOPHELES.

                    Sits about and frets,
not knowing what she wants or ought to do,   2850
thinks of the jewels day and night
and even more of him who brought them.

FAUST.

My sweetheart's trouble saddens me.
Go, get at once another ornament!
The first one was not very much.

MEPHISTOPHELES.

Oh yes, all this is child's play to the gentleman!

FAUST.

Move quickly and arrange things to my liking,
and worm your way into her neighbor's graces.
Are you a devil of molasses?
Go, get another set of precious stones for her!   2860

MEPHISTOPHELES.

Yes, gracious sir! My pleasure, sir!

                                        (FAUST *exits.*)

MEPHISTOPHELES.
>So ein verliebter Tor verpufft
>Euch Sonne, Mond und alle Sterne
>Zum Zeitvertreib dem Liebchen in die Luft.

(Ab.)

DER NACHBARIN HAUS

MARTHE (*allein*).
>Gott verzeih's meinem lieben Mann,
>Er hat an mir nicht wohl getan!
>Geht da stracks in die Welt hinein,
>Und läßt mich auf dem Stroh allein.
>Tät ihn doch wahrlich nicht betrüben,
>Tät ihn, weiß Gott, recht herzlich lieben.   2870
>   (*Sie weint.*)
>Vielleicht ist er gar tot!—O Pein!——
>Hätt' ich nur einen Totenschein!
>   (**MARGARET** *kommt.*)

MARGARET.
>Frau Marthe!

MARTHE.
>   Gretelchen, was soll's?

MARGARET.
>Fast sinken mir die Kniee nieder!
>Da find' ich so ein Kästchen wieder
>In meinem Schrein, von Ebenholz,
>Und Sachen herrlich ganz und gar,
>Weit reicher, als das erste war.

MARTHE.
>Das muß Sie nicht der Mutter sagen;
>Tät's wieder gleich zur Beichte tragen.   2880

MARGARET.
>Ach seh' Sie nur! ach schau' Sie nur!

MARTHE (*putzt sie auf*).
>O du glücksel'ge Kreatur!

MARGARET.
>Darf mich, leider, nicht auf der Gassen,
>Noch in der Kirche mit sehen lassen.

MEPHISTOPHELES.

> The lovesick fool. He'd blow away
> the sun and moon and all the stars,
> as a pastime for his sweetheart.

> > (*Exits.*)

THE NEIGHBOR'S HOUSE

MARTHA (*alone*).

> May God forgive my husband's escapades;
> he's done me a great injury!
> Suddenly he's off into the big wide world
> and leaves me on the straw alone.
> I never gave him cause for grief
> because, God knows, I dearly loved the man.   2870
> > (*She weeps.*)
> Perhaps he's dead by now! Oh, grief—
> and not to have it certified!
> > (MARGARET *enters.*)

MARGARET.

> Martha!

MARTHA.

> > Gretchen, what's up?

MARGARET.

> I thought my knees were giving out!
> I found another jewel box of ebony
> placed neatly on the wardrobe shelf.
> The things are beautiful beyond compare,
> far richer than the first ones yet.

MARTHA.

> This time you must not tell your mother.
> She'd promptly take it to a priest again.   2880

MARGARET.

> Just look at this. Oh my, just look and see!

MARTHA (*arranging the jewels on* MARGARET).

> You *are* a lucky creature, you!

MARGARET.

> I dare not walk about with these,
> and cannot show myself in church or street.

MARTHE.

Komm du nur oft zu mir herüber,
Und leg den Schmuck hier heimlich an;
Spazier ein Stündchen lang dem Spiegelglas vorüber,
Wir haben unsre Freude dran;
Und dann gibt's einen Anlaß, gibt's ein Fest,
Wo man's so nach und nach den Leuten sehen läßt.   2890
Ein Kettchen erst, die Perle dann ins Ohr;
Die Mutter sieht's wohl nicht, man macht ihr auch was vor.

MARGARET.

Wer konnte nur die beiden Kästchen bringen?
Es geht nicht zu mit rechten Dingen!
   (*Es klopft.*)
Ach Gott! mag das meine Mutter sein?

MARTHE (*durchs Vorhängel guckend*).

Es ist ein fremder Herr—Herein!
   (**MEPHISTOPHELES** *tritt auf.*)

MEPHISTOPHELES.

Bin so frei, grad' hereinzutreten,
Muß bei den Frauen Verzeihn erbeten.
   (*Tritt ehrerbietig vor* **MARGARETEN** *zurück.*)
Wollte nach Frau Marthe Schwerdtlein fragen!

MARTHE.

Ich bin's, was hat der Herr zu sagen?   2900

MEPHISTOPHELES (*leise zur ihr*).

Ich kenne Sie jetzt, mir ist das genug;
Sie hat da gar vornehmen Besuch.
Verzeiht die Freiheit, die ich genommen,
Will Nachmittage wiederkommen.

MARTHE (*laut*).

Denk, Kind, um alles in der Welt!
Der Herr dich für ein Fräulein hält.

MARGARET.

Ich bin ein armes junges Blut;
Ach Gott! der Herr ist gar zu gut:
Schmuck und Geschmeide sind nicht mein.

MEPHISTOPHELES.

Ach, es ist nicht der Schmuck allein;   2910
Sie hat ein Wesen, einen Blick so scharf!

MARTHA.

Come to me as often as you please;
put on your jewels secretly;
parade an hour, if you like, before my mirror,
so we can both enjoy the sight.
There'll soon be an occasion, some festivity,
where slowly, by degrees, you'll let the people see   2890
the necklace first, and then the earrings made of pearl.
Your mother will not notice, or else we'll think of what to say.

MARGARET.

Who could have brought the jewel boxes?
There's something not quite right.
    (A knock at the door.)
Oh, goodness! Could that be my mother?

MARTHA (peering through the blind).

A foreign gentleman—Come in!
    (MEPHISTOPHELES enters.)

MEPHISTOPHELES.

I take the liberty of stepping through your door.
I beg the gracious ladies' pardon.
    (Steps back reverently on seeing MARGARET.)
I seek a Mrs. Martha Schwerdtlein hereabouts.

MARTHA.

That's me. What is the gentleman's pleasure?   2900

MEPHISTOPHELES (softly to MARTHA).

I know now who you are, that is enough for me;
I see you're with a lady of high standing.
Forgive my bold demeanor,
I will return this afternoon.

MARTHA (aloud).

Just think, my dear, for heaven's sake!
He took you for a noble lady!

MARGARET.

I'm just a poor young girl;
I'm afraid the gentleman is much too kind.
These gems and spangles don't belong to me.

MEPHISTOPHELES.

Ah, but it is not the jewelry alone;   2910
it is the lady's presence and commanding eye!

Wie freut mich's, daß ich bleiben darf.

MARTHE.

Was bringt Er denn? Verlange sehr—

MEPHISTOPHELES.

Ich wollt', ich hätt' eine frohere Mär!
Ich hoffe, Sie läßt mich's drum nicht büßen:
Ihr Mann ist tot und läßt Sie grüßen.

MARTHE.

Ist tot? das treue Herz! O weh!
Mein Mann ist tot! Ach, ich vergeh'!

MARGARET.

Ach! liebe Frau, verzweifelt nicht!

MEPHISTOPHELES.

So hört die traurige Geschicht'!   2920

MARGARET.

Ich möchte drum mein' Tag' nicht lieben,
Würde mich Verlust zu Tode betrüben.

MEPHISTOPHELES.

Freud' muß Leid, Leid muß Freude haben.

MARTHE.

Erzählt mir seines Lebens Schluß!

MEPHISTOPHELES.

Er liegt in Padua begraben
Beim heiligen Antonius,
An einer wohlgeweihten Stätte
Zum ewig kühlen Ruhebette.

MARTHE.

Habt Ihr sonst nichts an mich zu bringen?

MEPHISTOPHELES.

Ja, eine Bitte, groß und schwer;   2930
Lass' Sie doch ja für ihn dreihundert Messen singen!
Im übrigen sind meine Taschen leer.

MARTHE.

Was! nicht ein Schaustück? Kein Geschmeid'?
Was jeder Handwerksbursch im Grund des Säckels spart,
Zum Angedenken aufbewahrt,
Und lieber hungert, lieber bettelt!

MEPHISTOPHELES.

Madam, es tut mir herzlich leid;

I am so pleased that I may stay awhile.

MARTHA.
What brings you here? Please be so kind—

MEPHISTOPHELES.
I wish I had some better news.
I only hope you won't be cross with me.
Your husband's dead and sends his greetings.

MARTHA.
Is dead? The faithful heart! Alas!
My husband's dead! Ah, how I suffer!

MARGARET.
Dear friend, dear neighbor, don't despair!

MEPHISTOPHELES.
Here is my sorrowful report!   2920

MARGARET.
I should never want to be in love;
a loss would make me die of grief.

MEPHISTOPHELES.
With joy goes sorrow, and with sorrow, joy.

MARTHA.
Please tell me of his final hours.

MEPHISTOPHELES.
His grave was dug in Padua,
the city of Saint Anthony.[30]
He lies in consecrated ground,
a cool eternal resting place.

MARTHA.
And have you nothing else for me?

MEPHISTOPHELES.
Oh yes, a grave and serious request;   2930
he wants three hundred masses for his soul.
Apart from that, my hands are empty.

MARTHA.
What? No token? Not one piece of jewelry?
Every craftsman stows away a thing or two
deep in his satchel as a souvenir
and would sooner starve and beg than lose it.

MEPHISTOPHELES.
It grieves me very much,

Allein er hat sein Geld wahrhaftig nicht verzettelt.
Auch er bereute seine Fehler sehr,
Ja, und bejammerte sein Unglück noch viel mehr.   2940

MARGARET.

Ach! daß die Menschen so unglücklich sind!
Gewiß, ich will für ihn manch Requiem noch beten.

MEPHISTOPHELES.

Ihr wäret wert, gleich in die Eh' zu treten:
Ihr seid ein liebenswürdig Kind.

MARGARET.

Ach nein, das geht jetzt noch nicht an.

MEPHISTOPHELES.

Ist's nicht ein Mann, sei's derweil ein Galan.
's ist eine der größten Himmelsgaben,
So ein lieb Ding im Arm zu haben.

MARGARET.

Das ist des Landes nicht der Brauch.

MEPHISTOPHELES.

Brauch oder nicht! Es gibt sich auch.   2950

MARTHE.

Erzählt mir doch!

MEPHISTOPHELES.

       Ich stand an seinem Sterbebette,
Es war was besser als von Mist,
Von halbgefaultem Stroh; allein er starb als Christ,
Und fand, daß er weit mehr noch auf der Zeche hätte.
„Wie", rief er, „muß ich mich von Grund aus hassen,
So mein Gewerb, mein Weib so zu verlassen!
Ach, die Erinnrung tötet mich.
Vergäb' sie mir nur noch in diesem Leben!"

MARTHE (weinend).

Der gute Mann! ich hab' ihm längst vergeben.

MEPHISTOPHELES.

„Allein, weiß Gott! sie war mehr schuld als ich."   2960

MARTHE.

Das lügt er! Was! am Rand des Grabs zu lügen!

MEPHISTOPHELES.

Er fabelte gewiß in letzten Zügen,
Wenn ich nur halb ein Kenner bin.

but your husband did not squander money.
He regretted all his errors too,
and his misfortunes even more. 2940

MARGARET.

Ah, why are people so unhappy!
Yes, I will gladly offer him some requiems.

MEPHISTOPHELES.

You ought to marry right away,
you're such a kindly and endearing creature.

MARGARET.

Ah no, it would never do, not yet.

MEPHISTOPHELES.

If not a husband, then perhaps a lover.
It would be among the greatest gifts from heaven,
to embrace a lovely woman like yourself.

MARGARET.

That is not the custom hereabouts.

MEPHISTOPHELES.

Custom or no custom. It can be arranged. 2950

MARTHA.

But please, continue your report.

MEPHISTOPHELES.

        His deathbed, where I stood,
was not exactly horse manure,
but rotted straw; but still and all he died a Christian.
He found he left a number of unsettled scores.
"How deeply must I hate myself," he cried,
"I left my wife and my profession!
Alas, the memory will do me in.
I crave her pardon while I still draw breath."

MARTHA (*crying*).

The dear good man. Long since I have forgiven him.

MEPHISTOPHELES.

"And yet, God knows, she was much more to blame
     than I." 2960

MARTHA.

The liar! What! He lied with one foot in the grave!

MEPHISTOPHELES.

I think he raved a bit before he breathed his last,
if I'm but half a connoisseur;

„Ich hatte", sprach er, „nicht zum Zeitvertreib zu gaffen,
Erst Kinder, und dann Brot für sie zu schaffen,
Und Brot im allerweitsten Sinn,
Und konnte nicht einmal mein Teil in Frieden essen."

MARTHE.

Hat er so aller Treu', so aller Lieb' vergessen,
Der Plackerei bei Tag und Nacht!

MEPHISTOPHELES.

Nicht doch, er hat Euch herzlich dran gedacht.   2970
Er sprach: „Als ich nun weg von Malta ging,
Da betet' ich für Frau und Kinder brünstig;
Uns war denn auch der Himmel günstig,
Daß unser Schiff ein türkisch Fahrzeug fing,
Das einen Schatz des großen Sultans führte.
Da ward der Tapferkeit ihr Lohn,
Und ich empfing denn auch, wie sich gebührte,
Mein wohlgemeßnes Teil davon."

MARTHE.

Ei wie? Ei wo? Hat er's vielleicht vergraben?

MEPHISTOPHELES.

Wer weiß, wo nun es die vier Winde haben.   2980
Ein schönes Fräulein nahm sich seiner an,
Als er in Napel fremd umherspazierte;
Sie hat an ihm viel Lieb's und Treu's getan,
Daß er's bis an sein selig Ende spürte.

MARTHE.

Der Schelm! der Dieb an seinen Kindern!
Auch alles Elend, alle Not
Konnt' nicht sein schändlich Leben hindern!

MEPHISTOPHELES.

Ja seht! dafür ist er nun tot.
Wär' ich nun jetzt an Eurem Platze,
Betraurt' ich ihn ein züchtig Jahr,   2990
Visierte dann unterweil nach einem neuen Schatze.

MARTHE.

Ach Gott! wie doch mein erster war,
Find' ich nicht leicht auf dieser Welt den andern!
Es konnte kaum ein herziger Närrchen sein.
Er liebte nur das allzuviele Wandern;

"I had no time," he said, "for fun or recreation:
First the children, then their daily bread,
and bread in all its broadest meaning;
I could hardly ever eat in peace."

MARTHA.

Then all my love and loyalty meant nothing,
nor the drudgery by day and night.

MEPHISTOPHELES.

Not so! His heart was deeply touched by it.   2970
He said: "When I embarked in Malta's harbor
I prayed for wife and children ardently;
and so the heavens smiled on us
and let us catch a Turkish merchant ship
which had a Sultan's treasure in its hold.
Then valor got its just reward
and, as is only right and proper,
I received my well-apportioned share."

MARTHA.

Oh really? Where? Has he buried it somewhere?

MEPHISTOPHELES.

Who knows; it could be anywhere.   2980
A pretty girl took him in tow
when all alone he walked the streets of Naples;
she gave him so much love and loyalty,
he felt the consequences to his dying day.

MARTHA.

The dirty thief! The robber of his children!
All our misery and dire need did not suffice
to draw his shameful life from sin.

MEPHISTOPHELES.

Well spoken, and for that, you see, he's dead.
But now, if I were in your place,
I'd spend a year in decent mourning   2990
while angling for a new prospective swain.

MARTHA.

Oh my! To find another one quite like my first
will be no easy undertaking in this world.
He was the sweetest little pickle-herring.
But he liked too much to roam about—

Und fremde Weiber, und fremden Wein,
Und das verfluchte Würfelspiel.

MEPHISTOPHELES.

Nun, nun, so konnt' es gehn und stehen,
Wenn er Euch ungefähr so viel
Von seiner Seite nachgesehen.   3000
Ich schwör' Euch zu, mit dem Beding
Wechselt' ich selbst mit Euch den Ring!

MARTHE.

O es beliebt dem Herrn, zu scherzen!

MEPHISTOPHELES (*für sich*).

Nun mach' ich mich beizeiten fort!
Die hielte wohl den Teufel selbst beim Wort.
        (*Zu* GRETCHEN.)
Wie steht es denn mit Ihrem Herzen?

MARGARET.

Was meint der Herr damit?

MEPHISTOPHELES (*für sich*).

                        Du gut's, unschuldig's Kind!
        (*Laut.*)
Lebt wohl, ihr Fraun!

MARGARET.

                        Lebt wohl!

MARTHE.

                        O sagt mir doch geschwind!
Ich möchte gern ein Zeugnis haben,
Wo, wie und wann mein Schatz gestorben und
        begraben.   3010
Ich bin von je der Ordnung Freund gewesen,
Möcht' ihn auch tot im Wochenblättchen lesen.

MEPHISTOPHELES.

Ja, gute Frau, durch zweier Zeugen Mund
Wird allerwegs die Wahrheit kund;
Habe noch gar einen feinen Gesellen,
Den will ich Euch vor den Richter stellen.
Ich bring' ihn her.

MARTHE.

                        O tut das ja!

foreign wine and foreign women,
and worst of all, those cursed dice.

MEPHISTOPHELES.
Oh, well, all this might yet have been just fine,
had he been smart enough to overlook
the things you overlooked in him. 3000
I swear to you, except for this condition,
I would myself exchange my ring with yours.

MARTHA.
The gentleman seems pleased to jest with me.

MEPHISTOPHELES (*aside*).
I'd better run while I'm still able,
or else she'd hold the devil by his word.
     (*To* GRETCHEN.)
And may I ask about your heart, young lady?

MARGARET.
What does the gentleman mean?

MEPHISTOPHELES (*aside*).
                                        You innocent, sweet thing!

     (*Aloud.*)
Ladies, farewell!

MARGARET.
                         Farewell!

MARTHA.
                                Oh, one more thing about my husband.
I should like to have a document to show
the when, the how and why of his demise. 3010
I always was a friend of law and order
and want to see him dead in our local paper.

MEPHISTOPHELES.
Why yes, by two attested statements
the truth is always well confirmed;
I have an excellent companion
whom I will ask to make a deposition.
I'll bring him here.

MARTHA.
                    Oh yes, please do.

MEPHISTOPHELES.

Und hier die Jungfrau ist auch da?—
Ein braver Knab'! ist viel gereist,
Fräuleins alle Höflichkeit erweist.   3020

MARGARET.

Müßte vor dem Herren schamrot werden.

MEPHISTOPHELES.

Vor keinem Könige der Erden.

MARTHE.

Da hinterm Haus in meinem Garten
Wollen wir der Herrn heut' abend warten.

STRASSE

Faust, Mephistopheles.

FAUST.

Wie ist's? Will's fördern? Will's bald gehn?

MEPHISTOPHELES.

Ah bravo! Find' ich Euch in Feuer?
In Kurzer Zeit ist Gretchen Euer.
Heut' abend sollt Ihr sie bei Nachbar' Marthen sehn:
Das ist ein Weib wie auserlesen
Zum Kuppler- und Zigeunerwesen!   3030

FAUST.

So recht!

MEPHISTOPHELES.

Doch wird auch was von uns begehrt.

FAUST.

Ein Dienst ist wohl des andern wert.

MEPHISTOPHELES.

Wir legen nur ein gültig Zeugnis nieder,
Daß ihres Ehherrn ausgereckte Glieder
In Padua an heil'ger Stätte ruhn.

FAUST.

Sehr klug! Wir werden erst die Reise machen müssen!

MEPHISTOPHELES.

Sancta Simplicitas! darum ist's nicht zu tun;
Bezeugt nur, ohne viel zu wissen.

MEPHISTOPHELES.

And our maiden here will then be present?—
A gallant youth! Has traveled much;
shows every courtesy to the ladies.   3020

MARGARET.

I would blush before a gentleman like that.

MEPHISTOPHELES.

Before no king on earth!

MARTHA.

Behind the house, there in the garden
we will await the both of you tonight.

A STREET

Faust, Mephistopheles.

FAUST.

How is it? Will it work? Are we ready?

MEPHISTOPHELES.

Bravo! Do I find you all afire?
It won't be long, and Gretchen will be yours.
Tonight you'll see her at her neighbor's house.
The woman there is without peer
in gypsy deals and pimping.   3030

FAUST.

Good!

MEPHISTOPHELES.

But something of a quid pro quo will be required.

FAUST.

Well, one good turn deserves another.

MEPHISTOPHELES.

All we do is make a proper deposition:
To wit, her husband's limp cadaver rests
in peace in Padua's consecrated ground.

FAUST.

That's wise! We'll have to make the journey first.

MEPHISTOPHELES.

Sancta Simplicitas! That is beside the point;
just testify, don't make a fuss.

FAUST.

Wenn Er nichts Bessers hat, so ist der Plan zerrissen.

MEPHISTOPHELES.

O heil'ger Mann! Da wärt Ihr's nun!   3040
Ist es das erstemal in Eurem Leben,
Daß Ihr falsch Zeugnis abgelegt?
Habt Ihr von Gott, der Welt und was sich drin bewegt,
Vom Menschen, was sich ihm in Kopf und Herzen regt,
Definitionen nicht mit großer Kraft gegeben?
Mit frecher Stirne, kühner Brust?
Und wollt Ihr recht ins Innre gehen,
Habt Ihr davon, Ihr müßt es grad' gestehen,
So viel als von Herrn Schwerdtleins Tod gewußt!

FAUST.

Du bist und bleibst ein Lügner, ein Sophiste.   3050

MEPHISTOPHELES.

Ja, wenn man's nicht ein bißchen tiefer wüßte.
Denn morgen wirst, in allen Ehren,
Das arme Gretchen nicht betören
Und alle Seelenlieb' ihr schwören?

FAUST.

Und zwar von Herzen.

MEPHISTOPHELES.

                Gut und schön!
Dann wird von ewiger Treu' und Liebe,
Von einzig überallmächt'gem Triebe—
Wird das auch so von Herzen gehn?

FAUST.

Laß das! Es wird!—Wenn ich empfinde,
Für das Gefühl, für das Gewühl   3060
Nach Namen suche, keinen finde,
Dann durch die Welt mit allen Sinnen schweife,
Nach allen höchsten Worten greife,
Und diese Glut, von der ich brenne,
Unendlich, ewig, ewig nenne,
Ist das ein teuflisch Lügenspiel?

MEPHISTOPHELES.

Ich hab' doch recht!

FAUST.

If you've got nothing better, our plan is null and void.

MEPHISTOPHELES.

You holy man! You image of a saint!   3040
Is this the only instance in your life
that you have borne false witness?
Have you not shown imposing power
defining God, the world, and every moving thing,
as well as man and all his inward stirrings,
with brazen face and swollen chest?
But if you probe the matter to the core,
you must confess you've never known much more
than now you know of brother Schwerdtlein's death.

FAUST.

You'll always be a sophist and a liar.   3050

MEPHISTOPHELES.

True enough; except I've peered a little deeper.
For will you not, in words of great propriety
befog poor Gretchen, [31] come tomorrow,
and swear your heart and soul belong to her?

FAUST.

And that with all my heart!

MEPHISTOPHELES.

                          That's good of you!
And then you'll speak of faith and love eternal,
of a single, overpowering urge—
will that flow so easily from your heart?

FAUST.

Enough, I say it *will*.—When I am deeply stirred
and through the raging tumult seek   3060
and grope in vain for name and speech,
sweep through the world with all my senses,
reach for the highest words that come to me,
and the ardor in which I burn
I call infinite, eternal fire—
can that be called a devil's game of lies?

MEPHISTOPHELES.

All the same, I'm right.

FAUST.

Hör! merk dir dies—
Ich bitte dich, und schone meine Lunge—:
Wer recht behalten will und hat nur eine Zunge,
Behält's gewiß.   3070
Und komm, ich hab' des Schwätzens Überdruß,
Denn du hast recht, vorzüglich weil ich muß.

GARTEN

*Margaret an Faustens Arm. Marthe mit
Mephistopheles auf und ab spazierend.*

MARGARET.

Ich fühl' es wohl, daß mich der Herr nur schont,
Herab sich läßt, mich zu beschämen.
Ein Reisender ist so gewohnt,
Aus Gütigkeit fürlieb zu nehmen;
Ich weiß zu gut, daß solch erfahrnen Mann
Mein arm Gespräch nicht unterhalten kann.

FAUST.

Ein Blick von dir, ein Wort mehr unterhält
Als alle Weisheit dieser Welt.   3080
   (*Er küßt ihre Hand.*)

MARGARET.

Inkommodiert Euch nicht! Wie könnt Ihr sie nur küssen?
Sie ist so garstig, ist so rauh!
Was hab' ich nicht schon alles schaffen müssen!
Die Mutter ist gar zu genau.
   (*Gehn vorüber.*)

MARTHE.

Und Ihr, mein Herr, Ihr reist so immer fort?

MEPHISTOPHELES.

Ach, daß Gewerb' und Pflicht uns dazu treiben!
Mit wieviel Schmerz verläßt man manchen Ort,
Und darf doch nun einmal nicht bleiben!

MARTHE.

In raschen Jahren geht's wohl an,
So um und um frei durch die Welt zu streifen;   3090

FAUST.

> Listen now! Mark this well,
> I beg of you, and let me save my breath—
> Anyone intent on winning,
> if he but use his tongue, will win.   3070
> But come, I'm tired of this idle chatter,
> for you have won your point, since what I do, I must.

MARTHA'S GARDEN

*Margaret on Faust's arm. Martha and
Mephistopheles walking up and down.*

MARGARET.

> I'm sure, sir, you're only being kind.
> You condescend and make me feel unworthy.
> A traveler becomes accustomed
> to be content with what he finds.
> My simple words could never entertain
> a gentleman of your experience.

FAUST.

> One glance from you, a single word, holds more
> than all the wisdom of this world.   3080
>   (*He kisses her hand.*)

MARGARET.

> Don't trouble yourself—how can you kiss my hand?
> It is a rough and ugly hand!
> Think of all the work that I have done.
> My mother is so very fussy.
>   (*They pass on.*)

MARTHA.

> And you, sir, do you travel all the time?

MEPHISTOPHELES.

> Ah yes, our trade and duty keep us on the move.
> With deep regret one leaves some charming place—
> but once for all, one cannot stay and rest!

MARTHA.

> It is all right, when one is young and gay,
> to roam the whole wide world at will;   3090

Doch kömmt die böse Zeit heran,
Und sich als Hagestolz allein zum Grab zu schleifen,
Das hat noch keinem wohlgetan.

MEPHISTOPHELES.

Mit Grausen seh' ich das von weiten.

MARTHE.

Drum, werter Herr, beratet Euch in Zeiten.
(*Gehn vorüber.*)

MARGARET.

Ja, aus den Augen aus dem Sinn!
Die Höflichkeit ist Euch geläufig;
Allein Ihr habt der Freunde häufig,
Sie sind verständiger, als ich bin.

FAUST.

O Beste! glaube, was man so verständig nennt,   3100
Ist oft mehr Eitelkeit und Kurzsinn.

MARGARET.

                                    Wie?

FAUST.

Ach, daß die Einfalt, daß die Unschuld nie
Sich selbst und ihren heil'gen Wert erkennt!
Daß Demut, Niedrigkeit, die höchsten Gaben
Der liebevoll austeilenden Natur—

MARGARET.

Denkt Ihr an mich ein Augenblickchen nur,
Ich werde Zeit genug an Euch zu denken haben.

FAUST.

Ihr seid wohl viel allein?

MARGARET.

Ja, unsre Wirtschaft ist nur klein,
Und doch will sie versehen sein.   3110
Wir haben keine Magd; muß kochen, fegen, stricken
Und nähn, und laufen früh und spat;
Und meine Mutter ist in allen Stücken
So akkurat!
Nicht daß sie just so sehr sich einzuschränken hat;
Wir könnten uns weit eh'r als andre regen:
Mein Vater hinterließ ein hübsch Vermögen,
Ein Häuschen und ein Gärtchen vor der Stadt.

but a bachelor who falls on evil days
and drags his person to the grave alone
is never truly happy and at peace.

MEPHISTOPHELES.

I shudder when I look at it that way.

MARTHA.

Hence, worthy sir, take counsel in good time.
   (*They pass on.*)

MARGARET.

Yes, out of sight is out of mind!
Your courtesy is second nature;
you have friends in many places
who are much cleverer than I.

FAUST.

What the world calls cleverness, my dearest,   3100
is really narrowness and rank conceit.

MARGARET.

                              How's that?

FAUST.

Why should simplicity and innocence
be unaware of self and of their sacred worth?
Why are humility and lowliness the finest gifts
of a loving, bounteous Nature—

MARGARET.

Think of me for just a little moment's time,
I shall have a lot of time to think of you!

FAUST.

Then you are much alone?

MARGARET.

Yes, our household's rather small,
but still it needs much looking after.   3110
We keep no maid, so I must cook and sweep and knit,
and sew and run, from morning until late at night.
And mother is so finicky
with every little chore!
Not that she needs to skimp with downright everything;
we're still much better off than many others:
My father left us quite a nice estate,
a house, a little garden just outside the town.

Doch hab' ich jetzt so ziemlich stille Tage;
Mein Bruder ist Soldat,   3120
Mein Schwesterchen ist tot.
Ich hatte mit dem Kind wohl meine liebe Not;
Doch übernähm' ich gern noch einmal alle Plage,
So lieb war mir das Kind.

FAUST.

                      Ein Engel, wenn dir's glich.

MARGARET.

Ich zog es auf, und herzlich liebt' es mich.
Es war nach meines Vaters Tod geboren.
Die Mutter gaben wir verloren,
So elend wie sie damals lag,
Und sie erholte sich sehr langsam, nach und nach.
Da konnte sie nun nicht dran denken,   3130
Das arme Würmchen selbst zu tränken,
Und so erzog ich's ganz allein,
Mit Milch und Wasser; so ward's mein.
Auf meinem Arm, in meinem Schoß
War's freundlich, zappelte, ward groß.

FAUST.

Du hast gewiß das reinste Glück empfunden.

MARGARET.

Doch auch gewiß gar manche schwere Stunden.
Des Kleinen Wiege stand zu Nacht
An meinem Bett; es durfte kaum sich regen,
War ich erwacht;   3140
Bald mußt' ich's tränken, bald es zu mir legen,
Bald, wenn's nicht schwieg, vom Bett aufstehn
Und tänzelnd in der Kammer auf und nieder gehn,
Und früh am Tage schon am Waschtrog stehn;
Dann auf dem Markt und an dem Herde sorgen,
Und immer fort wie heut so morgen.
Da geht's, mein Herr, nicht immer mutig zu;
Doch schmeckt dafür das Essen, schmeckt die Ruh.
    (*Gehn vorüber.*)

MARTHE.

Die armen Weiber sind doch übel dran:

But of late I've had some rather quiet days;
my brother is a soldier;   3120
my little sister's dead.
I spent some trying moments with the child,
but I would gladly take on twice the trouble;
she was so very dear to me.

FAUST.

       An angel if she resembled you.

MARGARET.

I brought her up. She loved me dearly too.
My father died before she came into the world.
My mother we had given up for lost,
her condition was so desperate,
but she recovered slowly, step by step.
After that, she could not even think of trying   3130
to nurse the little mite herself,
and so I reared it all alone
with milk and water.—She became my own.
In my arms and on my knee
she grinned and wriggled and grew strong.

FAUST.

You must have felt the purest bliss.

MARGARET.

But many fretful hours too.
At night I placed the little creature's cradle
beside my bed, and if she stirred the slightest bit,
I was awake immediately.   3140
I would feed her—or would place her next to me,
or else, to quiet her, I'd leave my bed
and rock her gently as I paced the room,
and bright and early I would do the wash,
then off to market, then stoke the kitchen range,
and on and on, tomorrow like today.
One does not always feel like smiling, sir,
but then the food tastes good, and sleep tastes even
  better.
 (*They pass on.*)

MARTHA.

We women get the worst of everything;

Ein Hagestolz ist schwerlich zu bekehren.   3150

MEPHISTOPHELES.

Es käme nur auf Euresgleichen an,
Mich eines Bessern zu belehren.

MARTHE.

Sagt grad', mein Herr, habt Ihr noch nichts gefunden?
Hat sich das Herz nicht irgendwo gebunden?

MEPHISTOPHELES.

Das Sprichwort sagt: Ein eigner Herd,
Ein braves Weib sind Gold und Perlen wert.

MARTHE.

Ich meine, ob Ihr niemals Lust bekommen?

MEPHISTOPHELES.

Man hat mich überall recht höflich aufgenommen.

MARTHE.

Ich wollte sagen: ward's nie Ernst in Eurem Herzen?

MEPHISTOPHELES.

Mit Frauen soll man sich nie unterstehn zu scherzen.   3160

MARTHE.

Ach, Ihr versteht mich nicht!

MEPHISTOPHELES.

                                    Das tut mir herzlich leid!
Doch ich versteh'—daß Ihr sehr gütig seid.
   (*Gehn vorüber.*)

FAUST.

Du kanntest mich, o kleiner Engel, wieder,
Gleich als ich in den Garten kam?

MARGARET.

Saht Ihr es nicht? ich schlug die Augen nieder.

FAUST.

Und du verzeihst die Freiheit, die ich nahm?
Was sich die Frechheit unterfangen,
Als du jüngst aus dem Dom gegangen?

MARGARET.

Ich war bestürzt, mir war das nie geschehn;
Es konnte niemand von mir Übels sagen.
Ach, dacht' ich, hat er in deinem Betragen   3170
Was Freches, Unanständiges gesehn?
Es schien ihn gleich nur anzuwandeln,

a bachelor is difficult to sway.   3150

MEPHISTOPHELES.
It would depend on women like yourself
to teach me what is better.

MARTHA.
Be frank, dear sir, you never found the real thing?
You haven't tied your heart to anyone?

MEPHISTOPHELES.
The proverb says: A hearth, a goodly woman of one's own,
are worth their weight in pearls and gold.

MARTHA.
What I meant was: Did you ever feel inclined?

MEPHISTOPHELES.
Everywhere I've been politely treated.

MARTHA.
I mean, were your intentions ever serious?

MEPHISTOPHELES.
One should never trifle with the ladies.   3160

MARTHA.
Ah, you do not grasp my meaning.

MEPHISTOPHELES.
                              I'm sincerely pained,
but I can grasp—that you are very good to me.
    (*They pass on.*)

FAUST.
You knew me, little angel, right away,
when I entered through your garden door?

MARGARET.
Didn't you see? I cast down my eyes.

FAUST.
Will you forgive the liberty I took,
the impertinence and my brazen words,
when you were coming out of church?

MARGARET.
I was upset. I could not cope with such a thing.
No one till now found fault with me.   3170
Could he have seen in me—I thought—
brazenness and a lack of modesty?
He showed no qualm or hesitation

Mit dieser Dirne gradehin zu handeln.
Gesteh' ich's doch! Ich wußte nicht, was sich
Zu Eurem Vorteil hier zu regen gleich begonnte;
Allein gewiß, ich war recht bös' auf mich,
Daß ich auf Euch nicht böser werden konnte.

FAUST.
Süß Liebchen!

MARGARET.
    Laßt einmal!
 (*Sie pflückt eine Sternblume und zupft die
 Blätter ab, eins nach dem andern.*)

FAUST.
       Was soll das? Einen Strauß?

MARGARET.
Nein, es soll nur ein Spiel.

FAUST.
     Wie?

MARGARET.
     Geht! Ihr lacht mich aus. 3180
 (*Sie rupft und murmelt.*)

FAUST.
Was murmelst du?

MARGARET (*halb laut*).
    Er liebt mich—liebt mich nicht.

FAUST.
Du holdes Himmelsangesicht!

MARGARET (*fährt fort*).
Liebt mich—Nicht—Liebt mich—Nicht—
 (*Das letzte Blatt ausrupfend, mit holder
 Freude.*)
Er liebt mich!

FAUST.
   Ja, mein Kind! Laß dieses Blumenwort
Dir Götterausspruch sein. Er liebt dich!
Verstehst du, was das heißt? Er liebt dich!
 (*Er faßt ihre beiden Hände.*)

MARGARET.
Mich überläuft's!

to strike a bargain with a wench.
Let me confess! I could not fathom why
I felt a sudden stirring in your favor.
And surely, I was angry with myself
because I was not angrier with you.

FAUST.
My sweet love.

MARGARET.
                    Wait awhile.
(She picks a daisy and plucks the petals, one by one.)

FAUST.
                    What is it? A bouquet?

MARGARET.
No, it's just a game.

FAUST.
                    A what?

MARGARET.
                         Go away, you'll laugh at me. 3180
(She plucks petals, murmuring to herself.)

FAUST.
What are you murmuring?

MARGARET *(half aloud)*.
                         He loves me . . . loves me not.

FAUST.
You countenance of Heaven!

MARGARET *(continues)*.
Loves me—Not—Loves me—Not—
    (Plucking the last petal, radiant with joy.)
He loves me!

FAUST.
                    Yes, my sweet! Oh, let this flower's word
be the pronouncement of the gods. He loves you!
Can you feel the word's profundity? He loves you!
    (He grasps both her hands.)

MARGARET.
I tremble so.

FAUST.

O schaudre nicht! Laß diesen Blick,
Laß diesen Händedruck dir sagen,
Was unaussprechlich ist: 3190
Sich hinzugeben ganz und eine Wonne
Zu fühlen, die ewig sein muß!
Ewig!—Ihr Ende würde Verzweiflung sein.
Nein, kein Ende! Kein Ende!

> (MARGARET *drückt ihm die Hände, macht*
> *sich los und läuft weg. Er steht einen Augen-*
> *blick in Gedanken, dann folgt er ihr.*)

MARTHE (*kommend*).

Die Nacht bricht an.

MEPHISTOPHELES.

                 Ja, und wir wollen fort.

MARTHE.

Ich bät Euch, länger hier zu bleiben,
Allein es ist ein gar zu böser Ort.
Es ist, als hätte niemand nichts zu treiben
Und nichts zu schaffen,
Als auf des Nachbarn Schritt und Tritt zu gaffen,   3200
Und man kommt ins Gered', wie man sich immer stellt.
Und unser Pärchen?

MEPHISTOPHELES.

               Ist den Grang dort aufgeflogen.
Mutwill'ge Sommervögel!

MARTHE.

                Er scheint ihr gewogen.

MEPHISTOPHELES.

Und sie ihm auch. Das ist der Lauf der Welt.

EIN GARTENHÄUSCHEN

*Margaret springt herein, steckt sich hinter die
Tür, hält die Fingerspitze an die Lippen,
und guckt duch die Ritze.*

MARGARET.

Er kommt!

FAUST.

Oh, do not tremble. Look into my eyes;
let my hands which press your hands convey to you
the inexpressible: 3190
to give oneself completely and to feel an ecstasy
which must be everlasting!
Everlasting!—the end would be despair.
No—no end! no end!

> (MARGARET *clasps his hands, frees herself,
> and runs off.* FAUST *stands for a moment in
> deep thought, then follows her.*)

MARTHA (*coming forward*).

The sky is darkening.

MEPHISTOPHELES.

We must be on our way.

MARTHA.

I would prefer to have you stay awhile,
but our town is mean and petty.
People here can think of nothing better
than spying on their neighbor's every move.
For this they'll gladly set aside their daily chores   3200
and gossip if they're given half a chance.
And what of our little couple?

MEPHISTOPHELES.

Flew up the garden path.
The willful birds of summer!

MARTHA.

He seems to like her well.

MEPHISTOPHELES.

And she likes him. The world keeps spinning.

A SUMMER CABIN

*Margaret rushes in and hides behind the door, puts
her finger to her lips and peeps through a crack.*

MARGARET.

He's coming!

FAUST (*kommt*).

> Ach Schelm, so neckst du mich!

Treff' ich dich!

(*Er küßt sie.*)

MARGARET (*ihn fassend und den Kuß zurückgebend*).

> Bester Mann! von Herzen lieb' ich dich!

(**MEPHISTOPHELES** *klopft an.*)

FAUST (*stampfend*).

Wer da?

MEPHISTOPHELES.

> Gut Freund!

FAUST.

> Ein Tier!

MEPHISTOPHELES.

> Es ist wohl Zeit zu scheiden.

MARTHE (*kommt.*)

Ja, es ist spät, mein Herr.

FAUST.

> Darf ich Euch nicht geleiten?

MARGARET.

Die Mutter würde mich—Lebt wohl!

FAUST.

> Muß ich denn gehn?

Lebt wohl!

MARTHE.

> Ade!

MARGARET.

> Auf baldig Wiedersehn!   3210
> (**FAUST** *und* **MEPHISTOPHELES** *ab.*)

MARGARET.

Du lieber Gott! was so ein Mann
Nicht alles, alles denken kann!
Beschämt nur steh' ich vor ihm da,
Und sag' zu allen Sachen ja.
Bin doch ein arm unwissend Kind,
Begreife nicht, was er an mir find't.

(*Ab.*)

FAUST.

               Oh, you rascal, you're teasing me!
I've caught you!
    (*He kisses her.*)

MARGARET (*clasps him and returns his kiss*).
Dearest man! With all my heart I love you so!
    (MEPHISTOPHELES *knocks.*)

FAUST (*stamping his foot*).
Who's there?

MEPHISTOPHELES.

             A friend!

FAUST.

               A beast!

MEPHISTOPHELES.

                         I think it's time for us to leave.

MARTHA (*entering*).
Yes indeed, good sir, it's getting late.

FAUST.

                     May I not see you to
    your home?

MARGARET.
My mother would—Farewell!

FAUST.

                  If I must really leave you
    then—
Farewell!

MARTHA.
      Adieu!

MARGARET.

            Until we meet again!   3210
    (FAUST *and* MEPHISTOPHELES *exit.*)

MARGARET.
Dear God! The many thoughts and weighty matters
to which this man can put his mind!
All I can do is stand abashed
and nod my "yes" to everything.
I'm such a silly child and cannot grasp
whatever he may find in me.
               (*Exits.*)

FAUST (*allein*).

Erhabner Geist, du gabst mir, gabst mir alles,
Warum ich bat. Du hast mir nicht umsonst
Dein Angesicht im Feuer zugewendet.
Gabst mir die herrliche Nature zum Königreich,   3220
Kraft, sie zu fühlen, zu genießen. Nicht
Kalt staunenden Besuch erlaubst du nur,
Vergönnest mir, in ihre tiefe Brust,
Wie in den Busen eines Freunds, zu schauen.
Du führst die Reihe der Lebendigen
Vor mir vorbei, und lehrst mich meine Brüder
Im stillen Busch, in Luft und Wasser kennen.
Und wenn der Sturm in Walde braust und knarrt,
Die Riesenfichte stürzend Nachbaräste
Und Nachbarstämme quetschend niederstreift,   3230
Und ihrem Fall dumpf hohl der Hügel donnert,
Dann führst du mich zur sichern Höhle, zeigst
Mich dann mir selbst, und meiner eignen Brust
Geheime tiefe Wunder öffnen sich.
Und steigt vor meinem Blick der reine Mond
Besänftigend herüber, schweben mir
Von Felsenwänden, aus dem feuchten Busch
Der Vorwelt silberne Gestalten auf
Und lindern der Betrachtung strenge Lust.

O daß dem Menschen nichts Vollkommnes wird,   3240
Empfind' ich nun. Du gabst zu dieser Wonne,
Die mich den Göttern nah und näher bringt,
Mir den Gefährten, den ich schon nicht mehr
Entbehren kann, wenn er gleich, kalt und frech,
Mich vor mir selbst erniedrigt, und zu Nichts,
Mit einem Worthauch, deine Gaben wandelt.
Er facht in meiner Brust ein wildes Feuer
Nach jenem schönen Bild geschäftig an.
So tauml' ich von Begierde zu Genuß,
Und im Genuß verschmacht' ich nach Begierde.   3250

FAUST (*alone*).

Sublime Spirit,[32] you gave me everything,
gave me all I ever asked. Not in vain
you turned your fiery countenance on me.
You gave me glorious Nature for my kingdom,   3220
the strength to feel and to enjoy Her. You gave me
more than a visit merely of cold wonderment;
you granted that I peer into Her boundless depths
as I peer into a friendly heart.
And you pass the ranks of living creatures
before me, and you acquaint me with my brothers
in silent bush, in airy heights and water.
When the winds roar in and rattle,
and giant spruces break and topple,
crushing neighbors and obstructing limbs,   3230
and the hill responds with inward thunder—
then you lead me to the sheltered cavern,
and show me to myself, and then reveal
to me profundities within my breast.
And when the pure moon rises
soothingly before my gaze,
the silver phantoms of a bygone age
drift toward me from rocky walls and dew-soaked bushes
and temper meditation's austere pleasure.

That nothing perfect ever can accrue to Man   3240
I know deeply now. With all my bliss
which brought me close and closer to the gods,
you gave me the companion which I even now
can no longer do without, though cold and insolent,
he humbles me before myself, and by a single breath
he transforms your gifts to nothingness,
and busily he fans within my bosom
a seething fire for that radiant image.
I stagger from desire to enjoyment,
and in its throes I starve for more desire.   3250

221

(**MEPHISTOPHELES** *tritt auf*.)

MEPHISTOPHELES.

　　Habt Ihr nun bald das Leben gnug geführt?
　　Wie kann's Euch in die Länge freuen?
　　Es ist wohl gut, daß man's einmal probiert;
　　Dann aber wieder zu was Neuen!

FAUST.

　　Ich wollt', du hättest mehr zu tun,
　　Als mich am guten Tag zu plagen.

MEPHISTOPHELES.

　　Nun, nun! ich lass' dich gerne ruhn,
　　Du darfst mir's nicht im Ernste sagen.
　　An dir Gesellen, unhold, barsch und toll,
　　Ist wahrlich wenig zu verlieren.　　　　　　　　　　3260
　　Den ganzen Tag hat man die Hände voll!
　　Was ihm gefällt und was man lassen soll,
　　Kann man dem Herrn nie an der Nase spüren.

FAUST.

　　Das ist so just der rechte Ton!
　　Er will noch Dank, daß er mich ennuyiert.

MEPHISTOPHELES.

　　Wie hättst du, armer Erdensohn,
　　Dein Leben ohne mich geführt?
　　Vom Kribskrabs der Imagination
　　Hab' ich dich doch auf Zeiten lang kuriert;
　　Und wär' ich nicht, so wärst du schon　　　　　　　3270
　　Von diesem Erdball abspaziert.
　　Was hast du da in Höhlen, Felsenritzen
　　Dich wie ein Schuhu zu versitzen?
　　Was schlurfst aus dumpfem Moos und triefendem Gestein,
　　Wie eine Kröte, Nahrung ein?
　　Ein schöner, süßer Zeitvertreib!
　　Dir steckt der Doktor noch im Leib.

FAUST.

　　Verstehst du, was für neue Lebenskraft
　　Mir dieser Wandel in der Öde schafft?
　　Ja, würdest du es ahnen können,　　　　　　　　　3280
　　Du wärest Teufel gnug, mein Glück mir nicht zu gönnen.

(MEPHISTOPHELES *enters.*)

MEPHISTOPHELES.
Are you not done yet with this kind of life?
How can you enjoy it for so long?
A taste of it is well and good,
but then come on, try something new!

FAUST.
I wish that you had other things to do
than to plague me with your presence.

MEPHISTOPHELES.
Well, well; I should be glad to let you be,
if you should ask for it in earnest.
The loss of such a mad and hostile fellow
is but a trifling business for me;   3260
I've got my hands full day and night;
there is no telling by his nose and bearing
what pleases him and what repels him at the moment.

FAUST.
This is just the tone I needed!
Demanding gratitude for boring me.

MEPHISTOPHELES.
How would you, miserable son of earth,
have lived your life without my help?
I think I cured you for some time to come
from the claptrap of your fantasy.
Except for me you would have made your exit   3270
from this globe some time ago.³³
What is the point of cowering like an owl
in fissured rocks and dismal mountain caves?
Why, toadlike, do you swill your nourishment
from soggy moss and dripping stones?
A darling way to pass the time!
The doctor's in your belly still!

FAUST.
Can you conceive what new and vital power
I draw from living in the wilderness?
If you could, I think you'd be   3280
devilish enough to envy me my happiness.

MEPHISTOPHELES.

Ein überirdisches Vergnügen!
In Nacht und Tau auf den Gebirgen liegen,
Und Erd' und Himmel wonniglich umfassen,
Zu einer Gottheit sich aufschwellen lassen,
Der Erde Mark mit Ahnungsdrang durchwühlen,
Alle sechs Tagewerk' im Busen fühlen,
In stolzer Kraft ich weiß nicht was genießen,
Bald liebewonniglich in alles überfließen,
Verschwunden ganz der Erdensohn,   3290
Und dann die hohe Intuition—
    (*Mit einer Gebärde.*)
Ich darf nicht sagen, wie—zu schließen.

FAUST.

Pfui über dich!

MEPHISTOPHELES.

           Das will Euch nicht behagen;
Ihr habt das Recht, gesittet Pfui zu sagen.
Man darf das nicht vor keuschen Ohren nennen,
Was keusche Herzen nicht entbehren können.
Und kurz und gut, ich gönn' Ihm das Vergnügen,
Gelegentlich sich etwas vorzulügen;
Doch lange hält Er das nicht aus.
Du bist schon wieder abgetrieben,   3300
Und, währt es länger, aufgerieben
In Tollheit oder Angst und Graus!
Genug damit! Dein Liebchen sitzt dadrinne,
Und alles wird ihr eng und trüb.
Du kommst ihr gar nicht aus dem Sinne,
Sie hat dich übermächtig lieb.
Erst kam deine Liebeswut übergeflossen,
Wie vom geschmolznen Schnee ein Bächlein übersteigt;
Du hast sie ihr ins Herz gegossen,
Nun ist dein Bächlein wieder seicht.   3310
Mich dünkt, anstatt in Wäldern zu thronen,
Ließ' es dem großen Herren gut,
Das arme affenjunge Blut
Für seine Liebe zu belohnen.
Die Zeit wird ihr erbärmlich lang;

MEPHISTOPHELES.

What supernatural delight!
To lie in nightly dew on mountain heights,
to encompass earth and heaven in a rapture
and inflate one's being to a godlike state,
to burrow to the core, inflamed by premonition,
to feel six days of God's creation in your bosom,
enjoy in pride and strength I know not what,
and flooding all in loving ecstasy,
the son of earth is canceled out—   3290
then comes the lofty intuition—
        (*Makes an obscene gesture.*)
to end in . . . Well, I'll keep it to myself.

FAUST.

You pig!

MEPHISTOPHELES.

                I see that this is hardly to your liking.
You may say "pig" in all propriety.
One must not say to chaste and modest ears
what chaste hearts can never do without.
Once for all, you are most welcome to the fun
of self-delusion now and then;
you cannot keep it up for very long;
you're driven on before you know,   3300
and should it last, you're ground to bits
by madness, torment, or sheer horror.
Enough of this, your sweetheart sits at home,
and to her the world seems close and dreary.
You live forever in her mind.
An overwhelming love for you has seized her soul.
At first your passion rose and overflowed
as when a brook will swell from melting snow;
you poured it all into her bosom—
and now the brook runs dry again.   3310
I think, instead of playing king in forest groves,
the gentleman might well see fit
to give the squirming little creature
a gift in gratitude for loving him.
The time hangs heavy on her hands;

Sie steht am Fenster, sieht die Wolken ziehn
Über die alte Stadtmauer hin.
Wenn ich ein Vöglein wär'! so geht ihr Gesang
Tage lang, halbe Nächte lang.
Einmal ist sie munter, meist betrübt,   3320
Einmal recht ausgeweint,
Dann wieder ruhig, wie's scheint,
Und immer verliebt.

FAUST.

Schlange! Schlange!

MEPHISTOPHELES (*für sich*).

Gelt! daß ich dich fange!

FAUST.

Verruchter! hebe dich von hinnen,
Und nenne nicht das schöne Weib!
Bring die Begier zu ihrem süßen Leib
Nicht wieder vor die halb verrückten Sinnen!

MEPHISTOPHELES.

Was soll es denn? Sie meint, du seist entflohn,   3330
Und halb und halb bist du es schon.

FAUST.

Ich bin ihr nah, und wär' ich noch so fern,
Ich kann sie nie vergessen, nie verlieren;
Ja, ich beneide schon den Leib des Herrn,
Wenn ihre Lippen ihn indes berühren.

MEPHISTOPHELES.

Gar wohl, mein Freund! Ich hab' Euch oft beneidet
Ums Zwillingspaar, das unter Rosen weidet.

FAUST.

Entfliehe, Kuppler.

MEPHISTOPHELES.

Schön! Ihr schimpft, und ich muß lachen.
Der Gott, der Bub und Mädchen schuf,
Erkannte gleich den edelsten Beruf,   3340
Auch selbst Gelegenheit zu machen.
Nur fort, es ist ein großer Jammer!
Ihr sollt in Eures Liebchens Kammer,
Nicht etwa in den Tod.

she stands and sees the clouds pass by her window
as they drift above the city walls.
"If I were just a little bird"—so goes her song
throughout the day and half the night.
Now she's cheerful, but mostly she is sad,   3320
now her tears are streaming down,
and then she's calm again, it seems,
and always, always loving you.

FAUST.

You snake! You snake!

MEPHISTOPHELES (*aside*).

Here now! So I've trapped you!

FAUST.

Get away from me, you cursed fiend,
and never speak her blessèd name!
Lash not again my tortured senses
to lust for her whom I adore.

MEPHISTOPHELES.

Then why the fuss? She thinks that you have left her,   3330
and more or less, that is what did occur.

FAUST.

I'm near her always, even when I'm far away;
I never can forget nor lose her.
I even grudge the Body of the Lord
when her lips approach to touch the Host.

MEPHISTOPHELES.

That's good, my friend! I've often envied you
the pair of roes that feeds among the lilies. [34]

FAUST.

Get out, you pimp!

MEPHISTOPHELES.

How nice! You rail away and I must laugh.
The God who fashioned boys and girls,
seeing quickly what was wanting,   3340
gave them their chance and opportunity.
But come. Why all this fussing?
You're going to your sweetheart's chamber
and not at all to death and doom.

FAUST.

Was ist die Himmelsfreud' in ihren Armen?
Laß mich an ihrer Brust erwarmen!
Fühl' ich nicht immer ihre Not?
Bin ich der Flüchtling nicht? der Unbehauste?
Der Unmensch ohne Zweck und Ruh',
Der wie ein Wassersturz von Fels zu Felsen brauste   3350
Begierig wütend nach dem Abgrund zu?
Und seitwärts sie, mit kindlich dumpfen Sinnen,
Im Hüttchen auf dem kleinen Alpenfeld,
Und all ihr häusliches Beginnen
Umfangen in der kleinen Welt.
Und ich, der Gottverhaßte,
Hatte nicht genug,
Daß ich die Felsen faßte
Und sie zu Trümmern schlug!
Sie, ihren Frieden mußt' ich untergraben!   3360
Du, Hölle, mußtest dieses Opfer haben!
Hilf, Teufel, mir die Zeit der Angst verkürzen!
Was muß geschehn, mag's gleich geschehn!
Mag ihr Geschick auf mich zusammenstürzen
Und sie mit mir zugrunde gehn!

MEPHISTOPHELES.

Wie's wieder siedet, wieder glüht!
Geh ein und tröste sie, du Tor!
Wo so ein Köpfchen keinen Ausgang sieht,
Stellt er sich gleich das Ende vor.
Es lebe, wer sich tapfer hält!   3370
Du bist doch sonst so ziemlich eingeteufelt.
Nichts Abgeschmackters find' ich auf der Welt
Als einen Teufel, der verzweifelt.

GRETCHENS STUBE

GRETCHEN (*am Spinnrade allein*).

Meine Ruh' ist hin,
Mein Herz ist schwer;
Ich finde sie nimmer
Und nimmermehr.

FAUST.

When in her arms, I need no joys of Heaven.
The warmth I seek is burning in her breast.
Do I not every moment feel her woe?
Am I not the fugitive, the homeless roamer,
an aimless, rootless, monstrous creature,
roaring like a cataract from crag to crag,   3350
madly racing for the final precipice?
And she along the banks with childlike, simple sense,
there in her cabin on an alpine meadow,
with all the homey enterprises
encompassed by her tiny world.
And I whom God abhors,
I was not satisfied
to seize the rocks,
and crush them into pieces.
It was her life, her peace I had to ruin.   3360
You, Satan, claimed this sacrifice!
Help, Satan, help abridge the time of fear!
What has to happen, let it happen now!
Let her fate come crashing down on mine,
let us both embrace perdition!

MEPHISTOPHELES.

How you burn and seethe again!
Go in and comfort her, you fool.
When you pinheads find no place to go,
you think at once, "It is the end!"
Long live he who stands his ground courageously!   3370
Till now I'd thought you pretty well en-deviled.
I can think of nothing tawdrier in the world
than a devil who despairs.

GRETCHEN'S ROOM

GRETCHEN (*alone at the spinning wheel*).

My peace is gone,
My heart is sore;
I'll find it never
And nevermore.

Wo ich ihn nicht hab',
Ist mir das Grab,
Die ganze Welt   3380
Ist mir vergällt.

Mein armer Kopf
Ist mir verrückt,
Mein armer Sinn
Ist mir zerstückt.

Meine Ruh' ist hin,
Mein Herz ist schwer;
Ich finde sie nimmer
Und nimmermehr.

Nach ihm nur schau' ich   3390
Zum Fenster hinaus,
Nach ihm nur geh' ich
Aus dem Haus.

Sein hoher Gang,
Sein' edle Gestalt,
Seines Mundes Lächeln,
Seiner Augen Gewalt,

Und seiner Rede
Zauberfluß,
Sein Händedruck,   3400
Und ach sein Kuß!

Meine Ruh' ist hin,
Mein Herz ist schwer;
Ich finde sie nimmer
Und nimmermehr.

Mein Busen drängt
Sich nach ihm hin.
Ach dürft' ich fassen
Und halten ihn,

To be without him
Is like the grave;
The sweet world all   3380
Is turned to gall.

Ah my poor head
Is so distraught;
Ah my poor mind
Can think no thought.

My peace is gone,
My heart is sore;
I'll find it never
And nevermore.

I stand by my window,   3390
I seek only him.
I run from my door
To be but with him.

His noble gait,
Lofty and wise;
The smile on his lips,
The force of his eyes.

In the flow of his words,
Is magical bliss.
The clasp of his hand   3400
Ah, what bliss!

My peace is gone,
My heart is sore;
I'll find it never
And nevermore.

My heart is yearning
To be at his side,
To clasp and enfold him
And hold him tight.

    Und küssen ihn,   3410
    So wie ich wollt',
    An seinen Küssen
    Vergehen sollt'!

MARTHENS GARTEN

Margaret, Faust.

MARGARET.
  Versprich mir, Heinrich!
FAUST.
                      Was ich kann!
MARGARET.
  Nun sag, wie hast du's mit der Religion?
  Du bist ein herzlich guter Mann,
  Allein ich glaub', du hältst nicht viel davon.
FAUST.
  Laß das, mein Kind! Du fühlst, ich bin dir gut;
  Für meine Lieben ließ' ich Leib und Blut,
  Will niemand sein Gefühl und seine Kirche rauben.   3420
MARGARET.
  Das ist nicht recht, man muß dran glauben!
FAUST.
  Muß man?
MARGARET.
              Ach! wenn ich etwas auf dich könnte!
  Du ehrst auch nicht die heil'gen Sakramente.
FAUST.
  Ich ehre sie.
MARGARET.
              Doch ohne Verlangen.
  Zur Messe, zur Beichte bist du lange nicht gegangen.
  Glaubst du an Gott?
FAUST.
                 Mein Liebchen, wer darf sagen:
  Ich glaub' an Gott?
  Magst Priester oder Weise fragen,

To love and to kiss,   3410
To murmur and sigh,
And under his kiss
To melt and to die!35

MARTHA'S GARDEN

Margaret, Faust.

MARGARET.
  Promise me, Heinrich!
FAUST.
                         Whatever I can!
MARGARET.
  Then tell me: How do you stand on religion?
  You are a dear and warmhearted man,
  but I don't believe you care for it.
FAUST.
  Let it be, my child. You know how dear you are to me.
  For those I love I'd give my blood and life;
  I grant to everyone his feelings and his church.   3420
MARGARET.
  That's not enough. One must have faith.
FAUST.
  One must?
MARGARET.
            Oh, if my words had some effect on you!
  You have no reverence for the Sacrament.
FAUST.
  I honor it, I do.
MARGARET.
                   But you lack desire.
  When were you last at mass or at confession?
  Do you believe in God?
FAUST.
                        My darling, who can really say:
  I believe in God!
  Ask any priest or sage,

Und ihre Antwort scheint nur Spott
Über den Frager zu sein.

MARGARET.

So glaubst du nicht?   3430

FAUST.

Mißhör mich nicht, du holdes Angesicht!
Wer darf ihn nennen?
Und wer bekennen:
Ich glaub' ihn.
Wer empfinden,
Und sich unterwinden
Zu sagen: ich glaub' ihn nicht?
Der Allumfasser,
Der Allerhalter,
Faßt und erhält er nicht   3440
Dich, mich, sich selbst?
Wölbt sich der Himmel nicht dadroben?
Liegt die Erde nicht hierunten fest?
Und steigen freundlich blickend
Ewige Sterne nicht herauf?
Schau' ich nicht Aug' in Auge dir,
Und drängt nicht alles
Nach Haupt und Herzen dir,
Und webt in ewigem Geheimnis
Unsichtbar sichtbar neben dir?   3450
Erfüll davon dein Herz, so groß es ist,
Und wenn du ganz in dem Gefühle selig bist,
Nenn es dann, wie du willst,
Nenn's Glück! Herz! Liebe! Gott!
Ich habe keinen Namen
Dafür! Gefühl ist alles;
Name ist Schall und Rauch,
Umnebelnd Himmelsglut.

MARGARET.

Das ist alles recht schön und gut;
Ungefähr sagt das der Pfarrer auch,   3460
Nur mit ein bißchen andern Worten.

FAUST.

Es sagen's allerorten

and their answer seems but mockery
of him who asks the question.

MARGARET.

> Then you don't believe?   3430

FAUST.

> Do not mistake me, sweetest light!
> Who may name Him,
> who profess:
> I believe in Him?
> Who dare think,
> who take the risk to say:
> I do not believe in Him?
> The All-Enfolding,
> All-Sustaining,
> does He not uphold and keep   3440
> you, me, Himself?
> Do you not see the vaulted skies above?
> Is our earth not firmly set below?
> Do not everlasting stars rise up
> to show their friendly light?
> Is my gaze not deeply locked in yours,
> and don't you feel your being
> surging to your head and heart,
> weaving in perennial mystery
> invisibly and visibly in you?   3450
> Fill your heart to overflowing,
> and when you feel profoundest bliss,
> then call it what you will:
> Good fortune! Heart! Love! or God!
> I have no name for it!
> Feeling is all;
> the name is sound and smoke,
> beclouding Heaven's glow.

MARGARET.

> All this is very well and good;
> the priest says pretty much the same as you;   3460
> though he says it differently.

FAUST.

> They say it everywhere,

Alle Herzen unter dem himmlischen Tage,
Jedes in seiner Sprache;
Warum nicht ich in der meinen?

MARGARET.

Wenn man's so hört, möcht's leidlich scheinen,
Steht aber doch immer schief darum;
Denn du hast kein Christentum.

FAUST.

Liebs Kind!

MARGARET.

       Es tut mir lang schon weh,
Daß ich dich in der Gesellschaft seh'.   3470

FAUST.

Wieso?

MARGARET.

      Der Mensch, den du da bei dir hast,
Ist mir in tiefer innrer Seele verhaßt;
Es hat mir in meinem Leben
So nichts einen Stich ins Herz gegeben,
Als des Menschen widrig Gesicht.

FAUST.

Liebe Puppe, fürcht ihn nicht!

MARGARET.

Seine Gegenwart bewegt mir das Blut.
Ich bin sonst allen Menschen gut;
Aber wie ich mich sehne, dich zu schauen,
Hab' ich vor dem Menschen ein heimlich Grauen,   3480
Und halt' ihn für einen Schelm dazu!
Gott verzeih' mir's, wenn ich ihm unrecht tu'!

FAUST.

Es muß auch solche Käuze geben.

MARGARET.

Wollte nicht mit seinesgleichen leben!
Kommt er einmal zur Tür herein,
Sieht er immer so spöttisch drein
Und halb ergrimmt;
Man sieht, daß er an nichts keinen Anteil nimmt;
Es steht ihm an der Stirn geschrieben,
Daß er nicht mag eine Seele lieben.   3490

all hearts beneath the skies,
each in his tongue and way;
why not I in mine?

MARGARET.

When you say it so, it seems all right,
and yet there's something wrong;
you have no proper Christian faith.

FAUST.

Dear child!

MARGARET.

        I've long been sick at heart
to see you go about with your companion.   3470

FAUST.

How so?

MARGARET.

        That person whom you have with you—
I hate him from the bottom of my soul;
nothing has in all my days
wounded me as deeply in my heart
as that repulsive person's horrid face.

FAUST.

My pet, be not afraid of him.

MARGARET.

His presence makes my blood run cold
—and yet I usually like everyone.
I yearn to feast my eyes on you,
but for him I feel a nameless terror,   3480
and consider him a scoundrel too.
God forgive me if I do him an injustice.

FAUST.

One comes across queer ducks sometimes.

MARGARET.

I would not want to live near such a type!
When he steps inside the door,
he peers about so sneeringly
and hatefully.
One can see he's cold as ice;
and by his brow one quickly knows
that he loves no one in the world.   3490

Mir wird's so wohl in deinem Arm,
So frei, so hingegeben warm,
Und seine Gegenwart schnürt mir das Innre zu.

FAUST.

Du ahnungsvoller Engel du!

MARGARET.

Das übermannt mich so sehr,
Daß, wo er nur mag zu uns treten,
Mein' ich sogar, ich liebte dich nicht mehr.
Auch, wenn er da ist, könnt' ich nimmer beten,
Und das frißt mir ins Herz hinein;
Dir, Heinrich, muß es auch so sein.   3500

FAUST.

Du hast nun die Antipathie!

MARGARET.

Ich muß nun fort.

FAUST.

                    Ach, kann ich nie
Ein Stündchen ruhig dir am Busen hängen,
Und Brust an Brust und Seel' in Seele drängen?

MARGARET.

Ach, wenn ich nur alleine schlief'!
Ich ließ' dir gern heut nacht den Riegel offen;
Doch meine Mutter schläft nicht tief,
Und würden wir von ihr betroffen,
Ich wär' gleich auf der Stelle tot!

FAUST.

Du Engel, das hat keine Not.   3510
Hier ist ein Fläschchen! Drei Tropfen nur
In ihren Trank umhüllen
Mit tiefem Schlaf gefällig die Natur.

MARGARET.

Was tu' ich nicht um deinetwillen?
Es wird ihr hoffentlich nicht schaden!

FAUST.

Würd' ich sonst, Liebchen, dir es raten?

MARGARET.

Seh' ich dich, bester Mann, nur an,
Weiß nicht, was mich nach deinem Willen treibt;

I feel so good when I'm in your arms,
so free, so warm, so yielding,
but his mere presence chokes me up inside.

FAUST.

You foreboding angel, you.

MARGARET.

I am so overcome by this,
whenever he comes near I feel
as if I'd fallen out of love with you.
Nor can I ever pray when he's about;
he poisons and corrodes my heart.
And, Heinrich, surely you must feel the same.   3500

FAUST.

There, there, it's just a strong antipathy.

MARGARET.

Now I must go.

FAUST.

     Oh, shall I never
hang upon your bosom one short hour,
pressing breast on breast, my soul into your soul?

MARGARET.

Oh, if I only slept alone,
I should gladly leave the door unlatched tonight,
but my mother's slumber is not deep,
and if she ever found us there together,
I should die in terror on the spot.

FAUST.

My angel, there is really no impediment.   3510
I have this little flask. A mere three drops
from it put in her glass will gently lull
her nature into heavy sleep.

MARGARET.

What would I not do for you?
It will not harm her in the least, I hope.

FAUST.

Would I suggest it then, my sweet?

MARGARET.

Dearest man, when I but look at you
I do not know what drives me to your will.

Ich habe schon so viel für dich getan,
Daß mir zu tun fast nichts mehr übrig bleibt.   3520
                                        (Ab.)

(MEPHISTOPHELES *tritt auf*.)

MEPHISTOPHELES.
Der Grasaff'l ist er weg?

FAUST.
                    Hast wieder spioniert?

MEPHISTOPHELES.
Ich hab's ausführlich wohl vernommen,
Herr Doktor wurden da katechisiert;
Hoff', es soll Ihnen wohl bekommen.
Die Mädels sind doch sehr interessiert,
Ob einer fromm und schlicht nach altem Brauch.
Sie denken: duckt er da, folgt er uns eben auch.

FAUST.
Du Ungeheuer siehst nicht ein,
Wie diese treue liebe Seele
Von ihrem Glauben voll,   3530
Der ganz allein
Ihr selig machend ist, sich heilig quäle,
Daß sie den liebsten Mann verloren halten soll.

MEPHISTOPHELES.
Du übersinnlicher sinnlicher Freier,
Ein Mägdelein nasführet dich.

FAUST.
Du Spottgeburt von Dreck und Feuer!

MEPHISTOPHELES.
Und die Physiognomie versteht sie meisterlich:
In meiner Gegenwart wird's ihr, sie weiß nicht wie,
Mein Mäskchen da weissagt verborgnen Sinn;
Sie fühlt, daß ich ganz sicher ein Genie,   3540
Vielleicht wohl gar der Teufel bin.
Nun, heute nacht—?

FAUST.
                    Was geht dich's an?

MEPHISTOPHELES.
Hab' ich doch meine Freude dran!

Already I have done so much for you
that little else remains undone.   3520

(*Exits.*)

(MEPHISTOPHELES *enters.*)

MEPHISTOPHELES.

The little monkey! Has she gone?

FAUST.

                              Did you spy on me again?

MEPHISTOPHELES.

I took in every small detail;
now Herr Doktor has been catechized—
I hope it will agree with you.
Those girls are always out to know
if you're devout according to tradition.
They think, "If he but yields a little, we've got him all the
    way."

FAUST.

You, monster, fail to see
how this trusting, loving soul,
imbued with her religion—   3530
her one and only road to beatitude—
torments herself in holy fear
lest her belov'd be lost and damned forever.

MEPHISTOPHELES.

You more than sensual, sensual lover,
the little girl has tied a string to you.

FAUST.

You scum, you misbegotten filth and fire!

MEPHISTOPHELES.

And she's quite an expert in physiognomy.
When I am there, she feels a vague constriction.
She reads a hidden sense behind the face I show
and is convinced I am a genius of sorts,   3540
and possibly the very devil.
Well, and tonight—?

FAUST.

                              What is that to you?

MEPHISTOPHELES.

I feel the keenest pleasure!

AM BRUNNEN

Gretchen und Lieschen mit Krügen.

LIESCHEN.

Hast nichts von Bärbelchen gehört?

GRETCHEN.

Kein Wort. Ich komm' gar wenig unter Leute.

LIESCHEN.

Gewiß, Sibylle sagt' mir's heute!

Die hat sich endlich auch betört.

Das ist das Vornehmtun!

GRETCHEN.

Wieso?

LIESCHEN.

Es stinkt!

Sie füttert zwei, wenn sie nun ißt und trinkt.

GRETCHEN.

Ach!   3550

LIESCHEN.

So ist's ihr endlich recht ergangen.

Wie lange hat sie an dem Kerl gehangen!

Das war ein Spazieren,

Auf Dorf und Tanzplatz Führen,

Mußt' überall die Erste sein,

Kurtesiert' ihr immer mit Pastetchen und Wein;

Bild't' sich was auf ihre Schönheit ein,

War doch so ehrlos, sich nicht zu schämen,

Geschenke von ihm anzunehmen.

War ein Gekos' und ein Geschleck';   3560

Da ist denn auch das Blümchen weg!

GRETCHEN.

Das arme Ding!

LIESCHEN.

Bedauerst sie noch gar!

Wenn unsereins am Spinnen war,

Uns nachts die Mutter nicht hinunterließ,

Stand sie bei ihrem Buhlen süß,

AT THE WELL

Gretchen and Lieschen, with earthen jugs.

LIESCHEN.
  What's the news from Barbara?

GRETCHEN.
  Not a word. I don't get out a lot, you know.

LIESCHEN.
  It's true, Sibylle told me so today!
  She's finally been taken in.
  So much for giving oneself airs!

GRETCHEN.
                                    What do you mean?

LIESCHEN.
                                                    It stinks!
  Now she must eat and drink for two.

GRETCHEN.
  Oh.   3550

LIESCHEN.
  At last she's got what she's been looking for.
  She's been fawning on that fellow all this time.
  All that promenading,
  to the village and to dancing places;
  she—first in line on all occasions,
  he—plying her with cakes and wine,
  and she parading her good looks.
  She was brazen, had no sense of shame,
  accepting all his presents.
  They kissed and coddled once too often,   3560
  and now her flower has been plucked.

GRETCHEN.
  Poor thing!

LIESCHEN.
              You have pity on her yet?
  While girls like us were spinning at the wheel,
  and our mothers never let us out at night,
  she was cooing with her lover,

Auf der Türbank und im dunkeln Gang
Ward ihnen keine Stunde zu lang.
Da mag sie denn sich ducken nun,
Im Sünderhemdchen Kirchbuß' tun!

GRETCHEN.
Er nimmt sie gewiß zu seiner Frau. 3570

LIESCHEN.
Er wär' ein Narr! Ein flinker Jung'
Hat anderwärts noch Luft genung.
Er ist auch fort.

GRETCHEN.
                    Das ist nicht schön!

LIESCHEN.
Kriegt sie ihn, soll's ihr übel gehn.
Das Kränzel reißen die Buben ihr,
Und Häckerling streuen wir vor die Tür!

                                    (Ab.)

GRETCHEN (*nach Hause gehend*).
Wie konnt' ich sonst so tapfer schmälen,
Wenn tät ein armes Mägdlein fehlen!
Wie konnt' ich über andrer Sünden
Nicht Worte gnug der Zunge finden! 3580
Wie schien mir's schwarz, und schwärzt's noch gar,
Mir's immer doch nicht schwarz gnug war,
Und segnet' mich und tat so groß,
Und bin nun selbst der Sünde bloß!
Doch—alles, was dazu mich trieb,
Gott! war so gut! ach war so lieb!

ZWINGER

*In der Mauerhöhle ein Andachtsbild der
Mater dolorosa, Blumenkrüge davor.*

GRETCHEN (*steckt frische Blumen in die Krüge*).
          Ach neige,
          Du Schmerzenreiche,
          Dein Antlitz gnädig meiner Not!

on a bench or in a darkened alley;
the time seemed never long to them.
Now it's her turn to duck and hide
and do penance in a sinner's shirt.

GRETCHEN.

Surely he will take her for his wife.   3570

LIESCHEN.

He'd be a fool! A smart young fellow
will look around for different air to breathe.
Well anyway, he's gone.

GRETCHEN.

                        But that is terrible!

LIESCHEN.

If she hooks him after all, she won't fare well.
The boys will tear her wreath from her
and scatter chaff before the door. [36]

                                    (*Exits.*)

GRETCHEN (*returning home*).

How once I felt so high and mighty
when some poor girl would go astray;
a stream of words flowed from my busy tongue
to rail at someone else's sins.   3580
When it seemed black, I blackened it some more.
I could never make it black enough,
and blessed myself with head held high,
and now it's me who's steeped in sin.
Yet—everything that drove me to this pass
was good, my God!—and ah, so sweet!

BY THE RAMPARTS

*In a niche of the city wall, a shrine with a
picture of the Mater Dolorosa. Earthen jugs filled
with flowers stand before it.*

GRETCHEN (*placing fresh flowers in the jugs*).
            Incline,
            O Merciful,
            Thy grieving countenance to me!

Das Schwert im Herzen,   3590
Mit tausend Schmerzen
Blickst auf zu deines Sohnes Tod.

Zum Vater blickst du,
Und Seufzer schickst du
Hinauf um sein' und deine Not.

Wer fühlet,
Wie wühlet
Der Schmerz mir im Gebein?
Was mein armes Herz hier banget,
Was es zittert, was verlanget,   3600
Weißt nur du, nur du allein!

Wohin ich immer gehe,
Wie weh, wie weh, wie wehe
Wird mir im Busen hier!
Ich bin, ach, kaum alleine,
Ich wein', ich wein', ich weine,
Das Herz zerbricht in mir.

Die Scherben vor meinem Fenster
Betau' ich mit Tränen, ach,
Als ich am frühen Morgen   3610
Dir diese Blumen brach.

Schien hell in meine Kammer
Die Sonne früh herauf,
Saß ich in allem Jammer
In meinem Bett schon auf.

Hilf! rette mich von Schmach und Tod!
Ach neige,
Du Schmerzenreiche,
Dein Antlitz gnädig meiner Not!

With sword in heart—   3590
A thousandfold pain—
Thy gaze rests on His death.

Thine eyes seek Our Father.
Thy sighs ascend
For His grief and Thine.

How they rage
Deep in my marrow,
The pangs of my heart!
Who can gauge and who assuage
My pain and my tears?   3600
Thou, oh, Thou alone!

Wherever I go,
Such woe! Such woe! Such woe
I feel in my breast!
No sooner alone,
I weep, I weep, I weep;
My heart is pierced within.

The flowers in my window,
I quenched them with my weeping;
I gathered them this morning   3610
And placed them for Thy keeping.

When the early morning sun
Shone brightly in my room,
I had risen from my pillow,
Deep in the grip of doom.

Help me! Save me from my shame and death!
Incline,
O Merciful,
Thy grieving countenance to me!

NACHT

Straße vor Gretchens Türe.

VALENTIN (*Soldat,* GRETCHENS *Bruder*).

Wenn ich so saß bei einem Gelag,   3620
Wo mancher sich berühmen mag,
Und die Gesellen mir den Flor
Der Mägdlein laut gepriesen vor,
Mit vollem Glas das Lob verschwemmt—
Den Ellenbogen aufgestemmt
Saß ich in meiner sichern Ruh',
Hört' all dem Schwadronieren zu,
Und streiche lächelnd meinen Bart,
Und kriege das volle Glas zur Hand
Und sage: Alles nach seiner Art!   3630
Aber ist eine im ganzen Land,
Die meiner trauten Gretel gleicht,
Die meiner Schwester das Wasser reicht?
Topp! Topp! Kling! Klang! das ging herum;
Die einen schrieen: Er hat recht,
Sie ist die Zier vom ganzen Geschlecht!
Da saßen alle die Lober stumm.
Und nun!—um 's Haar sich auszuraufen
Und an den Wänden hinaufzulaufen!—
Mit Stichelreden, Naserümpfen   3640
Soll jeder Schurke mich beschimpfen!
Soll wie ein böser Schuldner sitzen,
Bei jedem Zufallswörtchen schwitzen!
Und möcht' ich sie zusammenschmeißen,
Könnt' ich sie doch nicht Lügner heißen.

Was kommt heran? Was schleicht herbei?
Irr' ich nicht, es sind ihrer zwei.
Ist er's, gleich pack' ich ihn beim Felle,
Soll nicht lebendig von der Stelle!

    (FAUST, MEPHISTOPHELES.)

FAUST.

Wie von dem Fenster dort der Sakristei   3650

248

NIGHT

Street before Gretchen's door.

VALENTINE (*a soldier*, GRETCHEN's *brother*).

When I and my companions were carousing   3620
and we all saw fit to boast a little,
and would proudly raise our glasses
to the choicest women in our town,
the others drenched their praises deep in wine,
with their elbows planted on the table,
and I sat quietly and unconcerned,
took in the swaggering and the noisy babble
and stroked my beard and smiled in satisfaction.
And with my hand around the brimming glass
I said: "To each his own, my boys!   3630
But tell me of a single maiden in our land
who can measure up to Gretel, my dear sister,
who can hold a candle to the girl?"
And "clink!" and "clank!" "That's so!" It made the round,
and some exclaimed: "I think he's right.
She is the flower of all womankind!"
And all the braggarts bit their lips.
And now!—Oh, I could tear my hair
and dash my head against the wall!—
The sneers and needlings I must bear!   3640
Any scamp can thumb his nose at me!
And I must take it like a bankrupt gambler,
sweating blood at every casual allusion.
I'd smash them all to kingdom come
if I could call them liars to their faces.

What's moving there? Who's sneaking up the alley?
That's two of them, I think.
If he's the one, I'll break his neck!
He'll never leave this place alive!

   (FAUST, MEPHISTOPHELES.)

FAUST.

How from the window of the sacristy   3650

Aufwärts der Schein des ew'gen Lämpchens flämmert
Und schwach und schwächer seitwärts dämmert,
Und Finsternis drängt ringsum beil
So sieht's in meinem Busen nächtig.

MEPHISTOPHELES.

Und mir ist's wie dem Kätzlein schmächtig,
Das an den Feuerleitern schleicht,
Sich leis' dann um die Mauern streicht;
Mir ist's ganz tugendlich dabei,
Ein bißchen Diebsgelüst, ein bißchen Rammelei.
So spukt mir schon durch alle Glieder   3660
Die herrliche Walpurgisnacht.
Die kommt uns übermorgen wieder,
Da weiß man doch, warum man wacht.

FAUST.

Rückt wohl der Schatz indessen in die Höh',
Den ich dort hinten flimmern seh?

MEPHISTOPHELES.

Du kannst die Freude bald erleben,
Das Kesselchen herauszuheben.
Ich schielte neulich so hinein,
Sind herrliche Löwentaler drein.

FAUST.

Nicht ein Geschmeide, nicht ein Ring,   3670
Meine liebe Buhle damit zu zieren?

MEPHISTOPHELES.

Ich sah dabei wohl so ein Ding,
Als wie eine Art von Perlenschnüren.

FAUST.

So ist es recht! Mir tut es weh,
Wenn ich ohne Geschenke zu ihr geh'.

MEPHISTOPHELES.

Es sollt' Euch eben nicht verdrießen,
Umsonst auch etwas zu genießen.
Jetzt, da der Himmel voller Sterne glüht,
Sollt Ihr ein wahres Kunststück hören:
Ich sing' ihr ein moralisch Lied,   3680
Um sie gewisser zu betören.
    (*Singt zur Zither.*)

the flickering flame of the eternal light
grows weak and weaker on this side
and darkness presses in about us—
and night is spreading in my bosom.

MEPHISTOPHELES.

And I feel like a lonesome cat
that prowls about the fire ladders
and brushes stealthily along the walls;
I feel quite virtuous at that,
a little thievish, somewhat lecherous to boot.
Even now the glorious spirit of Walpurgis Night [37]   3660
is spooking through my bone and marrow.
Two nights from now will be the happy time
when insomnia is delightful and worthwhile.

FAUST.

The treasure I see glimmering over there—
will it rise above the ground?

MEPHISTOPHELES.

Very soon you will be pleased
to raise the little pot yourself.
Just recently I took a squint
and beheld some splendid Lion-Dollars. [38]

FAUST.

And did you see some jewelry, some gems,   3670
that might adorn my sweetheart's bosom?

MEPHISTOPHELES.

Yes, I saw a thing like that among the stuff,
something like a string of precious pearls.

FAUST.

That's excellent! I should be very sorry
to go to her without some presents.

MEPHISTOPHELES.

You ought not feel such great distaste if now and then
you can enjoy your pleasures free of charge.
Now that the heavens glow with many stars,
listen to my latest composition:
I will sing for her this moral ditty   3680
to make her putty in your hands.
    (*Sings accompanying himself on the zither.*)

    Was machst du mir
    Vor Liebchens Tür,
    Kathrinchen, hier
    Bei frühem Tagesblicke?
    Laß, laß es sein!
    Er läßt dich ein,
    Als Mädchen ein,
    Als Mädchen nicht zurücke.

    Nehmt euch in acht!   3690
    Ist es vollbracht,
    Dann gute Nacht,
    Ihr armen, armen Dinger!
    Habt ihr euch lieb,
    Tut keinem Dieb
    Nur nichts zu Lieb',
    Als mit dem Ring am Finger.

VALENTIN (*tritt vor*).
  Wen lockst du hier? beim Element!
  Vermaledeiter Rattenfänger!
  Zum Teufel erst das Instrument!   3700
  Zum Teufel hinterdrein den Sänger!

MEPHISTOPHELES.
  Die Zither ist entzwei! an der ist nichts zu halten.

VALENTIN.
  Nun soll es an ein Schädelspalten!

MEPHISTOPHELES (*zu FAUST*).
  Herr Doktor, nicht gewichen! Frisch!
  Hart an mich an, wie ich Euch führe.
  Heraus mit Eurem Flederwisch!
  Nur zugestoßen! ich pariere.

VALENTIN.
  Pariere den!

MEPHISTOPHELES.
         Warum denn nicht?

VALENTIN.
  Auch den!

MEPHISTOPHELES.
       Gewiß!

Why are you here
When daylight's near,
My little Catherine dear,
Before your lover's door?
He lets you in,
You enter a maid,
You slip through the door,
A maid no more.

If you don't run,   3690
It will be done;
Your virtue gone,
You poor, poor thing!
There will be grief,
His love is brief;
Don't love the thief,
Except with a ring on your finger. [39]

VALENTINE (*coming forward*).
  What are you piping? Hell and fire!
  Damn the Hamlin Piper! Blast your hide!
  To the devil with your zither first,   3700
  and then to hell with you, you troubadour!

MEPHISTOPHELES.
  The zither's smashed; so much for that, my friend.

VALENTINE.
  And now I'll split your head wide open!

MEPHISTOPHELES (*to* FAUST).
  Don't flinch, professor! At him now!
  Stay close by me and follow as I lead.
  Whip out your trusty feather duster
  and thrust it home! I'll parry his attack.

VALENTINE.
  Then parry that!

MEPHISTOPHELES.
                    Why not?

VALENTINE.
  And that!

MEPHISTOPHELES.
                    Gladly. Any more, my friend?

VALENTIN.

Ich glaub', der Teufel ficht!
Was ist denn das? Schon wird die Hand mir lahm.　　3710

MEPHISTOPHELES (*zu* FAUST).

Stoß zu!

VALENTIN (*fällt*).

O weh!

MEPHISTOPHELES.

Nun ist der Lümmel zahm!
Nun aber fort! Wir müssen gleich verschwinden:
Denn schon entsteht ein mörderlich Geschrei.
Ich weiß mich trefflich mit der Polizei,
Doch mit dem Blutbann schlecht mich abzufinden.

MARTHE (*am Fenster*).

Heraus! Heraus!

GRETCHEN (*am Fenster*).

Herbei ein Licht!

MARTHE (*wie oben*).

Man schilt und rauft, man schreit und ficht.

VOLK.

Da liegt schon einer tot!

MARTHE (*heraustretend*).

Die Mörder, sind sie denn entflohn?

GRETCHEN (*heraustretend*).

Wer liegt hier?

VOLK.

Deiner Mutter Sohn.　　3720

GRETCHEN.

Allmächtiger! welche Not!

VALENTIN.

Ich sterbe! das ist bald gesagt
Und bälder noch getan.
Was steht ihr Weiber, heult und klagt?
Kommt her und hört mich an!
　　(*Alle treten um ihn.*)
Mein Gretchen, sieh! du bist noch jung,
Bist gar noch nicht gescheit genung,
Machst deine Sachen schlecht.

VALENTINE.

                                              I think you are the
     devil's own disciple!
     What's that? My hand is growing lame!   3710
MEPHISTOPHELES (*to* FAUST).
     Thrust home!
VALENTINE (*falls*).
                    Ah!
MEPHISTOPHELES.
                    Now the lout is tame!
     Come away. It's time to disappear;
     there'll be a murderous hue and cry.
     I can handle the police quite well;
     the blood-ban, [40] though, is quite a different matter.
MARTHA (*at the window*).
     Come out! Come out!
GRETCHEN (*at the window*).
                         Quickly, a light!
MARTHA (*as above*).
     There's cursing and scuffling. It's a brawl!
THE CROWD.
     Someone's lying there, dead!
MARTHA (*coming out*).
     The murderers—did they get away?
GRETCHEN (*coming out*).
     Who is lying there?
THE CROWD.
                    Your mother's son.   3720
GRETCHEN.
     Almighty God! What horror!
VALENTINE.
     I die. That's quickly said
     and accomplished even quicker.
     Why do you women weep and wail?
     Come close and hear me to the end:
         (*All gather about him.*)
     My dear Gretchen, look, you are still young;
     you do not use your brains as yet,
     and now you've really made a mess of things.

Ich sag' dir's im Vertrauen nur:
Du bist doch nun einmal eine Hur'; 3730
So sei's auch eben recht.

GRETCHEN.

Mein Bruder! Gott! Was soll mir das?

VALENTIN.

Laß unsern Herr Gott aus dem Spaß.
Geschehn ist leider nun geschehn,
Und wie es gehn kann, so wird's gehn.
Du fingst mit e i n e m heimlich an,
Bald kommen ihrer mehre dran,
Und wenn dich erst ein Dutzend hat,
So hat dich auch die ganze Stadt.

Wenn erst die Schande wird geboren, 3740
Wird sie heimlich zur Welt gebracht,
Und man zieht den Schleier der Nacht
Ihr über Kopf und Ohren;
Ja, man möchte sie gern ermorden.
Wächst sie aber und macht sich groß,
Dann geht sie auch bei Tage bloß,
Und ist doch nicht schöner geworden.
Je häßlicher wird ihr Gesicht,
Je mehr sucht sie des Tages Licht.

Ich seh' wahrhaftig schon die Zeit, 3750
Daß alle brave Bürgersleut',
Wie von einer angesteckten Leichen,
Von dir, du Metze! seitab weichen.
Dir soll das Herz im Leib verzagen,
Wenn sie dir in die Augen sehn!
Sollst keine goldne Kette mehr tragen!
In der Kirche nicht mehr am Altar stehn!
In einem schönen Spitzenkragen
Dich nicht beim Tanze wohlbehagen!
In eine finstre Jammerecken 3760
Unter Bettler und Krüppel dich verstecken
Und, wenn dir dann auch Gott verzeiht,
Auf Erden sein vermaledeit!

I'll tell you in strict confidence:
You are a whore—you always were,   3730
and that's all right with me.

GRETCHEN.
  My brother! God! What's all this?
VALENTINE.
  Leave the Good Lord out of this!
What has happened cannot be undone.
It's sad, but things will take their course.
Since you started on the sly with one,
there will be others soon to follow,
and when a dozen get a taste of you,
all the town will taste you soon enough.

When Disgrace first issues from the womb,   3740
her birth takes place in secrecy.
A veil of night and furtive shadow
is quickly drawn about her head and ears,
and one would like to murder her.
And if she grows and throws her weight about,
she'll walk stark naked in the sun,
but her looks have not improved one bit.
The uglier her face becomes,
the more she seeks the light of day.

Even now I see the time   3750
when all the decent people of this town
will turn, as from a festering cadaver,
away from you, you slut!
May your heart convulse in you
when they look into your eyes!
You shall no longer wear your golden chain,
nor pray to God before the altar,
nor seek your pleasures at a dance
decked out in lace and finery.
You will hide in dismal nooks and corners   3760
among the cripples and the beggars,
and even if our God forgives you in the end,
you'll still be damned on earth until you die!

MARTHE.

Befehlt Eure Seele Gott zu Gnaden!
Wollt Ihr noch Lästrung auf Euch laden?

VALENTIN.

Könnt' ich dir nur an den dürren Leib,
Du schändlich kupplerisches Weib!
Da hofft' ich aller meiner Sünden
Vergebung reiche Maß zu finden.

GRETCHEN.

Mein Bruder! Welche Höllenpein! 3770

VALENTIN.

Ich sage, laß die Tränen sein!
Da du dich sprachst der Ehre los,
Gabst mir den schwersten Herzensstoß.
Ich gehe durch den Todesschlaf
Zu Gott ein als Soldat und brav.
  (*Stirbt.*)

DOM

*Amt, Orgel und Gesang. Gretchen unter
vielem Volke. Böser Geist hinter Gretchen.*

BÖSER GEIST.

Wie anders, Gretchen, war dir's,
Als du noch voll Unschuld
Hier zum Altar tratst,
Aus dem vergriffnen Büchelchen
Gebete lalltest, 3780
Halb Kinderspiele,
Halb Gott im Herzen!
Gretchen!
Wo steht dein Kopf?
In deinem Herzen
Welche Missetat?
Betst du für deiner Mutter Seele, die
Durch dich zur langen, langen Pein hinüberschlief?
Auf deiner Schwelle wessen Blut?

MARTHA.

Commend your soul to God Almighty!
Do not add blasphemy to your sins.

VALENTINE.

If I could smash your withered body,
you miserable pimping woman!
I would expect that all my sins
might yet be pardoned in full measure.

GRETCHEN.

My brother! Oh, what hellish pain!

3770

VALENTINE.

I tell you, stop your useless tears!
Once you said farewell to honor,
you dealt my heart a heavy blow.
I go to God through death's deep slumber
as a soldier, true and brave.

(*He dies.*)

CATHEDRAL

*Mass in progress, organ, choir. Gretchen among
the congregation. The Evil Spirit
behind Gretchen.*

EVIL SPIRIT.

How different, Gretchen, was it once for you
when you came to kneel before this altar,
pure and innocent,
and you lisped your prayers
from the worn and fingered little book,

3780

half in childlike play,
with God in your heart!
Gretchen!
What has happened to you?
What misdeed
is lodged in your heart?
Do you pray for the soul of your mother,
who through your doing passed to never-ending sleep?
Whose blood stains your doorstep?—

—Und unter deinem Herzen
Regt sich's nicht quillend schon
Und ängstet dich und sich
Mit ahnungsvoller Gegenwart?

GRETCHEN.

Weh! Weh!
Wär' ich der Gedanken los,
Die mir herüber und hinüber gehen
Wider mich!

CHOR.

Dies irae, dies illa
Solvet saeclum in favilla.
    (Orgelton.)

BÖSER GEIST.

Grimm faßt dich!   3800
Die Posaune tönt!
Die Gräber beben!
Und dein Herz,
Aus Aschenruh
Zu Flammenqualen
Wieder aufgeschaffen,
Bebt auf!

GRETCHEN.

Wär' ich hier weg!
Mir ist, also ob die Orgel mir
Den Atem versetzte,   3810
Gesang mein Herz
Im Tiefsten löste.

CHOR.

Judex ergo cum sedebit,
Quidquid latet adparebit,
Nil inultum remanebit.

GRETCHEN.

Mir wird so eng!
Die Mauernpfeiler
Befangen mich!
Das Gewölbe
Drängt mich!—Luft!   3820

Is something not stirring and swelling 3790
beneath your heart,
making itself and you afraid
with stark foreboding?

GRETCHEN.
Oh, God!
I wish that I could free myself
from terrible thoughts
marshaled against me!

CHOIR.
Dies irae, dies illa
Solvet saeclum in favilla.[41]
    (*Organ tone.*)

EVIL SPIRIT.
Despair seizes you! 3800
The trumpet sounds!
Sepulchers quake!
And your heart
from ashen sleep
arises, new,
trembling and throbbing,
to fiery torture.

GRETCHEN.
Oh, to escape!
I feel the sound
throttling my breath, 3810
and the chants melting
my inmost heart.

CHOIR.
Judex ergo cum sedebit,
Quidquid latet adparebit,
Nil inultum remanebit.[42]

GRETCHEN.
It's closing in!
The walls and pillars
imprison me!
The vaulted ceiling
crushes me!—Air! 3820

BÖSER GEIST.

Verbirg dich! Sünd' und Schande
Bleibt nicht verborgen.
Luft? Licht?
Weh dir!

CHOR.

Quid sum miser tunc dicturus?
Quem patronum rogaturus?
Cum vix justus sit securus.

BÖSER GEIST.

Ihr Antlitz wenden
Verklärte von dir ab.
Die Hände dir zu reichen,   3830
Schauert's den Reinen.
Weh!

CHOR.

Quid sum miser tunc dicturus?

GRETCHEN.

Nachbarin! Euer Fläschchen!—
(*Sie fällt in Ohnmacht.*)

WALPURGISNACHT

Harzgebirg. Gegend von Schierke und Elend.
Faust, Mephistopheles.

MEPHISTOPHELES.

Verlangst du nicht nach einem Besenstiele?
Ich wünschte mir den allerderbsten Bock.
Auf diesem Weg sind wir noch weit vom Ziele.

FAUST.

So lang' ich mich noch frisch auf meinen Beinen fühle,
Genügt mir dieser Knotenstock.
Was hilft's, daß man den Weg verkürzt!—   3840
Im Labyrinth der Täler hinzuschleichen,
Dann diesen Felsen zu ersteigen,
Von dem der Quell sich ewig sprudelnd stürzt,
Das ist die Lust, die solche Pfade würzt!

EVIL SPIRIT.

> Hide! Hide! Yet sin and shame
> will not remain concealed.
> Air? Light?
> Woe to you!

CHOIR.

> *Quid sum miser tunc dicturus?*
> *Quem patronum rogaturus?*
> *Cum vix justus sit securus.*[43]

EVIL SPIRIT.

> From you
> the blessed turn their faces.
> The pure recoil   3830
> from offering their hand.
> Woe!

CHOIR.

> *Quid sum miser tunc dicturus?*

GRETCHEN.

> Good neighbor! Please, your smelling salts!—
>   (*She faints.*)

WALPURGIS NIGHT[44]

The Harz Mountains. Region in the vicinity
of Schierke and Elend.
Faust, Mephistopheles.

MEPHISTOPHELES.

> Don't you want a broomstick to convey you hence?
> As for me, I'd like the toughest billy goat.
> By this road our goal is very distant still.

FAUST.

> While my legs feel fresh and strong,
> the knotted stick will serve me well.
> Why should I want to shorten the excursion?   3840
> To creep along the labyrinthine valleys,
> then to scale this sudden towering cliff,
> eternal source of spurting, plunging waters—
> those are the joys and seasonings of the trail!

Der Frühling webt schon in den Birken,
Und selbst die Fichte fühlt ihn schon;
Sollt' er nicht auch auf unsre Glieder wirken?

MEPHISTOPHELES.

Fürwahr, ich spüre nichts davon!
Mir ist es winterlich im Leibe,
Ich wünschte Schnee und Frost auf meiner Bahn.   3850
Wie traurig steigt die unvollkommne Scheibe
Des roten Monds mit später Glut heran,
Und leuchtet schlecht, daß man bei jedem Schritte
Vor einen Baum, vor einen Felsen rennt!
Erlaub', daß ich ein Irrlicht bitte!
Dort seh' ich eins, das eben lustig brennt.
He da! mein Freund! darf ich dich zu uns fodern?
Was willst du so vergebens lodern?
Sei doch so gut und leucht' uns da hinauf!

IRRLICHT.

Aus Ehrfurcht, hoff' ich, soll es mir gelingen,   3860
Mein leichtes Naturell zu zwingen;
Nur zickzack geht gewöhnlich unser Lauf.

MEPHISTOPHELES.

Ei! Ei! Er denkt's den Menschen nachzuahmen.
Geh' Er nur grad', in 's Teufels Namen!
Sonst blas' ich Ihm Sein Flackerleben aus.

IRRLICHT.

Ich merke wohl, Ihr seid der Herr vom Haus,
Und will mich gern nach Euch bequemen.
Allein bedenkt! der Berg ist heute zaubertoll,
Und wenn ein Irrlicht Euch die Wege weisen soll,
So müßt Ihr's so genau nicht nehmen.   3870

FAUST, MEPHISTOPHELES, IRRLICHT (*im Wechselgesang*).

In die Traum- und Zaubersphäre
Sind wir, scheint es, eingegangen.
Führ' uns gut und mach' dir Ehre,
Daß wir vorwärts bald gelangen
In den weiten, öden Räumen!

Seh' die Bäume hinter Bäumen,

Already Spring is weaving through these birches;
the fir itself is touched by it;
should Spring not quicken our limbs as well?

MEPHISTOPHELES.
Myself I notice no such thing.
I feel the winter in my belly
and wish for snow and frost to line my path.   3850
How sadly the unfinished, lunar disc
rises with belated, ruddy glow,
giving sparse illumination, and at every turn
one stumbles into trees and boulders.
Let me call upon a will-o'-the-wisp!
I see one over there that's burning merrily.
Hi there! My friend! Please join us over here!
Why cast your flickering flame for nothing?
Be good enough to shine your light up here!

WILL-O'-THE-WISP.
My reverence for you, I hope, will help control   3860
my inborn instability;
we are accustomed to a zigzag way of life.

MEPHISTOPHELES.
Well, well! It's man you aim to imitate.
Now in the devil's name, go straight!
Or else I'll snuff the fluttering life right out of you.

WILL-O'-THE-WISP.
I see you are the lord and master in this house;
I'll do my best to keep you satisfied.
But keep in mind, the mountain is magic-mad today,
and since you're asking me to light the way,
do not expect too much precision.   3870

FAUST, MEPHISTOPHELES, WILL-O'-THE-WISP (*singing
        alternately*).
We have arrived, so it appears,
In a sphere of magic dreams.
Lead us on and show no fears,
So we may move to further stations
Over broad and barren regions!

See the forest like a legion

Wie sie schnell vorüberrücken,
Und die Klippen, die sich bücken,
Und die langen Felsennasen,
Wie sie schnarchen, wie sie blasen!   3880

Durch die Steine, durch den Rasen
Eilet Bach und Bächlein nieder.
Hör' ich Rauschen? hör' ich Lieder?
Hör' ich holde Liebesklage,
Stimmen jener Himmelstage?
Was wir hoffen, was wir lieben!
Und das Echo, wie die Sage
Alter Zeiten, hallet wider.

Uhu! Schuhu! tönt es näher,
Kauz und Kiebitz und der Häher,   3890
Sind sie alle wach geblieben?
Sind das Molche durchs Gesträuche?
Lange Beine, dicke Bäuche!
Und die Wurzeln, wie die Schlangen,
Winden sich aus Fels und Sande,
Strecken wunderliche Bande,
Uns zu schrecken, uns zu fangen;
Aus belebten derben Masern
Strecken sie Polypenfasern
Nach dem Wandrer. Und die Mäuse   3900
Tausendfärbig, scharenweise,
Durch das Moos und durch die Heide!
Und die Funkenwürmer fliegen
Mit gedrängten Schwärmezügen
Zum verwirrenden Geleite.

Aber sag' mir, ob wir stehen,
Oder ob wir weitergehen?
Alles, alles scheint zu drehen,
Fels und Bäume, die Gesichter
Schneiden, und die irren Lichter,   3910
Die sich mehren, die sich blähen.

Flitting past us as we go;
And the cliffs inclining low,
Reaching for the forest floor,
Blow their noses, sneeze, and snore.   3880

Through meadows and by rocks we soar,
By brooks and reeds to which we cling;
Do they babble? Do they sing?
Are those ancient lovers' lays,
Languid voices out of blissful days?
We love and hope, and hope and love!
And the echo, like an age-old secret tale,
Rings below and sings above.

To-whit! To-whoo! Not far away
Are the plover, owl, and jay.   3890
Have they all remained awake?
Are there newts behind the reeds?
Skinny legs and swollen glands!
Here a root and there a snake,
Coiling through the roots and sands,
Sending strange and dewy threads
To frighten us and hold us here.
From living burls on crooked trees
They wind their fibrous polyp-tether
To trap the wanderer. And the mice   3900
Of myriad colors, far and near,
Scuttle through the moss and heather.
Glowworms gleaming in a crowd
Conjure up a sparkling cloud,
A shimmering escort of confusion.

But tell me if we stand and stay,
Or if we move along the way.
It all appears to turn and sway;
Rocks and trees are making faces,
Will-o'-the-wisps flit by   3910
And swell their teeming races.

MEPHISTOPHELES.

Fasse wacker meinen Zipfel!
Hier ist so ein Mittelgipfel,
Wo man mit Erstaunen sieht,
Wie im Berg der Mammon glüht.

FAUST.

Wie seltsam glimmert durch die Gründe
Ein morgenrötlich trüber Schein!
Und selbst bis in die tiefen Schlünde
Des Abgrunds wittert er hinein.
Da steigt ein Dampf, dort ziehen Schwaden,   3920
Hier leuchtet Glut aus Dunst und Flor,
Dann schleicht sie wie ein zarter Faden,
Dann bricht sie wie ein Quell hervor.
Hier schlingt sie eine ganze Strecke
Mit hundert Adern sich durchs Tal,
Und hier in der gedrängten Ecke
Vereinzelt sie sich auf einmal.
Da sprühen Funken in der Nähe,
Wie ausgestreuter goldner Sand.
Doch schau! in ihrer ganzen Höhe   3930
Entzündet sich die Felsenwand.

MEPHISTOPHELES.

Erleuchtet nicht zu diesem Feste
Herr Mammon prächtig den Palast?
Ein Glück, daß du's gesehen hast;
Ich spüre schon die ungestümen Gäste.

FAUST.

Wie rast die Windsbraut durch die Luft!
Mit welchen Schlägen trifft sie meinen Nacken!

MEPHISTOPHELES.

Du mußt des Felsens alte Rippen packen,
Sonst stürzt sie dich hinab in dieser Schlünde Gruft.
Ein Nebel verdichtet die Nacht.   3940
Höre, wie's durch die Wälder kracht!
Aufgescheucht fliegen die Eulen.
Hör', es splittern die Säulen
Ewig grüner Paläste.
Girren und Brechen der Äste!

MEPHISTOPHELES.

> Seize my coattail with a steady hand;
> we're flying by a central peak
> where we can marvel at the sight
> of Mammon glowing deep within.

FAUST.

> How strangely does the dawnlike, murky light
> seep through the trees and bushes.
> How it pries and even penetrates
> into ravines and gaping chasms.
> Here fumes arise, here vapors hover,   3920
> a fire glows from mists below;
> now it flickers like a tender thread,
> now it gushes in a bursting spring.
> Here it winds a crooked path
> through the valley in a hundred veins;
> there it crowds into a corner,
> only sparkling now and then.
> Suddenly there is a geyser
> of sparks like incandescent grains of sand.
> And look! The mountain wall from top to bottom   3930
> ignites and seems on fire.

MEPHISTOPHELES.

> Has not Sir Mammon lighted splendidly
> the palace for this great occasion?
> You are lucky to have seen the spectacle;
> some boisterous guests are fast approaching.

FAUST.

> How the wind-hag races through the air!
> How she slaps my shoulders with her blast!

MEPHISTOPHELES.

> You must grasp these ancient ribs of rock,
> or else she'll hurl you down headlong.
> A mist is thickening the night.   3940
> Hear how the timbers creak and moan;
> frightened owls are streaking through the trees.
> Hear through the palaces of evergreen
> the towering pillars crack and shatter,
> the squeal and crash of tumbling branches!

Der Stämme mächtiges Dröhnen!
Der Wurzeln Knarren und Gähnen!
Im fürchterlich verworrenen Falle
Übereinander krachen sie alle,
Und durch die übertrümmerten Klüfte   3950
Zischen und heulen die Lüfte.
Hörst du Stimmen in der Höhe?
In der Ferne, in der Nähe?
Ja, den ganzen Berg entlang
Strömt ein wütender Zaubergesang!

HEXEN (*im* CHOR).

       Die Hexen zu dem Brocken ziehn,
       Die Stoppel ist gelb, die Saat ist grün.
       Dort sammelt sich der große Hauf,
       Herr Urian sitzt oben auf.
       So geht es über Stein und Stock,   3960
       Es f—t die Hexe, es stinkt der Bock.

STIMME.

Die alte Baubo kommt allein,
Sie reitet auf einem Mutterschwein.

CHOR.

       So Ehre denn, wem Ehre gebührt!
       Frau Baubo vor! und angeführt!
       Ein tüchtig Schwein und Mutter drauf,
       Da folgt der ganze Hexenhauf.

STIMME.

Welchen Weg kommst du her?

STIMME.

                 Übern Ilsenstein!
Da guckt' ich der Eule ins Nest hinein.
Die macht' ein Paar Augen!

STIMME.

             O fahre zur Hölle!   3970
Was reitst du so schnelle!

STIMME.

Mich hat sie geschunden,
Da sieh nur die Wunden!

HEXEN (CHOR).

       Der Weg ist breit, der Weg ist lang,

The hollow thunder of the trunks!
The groaning of the roots below!
With a furious roar and rumble
they fall into a tangled heap;
the madly howling blasts careen 3950
through the wreckage-strewn ravine.
Do you hear the voices high above?
Far away and close at hand?
The entire mountainside has come alive
with frenzied chants of sorcery.

WITCHES (*in chorus*).

     The witches ride to Blockberg's[45] top.
     The stubble is yellow; green the crop.
     On top of the cackling horde
     Sits Urian[46] presiding as lord.
     Over rubble and stubble they stream in blustery
          weather, 3960
     Witches and billy goats stinking and leaping together.

VOICE.[47]

Our ancient Baubo[48] rides alone
with a mother sow beneath her buttocks.

CHORUS.

     We like to cheer when cheers are due!
     Let Lady Baubo lead the crew.
     With mother on a strapping swine
     The other hags will stay in line.

VOICE.

How did you fly?

VOICE.

          By way of Ilsenstein.[49]
I peeked at the owl in her nest.
Oh, how she stared at me!

VOICE.

          Oh, go to hell! 3970
Why must you gallop at such a pace?

VOICE.

The pig has flailed my buttocks;
just look at all my grievous sores.

WITCHES (*in chorus*).

     The way is broad, the way is long,

Was ist das für ein toller Drang?
Die Gabel sticht, der Besen kratzt,
Das Kind erstickt, die Mutter platzt.

HEXENMEISTER (*Halbes* CHOR).

Wir schleichen wie die Schneck' im Haus,
Die Weiber alle sind voraus.
Denn, geht es zu des Bösen Haus,   3980
Das Weib hat tausend Schritt voraus.

ANDRE HÄLFTE.

Wir nehmen das nicht so genau,
Mit tausend Schritten macht's die Frau;
Doch, wie sie auch sich eilen kann,
Mit einem Sprunge macht's der Mann.

STIMME (*oben*).

Kommt mit, kommt mit, vom Felsensee!

STIMME (*von unten*).

Wir möchten gerne mit in die Höh'.
Wir waschen, und blank sind wir ganz und gar;
Aber auch ewig unfruchtbar.

BEIDE CHÖRE.

Es schweigt der Wind, es flieht der Stern,   3990
Der trübe Mond verbirgt sich gern.
Im Sausen sprüht das Zauberchor
Viel tausend Feuerfunken hervor.

STIMME (*von unten*).

Halte! Halte!

STIMME (*von oben*).

Wer ruft da aus der Felsenspalte?

STIMME (*unten*).

Nehmt mich mit! Nehmt mich mit!
Ich steige schon dreihundert Jahr,
Und kann den Gipfel nicht erreichen.
Ich wäre gern bei meinesgleichen.

BEIDE CHÖRE.

Es trägt der Besen, trägt der Stock,   4000
Die Gabel trägt, es trägt der Bock;
Wer heute sich nicht heben kann,
Ist ewig ein verlorner Mann.

Then why this wild and crazy throng?
The broom has scratched, the fork has poked,
Mother bursts, the child is choked.

WIZARDS (*half-chorus*).

Like snails in their house we glide and we slither;
The women are all in a dither.
They race to the house of the Evil One   3980
To enjoy their advantage before they are done.

OTHER HALF-CHORUS.

We do not make astonished faces
If the women lead by a thousand paces.
Let them race and scramble without stop,
We the men can make it in one hop.

VOICE (*from above*).

Come here, come up, leave Rocky Lake behind!

VOICE (*from below*).

We'd like to be where you are now;
we are scrubbed and polished to the bone
but forever parched and sterile.[50]

BOTH CHORUSES.

The wind is still, the stars go by,   3990
The murky moon hides in the sky.
But a roaring, magic choir
Spews a million sparks of fire.

VOICE (*from below*).

Now wait! Please wait for me!

VOICE (*from above*).

Who clamors from the gorge below?

VOICE (*from below*).

Take me along! Take me with you!
I've been scaling for three centuries
and could never reach the summit,
yet I'd like to be among my peers.

BOTH CHORUSES.

The broom can fly, the stick's for you,   4000
A pitchfork and a goat will do;
Who cannot raise himself today
Is ever lost and doomed to stay.

HALBHEXE (*unten*).

    Ich tripple nach, so lange Zeit;
    Wie sind die andern schon so weit!
    Ich hab' zu Hause keine Ruh,
    Und komme hier doch nicht dazu.

CHOR DER HEXEN.

        Die Salbe gibt den Hexen Mut,
        Ein Lumpen ist zum Segel gut,
        Ein gutes Schiff ist jeder Trog;   4010
        Der flieget nie, der heut nicht flog.

BEIDE CHÖRE.

        Und wenn wir um den Gipfel ziehn,
        So streichet an dem Boden hin,
        Und deckt die Heide weit und breit
        Mit eurem Schwarm der Hexenheit.

    (*Sie lassen sich nieder.*)

MEPHISTOPHELES.

    Das drängt und stößt, das ruscht und klappert!
    Das zischt und quirlt, das zieht und plappert!
    Das leuchtet, sprüht und stinkt und brennt!
    Ein wahres Hexenelement!
    Nur fest an mir! sonst sind wir gleich getrennt.   4020
    Wo bist du?

FAUST (*in der Ferne*).

    Hier!

MEPHISTOPHELES.

        Was! dort schon hingerissen?
    Da werd' ich Hausrecht brauchen müssen.
    Platz! Junker Voland kommt. Platz! süßer Pöbel, Platz!
    Hier, Doktor, fasse mich! und nun, in e i n e m Satz,
    Laß uns aus dem Gedräng' entweichen;
    Es ist zu toll, sogar für meinesgleichen.
    Dort neben leuchtet was mit ganz besondrem Schein,
    Es zieht mich was nach jenen Sträuchen.
    Komm, komm! wir schlupfen da hinein.

FAUST.

    Du Geist des Widerspruchs! Nur zu! du magst mich
        führen.   4030
    Ich denke doch, das war recht klug gemacht:

HALF-WITCH (*below*).

  I stumble and straggle and cannot see
  how the others got ahead of me.
  Back home the children kept me busy;
  now the mountain makes me dizzy.

CHORUS OF WITCHES.

      The salve puts courage in a hag;
      For a sail we use a rag;
      A trough will make a splendid scow;   4010
      You'll never fly if grounded now.

BOTH CHORUSES.

      Approach the peak and fly around,
      Sweeping close along the ground!
      Take to the heath and fill the ditches
      With your cackling swarm of witches!

   (*They settle down.*)

MEPHISTOPHELES.

  They crowd and crush, they squeal and they clatter!
  They hiss and whirl, they pull and they chatter!
  They spew and sparkle, burn and stink;
  this is the proper sphere of witches!
  Keep close to me, or we'll be separated.   4020
  Where are you?

FAUST (*in the distance*).

  Here!

MEPHISTOPHELES.

      What! Carried out so far already?
  I must invoke my old prerogatives.
  Squire Voland[51] has arrived! Sweet rabble, let him through.
  Now, Doctor, seize my coat! We will escape
  in one leap to safer ground;
  this is too crazy even for the likes of me.
  Over there I see a very special glimmer,
  something draws me to that clump of bushes.
  Come, come, let us crawl in for now.

FAUST.

  You spirit of contradiction! Move along and I will
      follow   4030
  It seems to me we managed very cleverly so far:

Zum Brocken wandeln wir in der Walpurgisnacht,
Um uns beliebig nun hieselbst zu isolieren.

MEPHISTOPHELES.

Da sieh nur, welche bunten Flammen!
Es ist ein muntrer Klub beisammen.
Im Kleinen ist man nicht allein.

FAUST.

Doch droben möcht' ich lieber sein!
Schon seh' ich Glut und Wirbelrauch.
Dort strömt die Menge zu dem Bösen;
Da muß sich manches Rätsel lösen.   4040

MEPHISTOPHELES.

Doch manches Rätsel knüpft sich auch.
Laß du die große Welt nur sausen,
Wir wollen hier im Stillen hausen.
Es ist doch lange hergebracht,
Daß in der großen Welt man kleine Welten macht.
Da seh' ich junge Hexchen nackt und bloß,
Und alte, die sich klug verhüllen.
Seid freundlich, nur um meinetwillen;
Die Müh' ist klein, der Spaß ist groß.
Ich höre was von Instrumenten tönen!   4050
Verflucht Geschnarr! Man muß sich dran gewöhnen.
Komm mit! Komm mit! Es kann nicht anders sein,
Ich tret' heran und führe dich herein,
Und ich verbinde dich aufs neue.
Was sagst du, Freund? das ist kein kleiner Raum.
Da sieh nur hin! du siehst das Ende kaum.
Ein Hundert Feuer brennen in der Reihe;
Man tanzt, man schwatzt, man kocht, man trinkt, man liebt;
Nun sage mir, wo es was Bessers gibt?

FAUST.

Willst du dich nun, um uns hier einzuführen,   4060
Als Zaubrer oder Teufel produzieren?

MEPHISTOPHELES.

Zwar bin ich sehr gewohnt, inkognito zu gehn,
Doch läßt am Galatag man seinen Orden sehn.
Ein Knieband zeichnet mich nicht aus,
Doch ist der Pferdefuß hier ehrenvoll zu Haus.

We travel to the Brocken on Walpurgis Night,
to observe at will the magical proceedings.

MEPHISTOPHELES.

Just watch those varicolored flames below.
A lively club appears to be in session;
in smaller circles one is not alone.

FAUST.

But I prefer that higher region
where even now I see a smoky, churning glow,
and crowds advancing to the Evil One;
many riddles may be answered there.   4040

MEPHISTOPHELES.

But other riddles will be knotted.
Let the great world go to blazes
while we breathe and eat in peace.
It is an old transmitted custom
that little worlds are spawned within the great.
I see the younger witches go stark naked
and older ones more shrewdly veiled.
Be courteous now, if only for my sake;
the cost is small, the fun is great.
I hear the blaring of some instruments!   4050
Horrid twanging! I guess one finally gets used to it.
Come along! We cannot change the matter.
I will go and take you in with me
and bind you to me once again.
What say you, friend? The space is not so little.
Just look! You scarcely see the end of it.
One hundred fires burning in a row;
they dance, they chat, they cook and drink and kiss.
Can you tell me where one offers something better?

FAUST.

Will you effect our introduction   4060
in a wizard's or a devil's role?

MEPHISTOPHELES.

Though as a rule I go incognito,
one likes to show one's medals on a gala day.
A garter is too dull and undistinguished,
but cloven hooves are greatly honored here.

Siehst du die Schnecke da? Sie kommt herangekrochen;
Mit ihrem tastenden Gesicht
Hat sie mir schon was abgerochen.
Wenn ich auch will, verleugn' ich hier mich nicht.
Komm nur! von Feuer gehen wir zu Feuer,   4070
Ich bin der Werber, und du bist der Freier.
   (*Zu einigen, die um verglimmende Kohlen
   sitzen.*)
Ihr alten Herrn, was macht ihr hier am Ende?
Ich lobt' euch, wenn ich euch hübsch in der Mitte fände,
Von Saus umzirkt und Jugendbraus;
Genug allein ist jeder ja zu Haus.

GENERAL.

Wer mag auf Nationen trauen,
Man habe noch so viel für sie getan;
Denn bei dem Volk, wie bei den Frauen,
Steht immerfort die Jugend oben an.

MINISTER.

Jetzt ist man von dem Rechten allzu weit,   4080
Ich lobe mir die guten Alten;
Denn freilich, da wir alles galten,
Da war die rechte goldne Zeit.

PARVENU.

Wir waren wahrlich auch nicht dumm,
Und taten oft, was wir nicht sollten;
Doch jetzo kehrt sich alles um und um,
Und eben da wir's fest erhalten wollten.

AUTOR.

Wer mag wohl überhaupt jetzt eine Schrift
Von mäßig klugem Inhalt lesen!
Und was das liebe junge Volk betrifft,   4090
Das ist noch nie so naseweis gewesen.

MEPHISTOPHELES (*der auf einmal sehr alt erscheint*).

Zum jüngsten Tag fühl' ich das Volk gereift,
Da ich zum letzten Mal den Hexenberg ersteige,
Und weil mein Fäßchen trübe läuft,
So ist die Welt auch auf der Neige.

TRÖDELHEXE.

Ihr Herren, geht nicht so vorbei!

Watch the snail! It's slowly crawling our way,
and with its probing snout and feelers
it has already sniffed me out.
I could not hide here even if I tried my best.
But come! We'll move along the line of fires. 4070
I'll do the wooing, and you can be the squire.
(*Addressing some who are sitting around the
dying embers.*)
Good sirs, why dawdle on the outer fringes?
You should be sitting snugly in the middle,
engulfed by youthful zest and clamor;
at home you each have solitude enough.

GENERAL.
Who wants to put his faith in nations,
no matter what you've done for them?
For with the people just as with a woman
the prize goes always to the young.

MINISTER.
They have abandoned all that's good these days. 4080
Bring me back the older generation;
for when we better men held sway
it was a happy, golden age.

PARVENU.
We were not altogether stupid either;
here and there we made some tricky deals.
But now the world is topsy-turvy,
just when we meant to keep the status quo.

AUTHOR.
Who would want to read these days
a work of any depth and compass?
As for the touted younger generation, 4090
I never saw one more irreverent.

MEPHISTOPHELES (*who suddenly looks very old*).
Now that I scale this magic hill a final time,
I feel that men are ripe for Judgment Day;
and since my keg is running dry,
the world has reached the edge of time.

PEDDLER-WITCH.
Gentlemen, pray give me some attention!

Laßt die Gelegenheit nicht fahren!
Aufmerksam blickt nach meinen Waren,
Es steht dahier gar mancherlei.
Und doch ist nichts in meinem Laden,   4100
Dem keiner auf der Erde gleicht,
Das nicht einmal zum tücht'gen Schaden
Der Menschen und der Welt gereicht.
Kein Dolch ist hier, von dem nicht Blut geflossen,
Kein Kelch, aus dem sich nicht, in ganz gesunden Leib,
Verzehrend heißes Gift ergossen,
Kein Schmuck, der nicht ein liebenswürdig Weib
Verführt, kein Schwert, das nicht den Bund gebrochen,
Nicht etwa hinterrücks den Gegenmann durchstochen.

MEPHISTOPHELES.

Frau Muhme! Sie versteht mir schlecht die Zeiten.   4110
Getan geschehn! Geschehn getan!
Verleg' Sie sich auf Neuigkeiten!
Nur Neuigkeiten ziehn uns an.

FAUST.

Daß ich mich nur nicht selbst vergesse!
Heiß' ich mir das doch eine Messe!

MEPHISTOPHELES.

Der ganze Strudel strebt nach oben;
Du glaubst zu schieben und du wirst geschoben.

FAUST.

Wer ist denn das?

MEPHISTOPHELES.

                    Betrachte sie genau!
Lilith ist das.

FAUST.

            Wer?

MEPHISTOPHELES.

                Adams erste Frau.
Nimm dich in acht vor ihren schönen Haaren,   4120
Vor diesem Schmuck, mit dem sie einzig prangt.
Wenn sie damit den jungen Mann erlangt,
So läßt sie ihn so bald nicht wieder fahren.

FAUST.

Da sitzen zwei, die Alte mit der Jungen;

Don't pass up this golden opportunity!
Pay close attention to my wares.
Some curious things are on display.
You'll find no single object in my shop—   4100
the like of which you never saw on earth—
that has not caused at least on one occasion
some splendid hurt to man and nature.
No dagger here from which no blood has spurted,
no cup from which corrosive poison
has not flowed into a healthy body;
no gem that did not trip a lovely maiden,
no sword that did not slash through sacred trusts
or pierce an adversary from behind.

MEPHISTOPHELES.
Cousin, you are way behind the times.   4110
What's done is past! What's past is done!
You should go in for novelties!
Something new is what we want.

FAUST.
If only I could keep my mind from snapping,
I'd call this fair a fair to end all fairs!

MEPHISTOPHELES.
There is an upward swirl and jostle here;
he who's pushed imagines that he's pushing.

FAUST.
Who's that girl?

MEPHISTOPHELES.
                    Observe her very closely!
She is Lilith.

FAUST.
          Who?

MEPHISTOPHELES.
              The first of Adam's wives. 52
Be on guard against her lovely hair,   4120
against adornments that outshine all others.
When a man is tangled in its toils,
Lilith will not lightly let him go.

FAUST.
Two sit over there, one old and haggard and one young;

Die haben schon was Rechts gesprungen!

MEPHISTOPHELES.

Das hat nun heute keine Ruh.
Es geht zum neuen Tanz; nun komm! wir greifen zu.

FAUST (*mit der* JUNGEN *tanzend*).

   Einst hatt' ich einen schönen Traum:
   Da sah ich einen Apfelbaum,
   Zwei schöne Äpfel glänzten dran,   4130
   Sie reizten mich, ich stieg hinan.

DIE SCHÖNE.

   Der Äpfelchen begehrt ihr sehr,
   Und schon vom Paradiese her.
   Von Freuden fühl' ich mich bewegt,
   Daß auch mein Garten solche trägt.

MEPHISTOPHELES (*mit der* ALTEN).

   Einst hatt' ich einen wüsten Traum;
   Da sah ich einen gespaltnen Baum,
   Der hatt' ein————;
   So—es war, gefiel mir's doch.

DIE ALTE.

   Ich biete meinen besten Gruß   4140
   Dem Ritter mit dem Pferdefuß!
   Halt' Er einen————bereit,
   Wenn Er————nicht scheut.

PROKTOPHANTASMIST.

Verfluchtes Volk! was untersteht ihr euch?
Hat man euch lange nicht bewiesen:
Ein Geist steht nie auf ordentlichen Füßen?
Nun tanzt ihr gar, uns andern Menschen gleich!

DIE SCHÖNE (*tanzend*).

Was will denn der auf unserm Ball?

FAUST (*tanzend*).

Ei! der ist eben überall.
Was andre tanzen, muß er schätzen.   4150
Kann er nicht jeden Schritt beschwätzen,
So ist der Schritt so gut als nicht geschehn.
Am meisten ärgert ihn, sobald wir vorwärtsgehn.
Wenn ihr euch so im Kreise drehen wolltet,

both have danced and whirled about, it seems.

MEPHISTOPHELES.

Today there is no rest for you;
the dance resumes. Let's get into the fray.

FAUST (*dancing with the* YOUNG WITCH).

> Once I fell to pleasant dreaming:
> I saw a sturdy apple tree
> With two apples on it gleaming[53]— 4130
> I climbed it, for they tempted me.

PRETTY WITCH.

> You want apples of a pleasing size;
> You've looked for them since paradise.
> I am thrilled with joy and pleasure,
> For my garden holds such treasure.

MEPHISTOPHELES (*dancing with the* OLD WITCH).

> Once I had a savage dream:
> I saw an ancient, cloven tree
> In which a giant hole did gleam;
> Big as it was, it suited me.

OLD WITCH.

> Let me salute and welcome you; 4140
> The cloven hoof shows through your shoe!
> A giant stopper will ensure
> That you can fill the aperture.[54]

PROCTOPHANTASMIST.[55]

Shameless mob! What on earth is this?
Has it not been proven long ago:
Spirits do not walk on solid ground?
Now you presume to dance like one of us!

PRETTY WITCH (*dancing*).

What could he be doing at our ball?

FAUST (*dancing*).

You may find him anywhere, my dear.
When others dance, he's got to criticize, 4150
and if he fails to criticize a step,
that step might just as well have not been taken.
His chagrin grows most severe when we move forward.
If we would only spin around in circles,

Wie er's in seiner alten Mühle tut,
Das hieß' er allenfalls noch gut;
Besonders wenn ihr ihn darum begrüßen solltet.

PROKTOPHANTASMIST.

Ihr seid noch immer da! Nein, das ist unerhört.
Verschwindet doch! Wir haben ja aufgeklärt!
Das Teufelspack, es fragt nach keiner Regel.   4160
Wir sind so klug, und dennoch spukt's in Tegel.
Wie lange hab' icht nicht am Wahn hinausgekehrt,
Und nie wird's rein; das ist doch unerhört!

DIE SCHÖNE.

So hört doch auf, uns hier zu ennuyieren!

PROKTOPHANTASMIST.

Ich sag's euch Geistern ins Gesicht,
Den Geistesdespotismus leid' ich nicht;
Mein Geist kann ihn nicht exerzieren.
    (*Es wird fortgetanzt.*)
Heut', seh' ich, will mir nichts gelingen;
Doch eine Reise nehm' ich immer mit
Und hoffe noch, vor meinem letzten Schritt,   4170
Die Teufel und die Dichter zu bezwingen.

MEPHISTOPHELES.

Er wird sich gleich in eine Pfütze setzen,
Das ist die Art, wie er sich soulagiert,
Und wenn Blutegel sich an seinem Steiß ergetzen,
Ist er von Geistern und von Geist kuriert.
    (*Zu* FAUST, *der aus dem Tanz getreten ist.*)
Was lässest du das schöne Mädchen fahren,
Das dir zum Tanz so lieblich sang?

FAUST.

Ach! mitten im Gesange sprang
Ein rotes Mäuschen ihr aus dem Munde.

MEPHISTOPHELES.

Das ist was Rechts! das nimmt man nicht genau;   4180
Genug, die Maus war doch nicht grau.
Wer fragt darnach in einer Schäferstunde?

FAUST.

Dann sah ich—

the way he grinds his ancient mill,
he may at best abstain from censure,
especially if you loudly sing his praises.

PROCTOPHANTASMIST.

You are still here! Incredible, such insolence!
Clear out! We are enlightened, don't you know?
The devil's pack ignores all rules and standards.   4160
We are so smart, but still the ghosts haunt Tegel.[56]
How I have worked to clear the air of superstition!
But—such insolence—the folly still clings everywhere.

PRETTY WITCH.

Now go away, you're boring us to tears!

PROCTOPHANTASMIST.

I must tell you, spirits, to your face:
I won't accept your spectral impositions
because they can't be classified.
      (*The dancing continues.*)
Right now it seems that I can do but little,
but I am always pleased to take a trip.[57]
Before I take my final step,   4170
I'll vanquish both the devils and the poets.

MEPHISTOPHELES.

Now he will squat upon the nearest puddle—
in this manner he relieves his trouble;
and when the leeches gorge themselves on his behind
he will be cured of spirits and of mind.
      (*To* FAUST *who has left his dancing partner
      and stands alone.*)
Why did you ditch your dancing partner
who sang so sweetly to the music?

FAUST.

Ah, right in the middle of her melody
a scarlet mouse sprang from her lips.

MEPHISTOPHELES.

That's nothing much. You need not be alarmed;   4180
the mouse was after all not gray.
Who'd ask questions in so sweet an hour?

FAUST.

And then I saw—

MEPHISTOPHELES.

        Was?

FAUST.

                Mephisto, siehst du dort
Ein blasses, schönes Kind allein und ferne stehen?
Sie schiebt sich langsam nur vom Ort,
Sie scheint mit geschloßnen Füßen zu gehen.
Ich muß bekennen, daß mir deucht,
Daß sie dem guten Gretchen gleicht.

MEPHISTOPHELES.

Laß das nur stehn! dabei wird's niemand wohl.
Es ist ein Zauberbild, ist leblos, ein Idol.   4190
Ihm zu begegnen, ist nicht gut;
Vom starren Blick erstarrt des Menschen Blut,
Und er wird fast in Stein verkehrt,
Von der Meduse hast du ja gehört.

FAUST.

Fürwahr, es sind die Augen einer Toten,
Die eine liebende Hand nicht schloß.
Das ist die Brust, die Gretchen mir geboten,
Das ist der süße Leib, den ich genoß.

MEPHISTOPHELES.

Das ist die Zauberei, du leicht verführter Tor!
Denn jedem kommt sie wie sein Liebchen vor.   4200

FAUST.

Welch eine Wonne! welch ein Leiden!
Ich kann von diesem Blick nicht scheiden.
Wie sonderbar muß diesen schönen Hals
Ein einzig rotes Schnürchen schmücken,
Nicht breiter als ein Messerrücken!

MEPHISTOPHELES.

Ganz recht! ich seh' es ebenfalls.
Sie kann das Haupt auch unterm Arme tragen;
Denn Perseus hat's ihr abgeschlagen.—
Nur immer diese Lust zum Wahn!
Komm doch das Hügelchen heran,   4210
Hier ist's so lustig wie im Prater;
Und hat man mir's nicht angetan,
So seh' ich wahrlich ein Theater.

MEPHISTOPHELES.

What?

FAUST.

                    Mephisto, do you see
a pale and lovely child, far away and quite alone?
She is gliding slowly from her place;
she appears to move with fettered feet.
I must confess, it seems to me
that she resembles my dear Gretchen.

MEPHISTOPHELES.

Leave that be! It bodes no good to anyone.
It is a lifeless magic shape, an idol;   4190
it is unwise to meet it anywhere.
Its rigid stare congeals the blood of men
so that they nearly turn to stone.
You've heard of the Medusa, I suppose.

FAUST.

Now I see a dead girl's eyes
which were never closed by loving hands.
That is the breast which Gretchen yielded me,
the blessed body I enjoyed.

MEPHISTOPHELES.

You are too gullible, you fool! It's make-believe!
To all she seems their own beloved.   4200

FAUST.

What ecstasy! What anguish and despair!
I cannot turn my eyes away.
How strange a single crimson thread,
no broader than a razor's edge,
would look upon her lovely throat.

MEPHISTOPHELES.

Quite right. Now I can see it too. What's more,
she also holds her head beneath her arm,
since Perseus struck it from her trunk. [58]
Must you always hanker after phantoms?
Climb up that little hill with me;   4210
it is as lively as the Prater [59] there.
And unless I'm totally bewitched,
I see a ready stage and curtain.

Was gibt's denn da?

SERVIBILIS.

Gleich fängt man wieder an.
Ein neues Stück, das letzte Stück von sieben;
So viel zu geben, ist allhier der Brauch.
Ein Dilettant hat es geschrieben,
Und Dilettanten spielen's auch.
Verzeiht, ihr Herrn, wenn ich verschwinde;
Mich dilettiert's, den Vorhang aufzuziehn.   4220

MEPHISTOPHELES.

Wenn ich euch auf dem Blocksberg finde,
Das find' ich gut; denn da gehört ihr hin.

WALPURGISNACHTSTRAUM
oder
OBERONS UND TITANIAS
GOLDNE HOCHZEIT

Intermezzo

THEATERMEISTER.

Heute ruhen wir einmal,
Miedings wackre Söhne.
Alter Berg und feuchtes Tal,
Das ist die ganze Szene!

HEROLD.

Daß die Hochzeit golden sei,
Solln funfzig Jahr sein vorüber;
Aber ist der Streit vorbei,
Das Golden ist mir lieber.   4230

OBERON.

Seid ihr Geister, wo ich bin,
So zeigt's in diesen Stunden;
König und die Königin,
Sie sind aufs neu verbunden.

PUCK.

Kommt der Puck und dreht sich quer
Und schleift den Fuß im Reihen,
Hundert kommen hinterher,

What are they doing?

SERVIBILIS. [60]

> They will resume in just a moment.
> Another piece, the last of seven pieces.
> It is the custom here to show a lot.
> An amateur composed the play,
> and amateurs make up the cast.
> Allow me, sirs, to disappear
> and be an amateurish curtain-raiser.   4220

MEPHISTOPHELES.

> I am glad to find you on the Brocken,
> for that's the proper place for you.

WALPURGIS-NIGHT'S DREAM
or
OBERON AND TITANIA'S
GOLDEN WEDDING[61]

Intermezzo

THEATER MANAGER.

> Let us rest today for once,
> my excellent sons of Mieding.[62]
> "Ancient hill and greening vale"
> is all the scenery required.

HERALD.

> To hold a Golden Wedding feast
> one should be wedded fifty years;
> but once the struggle is composed,
> give me the gold to hold and keep.   4230

OBERON.

> Are you present and prepared?
> Then show your mettle, spirits;
> for the king and lovely queen
> have renewed their pledge today.

PUCK.

> Puck arrives and turns and twirls
> and stamps his foot in time.
> One hundred follow after him

Sich auch mit ihm zu freuen.

ARIEL.

Ariel bewegt den Sang
In himmlisch reinen Tönen;   4240
Viele Fratzen lockt sein Klang,
Doch lockt er auch die Schönen.

OBERON.

Gatten, die sich vertragen wollen,
Lernen's von uns beiden!
Wenn sich zweie lieben sollen,
Braucht man sie nur zu scheiden.

TITANIA.

Schmollt der Mann und grillt die Frau,
So faßt sie nur behende,
Führt mir nach dem Mittag Sie,
Und Ihn an Nordens Ende.   4250

ORCHESTER TUTTI (*Fortissimo*).

Fliegenschnauz' und Mückennas'
Mit ihren Anverwandten,
Frosch im Laub und Grill' im Gras,
Das sind die Musikanten!

SOLO.

Seht, da kommt der Dudelsack!
Es ist die Seifenblase.
Hört den Schneckeschnickeschnack
Durch seine stumpfe Nase.

GEIST (*der sich erst bildet*).

Spinnenfuß und Krötenbauch
Und Flügelchen dem Wichtchen!   4260
Zwar ein Tierchen gibt es nicht,
Doch gibt es ein Gedichtchen.

EIN PÄRCHEN.

Kleiner Schritt und hoher Sprung
Durch Honigtau und Düfte;
Zwar du trippelst mir genung,
Doch geht's nicht in die Lüfte.

NEUGIERIGER REISENDER.

Ist das nicht Maskeraden-Spott?
Soll ich den Augen trauen,

to share the pleasant hour.

ARIEL.

Ariel engenders song
of pure, angelic voices.   4240
The sound attracts some ugly faces
but lures some pretty ones as well.

OBERON.

You, spouses who want harmony,
look to us as an example!
Those who are to burn with love
merely must be separated.

TITANIA.

If he should pout and she be cross,
then take them both aside.
Send her off to southern climes,
and him to northern regions.   4250

ORCHESTRA, TUTTI (*fortissimo*).

Snouts of flies, mosquito jaws,
and all their kith and kin,
frogs and crickets in the grass:
These are the music men!

SOLO.

Look! The bagpipe comes this way!
It is a bloated hose.
Hear the snarky-snooky-snay
squeezing through its nose.

SPIRIT (*forming itself*).

Spider's foot and paunch of toad,
and winglets for the gnome!   4260
They will not make a horse or goat
but compose a pretty poem.

A YOUNG COUPLE.

A careful step, a bolder jump
beneath the honeydew and briar;
You trip along from stump to stump
and never can go higher.

INQUISITIVE TRAVELER.

Is this a blatant travesty?
Is it true or mere disguise

Oberon den schönen Gott
Auch heute hier zu schauen!   4270

ORTHODOX.

Keine Klauen, keinen Schwanz!
Doch bleibt es außer Zweifel:
So wie die Götter Griechenlands,
So ist auch er ein Teufel.

NORDISCHER KÜNSTLER.

Was ich ergreife, das ist heut
Fürwahr nur skizzenweise;
Doch ich bereite mich bei Zeit
Zur italien'schen Reise.

PURIST.

Ach! mein Unglück führt mich her:
Wie wird nicht hier geludert!   4280
Und von dem ganzen Hexenheer
Sind zweie nur gepudert.

JUNGE HEXE.

Der Puder ist so wie der Rock
Für alt' und graue Weibchen;
Drum sitz' ich nackt auf meinem Bock
Und zeig' ein derbes Leibchen.

MATRONE.

Wir haben zu viel Lebensart,
Um hier mit euch zu maulen;
Doch, hoff' ich, sollt ihr jung und zart,
So wie ihr seid, verfaulen.   4290

KAPELLMEISTER.

Fliegenschnauz' und Mückennas',
Umschwärmt mir nicht die Nackte!
Frosch im Laub und Grill' im Gras,
So bleibt doch auch im Takte!

WINDFAHNE (*nach der einen Seite*).

Gesellschaft wie man wünschen kann.
Wahrhaftig lauter Bräute!
Und Junggesellen, Mann für Mann,
Die hoffnungsvollsten Leute.

WINDFAHNE (*nach der andern Seite*).

Und tut sich nicht der Boden auf,

that Oberon, the handsome god,
is here before my eyes?   4270

AN ORTHODOX PERSON.

I see no claws, no tail,
and yet the case is crystal clear:
just like the gods of ancient Greece,
he can be a devil too, I fear.

NORDIC ARTIST.

What I can seize and fix today
is only rough and vague.
I must prepare without delay
for my Italian journey.

PURIST.

Ah! My misfortune leads me here:
Such lewdness, such disgrace!   4280
Of the twitching horde of witches
only two have a powdered face!

YOUNG WITCH.

A powdered face is like a skirt
for old and graying wives;
so I sit naked on my buck
and show my eager thighs.

MATRON.

We are too civilized and proud
to argue with the younger crowd.
I wish the young and juicy fry
would wither up and putrefy.   4290

ORCHESTRA LEADER.

Snouts of flies, mosquito jaws,
do not crowd the naked girls!
Frogs and crickets in the grass,
keep the beat and stop your twirls.

WEATHER VANE (*pointing one way*).

This is congenial company,
brides galore, more plentiful than ever.
And bachelors as far as I can see,
full of hope in their endeavor.

WEATHER VANE (*pointing the other way*).

If the earth won't open wide

    Sie alle zu verschlingen,   4300
    So will ich mit behendem Lauf
    Gleich in die Hölle springen.

XENIEN.

    Als Insekten sind wir da,
    Mit kleinen scharfen Scheren,
    Satan, unsern Herrn Papa,
    Nach Würden zu verehren.

HENNINGS.

    Seht, wie sie in gedrängter Schar
    Naiv zusammen scherzen!
    Am Ende sagen sie noch gar,
    Sie hätten gute Herzen.   4310

MUSAGET.

    Ich mag in diesem Hexenheer
    Mich gar zu gern verlieren;
    Denn freilich diese wüßt' ich eh'r
    Als Musen anzuführen.

CI-DEVANT GENIUS DER ZEIT.

    Mit rechten Leuten wird man was.
    Komm, fasse meinen Zipfel!
    Der Blocksberg, wie der deutsche Parnaß,
    Hat gar einen breiten Gipfel.

NEUGIERIGER REISENDER.

    Sagt, wie heißt der steife Mann?
    Er geht mit stolzen Schritten.   4320
    Er schnopert, was er schnopern kann.
    „Er spürt nach Jesuiten."

KRANICH.

    In dem Klaren mag ich gern
    Und auch im Trüben fischen;
    Darum seht ihr den frommen Herrn
    Sich auch mit Teufeln mischen.

WELTKIND.

    Ja für die Frommen, glaubet mir,
    Ist alles ein Vehikel;
    Sie bilden auf dem Blocksberg hier
    Gar manches Konventikel.   4330

to swallow all this rabble,   4300
then I will walk with nimble stride
and leap into perdition.

XENIES.[63]

As insects are we here
with little sharpened shears
to honor Satan, Papa dear,
whom everyone reveres.

HENNINGS.[64]

In its crude and silly vein
the rabble acts so bold,
and in the end they will maintain
that they have hearts of gold.   4310

MUSAGET.[65]

I should like to use my ruses
upon this band of witches,
for I can guide the witches
far better than the muses.

CI-DEVANT GENIUS OF THE AGE.[66]

You've got to know the proper people;
take my coattail as we go.
The Blocksberg has a spacious top,
and so has Germany's Parnassus.

INQUISITIVE TRAVELER.[67]

What's that rigid fellow's name,
strutting up and down these places?   4320
He sniffs in every nook and cranny.
"He's on the Jesuits' traces."[68]

A CRANE.

I like to catch my fish
in clear and troubled waters;
hence you see that pious fellow
making small talk with the devil.

WORLDLING.[69]

For those of strong religious faith
all things will serve their pious ends.
They erect their little churches
right here on this mountain.   4330

TÄNZER.

> Da kommt ja wohl ein neues Chor?
> Ich höre ferne Trommeln.
> Nur ungestört! es sind im Rohr
> Die unisonen Dommeln.

TANZMEISTER.

> Wie jeder doch die Beine lupft!
> Sich, wie er kann, herauszieht!
> Der Krumme springt, der Plumpe hupft
> Und fragt nicht, wie es aussieht.

FIDELER.

> Das haßt sich schwer, das Lumpenpack,
> Und gäb' sich gern das Restchen;   4340
> Es eint sie hier der Dudelsack,
> Wie Orpheus' Leier die Bestjen.

DOGMATIKER.

> Ich lasse mich nicht irre schrein,
> Nicht durch Kritik noch Zweifel.
> Der Teufel muß doch etwas sein;
> Wie gäb's denn sonst auch Teufel?

IDEALIST.

> Die Phantasie in meinem Sinn
> Ist diesmal gar zu herrisch.
> Fürwahr, wenn ich das alles bin,
> So bin ich heute närrisch.   4350

REALIST.

> Das Wesen ist mir recht zur Qual
> Und muß mich baß verdrießen;
> Ich stehe hier zum ersten Mal
> Nicht fest auf meinen Füßen.

SUPERNATURALIST.

> Mit viel Vergnügen bin ich da
> Und freue mich mit diesen;
> Denn von den Teufeln kann ich ja
> Auf gute Geister schließen.

SKEPTIKER.

> Sie gehn den Flämmchen auf der Spur,
> Und glaub'n sich nah dem Schatze.   4360
> Auf Teufel reimt der Zweifel nur,

DANCER.

> Another band is now approaching.[70]
> I hear the beat of drums. Don't be concerned,
> This is the bitterns' monotone encroaching
> on the reeds and willows by the pond.

DANCING MASTER.

> How nimbly each one lifts his thigh,
> slyly skirting his dilemma!
> The bent ones leap, some others try,
> they never worry how they look.

FIDDLER.

> The ragged pack is full of hate;
> they'd gladly see each other dead,   4340
> but by the bagpipe does their wrath abate
> much as Orpheus' lyre tamed the beasts.

DOGMATIST.

> Let them shout their awful drivel;
> their doubts and carpings leave me cold.
> There must be something to the devil;
> else how could devils come to be?

IDEALIST.

> What's been imagined in this fray,
> to my mind is overblown,
> and I'd be but a fool today,
> if I believed what has been shown.   4350

REALIST.

> These doings are a pain to me;
> I've had my fill of them by now.
> For the first time I have found
> that I stand on shaky ground.

SUPERNATURALIST.

> I derive some real satisfaction
> from being witness to this view.
> For the presence of the devils
> implies good spirits too.

SKEPTIC.

> They would like to find the treasure
> employing flames to find their route,   4360
> and I will have the keenest pleasure,

Da bin ich recht am Platze.

KAPELLMEISTER.

Frosch im Laub und Grill' im Gras,
Verfluchte Dilettanten!
Fliegenschnauz' und Mückennas',
Ihr seid doch Musikanten!

DIE GEWANDTEN.

Sanssouci, so heißt das Heer
Von lustigen Geschöpfen;
Auf den Füßen geht's nicht mehr,
Drum gehn wir auf den Köpfen.   4370

DIE UNBEHÜLFLICHEN.

Sonst haben wir manchen Bissen erschranzt,
Nun aber Gott befohlen!
Unsere Schuhe sind durchgetanzt,
Wir laufen auf nackten Sohlen.

IRRLICHTER.

Von dem Sumpfe kommen wir,
Woraus wir erst entstanden;
Doch sind wir gleich im Reihen hier
Die glänzenden Galanten.

STERNSCHNUPPE.

Aus der Höhe schoß ich her
Im Stern- und Feuerscheine,   4380
Liege nun im Grase quer—
Wer hilft mir auf die Beine?

DIE MASSIVEN.

Platz und Platz! und ringsherum!
So gehn die Gräschen nieder,
Geister kommen, Geister auch
Sie haben plumpe Glieder.

PUCK.

Tretet nicht so mastig auf
Wie Elefantenkälber,
Und der Plumpst' an diesem Tag
Sei Puck, der Derbe, selber.   4390

ARIEL.

Gab die liebende Natur,
Gab der Geist euch Flügel,

since the devil lives on doubt.

ORCHESTRA LEADER.

> Frogs and crickets in the grass:
> You are the rankest amateurs.
> Snouts of flies, mosquito jaws,
> as musicians you are boors.

THE VERSATILE ONES.[71]

> *Sans Souci* they call the corps
> by merry creatures led,
> and when our feet are tired and sore,
> we walk on our heads instead.   4370

THE AWKWARD ONES.

> In former times the people fed us well,
> but now may Heaven help us eat!
> We pranced and danced until we fell
> and limped about on naked feet.

WILL-O'-THE-WISPS.

> We arrived from swampy regions
> where once we came to be.
> But now we join the Brocken's legions,
> a gallant troop are we.

SHOOTING STAR.

> I darted downward from the heights
> in astral light and flame.   4380
> I now lie sick and crumpled—
> Who'll help me up? I'm lame!

THE STOCKY ONES.

> Make room! And do as you are told!
> Watch us crush the tender green.
> We may be ghosts, and yet behold:
> We're clumsy and we're mean.

PUCK.

> You move like elephantine calves;
> such is your ponderous tramp.
> Let the clumsiest on this day
> be Puck, myself, the well-known scamp.   4390

ARIEL.

> If loving Nature or the Spirit
> gave you wings to lighten you,

> Folget meiner leichten Spur,
> Auf zum Rosenhügel!

ORCHESTER (*Pianissimo*).

> Wolkenzug und Nebelflor
> Erhellen sich von oben.
> Luft im Laub und Wind im Rohr,
> Und alles ist zerstoben.

TRÜBER TAG · FELD

Faust, Mephistopheles.

FAUST.

Im Elend! Verzweifelnd! Erbärmlich auf der Erde lange
verirrt und nun gefangen! Als Missetäterin im Kerker zu
entsetzlichen Qualen eingesperrt das holde unselige Geschöpf! Bis dahin! dahin—Verräterischer, nichtswürdiger
Geist, und das hast du mir verheimlicht!—Steh nur, steh!
Wälze die teuflischen Augen ingrimmend im Kopf herum!
Steh und trutze mir durch deine unerträgliche Gegenwart!
Gefangen! Im unwiederbringlichen Elend! Bösen Geistern
übergeben und der richtenden gefühllosen Menschheit!
Und mich wiegst du indes in abgeschmackten Zerstreuun-
gen, verbirgst mir ihren wachsenden Jammer und lässest
sie hülflos verderben!

MEPHISTOPHELES.

Sie ist die Erste nicht.

FAUST.

Hund! abscheuliches Untier!—Wandle ihn, du unendlicher
Geist! wandle den Wurm wieder in seine Hundsgestalt, wie
er sich oft nächtlicher Weile gefiel, vor mir herzutrotten,
dem harmlosen Wandrer vor die Füße zu kollern und sich
dem niederstürzenden auf die Schultern zu hängen. Wandl'
ihn wieder in seine Lieblingsbildung, daß er vor mir im
Sand auf dem Bauch krieche, ich ihn mit Füßen trete, den
Verworfnen!—Die Erste nicht!—Jammer! Jammer! von
keiner Menschenseele zu fassen, daß mehr als ein Geschöpf
in die Tiefe dieses Elendes versank, daß nicht das erste
genug tat für die Schuld aller übrigen in seiner windenden

then follow out my airy trail,
then join me on the Hill of Roses!

ORCHESTRA (*pianissimo*).

The drifting clouds and sifting fogs
receive the sun's awakening ray;
breezes ruffle reeds in bogs,
and all that was has gone away.

GLOOMY DAY—FIELD

Faust, Mephistopheles.

FAUST

In misery! Despairing! Pitiably stranded on the face of the earth, and now caught in the net. Thrown into prison as a common criminal and suffering fearful torment, the unhappy creature, my beloved. It has come to this. To this! Treacherous, contemptible spirit, and that you concealed from me. Stand there! Your satanic, bitter eyes wrathfully rolling in your head. Stand there and mortify me by your unbearable presence! In prison! In irremediable misery! Given over to evil spirits and to the unfeeling who presume to dispense justice! And meanwhile you soothe me with stale, insipid diversions, hide her ever-growing anguish from me, and let her perish without help and without hope.

MEPHISTOPHELES.

She is not the first.

FAUST.

Cur! Loathsome monster!—Transform him, Infinite Spirit! Transform the viper back into a dog, the shape in which he capered before me at night, entangling the feet of the unknowing wanderer and—when he stumbled and fell—hanging upon his shoulder. Change him back into his favorite shape; make him crawl on his belly before me; I want to kick his cursed belly!—Not the first!—Oh, the sorrow, the grief! A human soul cannot conceive that more than one creature should have sunk to such bottomless wretchedness, that the First in His writhing agony should not have been sufficient to expiate the guilt of all the others

Todesnot vor den Augen des ewig Verzeihenden! Mir wühlt
es Mark und Leben durch, das Elend dieser Einzigen; du
grinsest gelassen über das Schicksal von Tausenden hin!

MEPHISTOPHELES.

Nun sind wir schon wieder an der Grenze unsres Witzes,
da wo euch Menschen der Sinn überschnappt. Warum
machst du Gemeinschaft mit uns, wenn du sie nicht durch-
führen kannst? Willst fliegen und bist vorm Schwindel
nicht sicher? Drangen wir uns dir auf, oder du dich uns?

FAUST.

Fletsche deine gefräßigen Zähne mir nicht so entgegen!
Mir ekelt's!—Großer herrlicher Geist, der du mir zu erscheinen würdigtest, der du mein Herz kennest und meine
Seele, warum an den Schandgesellen mich schmieden, der
sich am Schaden weidet und am Verderben sich letzt?

MEPHISTOPHELES.

Endigst du?

FAUST.

Rette sie! oder weh dir! Den gräßlichsten Fluch über dich
auf Jahrtausende!

MEPHISTOPHELES.

Ich kann die Bande des Rächers nicht lösen, seine Riegel
nicht öffnen.—Rette sie!—Wer war's, der sie ins Verderben
stürzte? Ich oder du?

   (FAUST *blickt wild umher.*)

Greifst du nach dem Donner? Wohl, daß er euch elenden
Sterblichen nicht gegeben ward! Den unschuldig Entgeg-
nenden zu zerschmettern, das ist so Tyrannenart, sich in
Verlegenheiten Luft zu machen.

FAUST.

Bringe mich hin! Sie soll frei sein!

MEPHISTOPHELES.

Und die Gefahr, der du dich aussetzest? Wisse, noch liegt
auf der Stadt Blutschuld von deiner Hand. Über des Er-
schlagenen Stätte schweben rächende Geister und lauern
auf den wiederkehrenden Mörder.

FAUST.

Noch das von dir? Mord und Tod einer Welt über dich

before the eyes of the Eternal Redeemer! I am pierced to the marrow of my being by the agony of one alone—while you grin complacently at the fate of thousands.

MEPHISTOPHELES.

Now once again we've reached the threshold of our wit where the mind of mortals runs amok and snaps. Why do you make common cause with us if you cannot see it through? You wish to fly and yet are prone to vertigo? Did we thrust ourself on you, or you on us?

FAUST.

Don't bare your voracious teeth at me! You make me sick!—O great and glorious Spirit, you who deigned to appear to me, who know my heart and soul, why must you weld me to this odious creature that gloats on suffering and revels in destruction?

MEPHISTOPHELES.

Have you finished?

FAUST.

Save her! Or else beware! The most dreadful curse on you for ages!

MEPHISTOPHELES.

I cannot undo the bonds of the Avenger, nor draw back the bolts.—Save her!—Who was it that plunged her into ruin? I or you?

(FAUST *gazes wildly about him.*)

Are you reaching for a thunderbolt? Luckily, it was not handed to you mortals. To smash the innocent who cross your path—that is the tyrant's way to dispose of his embarrassments.

FAUST.

Take me to her! She shall be free!

MEPHISTOPHELES.

And the risk that you would run? Let me tell you: The blood-guilt by your hand still lies upon the town. Avenging spirits hover over the site of the murder, lying in wait for the returning killer.

FAUST.

That too from you? A world of murder and death upon your

Ungeheuer! Führe mich hin, sag' ich, und befrei sie!

MEPHISTOPHELES.
Ich führe dich, und was ich tun kann, höre! Habe ich alle
Macht im Himmel und auf Erden? Des Türners Sinne will
ich umnebeln, bemächtige dich der Schlüssel und führe
sie heraus mit Menschenhand! Ich wache! die Zauberpferde
sind bereit, ich entführe euch. Das vermag ich.

FAUST.
Auf und davon!

NACHT · OFFEN FELD

*Faust, Mephistopheles, auf schwarzen Pferden
daherbrausend.*

FAUST.
Was weben die dort um den Rabenstein?

MEPHISTOPHELES.
Weiß nicht, was sie kochen und schaffen.   4400

FAUST.
Schweben auf, schweben ab, neigen sich, beugen sich.

MEPHISTOPHELES.
Eine Hexenzunft.

FAUST.
Sie streuen und weihen.

MEPHISTOPHELES.
Vorbei! Vorbei!

KERKER

FAUST (*mit einem Bund Schlüssel und einer Lampe, vor einem
        eisernen Türchen*).
Mich faßt ein längst entwohnter Schauer,
Der Menschheit ganzer Jammer faßt mich an.
Hier wohnt sie, hinter dieser feuchten Mauer,
Und ihr Verbrechen war ein guter Wahn!
Du zauderst, zu ihr zu gehen!

monstrous head! Take me to her, I tell you, and set her free!

MEPHISTOPHELES.

I will take you there. And now listen. This is the limit of what I
can do—after all, am I all-powerful on earth and in
Heaven?—First I will befog the jailer's senses, then you seize
the keys and lead her out yourself. I will keep watch; the magic
horses are at the ready. I will whisk you both away. That much
I can do.

FAUST.

Let us move. Now!

NIGHT—OPEN FIELD

Faust; Mephistopheles, racing by on black horses.

FAUST.

What are they plotting 'round the Raven Stone?[72]

MEPHISTOPHELES.

Who knows what they're brewing and hatching.   4400

FAUST.

Soaring, swooping, bowing, bending.

MEPHISTOPHELES.

A covey of witches.

FAUST.

Sprinkling and murmuring spells.

MEPHISTOPHELES.

On! Move on!

DUNGEON

FAUST (*a bunch of keys and a lantern in his hands, standing
        before a small iron door*).

An unfamiliar shudder seizes me;
all the misery of Man is mine.
Here she lives, behind these humid walls;
her crime was but a fond delusion!
I hesitate to go to her.

Du fürchtest, sie wiederzusehen!   4410
Fort! Dein Zagen zögert den Tod heran.
   (*Er ergreift das Schloß. Es singt inwendig.*)
       Meine Mutter, die Hur',
       Die mich umgebracht hat!
       Mein Vater, der Schelm,
       Der mich gessen hat!
       Mein Schwesterlein klein
       Hub auf die Bein',
       An einem kühlen Ort;
       Da ward ich ein schönes Waldvögelein;
       Fliege fort, fliege fort!   4420

FAUST (*aufschließend*).
  Sie ahnet nicht, daß der Geliebte lauscht,
  Die Ketten klirren hört, das Stroh, das rauscht.
    (*Er tritt ein.*)
MARGARET (*sich auf dem Lager verbergend*).
  Weh! Weh! Sie kommen. Bittrer Tod!
FAUST (*leise*).
  Still! Still! ich komme, dich zu befreien.
MARGARET (*sich vor ihn hinwälzend*).
  Bist du ein Mensch, so fühle meine Not.
FAUST.
  Du wirst die Wächter aus dem Schlafe schreien!
    (*Er faßt die Ketten, sie aufzuschließen.*)

MARGARET (*auf den Knieen*).
  Wer hat dir, Henker, diese Macht
  Über mich gegeben!
  Du holst mich schon um Mitternacht.
  Erbarme dich und laß mich leben!
  Ist's morgen früh nicht zeitig genung?   4430
    (*Sie steht auf.*)
  Bin ich doch noch so jung, so jung!
  Und soll schon sterben!
  Schön war ich auch, und das war mein Verderben.
  Nah war der Freund, nun ist er weit;
  Zerrissen liegt der Kranz, die Blumen zerstreut.

Am I afraid to see my love again?   4410
Quickly! Death creeps closer as I waver.
   (*He grasps the lock. Sound of singing within.*)
        My mother, the whore,
        Who put me to death!
        My father, the rogue,
        Who fed on my flesh!
        My sweet little sister,
        She buried my bones
        Beneath cool stones.
        Then I was a wood-bird gay;
        Fly away! Fly away![73]   4420

FAUST (*unbolting the door*).
   She cannot know her lover listens
   and hears the clanking chains, the rustling in the straw.
     (*He enters.*)
MARGARET (*cowering on the pallet*).
   Oh! Oh! They've come! Oh, bitter death!
FAUST (*softly*).
   Be still! Hush! I've come to set you free!
MARGARET (*throwing herself at his feet, thrashing the ground*).
   If you are human, feel my misery.
FAUST.
   You will rouse the night guards from their sleep!
     (*He takes hold of her chains in order to un-
     lock them.*)
MARGARET (*on her knees*).
   Who has given you this power,
   hangman, over me!
   It's only midnight, yet you've come for me.
   Show mercy, man, and let me live!   4430
   Is the morning not soon enough?
     (*She stands up.*)
   Look, how young I am, how young!
   And I must die today!
   I was pretty once, and that was my undoing.
   The friend was close, but now he's far away;
   the wreath lies torn, the flowers scattered.

Fasse mich nicht so gewaltsam an!
Schone mich! Was hab' ich dir getan?
Laß mich nicht vergebens flehen,
Hab' ich dich doch mein Tage nicht gesehen!   4440

FAUST.

Werd' ich den Jammer überstehen!

MARGARET.

Ich bin nun ganz in deiner Macht.
Laß mich nur erst das Kind noch tränken.
Ich herzt' es diese ganze Nacht;
Sie nahmen mir's, um mich zu kränken,
Und sagen nun, ich hätt' es umgebracht.
Und niemals werd' ich wieder froh.
Sie singen Lieder auf mich! Es ist bös von den Leuten!
Ein altes Märchen endigt so,
Wer heißt sie's deuten?   4450

FAUST (wirft sich nieder).

Ein Liebender liegt dir zu Füßen,
Die Jammerknechtschaft aufzuschließen.

MARGARET (wirft sich zu ihm).

O laß uns knien, die Heil'gen anzurufen!
Sieh! unter diesen Stufen,
Unter der Schwelle
Siedet die Hölle!
Der Böse,
Mit furchtbarem Grimme,
Macht ein Getöse!

FAUST (laut).

Gretchen! Gretchen!   4460

MARGARET (aufmerksam).

Das war des Freundes Stimme!
    (Sie springt auf. Die Ketten fallen ab.)
Wo ist er? Ich hab' ihn rufen hören.
Ich bin frei! Mir soll niemand wehren.
An seinen Hals will ich fliegen,
An seinem Busen liegen!
Er rief: Gretchen! Er stand auf der Schwelle.
Mitten durchs Heulen und Klappen der Hölle,
Durch den grimmigen, teuflischen Hohn

Don't seize me so harshly!
Spare me! What have I ever done to you?
Don't let me plead in vain!
I never saw you in my life!   4440

FAUST.
  Will I survive such misery?

MARGARET.
  I am now completely in your power,
  but let me nurse my baby just once more;
  I held it close to me all night;
  they meant to hurt me, so they took it,
  and now they say I killed it.
  And I shall not recover, ever.
  They taunt me with their songs. Cruel people!
  I know an ancient tale with such an ending.[74]
  Who bade them to construe it so?   4450

FAUST (falling on his knees).
  Your lover, kneeling at your feet,
  has come to free you from your chains.

MARGARET (impulsively kneeling with him).
  Oh, let us kneel and call upon the saints!
  See! Beneath the stair,
  beneath the sill
  Hell is seething!
  The Evil One
  in horrible wrath
  rants and rages!

FAUST (exclaiming loudly).
  Gretchen! Gretchen!   4460

MARGARET (listening attentively).
  That was the voice of my beloved!
    (She springs to her feet. Her chains fall off.)
  Where is he? I heard him calling me.
  I am free! No one shall bar me!
  I want to fly into his arms,
  hang on his breast!
  He called "Gretchen!" He stood in the door.
  Amidst the shrieks and clatter of Hell,
  through Satan's ice-cold scorn

Erkannt' ich den süßen, den liebenden Ton.

FAUST.

Ich bin's!

MARGARET.

Du bist's! O sag' es noch einmal!   4470

(*Ihn fassend.*)

Er ist's! Er ist's! Wohin ist alle Qual?

Wohin die Angst des Kerkers? der Ketten?

Du bist's! Kommst, mich zu retten!

Ich bin gerettet!—

Schon ist die Straße wieder da,

Auf der ich dich zum ersten Male sah.

Und der heitere Garten,

Wo ich und Marthe deiner warten.

FAUST (*fortstrebend*).

Komm mit! Komm mit!

MARGARET.

O weile!

Weil' ich doch so gern, wo du weilest.   4480

(*Liebkosend.*)

FAUST.

Eile!

Wenn du nicht eilest,

Werden wir's teuer büßen müssen.

MARGARET.

Wie? du kannst nicht mehr küssen?

Mein Freund, so kurz von mir entfernt,

Und hast 's Küssen verlernt?

Warum wird mir an deinem Halse so bang?

Wenn sonst von deinen Worten, deinen Blicken

Ein ganzer Himmel mich überdrang,

Und du mich küßtest, als wolltest du mich ersticken. 4490

Küsse mich!

Sonst küss' ich dich!

(*Sie umfaßt ihn.*)

O weh! deine Lippen sind kalt,

Sind stumm.

Wo ist dein Lieben

Geblieben?

I recognized, I knew the sweet, the loving sound.

FAUST.

I am here!

MARGARET.

          It's you! Oh, say it once again!   4470
  (*She clasps him.*)
It's he! It's he! Now where is my anguish,
where the terror of the dungeon, of my chains?
You are here! You've come to save me!
I am saved!—
I'm transported to the street again
where first I saw you passing by,
and to the cheerful garden
where I awaited you with Martha.

FAUST (*impatiently*).

Come with me! Come!

MARGARET.

               Oh, stay!
Where you are, there I always want to be.   4480
  (*Caressing him.*)

FAUST.

Make haste!
Unless you hurry now,
we'll have to pay a heavy penalty.

MARGARET.

What? Have you forgotten how to kiss?
My friend, you went away but recently,
and you've unlearned so quickly how to kiss?
Why am I so fearful in your arms?
Once at a word or glance from you
an entire heaven would descend;
your kisses almost smothered me.   4490
Kiss me!
Or I'll kiss you!
  (*Clutching him.*)
Oh no! Your lips are cold,
your mouth is clenched.
Where is your love,
my love!

Wer brachte mich drum?
   (Sie wendet sich von ihm.)

FAUST.

Komm! Folge mir! Liebchen, fasse Mut!
Ich herze dich mit tausendfacher Glut;
Nur folge mir! Ich bitte dich nur dies!   4500

MARGARET *(zu ihm gewendet).*

Und bist du's denn? Und bist du's auch gewiß?

FAUST.

Ich bin's! Komm mit!

MARGARET.

              Du machst die Fesseln los,
Nimmst wieder mich in deinen Schoß.
Wie kommt es, daß du dich vor mir nicht scheust?—
Und weißt du denn, mein Freund, wen du befreist?

FAUST.

Komm! komm! schon weicht die tiefe Nacht.

MARGARET.

Meine Mutter hab' ich umgebracht,
Mein Kind hab' ich ertränkt.
War es nicht dir und mir geschenkt?
Dir auch.—Du bist's! ich glaub' es kaum.   4510
Gib deine Hand! Es ist kein Traum!
Deine liebe Hand!—Ach aber sie ist feucht!
Wische sie ab! Wie mich deucht,
Ist Blut dran.
Ach Gott! was hast du getan!
Stecke den Degen ein,
Ich bitte dich drum!

FAUST.

Laß das Vergangne vergangen sein,
Du bringst mich um.

MARGARET.

Nein, du mußt übrigbleiben!   4520
Ich will dir die Gräber beschreiben.
Für die mußt du sorgen
Gleich morgen;
Der Mutter den besten Platz geben,
Meinen Bruder sogleich darneben,

Who wrenched you from me?
   (*She turns away from him.*)

FAUST.

Come! Follow me! Beloved, be strong!
I'll love you with thousandfold passion;
only come with me! This is all I beg of you!   4500

MARGARET (*turning to him*).

Is it really you? Are you quite certain?

FAUST.

Yes! Come with me! Come!

MARGARET.

                      You loose my chains;
you hold me close to you again.
Why is it that you don't recoil from me?—
Do you know, my friend, whom you set free?

FAUST.

Come! Come! The night is almost done.

MARGARET.

I killed my mother,
drowned my child;
was it not a gift for you and me?
For me and *you*. It's you! I can scarce believe it.   4510
Give me your hand. No, it is no dream!
Your dear hand!—Oh, but it is wet!
Wipe it! I believe
there's blood on it.
My God! What have you done!
Put your sword away,
I beg of you!

FAUST.

Let the past be past.
You are killing me!

MARGARET.

No, no! You must remain among the living.   4520
I will describe the graves for you.
You must begin tomorrow
to prepare them carefully.
Give the best place to my mother,
and lay my brother next to her;

Mich ein wenig beiseit',
Nur nicht gar zu weit!
Und das Kleine mir an die rechte Brust.
Niemand wird sonst bei mir liegen!
Mich an deine Seite zu schmiegen,   4530
Das war ein süßes, ein holdes Glück!
Aber es will mir nicht mehr gelingen;
Mir ist's, als müßt' ich mich zu dir zwingen,
Als stießest du mich von dir zurück;
Und doch bist du's und blickst so gut, so fromm.

FAUST.

Fühlst du, daß ich es bin, so komm!

MARGARET.

Dahinaus?

FAUST.

Ins Freie.

MARGARET.

         Ist das Grab drauß,
Lauert der Tod, so komm!
Von hier ins ewige Ruhebett   4540
Und weiter keinen Schritt—
Du gehst nun fort? O Heinrich, könnt' ich mit!

FAUST.

Du kannst! So wolle nur! Die Tür steht offen.

MARGARET.

Ich darf nicht fort; für mich ist nichts zu hoffen.
Was hilft es fliehn? Sie lauern doch mir auf.
Es ist so elend, betteln zu müssen,
Und noch dazu mit bösem Gewissen!
Es ist so elend, in der Fremde schweifen,
Und sie werden mich doch ergreifen!

FAUST.

Ich bleibe bei dir.   4550

MARGARET.

Geschwind! Geschwind!
Rette dein armes Kind.
Fort! Immer den Weg
Am Bach hinauf,
Über den Steg,

place me a little to one side—
but not so very far away!
And place my baby by my breast.
No one else will lie beside me!
To nestle at your side, my love,   4530
that was a sweet and golden bliss!
It is not granted to me anymore;
I feel that I must force myself on you,
that you are thrusting me from you.
And yet it's you; you seem so good and kind.

FAUST.

Trust me, come with me!

MARGARET.

Out there?

FAUST.

To freedom!

MARGARET.

        If the grave is there,
and death lurks there, then come!
From here to my eternal rest,   4540
and not another step—
Must you go? Oh, Heinrich, could I go with you!

FAUST.

You can! Only will it! The door stands open.

MARGARET.

I dare not leave; for me there's nothing more to hope.
Why escape? I know they lie in wait for me.
It's misery to go begging,
and with a guilty conscience too.
It's misery to wander where I am not at home,
and in the end they'll come to hunt me down.

FAUST.

I will stay with you.   4550

MARGARET.

Quickly! Quickly!
Save your poor child.
Go! Follow the trail
that leads along the brook,
over the bridge

In den Wald hinein,
Links, wo die Planke steht,
Im Teich.
Faß es nur gleich!
Es will sich heben,   4560
Es zappelt noch!
Rette! rette!

FAUST.

Besinne dich doch!
Nur e i n e n Schritt, so bist du frei!

MARGARET.

Wären wir nur den Berg vorbei!
Da sitzt meine Mutter auf einem Stein,
Es faßt mich kalt beim Schopfe!
Da sitzt meine Mutter auf einem Stein
Und wackelt mit dem Kopfe;
Sie winkt nicht, sie nickt nicht, der Kopf ist ihr
      schwer,   4570
Sie schlief so lange, sie wacht nicht mehr.
Sie schlief, damit wir uns freuten.
Es waren glückliche Zeiten!

FAUST.

Hilft hier kein Flehen, hilft kein Sagen,
So wag' ich's, dich hinweg zu tragen.

MARGARET.

Laß mich! Nein, ich leide keine Gewalt!
Fasse mich nicht so mörderisch an!
Sonst hab' ich dir ja alles zu Lieb' getan.

FAUST.

Der Tag graut! Liebchen! Liebchen!

MARGARET.

Tag! Ja es wird Tag! der letzte Tag dringt herein;   4580
Mein Hochzeittag sollt' es sein!
Sag niemand, daß du schon bei Gretchen warst.
Weh meinem Kranze!
Es ist eben geschehn!
Wir werden uns wiedersehn;
Aber nicht beim Tanze.
Die Menge drängt sich, man hört sie nicht.
Der Platz, die Gassen

into the wood to the left
where the plank is thrust
into the pond.
Grasp it! Be quick!
It wants to rise,   4560
it wriggles still!
Save it! Save it!

FAUST.

Collect your wits!
One single step and you are free!

MARGARET.

If we were only past the mountain!
There my mother sits on a stone—
icy claws have seized my hair!
There my mother sits on a stone,
her head is swaying to and fro.
She does not nod nor beckon me, her head is
    very heavy,   4570
she slept so long, she wakes no more.
She slept, so we could be content.
We had some happy hours!

FAUST.

My words and pleadings are of no avail;
I must carry you away from here.

MARGARET.

Leave me! No! I will not be forced!
Do not hold me in that murderous grip!
There was nothing, once, I would not do for you.

FAUST.

Dear love! My love! The day is dawning!

MARGARET.

The day. It's coming, yes. The final day is breaking;   4580
it was meant to be my wedding day!
Tell no one that you were in Gretchen's room.
My poor wreath!
Now it has happened!
We shall meet again,
but not at the dance.
The crowd is pressing—a silent crowd.
The streets, the square,

Können sie nicht fassen.
Die Glocke ruft, das Stäbchen bricht.   4590
Wie sie mich binden und packen!
Zum Blutstuhl bin ich schon entrückt.
Schon zuckt nach jedem Nacken
Die Schärfe, die nach meinem zückt.
Stumm liegt die Welt wie das Grab!

FAUST.
O wär' ich nie geboren!

MEPHISTOPHELES (*erscheint draußen*).
Auf! oder ihr seid verloren.
Unnützes Zagen! Zaudern und Plaudern!
Meine Pferde schaudern,
Der Morgen dämmert auf.   4600

MARGARET.
Was steigt aus dem Boden herauf?
Der! der! Schick' ihn fort!
Was will der an dem heiligen Ort?
Er will mich!

FAUST.
                    Du sollst leben!

MARGARET.
Gericht Gottes! dir hab' ich mich übergeben!

MEPHISTOPHELES (*zu* FAUST).
Komm! komm! Ich lasse dich mit ihr im Stich.

MARGARET.
Dein bin ich, Vater! Rette mich!
Ihr Engel! Ihr heiligen Scharen,
Lagert euch umher, mich zu bewahren!
Heinrich! Mir graut's vor dir.   4610

MEPHISTOPHELES.
Sie ist gerichtet!

STIMME (*von oben*).
                    Ist gerettet!

MEPHISTOPHELES (*zu* FAUST).
                              Her zu mir!
    (*Verschwindet mit* FAUST.)

STIMME (*von innen, verhallend*).
Heinrich! Heinrich!

they cannot hold all the people.
The death bell tolls, the staff is broken.   4590
How they bind me and grip me!
I am now transported to the block.
The blade quivers over every neck
as it quivers over mine.
The world lies silent as the grave!

FAUST.
  Oh, if only I had not been born!

MEPHISTOPHELES (*appears outside*).
  Off! Or else you'll both be lost.
  Useless conversation! Dally and prate!
  My horses shudder;
  the day has now begun.   4600

MARGARET.
  What rises from the ground?
  He! He! Send him away!
  What does he want here in this holy place?
  He wants me!

FAUST.
                    You shall live!

MARGARET.
  Judgment of God! To Thee I surrender!

MEPHISTOPHELES (*to* FAUST).
  Come now! Come! Or I will desert you both.

MARGARET.
  Save me, Father! I am Thine!
  Angels! Sacred Hosts!
  Gather about and keep me!
  Heinrich! I shudder to look at you.   4610

MEPHISTOPHELES.
  She is condemned!

VOICE (*from above*).
                    Is saved!

MEPHISTOPHELES (*to* FAUST).
                    You come with me!
    (*He vanishes with* FAUST.)

VOICE (*from within, dying away*).
  Heinrich! Heinrich!

NOTES

1. DEDICATION. Composed in 1797, when the poet, under the prodding of his friend, Friedrich Schiller, decided to resume work on his *Faust*, which had been left unfinished for some years.

2. PROLOGUE IN HEAVEN. Goethe drew inspiration for this scene from the Book of Job.

3. Nostradamus. French physician and astrologer (1503–1566). Famous for his prophecies, which some believe are still coming true.

4. Earth Spirit. Goethe not only drew on archetypal myths but occasionally created his own. Stage directors have always felt free to represent the Earth Spirit in accordance with their own inspiration and requirements. The poet in a well-known pencil sketch gave his own interpretation. The drawing suggests a colossal face with Grecian features.

5. Note the contrast between Faust's unrestrained emotion in his present mood, and Wagner's reliance on the rules of rhetoric and philistine, rational analysis.

6. This is a rendering of the Latin *"ars longa, vita brevis,"* attributed to Hippocrates. This old saw typically expresses the eighteenth-century rationalist's reliance on accepted writings of classical antiquity.

7. It is significant that the joyous Easter choirs celebrating the Resurrection turn Faust's thoughts away from suicide.

8. BEFORE THE GATE. This scene is commonly known as *Osterspaziergang*, or "Easter Walk."

9. Burgdorf. A small village.

10. St. Andrew's Night. Saint Andrew is the legendary patron saint of unmarried girls looking for husbands.

11. "Black kitchen" was the alchemists' laboratory. "Red Lion" and "Lily" are chemicals. "Bridal Chamber" is the chemical retort. The "Queen" is the miraculous drug. These terms are all part of the alchemists' jargon.

12. Gospel of John 1:1. Faust is confronted with the ancient problem of translating the Greek *logos*. Note how throughout *Faust I* "the word" is denigrated in favor of "feeling."

13. The SPIRITS stand in close though undefined relationship to Mephistopheles.

14. Allegorical names representing the four traditional elements: fire, water, air, earth.

15. The crucifix.

16. The sign of the Trinity.

17. Pentagram. Sign representing the five letters of the word "Jesus." Known to alchemists and pansophists of the Baroque period; a sacred sign and hence anathema to hellish spirits.

18. A decisive line. Faust and Mephisto make a wager. In earlier versions of the story, for example in Marlowe's drama, Faust and Mephisto conclude a *pact*, according to which Faust simply signed away his soul in payment for services rendered.

19. Spanish boots. An instrument of torture used during the Spanish Inquisition.

20. *Encheiresis Naturae*. Technical jargon meaning something like "nature's special touch."

21. "You will be like God, knowing Good and Evil."

22. Block Mountain. Dominant peak in the Harz Mountain range in Germany, where, according to legend, devils, witches, and other evil spirits congregate on Walpurgis Night (April 30–May 1). The same peak is also referred to as *Blocksberg* or *Brocken*, the latter being the modern designation. (See also lines 3661, 4221, 4317.)

23. This song cruelly anticipates Gretchen's tragic fate.

24. In Goethe's time, the city of Leipzig was known for its culture and elegance. It was often referred to as "a little Paris."

25. A reference to "Hans Arsch von Rippach" of folklore fame, a figure of ribald student humor. Rippach is a village near Leipzig.

26. The magic mirror is a well-known device in fairy tales and folklore. Faust sees in it a shape of ideal feminine beauty. It may be regarded as a prefiguration of both Gretchen and Helena (*Faust II*).

27. The witch's numbers-game is pure mumbo-jumbo. No allegorical or symbolic meanings are indicated.

28. Walpurgis Night. (See note 22.)

29. A song about Ultima Thule, a fabled northern island believed to be the resting place for the setting sun. While the ballad does not apply directly to Gretchen's situation, it does evoke an appropriate mood. It has been set to music by such composers as Zelter, Schumann, Liszt, and Gounod.

30. This is calculated irony. Saint Anthony is the patron saint of loving wives and brides.

31. "Gretchen" and "Margaret" are used interchangeably.

32. Only the Earth Spirit (see note 4) can be meant, although such an interpretation jars with line 3243 because it was the Lord, not the Earth Spirit, who gave Faust Mephistopheles as a companion. It is never safe in Goethe's *Faust* to construct exact relationships between mythical forces.

33. Mephistopheles refers to Faust's rejuvenation in the witch's kitchen. The line is fairly typical of Goethe's treatment of time in this drama. Sequence and duration are generally kept open and vague.

34. Mephisto's flippant reference to breasts. (See the Song of Solomon 4:5.)

35. In contrast to Gretchen's previous song (2759–82), this song refers directly to her situation.

36. A demonstration of moral outrage; a motif in social ostracism. Other, similar motifs appear with increasing frequency. (See, for example, Valentine scene, 3620–3775.)

37. Walpurgis Night. (See note 22.)

38. Lion-Dollar. Valuable silver coin minted in Holland and used primarily for international trade.

39. A borrowing from Ophelia's song in *Hamlet* IV, 5.

40. Blood-ban. Thought to be a judgment stemming directly from God. Mephistopheles was therefore powerless to intervene.

41. "Day of wrath; that day will crumble the century to ashes." Two lines from a well-known medieval requiem attributed to Thomas of Celano.

42. "Before the judge all hidden things shall become apparent. Nothing will remain unavenged."

43. "What shall I say, I who am wretched? Whom shall I implore on my behalf when even the just are scarcely secure?"

44. WALPURGIS NIGHT. (See note 22.)

45. Blocksberg. (See note 22.)

46. Urian. The origin of this word is not certain, though it is probably a corruption of the German *Urhahn*. Here, simply another name for Satan.

47. This and subsequent VOICES should be understood as those of individual witches.

48. Baubo. In Greek mythology, Demeter's midwife; in German folklore, sometimes used as a name for a witch.

49. Ilsenstein. Granite rock formation near the peak of the Brocken.

50. Polemic against rationalist critics of Goethe.

51. Voland. Derived from the Middle High German *valant*, meaning "seducer." Here, another name for the devil.

52. Lilith, according to rabbinic tradition, was Adam's first wife. First mention of her name occurs in Isaiah 34:14. She was said to have left Adam and mated with demons, begetting dangerous spirits. In medieval and Renaissance books of magic she occurs as a frightening spirit. Lilith is also known as a *succuba*.

53. See the Song of Solomon 4:13.

54. For reasons of propriety Goethe deleted certain words when *Faust I* was published. It is felt, however, that the modern reader will not object to a translation of the full text as given in the poet's original manuscript.

55. PROCTOPHANTASMIST. A facetious coinage by Goethe meaning approximately "buttock ghost-imaginer." This is a reference to Friedrich Nicolai (1733–1811), Goethe's literary adversary and an undeviating rationalist, who believed that hallucinatory visions of ghosts could be treated effectively by the application of leeches to the buttocks.

56. Although Nicolai had repeatedly—by rational and "enlightened" argument—demonstrated the impossibility of ghosts, the castle at Tegel (near Berlin) continued to be haunted under his very nose, so to speak. It was a well-publicized affair, which angered Nicolai.

57. Nicolai had written a travelogue of no less than twelve volumes, covering his voyage through Germany and Italy.

58. Allusion to an episode in Greek mythology where Perseus struck off Medusa's head.

59. Prater. A famous public park in Vienna, relatively new in Goethe's time.

60. SERVIBILIS. A huckster and announcer, such as one might find before a circus tent.

61. WALPURGIS-NIGHT'S DREAM, etc. This scene has no organic connection to the Faust drama. While somewhat patterned after Shakespeare's A *Midsummer Night's Dream*, the scene consists of polemic verses criticizing the contemporary literary scene. The piece was originally intended as so-called *Xenien* for the *Almanac of Muses* (*Musenalmanach*), a journal organized by Goethe's friend Schiller. As Schiller was disinclined to use these verses for the journal, Goethe cast about for another, appropriate setting for them, and for better or for worse, decided to include them as an "intermezzo" in his *Faust*. Actually some parallels between the rather personal polemics of the previous "Walpurgis Night" scene and those of the "Intermezzo" may be found. It is well to keep the designation "Intermezzo" in mind, as well as the operetta-like character of the piece.

62. Mieding. The manager of the Weimar theater where Goethe directed many plays, including his own.

63. XENIES. Personifications of polemic verses.

64. Friedrich von Hennings, a Danish author who had taken severe exception to Goethe's and Schiller's polemics in the *Almanac of Muses*.

65. MUSAGET is the title of a collection of poems by Hennings. See note above.

66. CI-DEVANT GENIUS. A satiric attack on Hennings's periodical *Genius der Zeit*.

67. INQUISITIVE TRAVELER. This is Nicolai (see note 55). In this case, however, he is not the speaker, but the person spoken to.

68. Nicolai was a militant Protestant.

69. WORLDLING is likely to be Goethe himself.

70. The dancer calls attention to a group of philosophers of various persuasions, now approaching.

71. Here begins the political satire.

72. Raven Stone. Block of stone and mortar used for executions. Traditionally, crows circle over it.

73. The Juniper Song. In the old legend, an evil stepmother slaughters her child and serves it as a dish to the father. The child's sister gathers up the bones and buries them under a juniper tree. Soon a bird arises from the bones, and its song lures the stepmother from her house. Once outside, she is crushed by a falling millstone. Goethe was familiar with this tale as a young boy.

74. The juniper tree legend seems to work on Gretchen's mind. See previous note.

SELECTED BIBLIOGRAPHY

Books in English concerned with Goethe's *Faust*

Atkins, Stuart. *Goethe's Faust: A Literary Analysis*. Cambridge: Harvard University Press, 1949.

Butler, E. M. *The Fortunes of Faust*. Cambridge: Cambridge University Press, 1952.

Dieckmann, Liselotte. *Goethe's Faust: A Critical Reading*. Englewood Cliffs, NJ: Prentice Hall, 1972.

Enright, Dennis J. *Commentary on Goethe's Faust*. Folcroft, PA: Folcroft Libriary Edition, 1980.

Fairley, Barker. *Goethe's Faust: Six Essays*. Oxford: Oxford University Press, 1953.

Friedenthal, Richard. *Goethe, His Life and Times*. Cleveland: World Publishing, 1965.

Geary, John. *Goethe's Faust: The Making of Part I*. New Haven: Yale University Press, 1981.

Gillies, Alexander. *Goethe's Faust, an Interpretation*. Oxford: Blackwell, 1957.

Gray, Ronald. "*Faust Part I*," *Goethe, a Critical Introduction*. Cambridge: Cambridge University Press, 1967, pp. 126–159.

_____. *Goethe the Alchemist*. Cambridge: Cambridge University Press, 1952.

Haile, H. G. *Invitation to Goethe's Faust*. University, AL: University of Alabama Press, 1978.

Jantz, Harold. *The Form of Faust: The Work of Art and Its Intrinsic Structures*. Baltimore: Johns Hopkins University Press, 1978.

_____. *Goethe's Faust as a Renaissance Man: Parallels and Prototypes*. Princeton: Princeton University Press, 1951.

Mason, Eudo C. *Goethe's Faust: Its Genesis and Purport*. Berkeley: University of California Press, 1967.

Palmer, Philip M., and Robert More. *Sources of the Faust Tradition*. New York: Haskell House, 1965.

Pascal, Roy. "Faust," *Essays on Goethe*, ed. W. Rose. London: Cassell, 1949.

Salm, Peter. *The Poem as Plant: A Biological View of Goethe's Faust*. New York: University Press Books, 1971.

Wilkinson, E. M., and L. A. Willoughby. "Faust, a Morphological Approach," *Goethe, Poet and Thinker*. New York: Barnes and Noble, 1962, pp. 95–117.

ABOUT THE TRANSLATOR

PETER SALM was born in Hameln, Germany, and received his early education in Rome. After emigrating to the United States in 1938, he studied at UCLA and at Yale University, where he received a Ph.D. in comparative literature. He has written on Dante, Goethe, and Thomas Mann, on the interrelations among the arts, and on theories of literature. His books include a study of three major European literary scholars entitled *Three Modes of Criticism*, also *The Poem as Plant*, a work that takes account of Goethe's endeavors in the natural sciences as they inform his poetry, especially his *Faust*. A recent book by Salm, which deals with the experience of time, is entitled *Pinpoint of Eternity: The Quest for Simultaneity in Literature*. He currently teaches in Cleveland at Case Western Reserve University, where he is Professor of Comparative Literature and German.

THE BANTAM SHAKESPEARE COLLECTION

The Complete Works in 29 Volumes

Edited with Introductions by David Bevington • Forewords by Joseph Papp

---

Ask for these books at your local bookstore or use this page to order.

Please send me the books I have checked above. I am enclosing $_____ (add $2.50 to cover postage and handling). Send check or money order, no cash or C.O.D.'s, please.

Name _____

Address _____

City/State/Zip _____

Send order to: Bantam Books, Dept. SH 2, 2451 S. Wolf Rd., Des Plaines, IL 60018
Allow four to six weeks for delivery.
Prices and availability subject to change without notice. SH 2 2/96

BANTAM CLASSICS ✪ BANTAM CLASSICS ✪ BANTAM CLASSICS

Bantam Classics bring you the world's greatest literature—timeless masterpieces of fiction and nonfiction. Beautifully designed and sensibly priced, Bantam Classics are a valuable addition to any home library.

The Brontës

_____21140-4	JANE EYRE, Charlotte Brontë	$3.50/$4.50 Canada
_____21243-5	VILLETTE, Charlotte Brontë	$5.95/$6.95
_____21258-3	WUTHERING HEIGHTS, Emily Brontë	$3.95/$4.95

Charles Dickens

_____21223-0	BLEAK HOUSE	$5.95/$7.95
_____21342-3	GREAT EXPECTATIONS	$3.95/$4.95
_____21386-5	OUR MUTUAL FRIEND	$5.95/$6.95
_____21244-3	A CHRISTMAS CAROL	$2.95/$3.95
_____21189-7	DAVID COPPERFIELD	$4.95/$5.95
_____21016-5	HARD TIMES	$3.95/$4.95
_____21102-1	OLIVER TWIST	$3.95/$4.95
_____21123-4	THE PICKWICK PAPERS	$4.95/$5.95
_____21176-5	A TALE OF TWO CITIES	$2.95/$3.50

Henry James

_____21127-7	THE PORTRAIT OF A LADY	$4.50/$5.50
_____21059-9	THE TURN OF THE SCREW	$3.95/$4.95

Jules Verne

_____21356-3	AROUND THE WORLD IN 80 DAYS	$2.95/$3.50
_____21252-4	20,000 LEAGUES UNDER THE SEA	$2.95/$3.50
_____21397-0	JOURNEY TO THE CENTER OF THE EARTH	$3.95/$4.95

Ask for these books at your local bookstore or use this page to order.

Please send me the books I have checked above. I am enclosing $_____ (add $2.50 to over postage and handling). Send check or money order, no cash or C.O.D.'s, please.

Name _____

Address _____

City/State/Zip _____

Send order to: Bantam Books, Dept. CL 3, 2451 S. Wolf Rd., Des Plaines, IL 60018
Allow four to six weeks for delivery.
Prices and availability subject to change without notice.   CL 3 11/95